D0371791

RED SEA

RED SEA

Emily Benedek

St. Martin's Press ≈ New York

This is a work of fiction. All of the characters, organizations, and events portrayed in this novel are either products of the author's imagination or are used fictitiously.

www.stmartins.com

ISBN-13: 978-0-312-35491-6
ISBN-10: 0-312-35491-6

First Edition: September 2007

10 9 8 7 6 5 4 3 2 1

For Jonathan

Preface

I was home in New York City on the morning of 9/11, when United Airlines Flight 175 and American Airlines Flight 11 smashed into the World Trade Center. I was shocked, furious, and scared. A couple days later I visited the still-burning hulk with my *Newsweek* editor. The devastation was appalling. I began to write. The first article was about Israeli counterterrorism experts. The next concerned cyber-terror. For another magazine, I wrote about an FBI special agent and SWAT operator working on counterterrorism at D/FW airport and an F-15C pilot who flew her fighter jet in Iraq during the American invasion.

Several months after the *Newsweek* article, I received a call from one of the experts I'd interviewed. He told me he was coming to New York for business and would I like to meet? He was smart, charming, and completely inscrutable. He had a prominent but faded scar on his face. A smile came easily to him and he had a happy laugh. Yet, on occasion, an expression of intense concentration passed over him that told me he was no stranger to death. A few more months. More meetings. Eventually, he asked if I would consider writing a book about airline security. His credentials told me he knew what he was talking about. I placed a tape recorder before him. For the first time in months, he seemed unable to talk. I snapped off the machine and asked him if it would be easier if I tried to tell the story in a work of fiction. Maybe, he said. Maybe.

Emily Benedek
January 2007
New York City

PART
ONE

Chapter One

At thirty thousand feet, American Airlines Flight 147 from Paris to Boston flew according to routine. Airline food wasn't what it used to be, but in first class at least, the drinks were good. The crew had just finished a meal specially prepared by a Parisian eatery catering to airline personnel. Captain Jack Kelly switched autopilot on and leaned back. "Did you see that new girl?" he asked his copilot. "The one with tits out to here?" He gestured with his hands toward the instrument panel.

At that moment, he felt a shock in the belly of his Boeing 767. He hurriedly scanned the instrument gauges, but before he had a chance to understand the readings, another explosion severed the cockpit from the cabin and Jack Kelly was hurtling through space, memories of the pretty girl lost to black sky and the flames of exploding fuselage.

Michelle Polito stood in the midcabin bathroom of British Airways' smart new Boeing 777. She hung over the sink, knees as weak as a baby's. Mother of God, she hated flying! The turbulence alone was enough to kill her, that awful sensation of the ground giving way beneath her. But what was she going to do, tell thirty kids in her Queens Spanish class that they couldn't go on a once-in-a-lifetime exchange program to Madrid because their teacher was afraid to fly? She checked her ashen face in the mirror and noticed that the turbulence was over. She waited another few seconds to make sure the calm was holding before she turned on the faucet and splashed cold water on her face. She dried her hands, gave her cheeks a few pinches to bring some color back, and stepped out of the bathroom.

Seeing the children jumping and playing brought a smile back to her face. She felt that everything was going to be fine when she heard a bang and then a dreadful thumping as a seam opened up in the cabin floor before her. A shriek tore through her as she watched Maryann Angelides and her American Girl doll get sucked through the hole. Right behind her went Ishmael Cordoba, seat and all, who was playing cards with his best friend, Anthony Apt.

Chang Lee, a flight attendant on Cathay Pacific's medium hop from Hong Kong to Singapore, had just begun beverage service when a businessman in row 3 asked for a Fresca. Finding none on his cart, Lee headed to the galley. He noticed a wisp of smoke curling from one of the forward overhead compartments. As Lee reached up to unclip the latch, a tremendous blast flung him backward and then he was floating, slipping, as if down a water slide. Cold and wet and dark. He thought of the Fresca, then drifted away, his arms and legs buffeted by the wind. His face was burning hot but he was cold as ice, and before he could think about what had happened, he could no longer take a breath.

Turquoise Coast, Turkey, May 5

Julian Granot cut a U-turn with his Jet Ski, churning the water into a tall fan of spray, then accelerated back toward his sons. The boys' parallel wakes converged toward the horizon, and the sun sparkled off the waters of the Mediterranean Sea at the Granot family's Turquoise Coast vacation spot. Lore held that the ancient peoples of this land had fashioned the word *turquoise* to describe the astonishing shade of the water, eventually deciding the country itself could be no better named: Turkuaz.

While Julian and his boys turned their games into sea-land strategy drills, his wife, Gabi, painted watercolors at water's edge. Her large kilim bag muffled the ring of her cell phone, as if trying to bar the outside world. She answered it. General David Ben-Ami grunted hello. He was head of Shabaq, Israel's internal security service, the Israelis' equivalent of the FBI, and Gabi knew the voice well. She and Ben-Ami had grown up together, and Julian had worked with Ben-Ami in the service for the last quarter century. She recognized the clipped syllables in his speech as a sign of controlled anger.

Somewhere, someone had died, or was about to.

Gabi told him Julian was on the water, far from shore. He asked how long it would take to get her husband's attention and wave him in. Maybe five minutes, she said. Ben-Ami added ten minutes: Julian would continue skiing after he saw his wife gesticulating with a telephone in her hand. A call at the beach invariably meant he'd be kissing his vacation good-bye. Ben-Ami knew Julian well, had commanded him and run missions with him. The man was a fine and loyal soldier, but also a stubborn son of a bitch. He needed latitude.

After attracting Julian's eye, Gabi returned to her work. The faded pastel hues she was trying to coax from the paint were slipping away from her into the bright sky, the shimmering silver of the mountains and coves. She blotted and dabbed while trying to block out the telephone call and what it would mean. After a few more brush strokes, she saw Julian pull up to shore. He was red-haired and strong, a fit forty-six-year-old with thick legs and a muscular chest. As he dragged the Jet Ski onto the sand, Gabi told him that Ben-Ami had called and would ring back. It wasn't thirty seconds before the telephone sounded again. The still-soaked Julian held the device away from his head. When Ben-Ami complained he couldn't hear him, Julian joked that there might be something more affecting in the phone than a good friend's voice. A few years back the two of them had caused a rather unhappy morning for a terrorist leader by planting a miniature bomb in his telephone earpiece.

Ben-Ami let out a short laugh. It was no time for jokes, he said, and explained: three commercial jets down within the last hour. Julian flushed deeply as he listened. He took these crashes personally, and though he was no longer directly responsible for the safety of airline passengers, he felt the familiar stomach-clenching reaction. His mind raced as if he were still on the job. Had he overlooked something, failed to make a crucial connection in the never-ending loop of intelligence clues? Habits of mind, forged through training, hard work, or even a long marriage, were hard to break. They never disappeared completely.

"I'll have a plane pick you up in ninety minutes," Ben-Ami was saying. "You'll be met at the airport in Tel Aviv and driven here." A fleet of private planes was available to the State of Israel on request, and the government had emergency landing rights for those planes at most of the world's major airports. Julian had negotiated many of those rights himself. He checked his watch. Ben-Ami hadn't asked whether he could make it. And Julian hadn't answered.

His sons splashed and shouted in the waves. They were getting big now, and muscular. The oldest one was almost a man. When Julian turned to his wife, he saw a shadow cross her face. Their life together had been full of interruptions and surprises. There had been ten years in an active unit that was routinely mobilized at any time of night or day, and ten more years of foreign postings. But who ever got used to the silence, the waiting for loved ones to come home? Who could?

"Three commercial jets have disappeared and are believed to have crashed." Julian spoke to Gabi in the combination of Hebrew and English that had developed into a family patois after years of living in the States. "David wants me to head a ministry task force to investigate."

Gabi winced, saddened at the thought of the planes and the deaths, the families left to their shock and pain, at night and alone with nothing for comfort but the official papers in their hands. She thought especially of the new orphans. Like most Israelis, Gabi was all too familiar with the nearness of death.

The worst of it, which came much later, was that the survivors would *never* find any sense in the deaths. Understanding brought no relief. There was nothing to understand. The terrorists didn't know their victims, didn't care about their particularities. To their killers, the dead weren't people, only statistics, body counts. Those who loved them didn't matter at all. The survivors were then left with an unbearable choice: to live choked with rage and hatred, or fight their way back to life through some form of forgiveness, bitter as it might be.

"When will it end?" she muttered, standing and pulling on her sweater. She wore a blue bandeau around her shapely hips and a wide-brimmed straw hat with a sage green ribbon. Her light-colored hair hung straight to her shoulders. She was two years younger than her husband and her face was still youthful and vibrant, not yet marked by the anxiety that prematurely aged the faces of many of her countrywomen. She looked out at the boys, playing so happily, and felt in her chest a familiar flutter. Soon these beautiful children would be in the army themselves. So would all their friends, girls and boys alike.

"What should we do?" she asked Julian, stepping toward him and placing her hand gently on his forearm.

"All airplanes have been grounded," he said, "so you can't leave." He grinned at her. "You're stuck here in this enchanted place with your two favorite boys!"

She stuck out her lower lip in a girlish way she usually didn't allow herself. She'd run missions for Mossad for fifteen years before leaving to teach college, and she'd earned her comrades' respect several times over. But these last few weeks of Julian's retirement had softened her, allowed her to imagine that life might return to normality, whatever that was. And she wanted him to be here. Julian put his arms around her waist and pulled her to him. "I'll let you know in a couple days how you can return. Everything will be okay," he said. "Kiss the boys for me, will you?" he asked, stepping back.

She nodded and he embraced her again, smelling the vanilla scent of her skin. "Be good," he said, his deep voice dropping off. Fatigue. Or was it sadness, she wondered, as he disappeared across the beach, his feet digging petal shapes in the fine white sand.

Chapter Two

It was as if the phrase had sprung spontaneously and independently to life in multiple languages across the world. They were referred to immediately as the "three angels": the trio of gleaming birds rising toward the sun, each from a different direction, all emerging into the blue plenum, soaring for a time on the cusp of sky and space, then exploding and crashing back to earth in a cascade of unholy violence. The first doomed plane was an American Airlines jet carrying a group of nuns home to Boston from Paris, where they had visited the ancestral home of their founder, for some of them the first departure from their Berkshires convent in forty years. World reaction was properly outraged, but there was an undercurrent of belief that the Americans had it coming. There was the occupation of Iraq, the standoff with Iran, and of course the United States' staunch support of Israel. European and Asian security experts were alarmed, not by the fact of another attempt on an airliner, but by the possibility that American security procedures might not have improved much since September 11, 2001.

The second angel was a British Airways jet headed to Madrid from

JFK with eighty schoolchildren on a cultural exchange program. Radio communication from the third plane ceased seconds later, before a worldwide alert could ground all flights; the Cathay Pacific jet was headed from Hong Kong to Singapore. Businessmen mostly, leaving a record 135 children without fathers. The victims came from three continents: America, Europe, and Asia.

International response was emotional, unrestrained. No one knew what would come next. No place seemed safe. The international business community panicked, and markets from the Dow to the Hang Seng took steep dives. Airline stocks fell 40 percent overnight; investors hadn't forgotten that the Lockerbie bombing killed Pan Am. Trade sputtered, including international transportation of food and medicines. Twenty-eight human organs bound for transplantation into ailing recipients in the U.S. couldn't reach their destinations and were discarded, though forty others were successfully transported by car and train. Seven million people in the United States alone were stranded with no way to get home until flights resumed. Cruise boats full of vacationers remained docked in ports from Miami to the Gulf of Thailand, passengers languishing aboard or on shore.

Fear gripped the world. In Japan, a couple jumped from the Tokyo Tower. Gun sales rose in the United States by 40 percent and the price of gas masks reached $250 from its usual base retail of $78. Demonstrators took to the streets in major Western cities protesting the lack of security.

Meanwhile, in the cities of the Arab Muslim world, there was joy in the streets. From Yemen to Egypt spontaneous rallies hailed the latest victory over the infidel, though the cause of the disappearances was officially unknown. No group made a credible claim of responsibility.

Within an hour of the crashes, before the president addressed the American public from the Oval Office, the defense minister of Israel called an emergency meeting of his Security and Defense Committee. Though the Israeli airline El Al was not involved, nor were any Israeli citizens aboard the doomed aircraft, it was Israel's practice to conduct its own investigations of incidents considered relevant to its safety.

The meeting began even before the secretary-general of the UN issued his boilerplate statement condemning "barbaric acts" against humanity; before the prime minister of Great Britain promised "a full commitment of our intelligence and special units to an investigative force"; and before Spain declared "a national day of mourning." In the secrecy of the Ministry of Defense in Tel Aviv, select members of the Israeli cabinet, the army chief of staff, the heads of army and air force intelligence, and the heads of Mossad and Shabaq convened an emergency task force.

It was a warm afternoon, and the sweet scents of orange blossom and honeysuckle caressed the cabinet ministers as they walked through the interior garden of the Tel Aviv headquarters of the Israel Defense Forces. Inside the drab, no-nonsense building, however, there was no late spring languor; the atmosphere was brisk, orderly, staccato. The men—and they were all men except for a female major in the legal department—had assembled in a large conference room. There they listened carefully to General Nir Arens, head of Aman, army intelligence, a gray-haired, distinguished-looking man of sixty-three.

Arens spoke Hebrew with a British accent and stood with his thumb hooked into his belt, a gesture his subordinates liked to mimic while slapping an imaginary riding crop against their legs. They liked to say he modeled himself on a movie actor: Alec Guinness in *The Bridge on the River Kwai*. As a fifteen-year-old immigrant, he'd changed his name from Godfrey to Nir, but he had otherwise retained his British mannerisms. Israelis are uncommonly casual, the polar opposite of the British, and though Arens was recognized as a brilliant tactician, he was just English enough to provoke good-natured ribbing from his colleagues.

But not today. The situation at hand was anything but lighthearted: three planes down, 723 people missing. All presumed lost.

"The defense minister has asked me to form a panel," said Arens, looking around the room full of battle-hardened men, "to determine the cause or causes of the crashes. We'll of course rule out technical failures before going on to further issues, but the downing of three planes in one day seems to stretch the limits of chance."

Now there's an understatement worthy of a Brit, thought Ben-Ami, sitting at Arens's right, though he didn't say a word.

"Were bombs stowed in luggage?" Arens asked. "We need to look at that possibility. Or were they carried on by suicide bombers? Maybe two or more bombers separately smuggled the ingredients onto each plane and assembled the bombs in flight."

"What about missiles launched from boats in the ocean?" asked the representative of Israel's tiny navy.

"Unlikely," said Arens. "That's beyond the capacities of any terrorist group we know of. Unless, of course, they had help from an unfriendly government."

"Like Iran?"

Arens shrugged. "Who knows? But you're right: it's a possibility we can't rule out, at least not yet."

A thoughtful silence settled over the room.

"And of course," Arens continued, "room must be left for surprise. Something we haven't anticipated. Use of a pigeon, maybe." He mentioned Anne-Marie Murphy, a pregnant young Irishwoman whose Palestinian boyfriend in 1986 tried to slip a bomb into her bag before she boarded an El Al flight. He didn't bother to tell her.

"How about a sleeper?" asked a Mossad man.

"What do you have in mind?"

"That guy Richard Reid, the weird Brit convert to Islam, the one with the scraggly beard, the punk who tried to touch off a bomb in his shoe on an American plane a couple of months after September 11."

"Also a possibility," said Arens. He cupped his hands together. "You see what we're up against. The enemy knows, but we don't."

An animated discussion followed. Who would conduct the investigation? To whom would the investigator answer? Where in the military hierarchy would the team fit? Arens, who had yielded the podium, was reminded of the old joke: put ten Jews in a room and you'll come out with eleven opinions. To his surprise, the answer emerged in less than half an hour. The various powers seemed almost relieved to hand off responsibility to Shabaq's David Ben-Ami, not least because the gruff old soldier had a trump card: Julian Granot, at this moment en route from Turkey.

Julian was recently retired from Shabaq. Although choosing a man

from outside the active military services usually generated opposition—
"Why not one of ours?"—he and his history were well known. He had
commanded a unit of one of Israel's most secret special forces, a unit
akin to the army Rangers and navy SEALs combined, which answered
directly to the army chief of staff. It performed the most daring of Israel's intelligence and reconnaissance operations abroad.

After his service there, Julian joined Shabaq and found his way into
aviation, becoming one of the country's experts in airline security and
eventually heading security operations for the national airline. Through
family ties, he was also connected with the air force, so Ben-Ami could
comfortably expect support from different branches of the service.

"If Granot does the job like he did with Sami," said Eliyahu Mordechai,
a member of the Knesset, "then we'll get back to regular business in no
time."

To a man, the crowd laughed. Everyone knew how Julian had foiled
Sami Kuntar, the Syrian pilot who plotted to crash his jet fighter into
Ben Gurion Airport, but instead was lured off course by Israeli-owned
Su-24s, Soviet-era planes purchased from Ukraine and repainted in Syrian colors. Puffed up with pride at the unexpected escort his bloated
psyche regarded as his due, Kuntar was escorted out to sea before realizing he'd been duped. Seconds later, his jet was unceremoniously blown
out of the sky by an air-to-air missile from an F-15 on his tail.

"The difference this time," intoned Arens, "is that people are already
dead." The group agreed gravely and without further ado to sign a letter
laying out the lines of responsibility and a timetable of goals. Ben-Ami,
a smooth operator as well as a respected former field man, reassured the
politicians that only good news would be traceable back to them. And
the military leaders were pleased: in Julian Granot, they most definitely
had the right man.

Chapter Three

The sudden clatter of a Teletype machine startled Marie Peterssen as she walked into the offices of the trade magazine *Aviation Monthly.* It was the newswire. The hour seemed early for the business releases that sometimes rattled off the ancient gadget, a relic of pre-Internet days kept around more for sentimental reasons than for any real value. She dropped her heavy sports bag, took a few easy strides to the machine, and tore off the long roll of paper that had fallen behind the printer. A reporter's adrenaline seized her. She glanced up at the four televisions running silently on the wall. The coverage hadn't caught up with the wire services; she saw no news of the airplane crashes.

Marie carried her bag into her cubicle. She needed to think, and at times it seemed easier to do so while performing mindless tasks. She pulled out a small nylon sack of foils and slid them under her desk. She hung her fencing helmet on the coatrack, then pulled her hair back from her face and held it on top of her head, as if to clear away interference. Piled on her desk and the floor around it were stacks of magazines, newspapers, and technical manuals. She took a moment to survey the mess, then dropped her hair, which fell straight to her shoulders, and pulled open the top drawer of an overstuffed file cabinet. She lifted out a folder labeled "Maintenance Vulnerabilities and etc.," and pulled from it an article outlining how an explosive device could be delivered to an airplane via the duty-free shops. She remembered with a tremor of anxiety the scenario: a bomb surreptitiously placed in a passenger's duty-free bags by a terrorist, and then unwittingly carried into the secure areas behind the checkpoints by the duty-free employees themselves.

Marie sat at her desk and dialed her editor's home number.

"Sorry to wake you," she said, hearing his groggy voice.

"No problem, Marie. What's up?"

"There's been an accident," she said.

"Are you okay?" he asked, suddenly alert.

"Yes, I'm fine. There've been three plane crashes." And she told him the little she knew.

"What's your theory?" he asked, knowing she'd have one. She always did. She had superb instincts. He would miss her when she went on to a big-city paper, and it wouldn't be long before she did.

"I'm thinking about vulnerabilities in maintenance."

"What about bombs?" he asked.

"Yes, bombs, of course bombs, but not bombs carried on by passengers. Bombs that got on the planes some other way, maybe through duty-free shops or through maintenance."

"Why do you think that?"

"A hunch. It'd be just about impossible for terrorists with bombs on their bodies to get through today's security screening at three different airports."

"Who will you talk to?" he asked.

"Oh, the usual suspects, but I don't expect to get much out of them. I do have a good source at the Port Authority Police at JFK. And I'll call a guy I know at MI5 in London. Maybe the French Interior Ministry; they take a lot of preemptive action against terrorists. Something we couldn't do here."

"Tell me about it," her boss grunted. "I'll be in soon. By the way, what brought you in early today?"

"Fencing practice," she said.

"The old college passion."

"Right," she said. She was not about to let him know she was training for the Olympic team again. She'd rather avoid the overly personal references to tight clothing and the salacious comments about swordsmanship that he found so amusing.

"Okay, work those phones."

"Sure thing," said Marie, hanging up. One day she hoped to have a really smart boss. Not a seat cushion like this guy.

Bangkok, Thailand, May 5

Mansour Obaidi lay in the middle of his king-sized bed at the Olympia Hotel on Sukhumvit Road. To the untutored eye, the area was a far cry from the seediness of the Patpong district with its live-sex bars. Sukhumvit Road was a haven of gentlemen's clubs with leather-upholstered booths, multilingual Russian hostesses, and single-malt scotch whiskies. But it was all facade. Behind the handsome mahogany doors, Sukhumvit Road provided its foreign guests with the traditional satisfactions, albeit wrapped in more expensive packaging: beautiful women, sensual massages, and the fulfillment of unusual tastes. The aura of luxury and discretion was an attraction for wealthy Muslims from North Africa to Indonesia. It offered them an escape from Islam's inconvenient strictures. Arab businessmen preferred Arab-controlled hotels like the Olympia. They were at ease here—with each other, and with the services provided.

Obaidi was dressed in tan slacks and a new shirt he'd had custom-made by a tailor across the street from his hotel. He didn't have to fret about prices, but still, he was proud that the same shirt custom-made in Hong Kong would have cost 50 percent more. The garment itself, a blue striped Egyptian cotton with white collar and cuffs, was an odd choice for him, though rather than fight the enthusiasm he felt for it, he embraced it. Other things were changing inside him as well, loosening up, breaking free.

He was feeling full, as if his emotions, usually competing for attention and gratification, had found a balance. All were momentarily content. He thought of some lines from the Koran that he had memorized as a child. "Ye asked for succor from your Lord, and He answered you, 'I will assist you with a thousand angels, with others in reserve.'"

Obaidi sat up and drew a newspaper onto his lap. One after the other, the papers were filled with news of the plane crashes. Headlines in German, Italian, English, and French, all describing the fiery curse.

But for him it was a blessing. Glory to Islam and death to the unbelievers. All over Europe, people were unhinged, governments indecisive. American politicians talked about a second invasion of Afghanistan, but terrorism analysts noted that the crashes didn't bear the marks of bin Laden. How perceptive of them, he thought drily. His blueblood friend Osama was overly enamored of spectacular gestures. He, on the other hand, was thoroughly practical. And fast on his feet. No big entourages with harems and children to slow him down. And no Muhammad complex. Yes, he had seen that even back in the eighties.

But Afghanistan had been a great experience for them all. They'd successfully fought the Russians and created a modern jihad, eventually imposing sharia on the country. En route, they'd learned a great deal, both from the failure of the Russians and from the mujahideen's helpers, the CIA. Each regime had put modern technology into their hands, as well as introducing unfamiliar cultures and ideas. Of course, most was disposable, the garbage of decadent, declining societies. But some was useful.

Obaidi's thoughts turned back toward the Middle East. For millennia it had served as a cauldron of exchange. Visitors from the four corners of the world came in search of enlightenment or riches. Once in the holy land, they learned, taught, and traded, and then they carried their new ideas and goods back home, fueling revolutionary change all over the globe.

It was Obaidi's fervent belief that Islam would once again regain its proper role at the epicenter of that process. That's what they had spoken about, dreamed of, and planned for back in those heady days in Afghanistan.

He looked again at the papers. His remorse over the deaths of Muslims had been tempered with exultation at the reach of his accomplishment, the breadth of the confusion it had wrought, and the clamorous denunciations that flew in every direction but the correct one. Confusion was the oxygen in which Obaidi burned with life. And those few Arabs and Muslims from Asian countries who were lost had died as *shahids,* holy warriors, and they were guaranteed tickets straight to paradise.

The telephone rang. Obaidi answered it. "Very good, thank you. Send them up."

He stood and straightened his shirt, gathered the papers into a desk drawer. He looked at himself in the mirror appraisingly and brushed his mustache into place. Yes, now he was in the mood. He'd had a lovely Thai massage earlier, then a quick trip to the go-go bar.

A few moments later, there was a knock on the door and he opened it, exhaling in satisfaction. Two girls walked in, dressed in fanciful costumes beneath their dark overcoats. Each had her hair pulled up tight like a dancer's and looked like a glittering ornament. He deserved a bit of a reward after all this, and he had scheduled some private entertainment for himself tonight. "They who are true believers—theirs shall be great dignity in their Sustainer's sight and forgiveness of sins, and a most excellent sustenance."

Behind them, timid, dressed in brocade and silk, was Obaidi's prize, the fruit of the evening. The young man was dark-skinned with a complexion as smooth as poured chocolate. Obaidi smiled and felt that movement again, the electricity that jumped in him, and made him forget everything but his quarry. With his three guests inside, Obaidi closed the door.

Ninety minutes later, having gratified himself, he sent his guests on their way. In the past, when he'd indulged in this particular type of commerce, he'd allowed himself a good deal more leeway, even at additional cost. But today he was hurried, impatient. It was time to return home.

Chapter Four

Tel Aviv, May 5

Julian pulled up to Shabaq's nondescript cement-block headquarters in Tel Aviv and parked on the street. The moon, almost full, shone brilliantly off the city's rooftops. As a young soldier he had studied lunar movements; missions depended on the moon's location and brightness. A helicopter drop in the Iraqi desert worked best when it was dark. Other missions required a full moon but a late rising. There were tables to memorize and rhymes to learn to determine the location of the moon and whether it was waxing or waning, but he did it by instinct. He'd grown up on a farm; the phases of the moon were as familiar to him as the cycles of planting and harvesting.

Julian swiped his ID card, waited for the buzz, then put his hand on a biometric hand sensor. He avoided the elevator. It was slow, and besides, Julian suffered from claustrophobia. Instead, he jogged up the stairs to the second floor and a shabby conference room. Military offices in Israel tended to be spartan; resources went where they were most needed. When soldiers slept in old sleeping bags or lacked bulletproof vests for patrols, there was no question of fine furniture or mahogany paneling. This room was no exception.

Ben-Ami greeted him with a nod and a handshake.

"Ride okay?" he asked. As often as Julian flew on planes, he still detested them. It took real willpower to control his anxiety about confined spaces. Ben-Ami knew this.

"I'd rather have ridden my Jet Ski all the way here than fly in that sardine can you arranged for me," he said. "Other than that, it was lovely." Julian's hair was rumpled as usual. He wore light corduroy slacks and a cotton knit short-sleeved shirt. Ben-Ami chuckled.

Julian looked appraisingly at his friend. Ben-Ami looked sharp and in good shape, Julian thought. The man was of medium height, his eyes were deep set and intelligent, his nose fine, body wiry and fit. Ben-Ami wore a crisp white short-sleeved shirt and khaki pants. Members of Shabaq and Mossad did not distinguish themselves from the populace and wore no military uniforms. In fact, until recently their leaders' identities, their voices and photos, had been state secrets.

Ben-Ami gestured toward a chair. Julian greeted the six men at the table with hellos and handshakes before sitting down.

"How's soccer?" asked one, to the amusement of all. These men were all from Ben-Ami's organization and had worked with Julian until his recent departure. He knew them all, and they knew him. They also knew of his dreams to quit the military and manage an amateur soccer team. That hadn't happened yet—in part because of intermittent requests for his help on jobs like this.

Julian smiled and shook his head.

In front of each man at the table was a laptop connected to an intranet where they could get whatever data they needed for the discussions ahead. It was a secure network, one firewall inside another. Security clearance was automated. Each user's screen name and password told the network exactly how much information to release. Only the most senior people had access to the innermost ring, containing such information as the real identities of agents inside hostile Middle Eastern countries.

The system allowed quick responses by elite teams that needed to act immediately on intelligence reports. It also allowed others full access to up-to-the-minute intelligence, on a need-to-know basis. And it took the place of hard documents that could be smuggled out and photocopied.

Before Ben-Ami began to speak, a young female army recruit with a brown ponytail and green fatigues placed on the table a pen and the only paper that would appear at this meeting. On it, the participants wrote down what they wanted to drink. The choices were as basic as the room: coffee, tea, mineral water. Then all chatter stopped and the men turned to Ben-Ami.

"I think you all know Julian Granot," he said. "And you, Shimon, have had regular dealings with him, right?" The men laughed, a brief release of tension, a temporary reprieve before what was to come. Shimon, a high-ranking air force intelligence officer, was Julian's brother-in-law. It ran in the family.

"As you know," continued Ben-Ami, his face grave once again, "we're here because three planes have disappeared almost simultaneously from radar while in flight and are presumed lost. Two were over the Atlantic Ocean when they went down. The third was over the South China Sea. Other pilots in the vicinities reported seeing flashes at the times of the disappearances. American coast guard and British, Japanese, and Chinese naval crews are searching for the crash sites. British Airways Flight 134 from New York to London, bound for Madrid, lost touch with the control tower two hours after takeoff. Wreckage has been located by the American coast guard a hundred miles off the coast of Newfoundland, in seas that are a mile deep. American ships have found a few suitcases, some seat cushions.

"As far as the other two flights are concerned, the debris fields have not yet been found. American Flight 147 from Paris to Boston lost contact with air traffic control three hours after takeoff. Cathay Pacific's Flight 715 from Hong Kong to Singapore was lost forty-five minutes after departure.

"Aman has given us passenger lists," continued Ben-Ami. They're appended to the agenda you'll find on the laptops. Aman is analyzing the lists for any connections among passengers of the flights. Our people are looking for connections to our own 'black list' of terrorists. If you look at the agenda, you'll also see links to maps of the flight routes, supplied by Shimon and his friends at air force intelligence. You'll also see an item on the agenda called 'news.' Clicking on the link will give you a compilation of all potentially interesting media reports for the next seventy-two hours."

The female soldier returned with a tray of drinks and set it down on the table. Ben-Ami accepted a bottle of mineral water and took a swig.

"Now, no Israeli aircraft were involved. No Israeli was on any of the planes. But if we do nothing, our turn will come." He looked around the table. "Our turn will come."

Every man nodded.

"That's why we have to do what we can. You've all been selected for a task force to figure out where to go from here. Julian here is heading up the show. He'll make sure you get everything you need. And he'll name additional members to the team as he sees fit. Though he's just arrived from vacation and hasn't had time to analyze the situation any longer than you, I'm sure he'll have something interesting to say. Julian, why don't you take it from here?"

Julian took off his glasses, folded them carefully, and placed them in their case.

"Hello, everybody," he said in a deep basso, gentler than one expected from his leonine appearance. "I know we all wish we were elsewhere. It's a sad day for too many families. I also wish I weren't here, because I left *my* family on the most beautiful beach in the world."

"Should have called the meeting there," murmured Shlomo, a young army lieutenant. "Flown us all over."

A chorus of affirmatives arose around the table.

"Violates Code PAC 1.01.05," said an officer from Shabaq's law office in an officious voice. Everyone laughed. Israelis lived with tragedy every day. Humor was a lifeline.

"Okay, okay," said Julian, smiling, turning the eyeglass case over in his hands. "First, we all know how hard it is to find clues when a plane crashes into deep water. Pieces of metal wreckage are small and sink straight to the bottom. Maybe cloth and plastic in suitcases or chair covers will be left floating, and maybe not. The pieces of TWA Flight 800 that went down in Long Island Sound were recovered only because the plane fell into relatively shallow water and from a low altitude. Then there was Swissair Flight 111, which went down off Nova Scotia in 1998, due to a technical failure. The wreckage lay in small pieces only fifty-five meters deep. Still, the flight data recorder and black box were never found.

"I mention this because the three flights we're talking about today had reached cruising altitude—thirty thousand feet. And they were all flying over deep ocean. So it's unlikely we'll find our most significant clues in the remains of the planes.

"I'll make one more point before opening up this discussion," Julian continued, looking each man in the eye, one by one. "The key to solving the cause of the explosion of Pan Am Flight 103 over Lockerbie, Scotland, was a piece of electronic circuit board only centimeters in diameter. And it was found because the bomb misfired and went off too soon. The plane exploded over land. Imagine finding a tiny piece of a circuit board three miles below the ocean surface. Before the salt water ruined it."

The men considered Julian's words in silence.

"So," Julian said, pushing himself back from the table a few inches. "Having said all that, to make this process a little easier, I'm going to assume that the same PMO was at work on all flights." Julian was referring to the possible means of operation. "It's unlikely that someone worked out three different simultaneous attack scenarios."

"What about surface-to-air missiles?" asked Nadav Rosenberg, a lanky young man of twenty-seven with a head full of dark brown curls. Nadav was one of Julian's favorite lieutenants, and a member of his former core team. "They could have been launched from ships large enough to hold missile batteries. One placed in the Atlantic could have been responsible for the first two attacks, and another in the South China Sea for the third."

"For sure, missiles must be considered," said Julian. "But as a PMO? I think not. Terrorists would have a hard time maintaining two ships outfitted with missile batteries—even a terrorist as wealthy as Osama bin Laden. Besides, if they're going to hit a target at thirty thousand feet, the missiles would have to be long-range, like the Soviets' SA-2 or SA-8. Our intelligence has no evidence that terrorists have anything like that."

Nadav nodded. "What about state-sponsored terrorism?" he asked. "Syria? Iran?"

"This we can't dismiss. But our intelligence has nothing to support the idea."

"Our intelligence," spat Daniel Orlovsky, an air force analyst. "Our intelligence missed the Yom Kippur War, it missed both intifadas. I think one of our neighbors is flexing its muscles. We know Libya was behind the Pan Am bombing over Lockerbie. We know Iran has a spectacular track record in sponsoring global terrorism and is now actively fomenting trouble in Iraq."

"Do we?" asked Julian mildly. "Has Iran ever mounted an operation like this? I don't trust them either, but my gut tells me here that we're dealing with freelance terrorists, and with a very simple device, like a bomb aimed to explode the aircraft in midair."

"A shoe bomb or explosives in a radio?" asked Nadav.

"Yes, though I don't see how three different people in three separate airports could smuggle explosive devices on board. Unless of course the explosive material was RDX."

"Because it can be soaked into the suicide bombers' clothes, and is undetectable," filled in Nadav.

"Correct," said Julian.

"Another possibility is that bomb parts were smuggled on board by multiple terrorists and assembled on the planes," said Benjamin Harel, a blond so fair his eyebrows and lashes were almost invisible. Born in Sweden to Israeli parents who were fair themselves, he was very useful to Julian because of his Swedish passport. He could pass as a native Swede for undercover operations. "This is basically the same strategy used in the 9/11 attack," he continued, "when four terrorists boarded the same flight, and then used the plane itself as the bomb."

Julian nodded. "Also there's a possibility that the bomb went inside a suitcase," he said, his thoughts falling into place neatly, as if he were not in fact thinking on the fly. "But to knock down that theory, all we have to do is prove that one of the airports screened the suitcases with an explosive-detection system."

"Like a CTX machine," said Benjamin.

"Yes," said Julian. "And we know that all American airports do that. So that's an unlikely PMO."

"What about cargo?" asked Benjamin. "I mean, that's the Wild West of opportunity for terrorists."

"That's an area of great concern," said Julian. "A bomb could have been sent in cargo. If so, it would have gone as personal-effects cargo by courier. If they sent it as bulk cargo, the terrorists couldn't be sure that their bomb would go on the flights they were targeting. Bulk cargo can be taken off one flight and put on another—even another airline. That wouldn't have been an option for so carefully planned an operation as this one, with the planes intended to go down over open water."

"All you need to do to dismantle that theory is to check the airline records," said Nadav. "If even one flight had no courier on board, we can eliminate it."

"And there's always my personal nightmare," Julian said, picking up his glasses again. "Catering and maintenance. The weak link in airline security. I know it and you know it. It's far too easy for unauthorized personnel to gain access to the tarmac. El Al is the safest airline in the world. But even our planes need constant maintenance. Hydraulic pumps must be checked and overhauled frequently. The GPS equipment needs to be adjusted. Radio systems sometimes need repair. You can't put a bomb in any of these, because the systems will register technical failures, but the mechanics making repairs have access to the cabin, to cargo.

"Catering is always vulnerable, but after September 11, all American flights and most international airlines have imposed strict security procedures including X-rays of the food carts."

"And then there are the duty-free shops," said Benjamin.

"Very enticing opportunities there," said Julian, nodding. "The delivery of goods in many airports takes place on the wrong side of the firewall."

He paused. "Let's go back for a moment to what we know about this series of crashes." Julian was reviewing as much for his own benefit as the others'. The discussion was moving too quickly, in too many directions, and he needed to regain focus.

"Think about it," he said. "All three planes went down over open water. This reduces evidence and increases fear. The explosions were carefully timed, and the triggers were clearly tied to a dependable and stable electronic device. Now, what if the planners used a mechanism that was already present in the aircraft? Part of its avionics, or other equipment? Something Boeing or Airbus built in, and that the terrorists took advantage of? Think, gentlemen: what is already present on a plane, is an electronic device, and is programmable?"

"What is large enough to hold some plastic explosives and an altimeter and can also supply an electric charge to set off the bomb?" asked Nadav, jumping in.

"What on a flight is programmable?" Julian repeated, to a sudden, sickening flash of memory. Seven years before, he'd visited a repair shop in London that maintained the on-board entertainment kits—the video machines that played movies, news, and safety instructions. Something about the shop had unnerved him, and he'd asked his British counterparts if they'd checked the backgrounds of three Moroccans who worked there. The Brits had laughed him off, insisting his Israeli paranoia was getting the best of him.

"The in-flight phones?" Yossi Nimrodi suggested. He was a telecommunications expert.

Julian waved the idea away. "No," he said. "The video machines that play the movies. They're programmable for up to a year. But they're complex systems, and they break down. When they do, they're not serviced on board, nor by anyone at the airports. Instead, they're sent off location to local repair shops. There are only a handful of companies that operate them."

"Don't tell me, let me guess," said Nadav. "When the video machines are returned to the airports and the planes, they're not sent through explosive-detection systems."

"That's right," said Julian, his voice quickening. "If the airport worker accepting the delivery is really conscientious, he may run the machine through an X-ray, but he won't see anything, because even a well-trained operator will have trouble analyzing the image of such a dense electronic device. All you need is a couple kilos of plastic explosive stuck inside the lid and a fuse that is set to turn on at a certain programmed time. The machines have clocks that are perfect for this. A small switch and an altimeter attached to a second circuit will do the trick."

Julian shook his head and thumped his fingers on the table before continuing. "There was a Mitsubishi repair shop in London I visited seven years ago. Three Moroccans worked there. When I checked their names, they didn't come up clean. It worried me. I personally ordered that all video kits on El Al be repaired only by our own people. I caught hell from passengers whenever that meant there was no in-flight movie. But that was it."

He paused, the image clawing at his mind: innocent passengers in their seats, watching Reese Witherspoon or Cameron Diaz or Matt Damon when suddenly the world ended. The room was silent.

"Okay, men. We have a lot of work to do," he said. "First, we have to get as much paperwork as we can about each of the three flights, and we must look for a pattern. For now, focus on this: Get the records for duty-free shops; get the names of the flight attendants who delivered the goods and the names of the passengers who purchased them. Find all repair and maintenance records for the three planes, including electronic components. We need to check cargo shipments and catering."

He looked at them one by one and spoke slowly. "This is very important," he said. "Avoid official channels if at all possible. They'll set us back weeks. I, for example, will get the repair and maintenance records of the planes myself, through my own contacts. All of you: use your personal contacts. Call in favors. Buy people off. Do whatever the hell it takes."

He looked at Ben-Ami. "You didn't hear that, right?"

"Good work, Julie," said Ben-Ami, nodding to the group. They got up quietly and filed out of the room, each to his own assignment.

"I have an office for you," said Ben-Ami, leading Julian out. "I think you'll remember it—it's your old one."

The office was as unremarkable as ever: metal desk and chair, bookshelf, an old leather armchair. Julian took off his windbreaker and hung it neatly on the back of the chair. He absently opened a drawer of the desk and saw his old table lamp still there. He set it on the desk and plugged it in. Julian hated fluorescent lights.

He sat down at his desk and pulled out his handheld PDA. He scrolled down to the office number of his old friend James Sylvestre, the top cop at the Port Authority of New York and New Jersey. They'd become friends when Julian ran El Al's security operation in the U.S. years before. As head of the "local authorities," Sylvestre had been in a position to make life easier for Julian and his operational men.

In return, Julian shared intelligence reports with Sylvestre that involved his airports. Sylvestre understood their significance and America's vulnerability, though his bosses did not. He confided to Julian that he was often prevented by higher-ups from conducting the investigations he knew were necessary.

Before 9/11, most American officials never imagined America could be the target of a terrorist attack. Julian thought of all the Middle Eastern students enrolled in American flight schools, but not interested in learning to land their planes. When a dismayed FBI agent tried to alert her superiors to the risk of one of them, a Frenchman of Moroccan descent, she was shouted down. With silence. When she complained, she was drummed out of her job.

The Americans were so naive! If they'd heard the chants and slogans of the terrorists in their training camps, the bloodlust and hatred, swearing to murder infidels wherever they could find them; if they'd only interviewed a terrorist who'd strapped a suicide belt on his girlfriend's body—a body he'd just made love to—and sent her out to blow up a jumbo jet or a pizza parlor, then they might have questioned their assumptions about shared humanity. They might have thought differently.

Sylvestre had. He'd learned about thugs and punks from his own childhood. He knew that terrorists were like the wise guys who ran his Brooklyn neighborhood, turning the system's weaknesses to their advantage. They hid behind the protections of American society and law. And, as he learned later as a law enforcement officer, it took extraordinary means to stop them.

But they'd got him first. When the initial police calls went out about the World Trade Center fire, Sylvestre was at a meeting in midtown. He jumped into his police cruiser, drove to the site, and entered the north tower. Julian imagined him running up the smoky stairwells and into offices to help the weak and the unsteady. Reports from colleagues indicated he'd made several trips up and down before World Trade Center One collapsed on him.

Julian looked away and took a deep breath. He dialed the number in his book. Sylvestre's former assistant, John Willoughby, answered.

"Willoughby. Julian Granot calling from Tel Aviv."

"Hey Julie, what's up?"

"I'm very sorry about your plane."

"Yeah, you wouldn't believe the shitstorm," said Willoughby. "Ain't a man here who can grab his ass with both hands. The TSA is off in front of one podium saying one thing, and the head of Homeland Security is at another saying something else. Everyone's freaked."

"John, I'm calling to ask you a favor."

"You just tell me, Julie," said Willoughby in his tough-guy Bronx accent. "I'm sure Jimmy woulda done it, so I'm happy to help you out. Go ahead, shoot."

"I need the maintenance reports from the American Airlines flight. I want everything—all the checks and repairs made on that plane from the engines right down to the coffeemakers for the week preceding the wreck. Is that something you can do without stirring up too much attention?"

"I think I could do that for you. Can I ask why?"

"I have a theory about your plane, and if it pans out, you'll be the first man in New York to know."

"I'd like that. You got what you want."

"Thanks, John. By the way," said Julian, his tone softening. "How is Jimmy's wife doing?"

"Oh, you know Lorraine," said Willoughby. "She's a tough one. Yeah, we see her sometimes, my wife and I. I think she's putting her life back together."

"Time flies, doesn't it?" said Julian.

"Hey, I just remembered," said Willoughby. "A reporter called me an hour or so ago. Used to talk to Jimmy, so she can't be bullshit like most of them people. And you know what? She was asking me the same kind of questions that you just asked. Maybe you want to talk to her. Maybe you and her could trade information."

Julian's alertness went up a notch. "What questions?"

"Like about who has access to the planes when they're on the ground, and who has maintenance contracts. You want me to give her your number?"

Julian paused. It was a breach of procedure to let someone contact him. But if he wanted to maintain any kind of cover, he couldn't act like who he was. Besides, her questions suggested she might know something. Julian liked information, he craved information, and he preferred data that came from outside the usual networks.

"No," said Julian. "Tell her I'm traveling and I'll call her. Also—tell her I'm an aviation consultant in private industry."

"Gotcha. Her name's Marie Peterssen."

Julian paused. He was surprised by the sudden butterflies in his stomach. "Okay, thanks," he said. "I know the name. She writes for one of the aviation magazines."

"Happy to help," said Willoughby, reading out Peterssen's telephone number. "But now I gotta get back to the meat grinder we call JFK."

Julian laughed in sympathy, then furrowed his brow. Marie Peterssen, he thought. Marie Mercier Peterssen. A long time ago.

He picked up the phone again and continued his calls, this one to a former colleague at Heathrow Airport in London. Again, he asked for a favor and copies of the British Airways plane's maintenance records. Then a colleague in Hong Kong. Finally, he buzzed an operator two floors below. "Give me a direct line to New York, area code 212," he said. He didn't identify himself. "And route it through Zurich. I don't want this country code popping up on anyone's caller ID."

Chapter Five

Jerusalem, May 6

"Abba Eban famously used to say that 'the Palestinians never miss an opportunity to miss an opportunity.'" The shop owner polished a copper coffeepot as he lectured a customer in his junk shop on Shlomzion Ha-Malka, just off Jaffa Road, hard by the Old City. Gil Kizner, a wiry man with curly black hair, was engaged in a lively conversation with a retired history professor from New Jersey about the current state of the peace process.

"Ah," said the professor, "Eban's error was in thinking the Palestinians' opportunity was the same as his own. Yassir Arafat never missed an opportunity to remain in control of the Palestinians' hearts and their money."

"But now Arafat's gone," said Gil, "and the Palestinians continue with their self-destructive ways. The mainstream doesn't have the guts to stand up and say 'Enough!' to the terrorists who have taken over— and if you ask me, derailed—their cause."

"It's an interesting time," said the bearded professor, who found an antique measuring device on the wall. "And what is this charming instrument, may I ask?" he said.

Kizner stepped beside the man and looked appreciatively at the walnut-and-rosewood wall hanging. "That is a hygrometer—an instrument for measuring humidity. Its working mechanism consists of a single human hair. The hair stretches as the humidity increases, and it moves an exquisitely sensitive dial. See, we can read it right here." He pointed to a hand-painted dial. "Today, the humidity in Jerusalem is twenty percent, not so bad."

The bell on the front door tinkled and a familiar figure entered the shop. Kizner watched with surprise and barely concealed pleasure as Julian approached. Kizner gave his friend a handshake and a soldier's hug.

"Everything okay with you?" asked Julian, smiling broadly.

"Couldn't be better," said Kizner. "It's me and my junk, just the way I like it."

Julian nodded, and Kizner knew he wanted to talk. The professor had decided to buy the hygrometer. Kizner convinced him to come and pick it up, all wrapped for travel, in one hour. As soon as the bell on the door stopped jangling, Julian began to speak.

"I have a little project I want your help with."

"Well, Julie, you never gave an order that I didn't follow." Kizner stood behind a glass counter, unwrapping delicate ceramic coffee cups from newspaper printed in Arabic.

"It's not an order. It's a request, nothing more. You can say no if your politics—whatever they happen to be at the moment—tell you to. I'll walk right out. I'm retired, remember?"

Kizner placed the cups carefully on the counter. He had never married, contenting himself to take care of the shop where his father had worked for forty years before him. It was a relief from military life, just standing among his stuff and shepherding items to their new homes.

"These cups belonged to a Syrian Jewish family, the Benvenistes," he said, holding one to the light and admiring its eggshell delicacy, its lustrous finish. "The porcelain was made in Spain in the eighteenth century.

Beautiful, eh? After the partition of Palestine in 1948, the family was expelled along with all the other Jews in Arab countries. But they didn't believe they would be gone for long, because they'd been settled in Syria for five hundred years. So they buried their valuables beneath a grove of orange trees. Of course, they never did go back, and it took fifty years for them to accept that fact.

"The children eventually contacted their former Syrian neighbors and asked them if they would dig up their possessions. The Benvenistes sent them money to return the objects via Cyprus to avoid any suspicion of collaboration with Israelis. So their neighbors dutifully dug up the stuff and returned it to the family."

"Beautiful story," said Julian. "I don't believe a word of it. After such an adventure, why would the family let go of the cups? For a few shekels? Shut the store for me for a moment, will you? And walk with me across the street." Julian appreciated his friend's imagination. It had saved both of them in tight spots in the past. But it was also an inescapable fact that in a life of subterfuge, reality and fantasy had the habit of blurring. For that, Julian was always on the lookout.

Kizner sighed and did as he was told. "Yes sir," he said, realizing that in a matter of a few moments, he had reverted to old manners with his beloved former commander. "We'll go for a little walk where no one can hear us, you'll ask me for help with an impossible task and I'll say yes, and then we'll celebrate with a drink back here. I have some lovely rum from Havana. I got it from a recent visitor."

They turned the corner onto Jaffa Road. Julian stepped into a bakery to buy *bourekas*, a Middle Eastern savory made from phyllo pastry filled with spinach, potato, and a salty cheese called *kachkaval.* Handing one to Kizner as he emerged, he began describing the crash investigation he was heading up. He needed someone who could trawl databases like a fisherman on Lake Kinneret, and Kizner was his man.

"Okay, so this is what brought you back," Kizner said. "I should have known right away." He stopped at the curb, but Julian was already halfway across the street, waving the bag of *bourekas* at him. "Call me and tell me what you've decided. I know it's hard to leave your shop, but think about it. We'll have that rum later."

New York City, May 6

The newswire transmission had been on Marie's desk since morning, but she hadn't had a chance to look it over. Just now she was filling out a form her boss had told her was of utmost importance, due last week, etc. She hated these things. Name of mother, name of father, place of birth, place of father's birth. She didn't know her father's name, although there was a name on her birth certificate: Sven Peterssen, one of her mother's favorite ballet partners. In spite of her mother's undeniable beauty and considerable charms, neither she nor anyone else had ever suggested Sven had ever been inclined, even momentarily, in any other direction other than his chosen one: gay.

So she made up names for her own amusement. Thomas Mann, Hermann Hesse. Ludwig von Beethoven. The wilder the better. So far, she'd never been called on it. Anyway, she finished up the form, threw it on her boss's desk, returned to her cubicle, and saw the newswire. When she finally picked it up, she saw that it contained the passenger lists for the downed planes. Marie ran down the names with dread. She cringed when she saw the ages of the victims. The numbers punctuated the names, which on their own seemed anonymous enough: Neal Whitton. The ages carved their silhouette: Mary Ann Jones, twenty-seven. Children, when they were lost, were the worst. Hillary Smith, four. Nicholas Martin, six. Four, six—those were ages for a birthday party, not a funeral.

Marie thought she owed it to the victims to read every one. Their lives had been cut short in a violent act, they'd had no chance for final words, but at least someone in the wider world would notice their passing.

Working her way down the list, she stopped. Nicolas Duras. Could it be him? From Paris. She'd heard he'd become a wine exporter. He could do that from Paris for sure. Age twenty-nine. That would be about right. Oh dear. He'd been a childhood friend. Nicolas. He was funny and quirky and rode a unicycle. She could hear his laughter after he'd crashed to earth for the millionth time. He kissed her once when they were nine, then ran away and didn't speak to her for a week.

Tears rushed to her eyes as she thought of him and the happy summers they'd spent together in Arles. She wondered if she still had a phone number for his parents so she could send her condolences. His father, Pierre, she'd always called Pere Jolie, a play on Pierre, she'd guessed, though she couldn't remember exactly where the name had come from. He had been a kind of substitute father for her, and a sweet, caring one at that, always including her when he played soccer with his son or took him out fishing. She got up to get a drink of water and was hit with a wave of sadness that brought tears to her eyes once again. Nicolas had brown hair. He wore kneesocks and short pants and brown tie shoes, and collected rocks. He'd called her Marie de Paris. She decided to leave the office and get a breath of fresh air.

These crashes had just got personal.

New York City, May 7

The door of the Greenwich Village restaurant was unexpectedly heavy, so Marie Peterssen propped it open with the heel of her suede shoe, and promptly dropped her umbrella. Bending over to retrieve it, she dropped her handbag on the floor. A waiter hurried to help, but Marie had already scooped up everything. She was a graceful, athletic woman, but prone to embarrassing pratfalls.

She saw the man who had called from Switzerland two nights before seated as promised. He'd chosen a small table, with his back to the wall so he had a full view of the room as well as the door. She knew it was him. He was using a handheld wireless device. A drink she presumed was some kind of whiskey sat in front of him. That is exactly what Julian had told her about himself—no description about his appearance, only that he'd be holding a PDA and drinking Wild Turkey. She was ten minutes early, but he was already quite settled. He was tall and muscular with tousled red hair and looked solid as a bull. Military, she figured right away. And although he hadn't yet looked up, she was sure he was aware of her presence.

He looked anywhere from thirty-five to fifty years old. When she got within four feet of his table, he finally looked up and searched her face with intelligent, alert green eyes.

"Marie Peterssen," she said steadily. He stood and offered his hand, which was large and warm. His face was friendly but inscrutable. She found in it no expression other than patience. He watched, taking in everything but giving little back. She thought he looked vaguely Irish or Scottish.

Marie slipped off her rain jacket and hung it over the back of her chair. She wore black bell-bottom slacks and a filmy V-neck top. She was tall with a lovely figure, Julian noticed. Chic, but unmannered. Her face was oval and framed by straight dark hair that hung to her shoulders. Her blue eyes were shaded by long black lashes. As she leaned forward to pull out her chair, her hair swung in front of her face and she pushed it back with a delicate movement of her left hand. Her appearance had changed since the last time he'd seen a photo of her. Her face had become more exotic. She'd grown up. She had an alluring beauty that stemmed, Julian saw, from a mysterious inner quiet. The waiter arrived and she ordered a glass of wine.

"I'd have bourbon with you," she said, looking quickly at his drink, "but I see much better with my eyes uncrossed."

Julian laughed. He had a deep voice, strong, sure, with a jovial aspect, suggesting a willingness to be surprised.

Female journalists on occasion tried to be tougher than their male counterparts, who, for their part, tended to make fools of themselves, particularly with military men, trying to act macho. Julian was glad she wasn't one of them. Not too long ago he had met with an American journalist, who after two years in Russia wanted to show off his vodka-drinking skills to his new Israeli military contacts. Julian had been obliged to deliver him to his hotel in a less than battle-ready state.

The restaurant Julian had chosen was a comfortable Spanish joint, old-fashioned and slightly worn around the edges. The walls were exposed brick hung with dusty old paintings of Seville and Madrid. The long tables were rustic, made of heavy dark wood, and the drinking glasses were plain and straight. The place was loud and small, and the clientele was largely from the neighborhood. The general low-scale din was interrupted by a passel of children at a table in the back, when they broke out in a rendition of "Happy Birthday" as a waiter carried a cake to their table. Marie turned and saw a young-looking man accepting the cake with an expression of surprise and delight from what appeared to be his four children.

"Big happy family," she said, turning back to Julian. She was moved by the sight of a father with his young children. And then she blushed. And she blushed deeper when she realized how corny that sounded.

"Appears to be," he said, watching her steadily, trying to fight the sadness tugging at him from far away.

"That was kind of apropos of nothing," she said quickly, suddenly self-conscious, and determined to hide what she was really feeling. "I guess I noticed because they were so boisterous. Life goes on, doesn't it? Even after plane crashes." That was a lucky segue she grabbed on to, she thought, pausing to gather herself. "So, how did you get here?"

"I flew over on a private plane," said Julian slowly, watching her, moved by her sudden discomfort. "I caught a ride with a businessman who was kind enough to give me a lift. I had a few meetings here in the States, and thought it might be easier to answer your questions in person rather than over the phone."

"Yeah," she said, nodding. The ban on some private aircraft had been lifted the day before.

"I understand you were asking our mutual friend Willoughby about baggage and maintenance," he said, getting right down to business.

"Does he tell you everything?" she asked.

"No," said Julian. "But about you, yes."

Marie laughed. "May I ask why?"

"Because I inquired," said Julian.

She raised her eyebrows. "Is there a reason for that?"

"Perhaps," he said, smiling. Was that a playful smile? She couldn't tell.

Marie looked at him quietly, her mind working. "Willoughby said you were the man to ask about security vulnerabilities in airline maintenance. That's why I wanted to talk to you."

"Why don't you tell me what you're working on," he said, nodding for her to go on.

"I write stories about different aspects of the aviation industry, but I have a special interest in crashes." Her brow furrowed. "Not the cheeriest specialty, I guess."

Julian smiled.

"Any particular crashes you've worked on?" he asked.

"TWA Flight 800."

"Yes, an interesting case," said Julian. "Down on takeoff into Long Island Sound in 1996."

She speeded up. "American Airlines Flight 587, which crashed in Far Rockaway, Queens. Swissair 111, which went down after a cockpit fire off Nova Scotia in '98."

Julian had no reaction.

Marie paused. Her eyes narrowed. What was he up to? "There are more. In several cases," she said, "I think the government has withheld information and the real stories haven't been told."

She saw nothing in his face. "What do you mean?" he asked, sipping his drink.

"I think that in at least two of the cases, the planes went down as a result of terrorism. But no one is willing to admit it."

"What are you thinking?" he said.

"I'm not sure I should tell you what I think. I really don't know who you are."

Julian raised his eyebrows. "Didn't Willoughby tell you to talk to me?"

"Yes." She held his gaze.

"Do you trust *him*?" he asked.

She shrugged. "I guess so. Though his boss was the guy I really knew."

"Sylvestre was a great man," said Julian. "And I loved him."

Marie was startled by the ease and simplicity of Julian's declaration. Maybe she shouldn't have doubted him.

"You knew him when you were posted at JFK? That's what Willoughby said." She was stalling as she tried to sort out her thoughts.

Julian nodded.

"You worked for El Al then," she said.

He nodded. "I work for a private company now. I retired recently from the Israel Defense Forces, where for some time I was in charge of security for the national airline."

"Your security company is new?"

Julian nodded.

"So it wouldn't be familiar to me, but it would have its requisite number of retired generals and high-ranking intelligence officers?"

He nodded, smiling slightly.

"And am I right in assuming your most important client right now might be your former employer?"

Julian took a sip of his drink. "If it were I wouldn't tell you."

She laughed. "I guess, then, I am fairly safe in assuming you know what you're talking about," she said.

"I'm always trying," he said. He was clearly an expert. Head of security for El Al? The most secure airline in the world. She might as well tell him what she knew.

"TWA Flight 800 was exhaustively examined," he said, looking at her steadily. "Your government determined the cause of the crash to be a design flaw."

"I have a copy of the National Transportation Safety Board's complete report on the crash," she said. "You've read it, right?"

"Sure." He shrugged. "Explosion in an empty gas tank."

"Right," she said. "I think the NTSB report is bullshit." She watched him to see if he took offense. He gave no sign. "Oh sure, those guys did everything they could. Unless they were under instructions not to uncover . . . inconvenient facts. I think that plane went down from a bomb, a small one, about two kilos of plastic explosives, not big enough to breach the outer skin, but large enough to ignite the gas tank."

Julian nodded.

"The FBI was all over that wreckage," Marie went on. "And they did find traces of some kind of explosive. But then it turned out that the same plane had been used to test bomb-sniffing dogs. They had to use explosive chemicals for that."

"And so they decided," said Julian, "that what they found was from long ago."

"Okay," said Marie, her eyebrows rising. "But why assume that? There could have been two sets of traces—one from the dog test, and one from an actual explosion."

This time Julian's expression changed. He looked impressed. Slightly. But his mask had cracked. She reached over for her glass of wine and noticed him looking her over. Aha, she'd got his attention. Finally. She took a sip.

"I mean, it's not like these guys suddenly discovered airplanes on September 11," she continued. "You remember Ramzi Yousef back in '94?"

Julian nodded.

"He put a bomb under a wing strut on a Philippines Airlines 747," she continued. "I think he was trying to figure out which placement would do the most damage."

"And it did do some damage, and I'll bet Yousef learned a lot."

Julian took a breath as if he were about to say something else, but Marie interrupted.

"Do you remember where Richard Reid was sitting when he tried to light up his sneaker?"

"Under a wing strut," said Julian. "The same area."

"Kind of makes you wonder if these people pool their knowledge, doesn't it?" said Marie.

"I think we have to assume they do. It would be negligent not to. Sounds like you've done some serious work," Julian said.

Marie smiled and held up her glass. He did the same, and they drank.

Marie lowered her voice and leaned over the table toward Julian. "It was the same on September 11, you know. The government. I don't think they're telling us everything they know about how the hijackers got where they were."

"Tell me more," said Julian, leaning back in his seat.

"I can't believe the hijackers got access to the cockpit in four separate planes by rushing up from the passenger seats with box cutters they'd *each* carried through security. Okay, so box cutters weren't banned from carry-ons then. Still, four or five Middle Eastern men on each of four flights getting on board with potential weapons? Uh-uh. I don't buy it. I think the box cutters and whatever other weapons they had were stashed on board beforehand. Knives and box cutters were found on other planes that were grounded that day. We now know they used Mace on some of the passengers in at least one plane, and one passenger may have been shot." This time there was a flicker of interest on Julian's face.

He was more than interested. He was surprised. He had come all the way to New York to see her, thinking she might somehow be of use to Israel. He'd had no idea she was this resourceful, this energetic.

He had been thinking of sending professionals to the video-machine repair shops. But maybe an amateur would be better. Her cover story would be perfect—because it would be real. She was a reporter for the most influential air industry trade publication. Any owner of a repair shop would be delighted to appear in its pages. Not one would imagine a connection had been made between him and the crashes. He might not even know there was one.

Julian captured her gaze, and held it. "Don't ask me how I know this, but you're right," he said. "Weapons were already on board. Not only that, but in at least two of the planes, hijackers were likely already inside the cockpits. They were wearing pilots' uniforms and were flying according to FAA rules concerning pilots traveling to make connections, in the cockpit jump seats. Of course, I don't know whether this will be any good to you. You probably won't be able to confirm it, and I'll certainly deny having given it to you."

It took her a few moments to digest the information.

"There were arrests made at JFK on September 12 of men traveling with pilots' uniforms," she said. "What happened with that?"

"Good question." He shook his head. "After all air traffic was grounded on 9/11, there was a United flight to Los Angeles with three Middle Eastern men on board. They were angry, and demanded that the plane take off. I guess they realized this didn't look so good, because they disappeared before the feds got to the scene. Also two men who had gotten off a Newark flight that was grounded in St. Louis were found on a train in Fort Worth carrying box cutters and disguises in their luggage. Originally, I remember, there had been word about eight planes." Julian shifted in his seat again, and she noticed the well-defined muscles of his thighs.

"What do you mean by 'word'?" she asked. "Word where?"

"I can't tell you that, except that your government was warned of a plot. By more than one source."

She looked at Julian, her mind running. Was he playing games with her?

His face was impassive. He said nothing for a full ten seconds. "I have a proposition for you," he said, finally. "A story. It might not seem such a big deal to you, but it could lead to something much bigger."

She raised her eyebrows. "And what might that be?"

"Does the phrase 'dry goods' mean anything to you? In the airline business, I mean."

"Sure. Blankets, laundry, catering, all the supplies brought on board the plane when it's on the tarmac."

"Right. And it offers a hole in security so big you could fly an Airbus 320 through it," he said.

"And then there's maintenance," Marie added.

Julian made a face. "Do you have any idea how many unauthorized people have access to the guts of an aircraft?"

"Actually, I do. The FBI investigated several companies at the Dallas–Fort Worth airport that hired illegal aliens to clean planes and hangars. The workers had unlimited access to planes. But they were underpaid. The working conditions were poor and they got no benefits or vacation time. It was like inviting a terrorist to bribe them to put something on board. Cash transaction, and then adios, south of the border."

Even Julian could be surprised. He took a breath. "What I had in mind was more legitimate companies handling maintenance, those that would be very pleased to have a story written about them, how well they work, how good their turnaround time is, their record of dependability and how they have implemented post-9/11 TSA security directives for off-airport repair shops."

"That sounds pretty boring," said Marie.

"But there may well be a payoff down the line for you. A big payoff.

A story that will attract a lot of attention. All I want from you now are copies of your notes for the repair story, and transcripts of any interviews you do. I would also like your first draft. Can you do that for me?"

Marie frowned slightly as she tried to sort out the implications of his offer. "So, I'd give you information about a story of mine, and in return you'd give me some leads I otherwise wouldn't be able to get?"

"Yes," he said, returning her gaze evenly.

"And where would you want me to go for this repair story?"

"Somewhere in Europe, I think."

"And you don't think somebody might find it odd that a reporter from the U.S. just shows up to write an article about repair shops? Somebody like, say, the shop owners?"

"Marie, you're a reporter for a respected trade publication. Good publicity for them means more business. I think they'd be happy to show you the smooth operation they run."

Marie nodded, though she was not entirely convinced. "And who will benefit from the information that I gather?"

"I will. I need information. You're a journalist. Information is your currency. When you have some, you use it to trade for more. That's really all I'm asking you to do here. Get some information, share it with me, and I'll get you more information in return. What can be wrong with that?"

"It's a bit unusual. We never share raw files with outsiders. A reporter could get into trouble doing that. Besides . . ." Her voice trailed off as she cast about in her head for the right words.

"Besides what?" said Julian, still patient.

"I don't know what you would do with anything I'd let you see."

"As long as your information is accurate, what do you care?"

"I can think of situations where I definitely would care."

Now Julian paused, searching for the words. "I can't imagine you would have any trouble with my use of it," he said, looking her sharply in the eye. "We're both against terror. Aren't we?"

Marie was startled, and it showed. Julian laughed.

Recovering, Marie had another question. "If this is part of the quote unquote war on terror, why don't you get the information yourself?

If you were in the IDF, you have a hell of a lot more resources than I do."

"Resources, yes. But not anonymity. If I went to London, or sent somebody from the IDF in my place, it would attract too much attention. And we wouldn't have a cover anywhere near as good as yours."

Julian drained his glass and put it carefully on the table. He shrugged. "And maybe you won't give me anything I can use. You'll still get a few stories for yourself out of the deal."

Marie didn't like the suggestion that she might not come through. "I don't usually disappoint," she said, and as soon as the words were out of her mouth, she realized he had her. She'd taken the bait.

She smiled to acknowledge the silent transaction that had taken place, and changed tacks. "I've done a bit of research myself," she said, smiling, "and I am *almost* satisfied that any information I might provide to you will go into responsible hands."

Julian laughed. "What else do you need to be completely satisfied?" He reflected back her playfulness.

"I won't know that until I work with you. And you can be sure I'll let you know if you fail to pass the test."

Julian laughed again. Normally, he controlled his targets with unsavory details of their entanglements at home or at work. But this girl was clean. His only leverage was her competitiveness. He knew she was twenty-eight years old and up for a job as aviation writer for a large metropolitan newspaper and that a few scoops might help her get it.

"Now I wonder if I can get my editor to agree to the story and pay for this little junket," Marie said, almost to herself.

"Don't worry about that. I can cover your expenses."

"Now that, my friend, would definitely be over the line. No can do."

Julian smiled. The European journalists he'd worked with weren't so scrupulous. "Have it your way," he said. "In any event, I'll contact you tomorrow after you've had time to think it over." His tone had become businesslike, even brusque.

"Yes sir," she said, surprised at the apparent conclusion of their meeting. Not knowing quite how else to express her surprise at his officiousness, she brought her hand to her forehead and made a mock salute.

"I'm very sorry I can't stay here with you for a meal," he said, standing. "But I have another meeting yet tonight. Expect my call tomorrow morning, say around eleven o'clock.

"And remind me," he added, smiling, taking her hand in his own, standing just a fraction of an inch too close to her, "to teach you one day how to salute properly."

"I shall," she said, watching him turn and walk out. "I most certainly shall," she murmured to herself, sinking into her seat.

Chapter Six

Captain Boutros Hamid paced the bridge of his container ship, the *LB Venture,* smoking furiously. He'd been sitting in the gulf waiting for a berth for twelve hours now, and he and his crew of restless Indonesians were getting dangerously close to their expected departure date.

Hamid looked out to the blue sea and the rocky coast. He knew this coastline like his own hometown. He'd spent more than his fair share of time here, cooling his heels, just like now. During the international embargo of Iraq before the First Gulf War, Coalition forces set up a blockade here, and the ships could sit for days while inspectors prevented forbidden goods from entering Iraq. Of course, a lot got through anyway; and he and his shipper were responsible for a good portion of it.

He took a final drag of his cigarette and lit up another. It was risky business, though, this sailing to New York, he said to himself. Yes, the man he knew as Gandoor owned the shipping line, and yes, he was very good at these kinds of international deals, and yes, he was, as usual, making this trip well worth Boutros's while. But the cargo was . . . well, unorthodox.

As he stood on the bridge, a message came through on the VHF. The ship was cleared to enter the port. A tremor of apprehension shot through him. He picked up the phone and called his onshore contacts. Time to move.

At a strip of vacation bungalows in Aqaba, men in masks raided two beachside dwellings and rounded up the occupants. One housed an extended family of Jordanians; the other, to the kidnappers' surprise, was apparently a local brothel. The women, *abayas* thrown on quickly to cover their cheap European underclothes, squealed in indignation as the men bound them and bundled them into a waiting van.

A little boy ran out of the house. "Mama!" he cried as his mother vanished behind the van's doors.

"Shit!" said one of the masked men. He didn't want the boy to rouse the entire neighborhood. There were international travelers here, and private guards. He opened the van door and kicked the boy in too.

The vehicle sped off to a dockside yard where a ship container awaited. The masked men herded the captives and the boy into the container. They punched holes in its sides to allow the prisoners to breathe. They slid five drums of water in, and enough dried food to last for three weeks.

Then they slammed the door and locked it.

With any luck, it wouldn't be too long before the container was trucked to the port and its human cargo was loaded onto the *LB Venture.*

South Kensington Arms, London, May 10

Over her shoulder, Marie Peterssen wore an elegant shoulder bag. It had been delivered to her hotel room wrapped in crisp white tissue and folded into a heavy paper shopping bag from Harrods. The bag also held a note from Julian that read, "Something smart for your London trip. I'll bet it looks nice on you." Marie had turned the note over a couple of times, trying to read more from its few words. Quite the gesture, she thought. And a lovely handbag it was: supple leather in a strong and useful design. But what was the message of the note? Something smart. That was about her. He wanted her to do a good job. She thought it was also a vote of confidence that she would. The next line was something else. It placed him closer to her in space.

It was a pleasant day, almost sunny. She left her South Kensington hotel, walked down Gloucester Road, descended to the underground, and caught the eastbound District Line train. She looked over a copy of the *Daily Mirror.* It was a guilty pleasure: gossip about the royals, meaningless government scandals, an obsession with sports. After a few minutes' scanning of bizarre headlines (EXCLUSIVE: BID ON BRITNEY'S BRA), she was bored. She felt a sudden flutter of nerves about her interview at the electronics shop and decided she'd better go over her questions in her mind. What was it Julian really wanted to know? When they spoke the morning after their meeting in New York, he'd said he was interested in how the process of repairing the airplanes' video machines could be exploited by terrorists. What could she ask that would provide an answer?

Getting off the train at Whitechapel, Marie emerged to an uncharacteristically bright London day. It almost hurt her eyes.

She looked around. If London was the international city everybody said it was, this section certainly proved it. Close to Hoxton Square, a newly trendy area filled with boutiques and wine bars, was the largest Muslim neighborhood in Britain, perhaps in all of Europe. The traditional and the fashionable lived in uneasy coexistence: there was even a shop in Whitechapel run by a Pakistani that marketed religious clothing "with style" to Muslim women.

Marie followed a detailed map given to her by one Nadav Rosenberg, whom she'd met briefly at the airport in the back office of a travel agency. He was Julian's man and her contact with him for the trip. He was nice, a very tall young man with long curly hair and a kind, responsible face. He'd given her instructions for her interview and how to send him the information Julian needed.

Another block or so and she was in a typical lower-middle-class

London neighborhood. She passed curry shops, lots of them, most every one with the name Famous Curry House. She passed a betting parlor called Ladbroke's and laughed at the pun. Certainly not the right neighborhood for gambling. She walked past a real estate agent, which she saw was called an "estate agent," and a candy shop called Ayub's Sweet Centre. The news shops sold papers from Islamabad, Karachi, Punjab, and Bangladesh. A music store blasted popular Indian or Pakistani music— she couldn't tell which—from speakers above the front entrance.

She looked for the numbers above the doors and was surprised to see, beneath number 32, in faded letters, the name Levy. And several doors away was a bagel store called Beigel Bake. This must have been an old Jewish neighborhood, she thought, shaking her head. An interesting place for a Pakistani electronics repair shop to be located, an area of shifting ethnic mix.

Here she was: 42 Brick Lane. A buzzer sounded her in. She stepped into a reception area furnished with three chairs and a coffee table on which were scattered a few computer magazines. It seemed antiseptic and colorless compared to the neighborhood outside. On the other side of a glass partition was a workshop packed with electronics equipment and diagnostic tools. Four men sat at workbenches repairing various boxes: video players, computer printers, fax machines. Spare parts and machines were set on metal shelves against the walls. Seeing her, a man with dark straight hair, a white short-sleeved shirt, and black slacks approached.

He nodded as she told him her name, and then he disappeared into an adjoining room. He returned with another man, taller than he was but otherwise looking like his twin brother. Induk Hajaera rubbed his hands together and exclaimed his honor and gratitude at her arrival. He ushered her through the workshop back to the room where his brother had found him. It was a charming dining room, and he sat Marie down at a wooden table covered with a lace tablecloth. He encouraged her to make herself comfortable and use the table for her papers and equipment. She accepted his offer of tea.

She hardly needed to ask a single question, as Mr. Hajaera was only too happy to elaborate the details of the electronics repair business, how he and his workers complied with government regulations, maintained certification standards, and stayed up to date on the ever-changing technology. He described his employees by name and specialty and noted that India still produced the best technicians, though Pakistan was struggling to catch up.

Nevertheless, the shop seemed a security breach waiting to happen. Video machines came here for service and repair, and as far as Marie could tell from Hajaera, government inspections were infrequent and perfunctory. She decided not to ask him straight out. No point in making him wonder why she asked.

He gave her a tour of the workshop. She took out her digital camera and asked if she could take a few shots. He agreed, and she snapped pictures of his workers at their desks, of their state-of-the-art equipment, and of Mr. Hajaera himself. She made sure she got a clear picture of every worker.

At the end of the tour, Hajaera introduced his wife. Marie said hello and, hoping she had more information than Julian could ever want, prepared to leave. She thanked Mrs. Hajaera for the pastries—*kheer* and *burfee*—she pressed into the journalist's hands. After the requisite pleasantries, she exited the shop and walked back down Brick Lane to the Tube.

Tel Aviv, May 10

Julian pulled in his chair. It was the same conference room in which he had spoken at Ben-Ami's first meeting four days ago. This time he was surrounded by his own people, seven men between twenty-two and forty-eight years old he'd worked with over the years, people with special skills and personalities, discipline and strengths. They were also experienced IDF officers, trained to work cohesively as a unit, think problems through, and marshal all available resources. As a result of Ben-Ami's clout and Julian's persistence, the group was given a position in the military hierarchy as an independent entity just below the office of the Shabaq chief. This designation was important for Julian, giving him autonomy as well as access.

"Okay, let's get to it," Julian said, and the room became quiet. "Hello, everyone. Welcome. We'll try to keep this meeting short because I know you're all eager to get back to your work.

"First, Benjamin Harel. Have you got any information about plane maintenance prior to takeoff?"

The blond Harel raised his blue-green eyes and said, "Yes sir."

"What have you found?"

"Mechanics were called to all three planes prior to takeoff."

Julian looked surprised. "And have you run down the details?"

"Yes. In the American Airlines flight, a mechanic was called to work on an altimeter dial that was blinking inappropriately. Twenty minutes and the switch was changed."

"Okay," said Julian, following him closely.

"On the Cathay flight, the problem was a cabin light failure. It seemed to have resolved itself after a telephone conversation between a mechanic and the flight crew."

"So no mechanic arrived?"

"No."

Julian drummed the table with his fingers. Something about this report bothered him.

Benjamin continued. "On the flight originating from JFK, a mechanic spent twenty minutes getting the ILS display indicator to operate properly."

"Do you know the name of the mechanic?" asked Julian.

Benjamin scanned the copy of a work order on his laptop. "John McDermott."

"From British Airways?" asked Julian.

"Yes. A company mechanic."

"I know him. He's worked there for twenty years. No way is he a terrorist. Or hired by one." Julian pushed back his chair and exhaled. "It sounded like Benjamin might have been onto something, didn't it?" he said. "It's like studying ancient texts. Not that I did that as much as I should have. But first you have a sentence that looks interesting: we had three calls to mechanics. Looked liked a possible means of delivery. Then you analyze deeper: in one of the three, the mechanic never got there. In another, the mechanic is clean. We eliminate the mechanics. We look at the details. Either there is a pattern, or there isn't."

Gil Kizner, his Jerusalem shop closed "for a vacation," chuckled. "Maybe you'd better call up your old Talmud teacher and ask him for some help right here." The men laughed, including Julian.

"Maybe we should skip the teacher and call a rabbi," said Nadav, to more laughter.

"Okay, Benjamin, good job. Now one more thing," said Julian, playing with his glasses case. "I want you to see if there were any last-minute orders for special food. Maybe somebody in first class asked for a vegetarian meal. Or a kosher meal."

The laughter this time was uneasy.

"Don't laugh," said Julian. "For an Arab terrorist, that would be good tradecraft, and you know it." He sat up straight. The mood in the room was suddenly somber. "Look for any late deliveries to the plane that would offer the opportunity for a bomb to be smuggled on board. Any medical emergencies on the planes? Was an oxygen tank brought on for someone having difficulty breathing, or were paramedics brought in to tend to any sick on board?"

Julian turned to Nadav. "Have we found out anything about the duty-free shops?"

Nadav nodded toward Eliyahu Sorenson, a short, dark-haired young man with glasses and a goatee.

"I think we can rule out duty-free," said Sorenson, speaking Hebrew with an American accent. Sorenson was born in the United States and brought up there but volunteered for the IDF before going to medical school. "The BA flight from New York to Madrid had no duty-free goods delivered. The duty-free employee supposed to carry on the bags suddenly became ill. The duty-free goods were left behind. The items were flown out on another plane to be delivered to the passengers in Madrid as if they were lost luggage. Of the other two planes, each had a few duty-free customers."

Julian nodded. "Thank you," he said. "We're assuming the PMO is the same for all planes.

"Who's handling cargo?" Julian asked Nadav.

"Jerome Lieberman, and he has nothing definitive yet," said Nadav. "Cargo records live in their own force fields. Records emerge only after extraordinary displays of shouting and invective."

"Let us know when the force is with him, then," said Julian. "But if it isn't by tomorrow, you can let Lieberman know he'll be picking oranges on a kibbutz. I want that report."

Nadav nodded, and pretended to smile.

"Okay. Good," said Julian. "Gil. Can you tell us what you know about the entertainment kits?"

Kizner seemed happy to be back with his former boss. He adjusted the glasses on his nose and peered at his laptop through the graduated lenses that his middle age forced him to wear.

"Your calls to your friends, Julian, have generated more information than we ever would have gotten normally," he said. "But paper has a way of disappearing or not getting filled out in the first place. Still, the three airlines have given us partial documentation on the video machines. We have a patchwork.

"I've got signatures on work orders at a Kawai repair in Paris and a Panasonic repair in London for work done on the kits from two of the planes. We know that the kit from the American Airlines jet was sent to the Paris shop the day before the plane went down. The Cathay Pacific plane was in London three days prior to its last flight and, while there, sent its machine to the Panasonic repair shop. The plane flying from the U.S. to Madrid had been in London on its previous leg, but it's not clear from the paper trail if its kit was ever removed from the plane.

"It appears that the Cathay plane, and maybe also the AA plane, flew one or more legs with the kits on board before the planes blew up. That means that if the bomb was in the video kit, its timer was set for a specific flight. A very sophisticated job.

"Two of the three kits went through London. The third went

through Paris, less than an hour away by air. I think London should be the focus of our investigation into the video-machine scenario."

Gil looked up toward Julian, pulling his glasses off his nose, and continued, addressing himself now to the other members of the group.

"Julian has sent someone to London. A journalist. As we speak, the source is meeting with the manager of the Panasonic shop, a Pakistani named Induk Hajaera. He seemed quite pleased with the attention. Nadav expects to receive a report tomorrow evening by e-mail." Gil looked back to Julian.

"Thank you, Gil." Julian took a deep breath and looked around the room.

"Tantalizing, isn't it?" he said. "We had two visits to the planes by mechanics—but not three. We had duty-free deliveries to two of the planes, but not three. And we have clear records of the entertainment kits going out in two of the three planes. What does the picture tell us?

"We know a bit more," Julian continued. "As Gil told you, the man who runs the Panasonic shop is a Pakistani Muslim whose record seems clean. Three of his four employees are also clean. But the fourth is of interest. Zaki Aarif Sediki is one of the Moroccans whose names I gave the Brits in 1996. In 1997 he moved to Iraq, and hung out with Ahmed Jibril. You all remember him, a founder of the Popular Front for the Liberation of Palestine. The PFLP doesn't count for much anymore, so Jibril may be using international terrorism to get it back onstage.

"Sediki returned to London two years ago. Hajaera hired him for the repair shop. Gil is now gathering telephone records for him over the past two years. We'll see if any of the calls made from the shop were to people that are known terrorists or linked to terrorist groups. Or vice versa."

Julian sat up straight in his chair, stretching. He glanced at his large diver's watch. "Let's get back to work," he said.

The scraping of chairs on linoleum sounded like a wave breaking on the shore. The men filed out to their offices. How long had it been since he left the beach in Turkey? Six days. It seemed like a year. His back hurt. He'd had a vertebra broken years ago in a little mishap. Stress aggravated it. Julian longed for the beach and some cold beer.

South Kensington Arms, London, May 10

Back at her hotel, Marie ordered high tea from room service and began to work. She'd promised her editor a file the next day. Transcribing tapes was tedious and time consuming, but this was part of her agreement with Julian: full transcripts. So she kept on. Strong tea and finger sandwiches helped keep up her energy. Cucumber and watercress on buttered bread, ham and cheese, assorted pastries and cakes. After three hours she began to write and realized she had forgotten to ask how often video kits required maintenance.

She called Hajaera. He was out, his wife said, but would be back within the hour. They chatted for a bit; then Mrs. Hajaera said it was too bad Marie had left when she did, as she had just missed Mr. Ahmed al-Jizouri, who was an important part of the business. Very nice man. Yes, in fact he conducted an audit one night a week earlier, sending her husband and herself out to a lovely dinner.

Marie tried not to sound too interested, but she pulled over a pad and scribbled notes. "So this man came in to make an audit," she said. "When was that again?"

"Oh, it was Monday, May 3. I remember because it was my birthday. He came in with three other men and they left the place so neat and tidy." Marie scribbled down the date.

"And to whom was Mr. al-Jizouri going to report his audit results?" Marie asked. Mrs. Hajaera didn't know, but she supposed it was the big company that owned her husband's business as well as several others, Olive Tree Partners Ltd. They worked very late, until about three in the morning, and left very quietly, not waking the family.

Did Marie want her to ask her husband to call when he got back? Mrs. Hajaera asked. No, said Marie, it wasn't important, and she had to send her story off soon. Marie hung up. She finished the story at about 2 a.m., then showered and fell into a restless sleep. When she awoke, she read the story again, made a few changes, and e-mailed it to her editor. She downloaded her photos and sent them off as well. Then she sent the same material to Nadav Rosenberg, whose e-mail address she'd memorized, as well as notes from her conversation with Mrs. Hajaera.

"Send me everything you find out, no matter how trivial seeming," Nadav had told her. "One never knows what ends up being significant."

She glanced at her watch. Her plane was scheduled to leave in three hours. She scooped up her things from the bed and threw them in her duffel bag, turned off her laptop and slipped it into its case. Marie hailed a cab and asked the driver to take her to Heathrow. Opening the window, watching the sights pass by, she felt the tension drain from her body. She had done her job. She had written a decent if not riveting story, and she had passed her information on to Julian. She didn't know what that might lead to, but now that she had finished, she could no longer avoid thinking about what she had done.

Marie had agreed to give Julian information without really knowing what he would do with it. She was on safe ground trading information; journalists did that all the time. But they did that with each other, and with their sources. Julian was more than a source. He was an agent of a foreign government. She was in effect his recruit, or as the intelligence people said, his hidden asset. It made her uncomfortable.

Had she violated professional ethics? Probably. She had passed information to him that she hadn't put in the story: information about the "audit" at the shop. But, she thought, there was nothing she could do with that information right now. She couldn't just stick it in the story. She didn't know its significance. And it was only through Julian that she might find that out. She was passing on information in hopes of furthering her story.

And it wasn't as if cooperation were new to her: she had relationships with attachés at various embassies abroad, not to mention government officials, pilots, and airline executives around the world. She told them things on occasion to encourage them to spill something better to her.

Still, Julian was a man of action. She could see that right away. What if her information got somebody killed? She decided to put the thought out of her mind.

Besides, she was intrigued by Julian and his team. They were smart and organized, at the top of their game. And she liked secrets. Or she hated them. Lord knows she had been brought up with them. The cab rolled on, finally climbing the on-ramp to the Hammersmith flyover and on toward Heathrow. She first arrived at that airport as a little girl on a VC-10 aircraft when the British national carrier was called BOAC and all the flight attendants wore natty suits and crisp hats. She remembered this particularly because she and her mother fought before getting onto the plane. She was five years old and asked her mother who her father was. Her mother vowed she would never tell her.

And she never did.

Tel Aviv, May 11

Julian studied the photos before him on the desk. His men, watching the Whitechapel repair shop from a van, had photographed a man entering it not long after Marie Peterssen's interview ended. Though the man's face was different—the chin and cheeks changed in their contours—the eyes were unmistakable, the arched dark brows, long lashes, and brilliant blue irises. Images that Julian battled to keep at bay for twenty-five years forced their way back into his mind. Once again he could see nothing but that wretched Madrid apartment where his partner Ari was butchered one sunny Sunday afternoon.

Julian's face contorted as he remembered the details: the unforced lock on the door, the cat wandering near the body, mewling as if the world had come to an end, the jazz music wafting in from a neighboring apartment, John Coltrane's rendition of "My Favorite Things." God knows who was playing that or why, but it played, as if stuck, over and over as he took out the body and cleansed the apartment of evidence.

They were in Madrid together, trying to infiltrate a PLO cell, six years after the murder of eleven Israeli athletes at the Munich Olympics. The Munich strike had been one of the most successful terrorist attacks in history. It helped Yassir Arafat catapult himself from obscurity to a position of international prominence, celebrated by European leaders and invited to address the UN General Assembly. By the end of the 1970s, the PLO had forged diplomatic ties with eighty-six countries, compared with Israel's seventy-two. Terrorism had proved its effectiveness. And

Israel's fight against Palestinian terror was just beginning. Following Israel's operation to assassinate every individual involved in planning the Munich attacks, the Palestinians launched a spate of worldwide airplane hijackings.

The Israelis had limited ability in Europe at this time to conduct antiterror operations. The Europeans erroneously believed that as long as they didn't oppose the terrorists they wouldn't get hit themselves, so they offered little help. The Israelis were thus compelled to build operational networks from scratch. Ari and Julian were sent to Madrid to find a man named Mansour Obaidi, an expert at concealing bombs inside audiocassette players. To get to Obaidi, they tried to turn a PLO operative known to them as Hassan Salah. They thought they had some leverage: Hassan's brother was in an Israeli jail. Or so they believed. An arrangement might be made to get him out.

But something went terribly wrong. First Ari and Julian had quarreled over the French girl, and then Ari did what he had been trained never to do. He met with the Palestinian alone. There was no excuse for his doing it, no good reason to violate orders. "Never meet your target without your partner."

The man in the pictures was Hassan. There was no doubt about it. It was a face that had haunted Julian for years. He held clenched fists to his forehead, then stood up, gathering the photos with him.

He walked to Gil Kizner's desk and set the photo on it. "Today, this man goes by the name Ahmed al-Jizouri. In 1978 in Madrid, Ari Schiffrin and I knew him as 'Hassan.' One Sunday in late March, he arranged to meet Ari alone. I picked up Ari's body four hours later."

Kizner looked at Julian's face and quickly looked away. Although Kizner had worked with Julian for twenty years, and had known in outline about Ari Schiffrin's death, Julian had never spoken of it. The grief Gil saw unsettled him.

"Several years later," continued Julian, "I thought I'd picked up his trail in Bulgaria. No luck. After that, there was a rumor that he'd joined up with the PFLP in Iraq and that bastard Abu Ibrahim."

"Okay, Julian. I'll see what I can find," said Kizner. He, too, remembered Ari Schiffrin. "Ari was the smartest kid on the block," he said softly. "His mom was crippled from a nerve disease, but Ari was so good to her, wheeling her around. We all loved her. She was one of the most interesting people we knew, the stories she told about fighting with the Palmach. I could never understand how Ari got himself into such a bad place."

"You're not the only one who's wondered that, my friend," said Julian, who, much to Kizner's relief, seemed to have regained his composure. He patted Kizner on the shoulder, then walked on. "And it's been a long time for wondering."

Chapter Seven

Marie stood in the roof garden outside her small penthouse apartment, tending to a climbing rosebush. She wore shorts that hung low on her hips and a white bikini top. No one could see into her roof garden, so she wore as much or as little as she liked. It was warm today, and brilliantly sunny. Her hair was pulled into a messy ponytail.

She reached up to snip off some blooms, absently pushing back her hair with a gloved hand. She crouched to smell a cluster of perfect flowers, pulling the soft fresh blooms to her face, the off-white roses reflecting golden on her creamy skin. She loved this rose, a magnificent specimen that was close to twenty feet tall, growing on a trellis over the entire back of her apartment and drenched with blooms. She snipped off a few more flowers, then turned to the hydrangea, its lacy flowers reaching past the leaves like daintily proffered handkerchiefs. She snapped off a few dead leaves, then walked to the strawberry plants, whose green shoots were just peeking out from their mounded beds. When she bent down to pick up the basket of debris she'd collected, her shapely legs showed off her fencer's muscles. Her ankles were narrow and graceful; her toenails, painted a petal pink. She gathered the bouquet she'd picked and walked inside to get a cup of coffee.

As she poured, she flicked on the television. A photo of an airplane appeared on the screen behind the newsreader, and as she turned up the volume, she heard the anchor say something about another airplane crash.

"Jesus, Mary, and Joseph!" she shouted to the empty room. A plane headed to Athens from London had gone down outside of Munich. The debris field was large. Marie watched the footage taken by helicopters over the scene, silently, in shock. There was a dark puncture wound in the green countryside where the Royal Jordanian jet had plunged to the ground, a scatter pattern of debris around it. Passengers of the London–Athens–Amman flight included Greeks, some Dutch, and a large number of Brits headed to Greece for holiday. "What is going on in this world?" she said, pacing in a circle. She had to call her boss. She had to go to the office. Before she could reach for the phone, it rang, causing her to jump in surprise. It was Julian.

"Hi," he said. "How are you?"

Marie was silent. She didn't know what to say. She didn't know where to start.

"Bad," she said. "See the news?"

"Yes," he said.

"This one was a mistake," she said. Julian was silent. "It crashed over land. The others went down over deep ocean so there would be no trace."

"You don't always know what makes sense with terrorists," said Julian. "But I agree. It doesn't seem to fit the pattern."

Marie was silent. After a few seconds, Julian asked, "Do you want to go to Germany to investigate?"

"Are you kidding?" she said

"You've done well so far. I'd like you to take on another assignment. I guarantee it'll be more interesting than the last one."

"What story?"

"I can't talk to you about it over the telephone, so I propose meeting you in Munich."

"But there's no way for me to get out of here. The airlines are shut down again."

"I'll take care of that," said Julian.

"What should I tell my boss?" asked Marie. "I should be in the middle of reporting an article about the new crash."

"Tell him you will be, that you'll have a front-row seat to the investigation. Since 9/11 there are international agreements on sharing information regarding terrorist acts. And now that we have an accident scene with evidence, you can be sure we have a chance, finally, to piece together some solid parts of this puzzle."

"That won't be a hard sell. But how will I explain how I got access to the site?"

"Just tell him the truth. In the course of your reporting, you found a source who's doing you a favor now. If your boss has a problem with it, tell him to hold his breath until you send him your first story."

Marie giggled. "Okay. How long will I be gone?"

"Pack for two weeks. I'll call back in an hour with details, but you should be ready to leave tonight."

Marie hung up, looked at the clock, and tried to settle the flutter in her belly. She turned the volume back up on the television. As she listened, she began throwing things into a bag.

She stopped, looked at the television images again. Four planes, she thought. Is that possible? It's so many. And then she remembered there were four planes on September 11. And four trains in Madrid. And four explosions in London. Twice.

But why was this one separated from the rest? It seemed that the terrorists were in charge and that they were lurking everywhere, just waiting to spring into action. But they weren't everywhere, Marie knew. They were in certain places where they could do the most damage, such as one small shop in London. She'd felt it as soon as she'd walked in, and the feeling got worse the moment Mrs. Hajaera mentioned "that nice man" Mr. al-Jizouri and how he stayed until three in the morning before letting himself silently out. She just hadn't realized she knew.

But why would three planes have been so carefully engineered to go down at the same time, and then this long break before the fourth? Her instinct was that it was a mistake. Was it possible that a video kit didn't make it into the right plane?

She stepped back out to her rooftop garden and took a few aimless steps. She felt her heart racing and a familiar flutter of dread in her belly. God, she hated that! There was nothing she hated worse than feeling frightened.

She walked over to the ladder that led up the water tower, grabbed a rung, and began to climb. As she passed the halfway mark, she felt the first wave of vertigo. She stopped and looked down. This was her little trick. When anxiety began to pound in her heart and squeeze her stomach, she did something that really scared her. It served to put things in perspective. Up she climbed, stopping again to look up and see the clouds moving. She felt another lurch in her belly and then nothing. She'd got to the place where she no longer felt fear. She felt nothing. Calm returned. Her heart slowed, and she began her climb back down.

When Julian called again, she had everything packed. Julian's voice was solicitous, kind. The international teams were setting up headquarters in Munich under the direction of the BMVBS, the German Federal Transportation Ministry. He had reserved a room under her name at the Gasthof Nagerl hotel near the Freising Airport. They could meet for a drink at the bar.

After she hung up, Marie stood and puffed the pillows of the couch absently. She closed the drapes and made sure the windows were latched. She turned off the coffeepot and the television, gave a last check of her bags, and walked out to the street to hail a cab.

"La Guardia Marine Air Terminal," she told the driver. The ride was easy, the night clear. News of the crash wasn't keeping New Yorkers from their evening commutes, she noticed, though the traffic seemed lighter than usual, at least across Ninety-sixth Street and toward the FDR. Well, no one was going to the airports. Except her. Weird. TV news reported that people were staying indoors and keeping their children close. Not in New York City. As she passed the huge mosque at Ninety-sixth and Lexington Avenue, she noticed that it was shut tight as a drum. Not a light visible.

The cab let her of out in front of a porticoed art deco building from the dawn of the aviation industry. Inside, she found herself in a circular reception hall, where a grand WPA mural decorated forty-foot-high walls. Farther into the terminal hung photos of President Roosevelt and Mayor Fiorello La Guardia sitting in the first planes, called "air boats" in the captions. The art deco style was evident everywhere, from the door fixtures to the signs. She made her way to the Delta ticket counter. Behind it, just as Julian had instructed, was a door marked "Baggage." She knocked on it and waited. After a few seconds, the door was opened by a young man holding a large textbook.

"Daniel?" she asked, and he nodded.

"Come in," he said, leading her into a room with a small desk and two chairs. On the floor against a wall was a down jacket and a large backpack filled with books. It appeared that the young man had been reading. He pointed to a rolling office chair and said, "You are Marie?" When she nodded, he said, "Please make yourself comfortable." He picked up a cell phone and dialed a number. "I'll find out about your plane." She noticed the textbook he'd been reading was titled *Fluid Dynamics*. He spoke into the phone in a foreign language that she assumed was Hebrew.

"Yes, okay," he said, and hung up. He looked at Marie. "In ten minutes, I can bring you out to the plane. They are just doing some refueling and checking the equipment." He looked as if he hadn't the slightest idea what to do with her. She could see this and smiled.

"Why don't you go back to your studying," she said, sitting on the chair. "I'm fine here."

The boy shrugged. "Whatever you want," he said, standing awkwardly.

"What are you studying?" she asked him.

"Physics," he answered.

"Good for you. This your job?"

"Yeah, security," he said. "I'm going to run out and see what's going on with the plane." When Daniel returned, he was accompanied by another man, in white overalls.

"Marie Peterssen?" the white-suited man asked.

"That's me," said Marie.

"We're ready to board you. Do you have any luggage?"

"Yes, it's right here."

The man in white took her suitcase and duffel. "I assume you want the computer with you?"

"Yes."

"You'll have to walk with me across the tarmac. It's a small plane and there's no jetway."

Marie nodded and followed him out. Daniel returned to his place on the floor and his books. Outside, the air was crisp and the breeze up. She couldn't see the water, but she could sense it around her. The man in white walked her toward an Astra G-200 jet and showed her up the entry ladder. Inside were four other men, lifting their bags into the overhead compartments, settling themselves in their places. She recognized one of them. He was Ilya Popolovsky, a violinst. She'd recently seen him play with the Israel Philharmonic Orchestra in New York. She'd had good seats and been close enough to have a good view of both him and the conductor, Zubin Mehta. Popolovsky was tall and balding with a grand Russian manner, and appeared at once respectful of the great Maestro Mehta and also mildly superior. Russian arrogance, she recognized from her years of friendships with Russian ballet dancers, sometimes hid behind a mask of false obsequiousness. She felt nervous about sitting beside the great violinist. He nodded to her with an expression of largesse, or possibly resignation.

She settled herself in. As the plane climbed toward its cruising altitude of twenty-five thousand feet, Popolovsky drew some papers from his briefcase and placed them on his pull-down tray. He was, Marie saw, perusing some Schubert sheet music. After five minutes, she got up the nerve to talk.

"I'm sorry to interrupt," she said, haltingly, "but I heard you play at Carnegie Hall with the Israel Philharmonic a couple weeks ago. You played Mahler's Sixth."

"Ah, so you heard us play Mahler," he said in surprisingly good English. "The *Tragic* Symphony."

"Yes," said Marie. "It was incredible."

"It has a powerful sense of foreboding, doesn't it?" he said. Something in her eyes intrigued the concertmaster.

"I read that the piece prefigured events in Mahler's own life," she said, slowly, trying to collect her thoughts. "It was almost as if he had seen into the future while writing the piece."

"Yes, the 'hammer blows.' That is the interpretation of many. Before the first performance of the symphony in Essen in 1906—which Mahler planned to conduct himself—he began to sob and wring his hands. He was terribly distraught."

"What happened?"

"He persevered. But he changed the piece."

"What do you mean?"

"He had scored the symphony with three large percussion sounds," said Popolovsky, raising his right hand then dropping it as if conducting the sounds right then and there. "According to his wife, the first two 'hammer blows,' as they called them, represented events that weakened the hero. Mahler always spoke of his symphonies in terms of heroic protagonists. But the third was to 'fell him like a tree.'"

Marie murmured sympathetically.

"At the premiere in Essen, Mahler decided abruptly to change the scoring by eliminating the third hammer blow. It was as if he were afraid of what might transpire if he didn't."

Marie nodded. "I read that when he first played the work on the piano for his wife, they both wept. Without saying a word to each other."

"Yes, his wife was a musician as well. A composer."

"Such communication, it's unbelievable," said Marie. "Like they could read their own fates in his music."

Popolovsky nodded gravely. "Their two young daughters would soon become ill," he said. "One died from diphtheria or scarlet fever, they didn't know which. At about the same time, Mahler was told he had a fatal heart problem. He never knew the diagnosis was incorrect."

Marie digested what he said. "The three hammer blows," she murmured.

The violinist folded his hands. He smiled and didn't speak for several minutes. He cocked his head and Marie wondered if he was silently hearing the music.

"Do you like the symphony?" she asked.

"I first heard Mahler's Sixth when I was a young man living in St. Petersburg. I heard it on a recording made by Leonard Bernstein, with the Vienna Orchestra. I thought when I heard it that my heart would break. The drama, terror, the love of nature, the personal tenderness, the struggle against the encroaching beats of modernity, all in one musical piece.

"But maybe more important, Leonard Bernstein, the great conductor, was a Jew celebrated around the world. Because he lived in America, he was free to become whatever he wanted to be. Things were not so good for us Jews in Russia. Or for Mahler in Vienna. Although I was encouraged to study music and the state bought me my books and helped me buy an instrument, I knew that my future was limited. My father's status at the university where he taught was lower than it should have been based on his accomplishments. My mother became a linguist after being refused admission to the Russian literature department. She was told that as a Jew she would never understand the Russian soul."

A man offered them water bottles. It was the same man who had helped get her bags on board. She and Popolovsky each took one.

"You asked me if I liked the symphony," continued Popolovsky. "I can hardly answer the question. Hearing the piece marked the day I realized that a Jew could be a man in the world, could put his mark on culture and the arts. It led me to raise my sights."

Marie looked at him, at his expressive eyes, at his sad brow, and couldn't say a word.

Northern Iraq, May 12

Ibrahim al-Aziz saw the trail of dust several miles away. He was a Bedouin; nothing escaped him. Nothing took place in the desert reaches of his camp that he didn't see or hear about from his clansmen. Survival in the brutal extremes of the desert demanded it. Custom guaranteed it. Any caravan crossing his land paid him tribute for safe passage. The less informed might find themselves relieved of a few livestock or bags of goods. Nowadays, with the Bedouin's traditional grazing routes obstructed by national boundaries marked off somewhere on strangers' maps, and drought taking its toll, it was even more important to assert his tribal authority. It was also incumbent on him to guard the water holes and protect the scant vegetation for his own herds of sheep.

When the vehicles got closer, a mile away, he saw there were three of them in a row. He stood up and straightened his djellaba, a long A-line white robe. He'd been sitting in his *madfeh*, the men's tent, pondering the day and the condition of the world. Now he'd prepare tea for his guests. Ibrahim's brown, craggy skin was marked with hundreds of small lines, each one etched by sun and blowing sand. Only an oval of his face showed; the rest of his head was covered with a red-checked kaffiyeh. His movements had an efficient, simple elegance, a fluidity born of the desert.

When the Isuzu trucks pulled up, Ibrahim stood to meet his visitors. He welcomed them into his tent and motioned them to sit on the pillows and cloths laid on the floor. As Ibrahim poured tea, his eyes took in every detail of the five men. He saw their new boots, jeans, and sunglasses. They wore watches and sport shirts. One wore a T-shirt marked "New York." Two wore cologne. City Arabs. As they began to share pleasantries, his eldest daughter slipped in, her head covered with an embroidered kerchief, and set down a plate of fresh dates.

Ibrahim had buried the goods with his own hands and watched over them for the last two years. Praise to God the opportunity had been good for him. Every month he had received a fine sum. That money had allowed him to keep his herds strong even through droughts. It had allowed him to buy access to water and new animals when the weakest died. The money had made him the envy of his relatives, though that meant of course they'd come to him more often in hard times. But Allah be praised, he'd been able to help everyone who asked.

The men seemed eager to get on with the trip, so after a cup of tea, they all climbed into the trucks and headed off to the east. It was about a fifteen-minute drive. The desert here was not marked by blown sand and massive, undulating dunes as in the Sahara. It was scrubby, bleak, flat land, marked by hills and rock formations. He remembered the spot exactly: to the east of a large hillock shaped like camel's hump and inside an outcropping of rocks. He directed his driver right up to the stones. He walked seventeen paces in from a pink-hued rock and began to pull stones from the outcropping. The men joined in to help him, and after fifteen minutes of work, a natural cave was revealed. In another half an hour, the passage was opened. And there was the prize: three metal boxes, each four feet long and about two and a half feet deep and wide.

The men looked at the strange markings on the boxes and exclaimed among themselves. Stamped on the silver metal was a yellow square inside of which were three truncated triangles, the trefoil, the universal symbol for radioactivity. They dropped to the ground and prayed, waving their arms and crying. The boxes were heavy, about two hundred kilos each, and it was dark before they'd pulled out all three and loaded them into the trucks—one in each bed. At Ibrahim's insistence, they shared a meal of yogurt and cheese at his house before continuing on their journey. As instructed, they presented Ibrahim with a parting gift and final payment, one certain to guarantee his contentment and his silence.

Tel Aviv, May 12

Shimshon Ashkenazy, tall and skinny with long ringlets of brown hair, hunched over his laptop in a windowless room at Shabaq headquarters, furiously taking notes, the tip of his tongue lodged between his lips. Shimshon was the office's computer genius. Nobody understood what he did, but they had complete confidence in him because he got information like no one else could. "He has a brain like a machine," Nadav said of him. "Even when he explains what he does, no one understands."

Shimshon, the youngest member of the team at twenty-two, turned to pick up a piece of paper he'd just printed out. As he compared the paper with the document on his computer screen, a sly smile crossed his face. He leaned back in his chair and cranked up the volume of the Moby tape he was listening to through earphones. He'd got a name.

Shimshon retrieved the telephone logs for 42 Brick Lane, the electronics repair shop in London; he'd downloaded them to his computer, all five hundred megabytes of them. He then correlated the names of people receiving calls from or sending calls to the Brick Lane address with the names of people entering the UK in the past three months. Only someone who was as skillful as he at getting information by breaking into private networks would be in a position even to attempt such a search. Generally, one needed a warrant to get the phone records, but Shimshon knew how to get into almost any computer in the world.

The names Ahmed al-Jizouri—whose presence at the London electronics shop had been reported by the American journalist—or Hassan Salah—whom Julian had crossed paths with in Madrid—came up nowhere. But Shimshon found that a man who had traveled to the UK four times had put down the security deposit on a telephone line in Baghdad, though it wasn't registered under his name. Numerous calls had been made from this phone number to 42 Brick Lane. This correlation was not as simple to make as it appeared, for the man had traveled under four different names on four different passports. Shimshon compared photos from the passport databases, and the only authentic passport with the photo of the man with blue eyes and arched brows was issued to Mansour Obaidi.

Shimshon rocked in his chair for a few minutes, thinking over what he had done and wondering whether the answer was solid enough to show to the boss. He decided yes and stood up, walked to Julian's office, and waited by the door until Julian looked up from his work.

"Come in, Shimshon, come in," Julian said. "What have you got for me?"

"A name," Shimshon said.

"A name for?"

"It belongs to the only individual linked to the London electronics shop via phone records who has also legally entered the UK. That is, aside from the known employees."

"No suspense, please," said Julian. "What is it?"

"Mansour Obaidi."

"Obaidi?" Julian stood up behind his desk, then paced a few steps. Shimshon was startled by his reaction.

"You know this name?" Shimshon asked. But Julian barely heard the young man's question. His thoughts were swirling in the cloud of obfuscation he had constructed over the years, precisely for the purpose of keeping his mind away. But here it was, billowing and tempting and giving way. Mansour Obaidi was the terrorist bomb maker he and Ari had been after in Madrid. But the man in the surveillance van's picture, the man who had visited the London shop, the man with the distinctive blue eyes, was the man they knew as Hassan. He had no doubt about it. But Hassan, from all they could determine, had been a low-level PLO operative, the man they had thought might lead them to Obaidi, and the man, in the end, who had killed Ari. Could Hassan and Obaidi have been one and the same?

Images from their Madrid mission flashed back like dealt tarot cards. If Hassan had actually been the wanted bomb maker, that would explain how he'd been able to disappear so well and so quickly. Obaidi would have been given unlimited resources, so valuable was he for the cause. How could he and Ari have miscalculated so badly? Why hadn't they recognized Obaidi? They'd been given photos of him before their mission, but the pictures certainly had not resembled the man they knew as Hassan. Julian picked up the photo taken by the surveillance van, put his arm around Shimshon, and marched him into the main office, where staffers worked in their cubicles, on computers, on telephones. He steered Shimshon over to Gil Kizner, who stood up when he saw them.

"Kizner," Julian said, nodding, his face stiff with tension. He set the photo on the desk. "This man is the one we knew from Madrid as Hassan. Shimshon tells me he believes the man is most likely Mansour Obaidi."

"Obaidi himself, eh?" asked Kizner, rubbing his chin. "Well now, that would be interesting, wouldn't it?"

"Son of a bitch," said Julian quietly. "Son of a bitch."

Port of Aqaba, May 12

Thirteen containers lay on a wharf at the Port of Aqaba. It was Jordan's only seaport, dispatching freighters south through the

Gulf of Aqaba to the Red Sea and from there to the Indian Ocean, or north through the Suez Canal to the Mediterranean.

It was midnight, and the docks were illuminated by blinding spotlights. On the wharf, gantry cranes hovered over the waiting ships, their latticed working arms shadowed in the glittering water. Winches rattled and screeched as they lowered a heavy cable with four hooks to the first of the containers, a steel box forty feet long. The stevedores—three Arab men dressed in drab gray overalls—attached the hooks to the corners of the box, then signaled to the crane operator in a cab high above to start lifting. It swung over the hold of the *LB Venture,* a Middle East Shipping Lines container ship, and men aboard guided it into the hold as the crane lowered it belowdecks.

The process was repeated twelve more times, with the last container, the one with the oddly punched holes in it, left on deck. The job took a little more than an hour. Five minutes per transfer from shore to ship. Thirteen boxes, sixty-five minutes.

Aqaba was a busy port. It served not only the Hashemite Kingdom of Jordan but also Western Iraq and northern Saudi Arabia. It refueled military ships. As much as thirty million tons of crude moved through its giant oil terminal every year. Phosphorous, fertilizer, potash, and ammonia were exported through Aqaba. Factories both manufactured and loaded fertilizer products on ships for transport all over the world. Dockside silos took in five hundred tons of grain per hour for import.

In all of the bustle, nobody would notice or care about thirteen containers hoisted onto a rust bucket like the *LB Venture.* Mansour Obaidi was counting on it.

The ship was duly registered according to the new international shipping regulations, and the cargo was shipped by an Iraqi businessman to an American buyer through a well-known Swiss forwarding company. Because the forwarder was familiar to the shippers and officials, it was unlikely there would be any cargo spot checks.

A prominent businessman in Iraq, Obaidi was also an experienced shipper, having moved goods into Iraq for fifteen years through various entities. A creative thinker, he knew an opportunity when he saw one.

Hundreds of thousands of containers were arriving in Iraq, full of supplies from the United States. Iraq had little to export, so the ships were sailing back empty, a lost opportunity.

The U.S. government was paying for the round-trip shipping costs, but what shipper would pass up the opportunity to make a few extra dollars carrying goods back for the ride? When the price of scrap metal began to rise, and he learned the U.S. government itself was looking for supplies, he knew he was nicely situated to fill a need, having access to the steel as well as the shippers. The situation couldn't have been better if he'd cooked it up himself.

The only danger was the dogs. A well-trained K-9 dog anywhere near the cargo hold would detect the massive amount of explosives in a second. But this was the chance they were taking. They had made every arrangement to avoid times when a dog patrol might be on the docks at Aqaba.

A man in a white dishdasha, a long white tunic worn by Muslim men, and a red-checked kaffiyeh walked back along the dock, hands in his pockets. He had a graceful gait and a gentle demeanor. Mustafa Hanavi, Obaidi's point man in Baquba, surveyed the territory and was satisfied. Within three hours, the *LB Venture* would leave Aqaba. Then it would steer a course north through the Suez Canal into the Mediterranean, and sail west through the Strait of Gibraltar and into the Atlantic. New York Harbor would be fifteen days away.

Munich, May 13

They descended into Munich quickly, dropping from fifteen thousand feet to come in low and flat from the southeast. Out the window, Marie could barely see the familiar skyline in the dusk. Her mother had made many appearances here with the Stuttgart Ballet. At thirteen, Marie had met an apprentice with the Rotterdam Ballet, a boy she'd watched in practice for weeks before finally getting up the nerve to talk to him. Germany was to her a place of innocence and childhood self-absorption, of ballet costumes, floral headpieces, and sunny picnics. But then, she wasn't Jewish.

The plane parked near a hangar for private aircraft. She noted the large modern print of the avionics company emblazoned on the structure—"Hemlach"—and the fresh, new, modernistic feel of the airport. As she gathered her bags and coat, she realized she was the only one disembarking.

Popolovsky looked at her and nodded. "Good luck to you," he said, shaking her hand. "I hope you get to the bottom of your story." He handed her an envelope and she looked at him. "It's just a bit of music I found in my papers that I thought you might like," he said, smiling.

"Thank you so much," she said, smiling and blushing. "It was a great pleasure to talk to you." She wanted to say so much more: that she appreciated what he'd said, that she just hadn't known what it was like in Russia; but she felt all eyes were on her, and the passengers were eager to get on with their flight. She made a little wave with her hand and hoisted her bag over her shoulder, then turned and walked down the steps to the tarmac.

Inside the terminal, she put her bags down on a seat and opened the manila envelope. She saw a few pages of sheet music and, in front of them, a smaller piece of paper. She pulled out the note.

"Slight change in plans. Walk out to the curb and look for a cream-colored Mercedes taxi. The driver will be wearing a blue cap. Tell him to take you to the Munich Novotel." It was signed "Julian." The hotel was different from the one he had originally told her to go to.

She felt her face get hot. How had he got a message into Popolovsky's hands? Marie looked around at the empty terminal. This guy Julian was everywhere. She walked out of the building and stood by the curb. It was creepy to be in an airport with no activity. The air seemed heavy and the sky low, oppressive. Few cars of any kind drove by, but within minutes a Mercedes approached slowly, driven by a man with a narrow face. He wore a matching blue tweed vest and cap.

Marie put her bags on the seat beside her and pulled shut the door.

"Novotel München, bitte," she said in German.

Approaching the Suez Canal, May 13

Captain Hamid drummed his fingers on the rosewood desk in his quarters. He was on the telephone with his shipping agent. Yes, he knew they were thirty minutes late approaching the arrival buoys. But what could he do? The ship in front of him had got out of shape leaving its berth in Aqaba, blocking their way and holding them up for a half hour, and they'd already been late leaving the port because of the chronic backups there. But this was Egypt, not Singapore! Everyone was behind schedule. They *had* to make the 0400 convoy. Later was out of the question. He heard a lot of mumbling on the line, but he placed down the phone. They wouldn't delay a ship owned by Gandoor, he was pretty sure. Still, when he stepped across his cabin, he realized his shirt was soaked through with perspiration.

He climbed to the bridge and lit up a cigarette. Ahead, the wide mouth of the Suez Canal stretched out like a sleepy bay, belying the frenetic activity that descended on ships as soon as they entered transit. Then every local vendor and canal employee would attempt to board his vessel, hands out at every step.

If the Canal Authority decided to play tough, he'd be sent to the anchorage to wait for a spot in a later convoy. But that was impossible. The shipper and agent had arranged for his ship to be inspected by Omar, a longtime canal employee known to be as crooked as a ram's horn. Omar was expecting the *LB Venture* in the first convoy. At least the passage was prebooked and paid; that gave him an advantage.

Someone—Hamid didn't know who—had already wired Omar half a king's ransom. The rest would be paid as soon as he got the ship through inspection. He hoped it had been attractive enough, because the gig was up if they failed here. The Suez inspectors routinely carried Geiger counters and explosives detectors. Not to mention what might happen if the hostages heard inspectors walking over the boat. If they had any sense, they'd choose that moment to kick up a storm. He hoped the sedative put into their food in Aqaba was still working. Still, he just couldn't understand why his handlers hadn't sent him around the Cape of Good Hope. Sure it was a longer trip, but far superior to trying to get through Suez with his present cargo.

Hamid called his first mate. "Ignore any orders to the anchorage and proceed to the prearrival buoys," he instructed. This was a gamble. Hamid didn't know if they'd be allowed through or surrounded by police boats and black-clad divers. If someone was suspicious, they'd be stopped right here.

As they approached the buoys, Hamid saw two tugboats plowing toward them from the north. He let out a small breath. This was good news. The tugs were there to hold the ship in place for boarding by the pilot and inspector. But where was the inspection boat? It was only a few minutes before the tugs nudged alongside the ship. The pilot boat approached a few minutes later, and from the bridge Hamid observed the inspector and pilot climb up the gangway.

Hamid greeted the men as they climbed over the main deck. "Welcome aboard, gentlemen. Pilot, you are a most welcome sight," he said, rubbing his hands together. "Thank you for getting here so quickly. Would you care to accompany me to my office for some refreshment?"

"Let's take care of all the formalities," said the inspector, a small, wiry man with brown eyes and tiny white teeth. He made a quick glance at the pilot. "So as to get you on your way. Do you agree, Captain?"

"Yes sir. Absolutely," said Hamid.

Have you got your certificates in order, Captain?" asked the inspector.

"Yes sir," said Hamid, turning to escort them to his office. He prayed to Allah that the gift to Omar had been huge.

Omar looked quickly over the papers laid out on the captain's table.

"It looks like everything is in order. And I understand you're in quite a hurry to get in transit."

"Yes sir, we are," said Hamid. "Thank you very much sir. I'll let my company know right away that we'll be on our way. I'm sure they'll be very appreciative of your cooperation and will be thinking of the welfare of your beloved family." Omar smiled broadly.

The pilot proceeded to the bridge to steer the ship through the length of the canal. Hamid noticed Omar look around the office, assessing the value of every object there. As they made their way toward the door, the inspector reached for a carton of Marlboro cigarettes stacked atop the ship's safe.

"Please," said Hamid, handing Omar an additional carton and a bottle of Scotch as well, which the man took happily. He slipped the bottle into a linen sack he carried over his shoulder and hugged the cigarette cartons to his chest. Hamid watched the inspector exit the ship and climb down the ladder, not hampered in the slightest by the boxes clamped under his arm. Hamid shook his head.

He returned to his office and poured himself a drink. Captain's special stash. He deserved a little treat. The pilot would navigate the ship for the next twelve hours, so he could relax. He opened the safe to check on its contents. Twenty more cartons of cigarettes for his crew. He chuckled. He'd figured pretty well with respect to old Omar.

Munich, May 14

Julian pulled up in front of the Novotel Hotel in a blue Opel sedan. The sun had risen on a fine, fair morning. Light low clouds floated over a shimmering spring day. He saw Marie by the entrance. She was wearing slim jeans with a low-slung belt and a turquoise knit top with lacing at the neck. As he came to a stop, he pushed open the passenger door for her. She looked at him as she slid into her seat, and he saw that the shirt was the color of her eyes.

Marie felt a rush of comfort in Julian's presence. She wondered why, since she was used to traveling on her own and certainly wasn't uncomfortable in foreign cities. But there was something so solid, strong, and yes, attractive, about him.

Julian seemed pleased to see her too. His eyes smiled as he took her in with a quick glance before pulling away from the curb.

"How are you? Flight okay?"

"Fine," she said, throwing her bag in the back and adjusting herself on the seat. "How are *you*?"

"Same old aches and pains," he said, weaving his way into the traffic.

"Been busy, no doubt," she said, raising her eyebrows and looking at him. He glanced at her.

"As usual."

"I had a very stimulating conversation with Ilya Popolovsky on the way over."

"Did you now?"

"Yes, I did." She waited for Julian to say something. He didn't.

"You know, Julian," she said, turning toward him from the passenger's seat, "I couldn't quite figure out how you managed to get a note to him on the plane."

He shrugged. "It doesn't matter."

"Yes it does."

"Why?"

"Because I want to know."

"I radioed a message to the pilot. He must have gotten it to Popolovsky to hand to you."

"Okay," she said. "Can you tell me why the hotel plans changed?"

"No."

"Why not?"

He shook his head. "I just can't." His tone was firm, but she could tell he was sorry to be disappointing her.

"Okay," she said. "I understand." She looked away from him and out the windshield.

"Let's say something like this," Julian said. "We're always in the business of keeping our eyes on known terrorists. When we see movement, we take greater precautions, as the situation warrants. You're not in danger; the alert has nothing to do with you or your job. We're just being extra cautious now, under the circumstances."

She nodded. "All right."

"Good. You need to keep up your strength because it's not going to be an easy day, I'm afraid," he said. "We're going to go to the debris field."

"I don't have a press pass," she said.

"No problem. The press is not being allowed onto the location yet. I'll keep you with me for now, as part of my team."

As they approached the crash area, which was surprisingly close to the city limits, German military police checked identification. Julian handed over two ID cards. A blond MP looked them over, looked at Marie, waved them in. Julian handed Marie one of the cards. It had her photo and name on it.

"Nice picture. Where'd you get it?"

"Don't you recognize it? It's your automobile license picture of four years ago. I have a very clever helper who lifted it from a database. We thought we'd save you the trouble of waiting in line for an ID card."

"So thoughtful of you," she said, trying to decide if she was impressed with his ingenuity or disturbed by this invasion of her privacy. Actually, it thrilled her. She looked more closely at the ID. Yes, now she recognized the license photo, though this version was cropped closer and more exposed, making her look older. It was in her name, and listed her nationality as U.S. That was good, she thought, since it needed to agree with her passport and entry visa. But there the similarities ended. It listed her as an adjunct member of an Israeli investigative team. She looked out the window, savoring this. She rather liked it. Better than a press pass for sure.

Julian pulled into a large dirt parking area and brought the car to a halt. They got out and walked through another checkpoint, to a large field at the edge of a wood that was roped off. Various officials in uniforms were kneeling, packing, measuring items scattered on the ground. Marie and Julian walked along the perimeter of the field on a narrow pathway marked off by orange cones. Julian greeted someone he knew, and after standing and waiting for a few minutes, Marie continued south, walking and looking. She saw suitcases, some blasted apart, one whole and upright, as if waiting to be picked up by its owner. There were metal and plastic pieces, unidentifiable, scattered throughout. She saw a laptop computer, rather half a computer, the screen and keyboard broken apart, and a leather glove. The glove wasn't empty. Nearby an arm lay flayed down to muscle and bone, like a drawing in an anatomy book. A severed upper torso was a few feet away, the blood already congealed and black. She thought she was tough, but she wasn't quite prepared for this.

Julian came up to her. She pointed to the body parts, and he muttered a few words under his breath and led her away with his arm around her shoulders.

"Come on, let's try to get a long view of the area and see what it's telling us." He supported her as they walked toward the epicenter, the area with the greatest density of objects on the ground, including the plane's blackened hulk. Up ahead was a wooded area, like an island of trees in the middle of the field. She saw workers walking in and out carrying white evidence bags, and then an increase of activity. She and Julian continued to watch, and they saw men emerge from the woods with two bodies still strapped in their seats. One was a woman in a pink wool suit. The other was a young girl. Their fingers were intertwined, a last-minute embrace that the rescuers seemed bound to respect.

"Jesus," Marie whispered, digging her fingernails into Julian's arm. "Oh, that's awful." Marie walked away. She tried to breathe deeply, but it didn't stop the nausea. She tried looking at the trees and at the sky, but she couldn't erase the image of the woman and her daughter holding hands. She stopped, leaned over, and placed her hands on her knees. She waited, her head spinning and her stomach churning. She knew she'd feel better when it was over. A few more seconds of nausea and she vomited.

After she collected herself, she walked back to Julian, who led her by the arm to the rest area. He handed her a cup of water, then reached into his pocket and retrieved a clean cotton handkerchief. She thanked him and took it.

"That woman and child were clinging to each other," said Marie, losing her composure again, tears dripping from her eyes.

"These scenes are tough to look at," he said, putting an arm lightly around her shoulder. "The lucky ones are near the bomb and get killed instantly."

Marie took a deep breath. "You mean the others stay alive for a while?" She closed her eyes. She thought she might be sick again.

"What's important is to find the people responsible and stop them from doing it again," said Julian, trying to right her and get her back on the path.

Just then an official approached Julian. He wasn't wearing a uniform, but he had several official-looking ID tags around his neck. It appeared that he knew Julian well. They spoke in German, Julian fluent to Marie's ear. This guy was full of surprises. Julian appeared very interested in what the man had to say. He turned to Marie and gestured to her to follow them. The man led them to an evidence tent. As soon as the official moved out of hearing, Julian told her that they were going to see some pieces from the debris. He apologized for his gesture to her—it wasn't rudeness, but he hadn't wanted the man to overhear him speak to her in English and not Hebrew, because she was officially part of his team.

"What will we do while viewing the material?" she asked.

"I think English will be okay there," said Julian. "Other people will be around, and English is the language of international gatherings."

They followed the German man into a large green tent. Inside were several wooden tables covered with pieces of plastic, metal, luggage, wiring. The man picked up a Plexiglas box inside of which was a small irregular blackened bead.

"*Kommt Ihnen das bekannt vor?*" he asked Julian. Marie knew enough German to understand that he'd said, "Recognize that?"

"Can I smell it?" asked Julian, in English.

The German nodded and handed him the box, which Julian opened with great care. He sniffed the air about five inches from the bead, then a bit closer.

"It doesn't smell like burned hair, so it's probably not wool. Smells like burned paper, so maybe it's cotton."

"Perhaps," said the man.

"You were lucky to find this in all that mess."

"Very. We found it on the clothes of a flight attendant. He must have been very close to the explosion."

Julian looked at the German. "A cotton wool stabilizer," he said, his thoughts drifting away, back to the scene of a small explosion in a shopping mall in Cebu City, the Philippines. The small bomb had been built by Ramzi Yousef, who had attempted to bring down the World Trade Center in 1993. Youssef was developing plans for an astonishing number of terror attacks at the time, including one against the pope and another against U.S. president Bill Clinton.

Of greatest interest to Julian was his attempt to build tiny nitroglycerin bombs that could be smuggled into airplanes past airport security. His bombs were very sophisticated. The timer was a Casio watch. The explosive was a mix of nitroglycerin and other chemicals hidden in bottles of contact-lens solution. The spark was created by two lightbulb filaments powered by two nine-volt batteries—which he hid in the hollowed-out heels of his shoes.

He used cotton wool as a stabilizer. It was his signature.

"Ramzi Yousef's material," said Julian, "in his practice run for the Bojinka Plan."

"And the material his friend Khalid Sheikh Mohammed favored too," added the German. "But they're both in prison. And if this is in fact a piece of the stabilizer used in a bomb and not something else, then one of their friends might be involved. Or one of their students."

Julian knew Obaidi wasn't one of their students. He would have been their teacher. The uberteacher. The cotton balls had been an innovation he'd conceived of while in Bulgaria. He'd also concocted a stable form of nitroglycerin. Bomb makers tended to stick to materials they knew.

"Do you think this is the calling card?" asked the German.

"Possibly," said Julian, who wasn't quite ready to reveal his hunch. He looked back at the table of evidence. He saw an array of small black plastic pieces that could very well be parts of the video kit. If they were, it would indicate that the bomb hadn't been too big. A huge bomb would have obliterated the machines. As Marie had explained to him so presciently, all it took was a kilo or two of Semtex to make a hole big enough to ignite the plane's gas tank.

"These collected from all over the site?"

"Yes."

"Can I have one fragment?"

The man looked over the table. "I think we have enough for whatever testing we might do. Sure, you can take a piece. Souvenir?"

"Not quite," said Julian.

"Got an idea already, have you?" the German asked.

"You bet," said Julian. "That's how I'm paid, by the idea."

Both laughed.

The German picked up a piece of plastic with tweezers and placed it in an evidence bag. He made a note in the logbook. "You'll make sure you let me know your findings before you inform anyone else, right?"

"Scout's honor, as our American friends say."

The German laughed and waved him out. Julian nodded, clapped him on the shoulder, and ushered Marie through the flap of the tent.

As soon as they were out of earshot, he said, "Time to get you back for a cup of tea. It's been a big day."

"Yeah," said Marie, still overwhelmed. She couldn't say anything else. They made it to the car and Julian started the engine.

"Do you think the black plastic pieces might have come from the video player?" Marie asked.

Julian looked at her with surprise.

"Do you think it might be the one that I saw in the shop in London?"

"Why do you ask that?" he said.

"Oh please. I can add two plus two as well as you can. You're investigating the crashes. You sent me to the repair shop, and now you're collecting a piece of black plastic that looks like it could have been from a video player."

"You're quick," he said. "I'll tell you this: maybe."

The road led east out of Munich toward Passau and into the Bavarian forest. Like everything else in Germany, the woods were orderly; no fallen branches marred the grace of the rolling hills. Wildflowers bloomed on cleared land, and the forest was varied in geography. Lovely and deep. As they approached Passau, the great blue Danube rose to greet them.

"Mr. Hajaera showed me the box that was there, actually," said Marie, disturbing Julian from a reverie. "He picked it up and turned it over. Scary to think of now. Anyway, he was showing me something on the bottom of the box, a hole where his technicians could plug in a diagnostic tool, and I was kind of staring at the serial number. It was stamped on a piece of silvery metallic tape. And I remembered it because the first six digits were the same as a telephone number I once had."

The car veered onto the bumpy shoulder.

"Sorry," he said. "Are you kidding me?"

"No."

"Did you put that in your report to Nadav?"

"I wrote that I'd seen a video kit, ready to go back in a plane."

Julian frowned. "I don't know why he didn't tell me," he said.

"I told him about the machine, but I don't think I mentioned the serial number. I only remembered it right now, after seeing the river. For some reason, seeing the Danube made me remember the phone number we had in Vienna: 418902."

"Wow," said Julian. "Sigmund Freud lives." He laughed. "From Vienna—and through you—to an Israeli counterterror operation. How about that?"

"Works for me," she said, smiling.

"Do you remember the brand of the machine?" asked Julian, reminding himself to ask her later why she'd been in Vienna.

"No."

"Doesn't matter," he said, thinking. "It would be in the repair manifest. Or it might be visible on one of the photos you took in the shop."

They drove on in silence for several minutes.

"That is a very good bit of information," he said. "I'm impressed. For that, I'll buy you a beer."

She smiled.

"We'll have to hum a few bars of the 'Blue Danube' waltz and toast the old river," said Julian, chuckling. "With the fragment of plastic and the serial number, we might be able to identify the video box. If we're very lucky, it'll be the first step toward tracking its movement. And we might be able to find out, finally, how the plane—and the others—blew up."

He pulled out his cell phone and dialed. "Shimshon," he said. "Find out everything you can about video kits with serial numbers beginning with 418902. Do it now."

Holiday Inn, Lower East Side, Manhattan, May 14

"Red" fumbled with the key in the old lock, juggling his carton of coffee and a paper-wrapped raspberry Danish in one hand, keys in the other. As soon as he shot the lock, he walked in, his heavy platform shoes resounding over the bare wood floors. He put his food down on the cheap table and pulled off his wool cap and girl's red wig. Beneath the wig, his hair was also red, but cut short. His complexion was light, his nose aquiline. He kicked off his shoes, pulled off the black tights, left them where they fell, and poured milk for the cat that wove insistently in and out of his legs. He didn't like wearing these women's clothes, but his commander told him it was good cover. In America, he was told, women were cheapened, made into objects. However, if they weren't so, shall we say, attractive, they weren't seen. If he dressed as a woman, he wouldn't be as suspicious. He could be invisible. His commander failed to consider how many men dressed as women anyway, but Red thought it probably helped him. People left him alone. He just stayed off certain streets at night.

Red sat at the table to unwrap his food. The room was stifling, but he didn't open the window. Clothes hung from every ledge, food wrappers lay in piles all over the floor, and unwashed plates filled the sink.

He took a bite of the Danish, then walked into the bathroom. He opened the medicine cabinet, shook several bottles of pills, and, finding them all empty, dropped them on the floor. He returned to the kitchen and opened the refrigerator again. He lifted out a rack of test tubes and straightened up. He took two glass vials and shook them. Dissolved. In both concentrations. Good. Everything looked good. He walked to the sink, splashed a drop of the liquid on a sponge, and dropped the sponge into the sink. He reached into his pocket for a cigarette lighter. As soon as he set the light near the sponge, it ignited, bursting into flame with a loud pop. He smiled and kicked his way through a pile of clothes on the floor back to the table. He picked up his Danish and took another bite, savoring the sweetness, then washed it down with coffee. The cat climbed onto the table and licked at the edge of the pastry.

Budapest, May 14

With an ornate iron pull, Cyril Kaspi yanked shut the massive oak door of his apartment house on Szondi utka on the Pest side of the Danube. His eyes lit on the discreet brass nameplate on his door and, beneath it, "Private Piano Instruction." He reminded himself to give it a polish when he came back, as it was losing its luster. Kaspi taught three dozen students of varying talents who trekked to his apartment every week for lessons and then participated in his occasional evening soirees, where they played their instruments and the parents socialized, indulging their conceit that Budapest would be the Vienna of the twenty-first century. Kaspi stepped down to the street, fastening one button of his tweed jacket at the waist. He wore a neatly pressed light blue oxford shirt, wool slacks, and heavy-soled cordovan shoes. It was all a bit conservative for a music teacher, but appreciated by his clients— nouveaux riches who would just as soon see him as a businessman as an artist.

But tonight he would delight them on levels they could only imagine. He was hosting a gala recital on the most elegant boulevard in his lovely city. First several of the better students would play their Liszts and Bartóks; then his friend Andrasz Freitov, a world-renowned violinist, would perform three short pieces. The city's best caterer had been hired to pass hors d'oeuvres and Veuve Clicquot, while a magician would entertain the children in a separate chamber.

Kaspi stepped past the grand mansions of the Andrassy ut and turned up the walkway of number 3. The building had been constructed between 1884 and 1886, its three-story facade ornamented by statues and balustrated balconies. A grand fresco illustrating a Roman bacchanalia, the work of the famous Hungarian artist Károly Lotz, decorated the front stairway, offering a magnificent focus for the neo-Renaissance,

Romantic mansion. Even before touching the doorbell, Kaspi heard the door buzz open. He looked up at the TV camera scanning the entryway. Security for the evening would be tight, with a special team hired. They were his people, a fact that was and of course would remain unknown to his guests. The employees, dressed like Hungarian bourgeoisie, some musicians or pretending to be musicians, would keep their ears open for interesting tidbits of conversation, particularly from a well-heeled plastic surgeon known to cater to East Bloc apparatchiks and Arabs with pasts (and features) better off fading into history. Cyril would be socializing himself, of course, but he couldn't be expected to hear every bit of useful gossip. So it was important for his people to be spread widely throughout the hall.

The men from the florist delivered flowers in crystal vases, and the caterers whisked them off to the tables, mantelpieces, and marble columns where they belonged. The baroque silverware, bone china, and Austrian crystal sparkled under nineteenth-century chandeliers. Kaspi checked that security had its instructions, and that the children's posies were ready. As he walked across the gleaming parquet floor, his shoes squeaking on the wax, he heard the beeping of his cell phone and saw that a call was coming in from his boss, Julian Granot.

PART
TWO

Chapter Eight

Morgan Ensley heaved his rucksack onto the Humvee. He looked around the airport and wondered if he'd been lowered onto the moon. So this was Baghdad, the storied land of Ali Baba and his Forty Thieves. He half expected to see soaring minarets and a bustling souk, but all around him was desert, flat and drab, with scattered scrub. A few tumbleweeds blew past.

A corporal from the First Infantry Division waved Morgan into the front seat and handed him an armored vest. "Put that on," he said. "Clean-cut white guys are extra-credit targets here."

Morgan smiled, but he pulled on the vest, tightening the Velcro straps carefully to each side of his chest. Morgan, forty-two, was an FBI special agent from Washington, D.C., assigned to investigate smuggling and shipping irregularities in Iraq.

"What's your name, soldier?" asked Morgan, looking at the man's name tag. "Dennehy?" Then he glanced at Dennehy's arm patch and saw a red numeral 1. "Dennehy from the First Infantry."

"That's it."

"'The Big Red One.'"

"Like we say," said Dennehy, "'If you gotta be a prick, be a Big Red One.' But call me Black Jack," he added, nodding and putting out his hand. "Glad to make your acquaintance."

Morgan shook it. "Any relation to 'Black Jack' Pershing?"

"Uh-uh. Wished I was, though."

"Anything in particular you like about him?"

"Well, for starters, he stopped an uprising of Muslim guerrillas over in the Philippines. Story is he took a bunch of 'em captive, shot all but one, and dumped pigs' blood and guts into the grave with the bodies. That defiled them. Pershing let the one go so he could scare the crap out of his buddies."

"Right," said Morgan.

"You don't believe the story?"

"Let's just say it doesn't appear in any biography of Pershing I've ever read. And I think I've read them all. Too good to leave out if it was true, don't you think?"

Dennehy looked over at Morgan. "I'll tell you this: Muslim attacks on Americans quieted right down at around that time. Like for fifty years." He put the Humvee in gear and pulled into the midday Baghdad traffic.

"So, Dennehy," said Morgan, looking around. "Where are the lush palm trees, the dates, the figs, the hanging gardens?"

Dennehy snorted. "You have a good imagination. It'll serve you well here. You'll love Baghdad when summer comes. You can imagine being fed grapes by a fine maiden cooling you under a palm frond when really the shirt's burning off your back and your feet are turning to cottage cheese. You'll be able to smell ocean breezes when the air is boiling with dust."

Morgan smiled. "That bad, huh?"

"Worse. I'm here to tell you that if the heat don't get you, the boredom will. Ain't nothing to do at night. Not more'n a few dozen American girls here, total. And half of them are fucking reporters."

"How about the local talent?"

"Iraqis?" Dennehy answered by spitting out the window. "Tell you what, though: you've already got a head start with your long hair. Most of the Americans come through here with the standard buzz cut. The locals like hair on their men. Especially the men. Trust you more if you have at least a mustache. A buddy of mine in Afghanistan told me all about it. He's gone native now—beard, robes, everything. He's a Ranger."

"Appreciate the advice," said Morgan. "Anything else?"

"Put this on," said Dennehy, handing him a combat helmet. "Sheraton Hotel, right? I'll take you on the scenic route." Dennehy revved the engine and careened down a potholed street strewn with garbage and broken furniture. Half the shops were shuttered, their walls pockmarked by gunfire. Rivulets carried raw sewage along the road where stray dogs ran wild. Morgan recoiled at the rancid smell.

Munich, May 14

Marie was shaken. It had been a difficult day at the debris field. Now, as she waited for Julian at a small round table in the hotel bar, she found herself unable to get rid of the grisly images fresh in her mind: the black scar of fire where the cabin had crashed and burned, the broken bodies and sheared-open suitcases. In a way, the worst of all were the souvenirs carried home from London: toys from Hanley's for the children, blouses from Harvey Nichols for the wives, gold cuff links for the men, purchased at Turnbull and Asser, shirtmaker to Prince Charles. Every one of these objects spoke to Marie of a domestic life shattered.

She pulled her gray sweater tighter around her shoulders. A hot bath had calmed her, but not enough.

She started on her second beer, a lager from Spaten, the famed Munich brewery, then grabbed a napkin and began scribbling notes about the day. A journalist's self-therapy: if it upsets you, write about it. When she looked up after fifteen minutes, a pile of napkins in front of her, she saw Julian in the doorway of the bar. He looked every month of his forty-six years. He walked toward her deliberately, but with a grace belying his size.

"How are you doing?" he asked. "Feeling any better?"

"The beer's helping," she said.

"How many is that?" he asked, sitting down.

"Two."

"I'll have to catch up, then." He signaled the waiter. "It doesn't get any easier, if that's any comfort to you," he said quietly, acknowledging the pain he saw on her face. "You never get used to it. It's even worse when the crash is in a jungle or some remote mountainside. It can take days to reach the site. By then, putrefaction is well under way. I hope you never have to experience that odor."

"How do you deal with it?" Marie asked.

"Drinking?" he said as his beer arrived.

"Does that work?"

"For short periods. Until the next morning."

"What else helps?" asked Marie. "Are you religious?"

"No."

"What *do* you believe in?"

"Work, soccer, eating well, and enjoying friends. Not in that order. In fact, there is a prayer that says, 'We have come into being to praise, to labor, and to love.' "

"You just said you're not religious, but then you recited a prayer."

Julian shrugged. "I was brought up by a man who believed that human beings are redeemed by work. Labor is what he believed in. Not labor to make a living, but work for its own sake. Work as the root of life."

"That's not a bad thing to believe in," said Marie. Her eyes wandered out over the tables, and she suddenly felt very sad.

Julian saw the grief pass over her face. She was drifting away from him into her own thoughts, and he needed to draw her back. "This place reminds me of a bar I was in years ago. In Uzbekistan," he said, reaching out to cup her hand in his. She looked back at him.

"I was there as an official representative of the Israeli government to negotiate a business deal. In most of the former Soviet republics, any kind of official negotiation involved days and nights of drinking and eating, at the end of which the local leader and his henchmen and bodyguards would finally get around to beginning the talks. This wasn't the first deal I'd done, so I knew the drill." Marie still looked distracted, but she was trying to follow his words. He left his hand on hers.

"I entered a nightclub in Tashkent. This was in 1992, after the Soviet Union had fallen apart. But the habits of Soviet prudery combined with Muslim censoriousness made nightlife, let's say, interesting. The place was underground. You couldn't find it unless you already knew where it was. Anyway, there was a Russian rock band in the corner, playing the Mungo Jerry song 'In the Summertime.' They were wearing elephant pants and they had these muttonchop sideburns. It was like walking into a twenty-year time warp."

Marie smiled, enjoying the touch of his hand. "So as I walk in, somebody from the Soviet mission stands up and shouts, 'Ladies and gentlemen, the Israeli diplomatic delegation is entering the hall.'

"He's drunk, of course. But as I hug and shake the hands of all the local dignitaries, I realize they've been drinking since at least noon. So it's my turn. I have to catch up. So I say to Igor, my host, two things: first of all, give me some food, because I can't drink on an empty stomach; second, make sure that from now to the end of the evening, I have the same color bottles of vodka—make sure it's the same kind. Otherwise I'll die." Julian gently pulled his hand away from hers and sat up straight.

"During that time I was actually taking big chunks of meat and bread and butter and drinking the damned vodka. In two hours, a whole bottle. A liter bottle. Bigger than your bottles. I'm feeling that I'm doing my part. Keeping up my end. Russians drink competitively. I'm also feeling completely smashed. And then a lady asks me to dance with her, some kind of slow sentimental song. I say I can't do that. Igor whispers to me, 'You have to. Otherwise, you're offending them. Go dance.'

"So I take her to the dance floor. I'm astonished she understands English, and I say to her, 'I can't even begin to waltz you around. If I do I'll fall down. So I am going to hold you tight. Enjoy yourself as much as you can but for the rest of this dance I am standing still.'

"At the end of the song, I feel I've done my duty, and when I return to my seat, I tell one of my guys, 'If I'm going to die, make sure they put on my stone that I died happily in service to the State of Israel.'"

Marie looked at him. He told her he wasn't religious, and maybe that was true. But he did believe in something. And he was a loyal soldier.

She finished off her second beer and realized she was starting to feel its effects.

"Lucky lady could have had her way with you," Marie said smiling, idly wondering what her own chances might have been. Might be. Hypothetically speaking of course.

Julian shook his head. "No way. Training kicks in even in situations like that."

"Why situations like that?"

"A man is never more vulnerable than when he's with a woman. One, vulnerable to blackmail through photos. And that could have ruined my mission. Also, the Soviets were well known to have female assassins."

Marie blushed. She felt she'd been put in her place.

"What do you believe in?" she asked again.

"A world where civilians can fly in planes without fear of dying. A place where people can drink coffee in a café without thinking they might be blown to pieces."

"Would you die for such a world?" she asked.

"It's easy to say one would die for an ideal," said Julian. "It's harder to say one would kill for one."

"Would you do that? Would you kill?" asked Marie.

Julian didn't answer her question. "You're too young to remember this," he said, tipping his head to the side, his voice low, controlled, "but in 1972, a terrorist group calling itself Black September attacked the Israeli Olympic team in Munich, not far from this hotel."

"Steven Spielberg made a movie about it."

"A soap opera. But never mind. The real story was the murder of the athletes. And that shouldn't be forgotten. Two men were killed in their rooms the first night. One was Youssef Romano, a terrifically strong man, a weight lifter, and the father of three girls. They dumped his body in an apartment. He'd been bleeding like a sheep at slaughter. Seven other Israeli athletes were tied together there. The killers wanted them to see for themselves what would happen if they tried to resist. These were world-class athletes."

"And they were at the Olympic Games," said Marie, her face softening with emotion. "Meant to reflect and celebrate the best qualities of human beings around the world."

Julian nodded.

"Some were fencers, weren't they?" Marie asked.

"Yes they were," said Julian. "And also weight lifters and wrestlers and sharpshooters. They were tough and strong. Fighters. But the bastards ambushed them in the middle of the night in their beds. They never had a chance."

"Why weren't the Games stopped?" asked Marie.

"The Olympic Committee wanted the games to go on. But the Germans felt they had to do something. They couldn't believe that once again, Jewish blood was being spilled on German soil, this time in front of television cameras beaming the images around the world."

"Unbelievable," said Marie.

"It gets worse," Julian went on. "The Germans decided to negotiate with the terrorists. They agreed to transport them and the hostages to a military airport. Although we assembled an expert hostage-rescue team, the Germans refused our help. Willy Brandt—you remember who he was?"

"The German chancellor," said Marie.

"Right. He insisted that the Germans could run the operation," said Julian. "But he was wrong. The Germans made terrible mistakes. Foreseeable ones. Their snipers opened up on the Palestinians at the airport. But they missed more than hit their targets." Marie looked at Julian quizzically. His eyes seemed strangely detached, as if he were in a trance. She squeezed his hand and he looked back at her, seeming momentarily surprised she was there. "In the end, all the Israelis were killed. In one helicopter, where they were bound to their seats, they were incinerated by a grenade. In the other helicopter, they were machine-gunned."

Marie was disgusted. "Were the Germans incompetent? Unprepared?"

"Both," said Julian. "The commandos were undertrained. A decision was made that guards at the Olympic Village would carry no weapons. Germany wanted to portray an image of peacefulness in contrast to the

1936 Games. And although it should not have, the attack caught the government by surprise. Some officials were literally immobilized by fear," Julian said. "But there is more that you don't know."

"What?"

"The three surviving terrorists arrested at the airfield that day were later set free."

"They were?" asked Marie.

"Soon after the massacre, a Lufthansa jet was hijacked by the same terrorist organization, Black September. They threatened to blow up the plane if the Munich terrorists weren't released. The German government chickened out, as you Americans would say. It turned out that the hijacking was a setup. Between Black September and the German government."

"That can't be," said Marie. "It's too grotesque."

"You can look it up," said Julian. "The Germans gave up the killers of the Israeli athletes in a deal they thought would protect the country from further terrorist attacks. "Appeasement" is a dirty word in European history, but appeasement of terrorists was, in the 1970s, and, has remained, a European policy."

Marie covered her face with her hands.

"You can imagine what it was like in Israel," Julian went on. "Grief and fury. Golda Meir herself wrote up an order that Israeli special services should hunt down and kill every individual involved in that plot. The operation was called Wrath of God."

"Any reason it was given that name?"

"The purpose was to put the fear of God into the hearts of terrorists everywhere. Remember, this was a different time. The Palestinians were just beginning to use terror as a tactic. Our job was to do the same. Not only would we kill the perpetrators, we'd do it brutally and in public. And we'd do our best to terrify them first. One of the tactics we used was to run obituaries in Arab newspapers of terrorists when they were still in the pink of health. They'd enjoy the unique experience of reading about their own deaths."

Marie looked closely at Julian. "You say 'we,'" she said. "Were you one of the killers?"

He didn't flinch. "Yes," he said.

"You killed one of the terrorists?" asked Marie.

"I was part of a team that did. There were many teams."

"How did he die?"

"His car exploded in Beirut."

"What was his name?"

"Ali Hassan Salameh."

"How did you feel about killing him?"

Julian looked Marie in the eye. "Not a single soldier I knew—including several women involved—had second thoughts about that operation. Even after the mistake in Lillehammer when the wrong man was killed. The men who planned and carried out the murder of the Olympic athletes didn't deserve to live. On Salameh's return from Munich to Beirut after the attacks, he was personally welcomed by Yassir Arafat, who embraced him and referred to him as 'my son.' He was dangerous: charismatic, intelligent, and dedicated to terrorism. He was also quite the international playboy. But no matter. He had operated in East Germany under the protection of the Stasi. And he enjoyed other international connections, including, I might add, the CIA."

"The CIA?" she asked, shaking her head in confusion.

"Yes, he ingratiated himself with the Americans by tipping the CIA off to a plot to kill Henry Kissinger in Beirut in 1973. He also helped a group of Americans trapped in Beirut in 1975 to escape. And he used Arafat's Force 17 to protect them from other militias. The CIA saw him as an important contact, even as he continued to play an active role in international terrorism.

"Salameh would never be tried in a court of law. So Israel tried him on her own terms."

Julian let this sink in. The scene of the crash had unsettled her, put her on unstable footing. He'd counted on that. Now he was creating a new reality for her. When recruiting new agents, it was important to get them away from their home turf, to knock them off balance. Coupled with that, an emotionally draining experience offered the chance of bonding with them. It was then that they were primed for the approach. They almost recruited themselves.

Marie opened her mouth as if to say something. But she stopped and fell silent again. She couldn't look away from Julian.

"The man who owns the repair shop that Mr. Hajaera runs in London is another terrorist bastard," he said.

"Al-Jizouri? You mean if he is the one who planned the crashes," said Marie.

Julian gave a wry smile, tipping his head again. "Of course, *if* he did it. But the clues sure point in his direction. Just this morning, we found material that was a signature element of bomb makers associated with him—cotton wool. Plus, I recognize him—both his name *and* his appearance, though both have apparently been altered. We now believe that al-Jizouri's real name is Mansour Obaidi, a well-known bomb maker and businessman who has been operating for more than twenty years. I found out through a colleague in Budapest that he underwent facial surgery in Hungary ten years ago. The surgeon, distracted by a festive occasion and with an incentive to boast, revealed some salient details to an admiring woman of a certain age who was questioning him about his abilities to transform the appearance of individuals."

"So how can you recognize him?"

"He can't change the color of his eyes. And he didn't wear tinted contact lenses the day he visited the shop in London."

"How did you get such a close look at his eyes?"

"I had a van near the house with two men in it. They took high-resolution telephoto-lens pictures of everyone coming and going. Before, during, and after your visit."

"What?" Marie asked him, surprised.

"Standard operating procedure. I would never send you to a meeting alone. You won't know we're around, but any time you go anywhere for me, members of my team will be nearby. If something unexpected happens, you might need help."

Marie didn't say a word. This information wasn't easy to absorb. She would never ask why he'd put her in danger without first asking if she accepted the risk. She assumed that any risk was her own. Julian knew this. He knew it from her fencing record and her psychology. And he had no trouble using it to his advantage. Israel and Great Britain shared

a brutal view of intelligence work. They were completely without remorse. At the heart of espionage was a completely unsentimental im-
perative: get information on the enemy. It was Somerset Maugham, if
Julian remembered correctly, who put it best regarding the condition of
the intelligence recruit: "If you do well you'll get no thanks and if you
run into trouble you'll get no help."

"So you in fact know al-Jizouri," she said. "Or rather Obaidi."

"I wish I *had* known it was him. I met him. Twenty-five years ago.
But we—my partner and I—didn't see through his disguise. We thought
he was someone else. He set up a meet with my partner, and then he
killed him."

Julian's eyes were turned away from hers and focused on a spot in
the mid distance. His expression was pure concentration. And pure ice.
It was the look on a warrior's face before he went in for the kill, not in
the stylized world of fencing matches, but the real thing. After seeing
that expression, Marie had no doubt that Julian had killed other men.

"That is all another story, of another world and another city," he said,
his face in a matter of seconds completely changed. He met her eyes
and held her gaze. "Tomorrow, the debris field will be open to the press.
You have a twenty-four-hour start on them. You can write a story for
your magazine or for the *Washington Post* or the *New York Times*. Whoever you want. The only thing I care about is what you say to your edi-
tors about how you got in early. If you want to say you got access with a
privately employed airline security expert, fine. But no names. In any
case, that will be your first major scoop. And your next, if you agree, will
be in Iraq."

"About what?"

"A Baghdad businessman. One of Iraq's postwar tycoons."

"And his name is?"

"Mansour Obaidi."

Marie's face reddened to the roots of her hair. If Julian was right,
Obaidi was a cold-blooded killer. And she would meet with him? Write
about him? Nothing in her life had prepared her for this. She was frightened. At the same time, she was thrilled that Julian wanted her for another assignment, thrilled that he was pulling her closer. *He* was

thrilling. No temporizing, no intellectualizing. He was an existential man. He acted on the world. And he was asking her to be part of his team.

She'd never felt part of any group. She didn't even know what nationality she was: American or French? She'd grown up with dancers, but she wasn't one herself. She'd never had a best friend for more than a year before she and her mother had moved away. At college she was a fencer, but that was hardly a team sport. You competed individually. Your opponent was mostly yourself. Even reporting was single-handed competition: you versus your sources, you versus your editor, you versus the other reporters on your beat.

She wouldn't have been able to say it in so many words, but Julian had found the perfect temptation to hold out before her. He was offering her a mission, an identity, a place, and a sense of belonging that her wandering expatriate life had denied her. And a man to appreciate and protect her. She blushed because she had an instinctive desire to hide what was most important to her. She couldn't let him know.

"How would that fit in with your plans?" she asked cautiously.

"You will lead us to him. You will constantly be monitored and accompanied. Because you're a journalist, you'll be able to make contact with him and make arrangements to meet him. That will put him within our sights."

"So you're asking me to bring Obaidi to a place where you can kill him?" she asked.

"He's too valuable to kill. We want to watch him because we suspect he may have other terror attacks in the works, which we obviously want to stop. We need him to lead us into his world. Iraq is new territory for all of us."

"Who are you working for, actually?"

"I'm investigating the cause of the four airline crashes for the government of Israel."

"Why? No Israelis were killed."

"You can be sure Obaidi has bigger plans. I think he's positioning himself to be a major player in postwar Iraq."

"Have you ever been to Iraq?" Marie asked.

Julian took a deep breath. "Not recently."

"Ever?"

"A long time ago."

She looked at him. "No tour guide involved, I guess."

"No. We flew over in helicopters at very low altitude in the middle of the night. A night with no moon."

"An operation of some kind?"

"You could say that."

"Well, going to Iraq would be a challenge for me, too," said Marie. "My own low altitude and no moon. I have no contacts there and I know nothing about this guy."

"We'll supply you with information to start. You know what you're doing, and you'll soon make your own contacts."

"Well, I guess I haven't got much to lose," she said.

"We won't knowingly put you in danger," said Julian. "You won't be reporting on the fighting or the security situation in the cities. You'll be reporting on business. It's a dangerous place, no question about that. But you have a lot to gain if you do your job well. You could end up writing the stories of your life. Where you sell them is your business."

She knew he was working her. And he was succeeding. She wanted what he was offering. From all appearances, he was a highly placed source in the Israeli intelligence community. That could only be good for her. And if in return he wanted a little shoe leather, what was not to like? Except it was totally foolhardy.

"I guess I need to think about it," she said.

"That's fair." He knew that she was not calculating the risk. She liked risks. She just wanted to make the decision on her own terms and in her own time.

"Right now I need to write my story about the debris field. And find someone to buy it from me. Quickly."

"Let me know if I can help," said Julian.

"You bet." Marie stood up, folding the napkins she had scribbled on and stuffing them in her rear pocket. Julian watched her pause in front of the elevator, then turn toward the stairwell instead.

He turned back to his drink. She was staying on the fourteenth floor. He wondered if she was climbing for the exercise. Or to clear her head.

Marie was breathing hard when she reached the top, but she felt good. Exercise was good. She had never felt better than when she was training for competition. Like now, except for the past week because of all this. She slid the card key into her door and let herself into her temporary sanctuary. She poured herself a tall glass of water, and removed her computer from its case. As she pulled it out, a manila envelope fell to the floor. It was the envelope that Popolovsky had handed to her on the airplane. She'd read Julian's note but hadn't looked over the rest of the papers.

She pulled out several sheets and saw they were music for Mahler's Symphony no. 6, the piece they had talked about. On the last page, Popolovsky had written: "Gustav Mahler said he'd always felt homeless in the world: as a Bohemian among Austrians, as an Austrian among Germans, and as a Jew among all nations on earth. But now there is Israel. Best wishes for success in your endeavors and in expectation of seeing you one day in the Holy Land." He had signed his name in Cyrillic letters.

Tears rushed to her eyes. She sat down on the edge of her bed and put her hands over her eyes. After a few minutes, she raised her head. What was the matter with her? All this emotion. The plane wreck and Julian. Mahler and Popolovsky. Obaidi. The beer. She wiped her nose with the back of her hand.

She took a long drink of water, then started to laugh through her tears. Five days ago she was hoping for a boss who was more than a seat cushion. Julian was maybe too much more.

Chapter Nine

Mansour Obaidi paced back and forth across the interior courtyard of his villa in the middle-class Karada district, in eastern Baghdad. A number of Iraqi Christians lived there, which displeased Obaidi. He would have preferred to live to the west, in Mansour, but its huge population of Sunni Muslims made it a haven for insurgents, and a target for the Americans. Karada was said to be safer than most other neighborhoods. But "safe" was of course a relative term in Baghdad.

The house was one of the largest in the district, built in the 1920s for a merchant who owned a dress shop on the luxury shopping street called Arrassat al-Hindiya, where he provided wealthy Baghdad women with the latest fashions from Paris and London. Obaidi bought it from the merchant's son, a former party leader in need of cash after the de-Baathification of Iraq. The courtyard was lined with small palm trees. An early-afternoon sun turned the walls the color of straw.

As Obaidi paced, he smoked one cigarette after another. The plan was his most audacious one yet, and the West had gotten only a small taste of his skills. Soon it would know what measure of man it was up against.

He spread his fingers, placed them over the front panel of his silk shirt, and caressed the fabric. His fingertips had been losing sensation over the years from the chemicals he worked with. In fact, he could feel the fine silk only with his palms. Yet he craved tactility, turning his fingers to the sides, searching for spots of feeling.

He remembered the first time he'd felt real pain, debilitating pain. It was 1976. He was rounded up in Cairo with other student members of Jama'a Islamiyya and jailed for advocating the forced Islamization of Egypt. They were called a scourge, worse than the Zionists. And they were charged with conspiracy against the government. They were starved, kept naked in cold, damp cell blocks, immersed in ice water tanks, attacked by starving dogs. Obaidi's feet were beaten. For months after, he'd felt pain from his soles to his teeth—screaming, pulsating pain.

But the physical discomfort was insignificant compared to the humiliation. His Egypt—a country so grand it once ruled the ancient world—was brutalizing its own Muslim men.

How young we were, how naive, thought Obaidi as he paced. We thought we could change the world by following the writings of Sayyid Qutb. They made for heady reading: the entire non-Muslim world is spiritually sick, wrote Qutb, "steeped in *jahiliyya*," a pagan ignorance of divine guidance which cannot be diminished by "all the marvelous material comforts" of the West, all its "high-level inventions."

The West, Qutb maintained, lacked healthy values. Islam alone possessed them, and it was Islam's destiny to provide mankind with a new vision. There was one striking passage that as a student Obaidi had committed to memory. It was with him still: "The highest form of triumph is the victory of soul over matter, the victory of belief over pain, and the victory of faith over persecution."

Stirring words, Obaidi still felt, but now he knew better. Words could not resist the Egyptian secret police, or the Israel Defense Forces, or the American smart bombs dropped on Muslim cities.

That was where he came in, he said to himself, flicking a cigarette butt to the ground. After his release from prison, he fled Egypt and joined a PLO group training in the Iraqi desert. His trainers discovered that he had a way with explosives. It was sheer instinct. He could size up a target and calculate with unnerving accuracy how much dynamite or ammonium nitrate would be needed to make the right bomb.

He was recruited for Yassir Arafat's Force 17 and sent undercover to Spain. After his successes in Western Europe, Arafat rewarded him by sending him to university in Bulgaria. It was an excellent cover for his extracurricular studies of electronics and ordnance. From the Bulgarians he learned about sophisticated plastic explosives, the latest timers and detonators. But personally, it was difficult. His new teachers were agnostics, some of them Communists. They did not nourish his soul, but they served his larger purpose: learning about the enemy; learning about bombs.

When his mother became ill in 1980, Obaidi was obliged to return to Egypt. But after Anwar Sadat was murdered in 1981, he was caught up in the mass arrests that followed. When he got out of custody this time, Obaidi was determined to plot his future plans carefully. He could not remain in Egypt.

The PLO was no longer an option, since Arafat had been driven out of Beirut. In 1983, Obaidi returned to Iraq to join up with Abu Ibrahim, who had split with Arafat over Arafat's agreement to leave Lebanon. In 1986, Obaidi agreed to go to Afghanistan to help Osama bin Laden build camps for Arab fighters.

It didn't take long for the two men to quarrel. They were natural rivals. They had different skills: bin Laden, the son of a builder and himself an engineer, focused on logistics. Obaidi was technical, a details man. Bin Laden suspected that the Egyptian Obaidi looked down on him as an arriviste Gulf Arab. Obaidi thought bin Laden was too much in love with the sound of his own voice. The man was delusional, to Obaidi's way of thinking, and therefore dangerous to those around him.

More important, Obaidi thought, bin Laden was weirdly disconnected with the operational side of the work. He could raise the money. He could build the training camps. But when it came to planning an operation down to the last detail, bin Laden too often seemed bored. He liked to issue commands. He didn't like to follow up.

Of course, the last of the crashed four planes had been as much of a surprise to Obaidi as to anyone. Something had gone wrong in the delivery of the machine to its target plane. But no matter; it couldn't have happened to worse traitors than the Jordanians, with their Western hardons and Israeli alliances.

Baghdad, May 16

Morgan Ensley looked over the hangar at Baghdad International Airport. A crowd had been assembled to celebrate the reopening of the Iraqi national airline, and he had been told to come over to help fill up the seats on the American side of the aisle. The assembled group of Iraqi and American dignitaries sat in metal folding chairs listening to the interminable speeches of gratitude and acclaim, each preceded by the obligatory thanks to God, Allah, this imam, and that bureaucrat. It was spring now and heating up just as Black Jack had told him it would. One of the tables in the back was laid with fresh fruit, tea, and cold drinks.

"Coke, sir?" asked a soldier. Morgan shook his head, picking up a bottle of water instead. As he turned back to the crowd, he saw a girl—could she be American?—coming toward the table.

"Ma'am," he said with a nod as she passed, and Mother of God, she said hi back. She got a bottle of water herself and made her way to a spot beside him.

"Thrilling, isn't it?" she whispered, twisting the cap off her water bottle and taking a sip. Her forehead was damp with perspiration and she wiped it with her wrist.

"Yes, ma'am," he said, and smiled. Morgan wondered if he was sweating through his shirt. Probably. He hoped she wouldn't hold it against him. What was that Bellamy Brothers line, "If I said you had a beautiful body would you hold it against me?" He smiled to himself.

The newly elected president of the Iraqi government began to speak. The woman took a notebook from her pocket. A reporter, Morgan realized. He watched her scribble notes for a moment before finding a position in which he could no longer read over her shoulder. She appreciated the gesture. The guy was some kind of American military something-or-other, she figured, though the long hair wasn't standard issue. She wasn't entirely unhappy to meet someone she might be able to talk to. After fifteen minutes, the speeches could not be distinguished one from the other.

She stepped closer to Morgan. He had a respectful smile and an intelligent face. He was handsome, lean like a cowboy, with green eyes and brown hair over the collar of his shirt. Rakish.

"Maybe now that the new runways are open," she said, "they'll be able to fly in some decent American coffee."

Morgan laughed out loud. "Starbucks, right? In the middle of Baghdad. That would be priceless."

"I'm sure someone has thought of it already," she whispered. "And if they haven't, maybe *we* should. Here we have front-row seats, right? Front-row seats to the revolution."

"Except that you're supposed to be a dispassionate observer," he said, nodding at her notepad.

"Oh, I am, I am," she said. "With a rapacious capitalist trapped inside. And what about you? Some kind of spook? Or junior spook, since you still look pretty innocent."

Morgan laughed again. "My mother would appreciate that. About the rest, no comment."

"Okay, sure," she said. "I just wonder what makes you guys think you just blend in with the wallpaper."

He looked at her.

"The ostrich-head-in-the-sand school of covert operations? If you don't have any good dress-ups, just imagine nobody can see you?"

He smiled.

"Don't worry," she said. "I won't give you away. Even if I'm tortured."

News that morning had been bad. A television journalist kidnapped, a British civilian aide worker's body found mutilated after three weeks of captivity, three car bombs, a shooting attack on a Baghdad police station, two American soldiers killed.

"It's not fun out there, is it?" he asked.

"We're not in Kansas anymore, if that's what you mean," she said.

"Okay, Morgan, no fraternizing with the locals," said a man walking over. This one resembled an action hero. Tall, big shoulders, muscles bulging everywhere, hair cut like a marine's.

"This ain't no local." Morgan turned to the reporter. "She's American. I'm sorry, ma'am, I don't know your name."

"Marie Peterssen," she said, putting out her hand. Morgan took it and introduced himself first, then the other man, Danny Comstock.

Morgan looked at Comstock. "We gotta go?" he asked.

Comstock nodded.

Morgan turned to Marie. "Are you staying with the rest of the press corps?"

"You can leave a message for me at the Al-Rashid."

He shook her hand again and while doing so, palmed her a card. She slipped it into her pocket. After he left, she looked it over. "Morgan Ensley. Special Agent, Federal Bureau of Investigation. Fort Worth, Texas," it read.

Amman, Jordan, May 16

Julian entered the Fakr al-Din restaurant, on Taha Hussein Street in Amman. He was alone, dressed in casual slacks and a short-sleeved golf shirt. His friend Gassan Fahed, now Colonel Fahed, the official liaison between the King's Special Guard and the Israelis, had suggested the place. The two had met fifteen years ago, when each had humbler titles and ran covert operations, at times against each other. In the time-honored Middle Eastern logic of "once enemies, now friends," Julian had gone out on a limb and tipped Fahed off to a PLO plot against the chief of the royal court, the king's top aide. It made Fahed's career, and earned Julian his lifelong loyalty. Julian had not fared as well in that particular exchange. He won the enmity of his own boss, who couldn't stand risk taking and "creative" relationships. Luckily, the man fell victim to a scandal involving Mossad funds in a Zurich bank account. Legend held that Julian had something to do with the revelation.

Julian noted as many details as he could while walking to the back of the restaurant, trying to get a feel for the space and its patrons. Every-thing seemed calm. He got no sense of a brewing energy or strange movements. He took a table in the back facing the door and waited for his friend.

A waiter took his order for a glass of peach juice. Julian remembered the last time he was in Amman. The local Mossad team had bungled an operation against Hezbollah, implicating several Jordanian undercover agents in the process. Julian spent two days chain-smoking with Fahed, trying to figure out how to fix it. They succeeded, but not before taking, at Julian's calculation, at least three years off their lives.

Fahed appeared in a white button-down shirt, khaki pants, and black loafers. He had jet-black hair, still, and a full mustache. Julian stood to greet him, and the two men kissed—one cheek, then the other, the tra-ditional Jordanian greeting—before sitting down.

"It's been a long time, no?" asked Fahed in the south Levantine Arabic dialect common to both Jordanians and Palestinians. He looked around to see if it was safe to speak openly. Radical elements in Jordan were restive, as they were in the rest of the Middle East, especially after the downing of the Jordanian jet.

"Too long in one sense, as it's always a pleasure to see you," Julian replied in the same tongue. "But good also, because our borders have been calm."

Fahed nodded and raised his glass. "I'll drink to that. And also to your wonderful wife, Gabi. How is she? Beautiful as ever?"

Julian smiled. "Even better."

"And it has been—what?—ten years? You are a lucky man." Fahed gave Julian a conspiratorial smile.

"Yes."

"Changed her line of work, I understand."

"Retired," said Julian. "From time to time they ask her to advise youngsters, and she helps. But she is on to other things now. She teaches European history at Tel Aviv University."

"An estimable woman. But we're not here only to recall the good old days, are we?"

"I'm very sorry about the Jordanian plane," said Julian. "That's mainly why I'm here."

"You know that people in the street believe the Americans and Israelis brought down this last plane."

"Of course."

"And you know that means you can't be seen to have anything to do with the investigation. People will assume you're working on a cover-up. That probably goes for some government officials, too. Palestinians in the government, anyway."

Julian shrugged. "So I'll stay out of sight. But I'm not leaving unless you ask me to."

"No, no, we need you, Julie. I'm telling you we're getting nowhere fast. I think the Germans know something, but they're playing their cards close."

"Our old friend Gerhard, eh?" laughed Julian, remembering the man who let him sniff the burned cotton wool and pocket the plastic from the video machine. "Okay, Fahed, I need your go-ahead to set up a small operation here, two or three men. They will be undercover as distributors of home water purifiers. I'll keep you informed of any movement of personnel in or out of Jordan and what their business is and who they will contact."

Julian said all this knowing he could not meet his promise entirely and knowing that Fahed knew it too. But they were professionals; they understood the drill. In this business, the only thing you could count on was the few people with whom you had history.

Of course that didn't mean your friends wouldn't surprise you from time to time. What Fahed didn't know was that on this mission, Julian was operating way outside of channels. Tel Aviv had not approved his arrangements and with any luck would never know anything about them.

"No problem," said Fahed. "Just keep me informed in the usual way." The usual way was a note inside a delivery of chrysanthemums to Fahed's wife, Sana, at home.

"I'm sure Sana will be glad to hear from me. Also an estimable woman."

A waiter arrived, juggling several heavy platters. Fahed rubbed his hands together. "Ah, here is our food at last. Are you hungry? Good. Let us break bread. *Tefadal*," he said, meaning "the table is yours"—offering the ancient Bedouin welcome to his guest.

Tel Aviv, May 16

Julian's team leader, Nadav Rosenberg, opened a large envelope and checked his watch. Today's package to Julian would be picked up in thirty minutes. He slipped in a copy of the *Wall Street Journal* with Marie's story about the Royal Jordanian crash on page 1. He also included hard copy of an e-mail from Marie telling him that on the basis of the *Journal* story, she'd got an assignment from *Fortune* magazine to write about Iraq's emerging tycoons.

He added an analysis of the plastic remnants Julian had picked up in Munich. The plastic matched material that Panasonic used to make its video kits up until 2002. But the Jordanian airliner was built in 2003, so the video machine could not have been the plane's original. In addition, Nadav had tracked down the partial serial number Marie remembered from the machine in the London shop to an Air France jet. The machine had never made its way back into the plane. It seemed that the Air France plane might have been the true target of that bomb. Tantalizing, but no proof yet.

Nadav also learned that the head of Germany's Federal Airport Authority, Gerhard Wegener, had quietly ordered an investigation of every shop that had repaired the airplane parts of the downed planes. Julian hadn't told him to do so, but their brief conversation had been enough. That was how they communicated.

Most of the repair paperwork was a jumbled mess. Except for that of the shop of Induk Hajaera. His paperwork seemed all quite in order, and the video players from the downed planes had no record of being serviced at the shop on Brick Lane. When asked by M15 about Ahmed al-Jizouri, the alias Obaidi used, Hajaera freely offered the information he had, which was little. He was an owner of Olive Tree Partners, came occasionally to make audits of the company's books, and had indeed come on the night of May 3, and sent Hajaera and his wife out for a nice dinner. No, he didn't contact al-Jizouri directly as a rule. He gave the inspectors his contact information for OTP, which turned out to be a shell corporation and part of a large Muslim charity. He wasn't aware of telephone calls made from his shop to Iraq, but the telephone bills were paid directly by Olive Tree Partners and he didn't see them.

No, the name Mansour Obaidi was not familiar to him.

The Moroccan, Zaki Aarif Sediki, was no longer working for him. Sediki had told Hajaera that he had to return home because of family problems. He was a clever fellow with the machines, very nimble and smart. Was there a problem with Sediki?

By that time, the security services knew about Sediki's terror ties and the connections Julian had warned them about in 1996. Sediki left England the day the Jordanian jet crashed. He flew to Riyadh. The Saudi authorities were put on alert for him. The last piece of news sent to Julian was no surprise, but welcome confirmation. Explosive material was found on the inside of the Royal Jordanian plane, definitive evidence that an incendiary device had indeed gone off inside. They were getting closer.

Nadav sealed the envelope and left it at the front desk, where it would be picked up by Shabaq's courier service and sent from Tel Aviv to the Israeli embassy in Amman in a diplomatic pouch. Upon arrival at the embassy, the package would be brought to DHL, which would deliver it as regular express mail to the office of the Dutch businessmen. Everything to maintain Julian's and Gil's cover.

As Nadav walked back to his desk, he knew what Julian would tell him the next time they communicated directly: They had little choice but to wait for Obaidi to make his next move. And all they could do was pray to God they got a lead before more people got hurt.

Al-Rashid Hotel, Baghdad, May 16

Marie Peterssen looked around the lobby of the Al-Rashid. Surrendering to the jet lag that dogged her since her arrival the day before, she sank into an armchair and surveyed the scene: reporters comparing notes, fixers sidling up to government officials, businessmen huddled over laptop computers. She was wearing a long skirt and long-sleeved shirt to avoid the leering glances and rude remarks she'd met when wearing pants. She swirled the ice around in her glass of Coke and noticed a group of Iraqi men cross the lobby. They all appeared very important and were dressed in nicely tailored suits or Arab robes. The man behind the reception desk, whom she'd been sure to tip generously and as often as was seemly since her arrival, had let slip that there would be a gathering today of Iraqi bigwigs and that Mansour Obaidi might be present.

She put her glass down as the men moved in a slow group farther into the lobby. They didn't make much progress before stopping and forming smaller groups to chat. Was Obaidi there? She consulted the photo Julian had given her, and scanned the faces without being too obvious about it. She thought she might have found him, a light-skinned man with a short beard and well-cut clothes. She stole glances at him for a while. The photo showed Obaidi clean-shaven and a few pounds lighter. She decided she had a match. The man looked nice enough. Gracious, even courtly, to judge from the way he treated his companions. He wore a white cotton summer suit. So now what was she supposed to do, just sidle on up to him and say hello? "Hi, can we talk about the crash site in Munich? How's your buddy Osama doing these days? Wanna talk about sharia in Sarajevo?" Okay, stop, Marie. You really need some sleep.

Obaidi was surrounded by men in long robes and headdresses and others with sport jackets buttoned tightly over bulges that had to be handguns. Only slightly intimidating. But there they were, milling about and on the verge of moving along. She could sit there and let the moment pass, or she could do her job. She stood up and walked slowly toward Obaidi. She stopped a few feet away so his bodyguards wouldn't fear she was a suicide bomber and neutralize her in a shower of bullets. Obaidi noticed her and looked up.

"Mr. Obaidi?" She tried to make her voice as soft as possible.

He smiled and bowed his head to her in a respectful or obsequious manner, she couldn't quite tell.

"I'm writing a story for *Fortune* magazine," she said. "About the business climate in Iraq. And I wondered if I might arrange an interview with you?"

A couple of men in suits moved closer to Obaidi. He waved them back. "Here are my credentials," said Marie, reaching into her bag. She pulled out her wallet, and as she opened it up, a clutch of credit cards and business cards flew out of a pocket and onto the floor in the shape of a large fan.

"Oh, I'm so sorry," she said, leaning over to gather up her things.

Obaidi bent over to try to help, but then demurred, making helpful motions with his hands in the air.

When she had gathered everything together, she stood, her face red.

"Well, that was quite an introduction," he said.

"I'm so sorry," she said again. "My name is Marie Peterssen." She didn't put out her hand, knowing that no Muslim man would take it. He smiled, as if in silent appreciation of her sensitivity.

"Pleased to meet you, Miss Peterssen. I would be happy to help you if I can. Why don't you send me a note describing in more detail what you had in mind." He reached into his pocket and pulled out a gold case, snapped it open efficiently, and handed her a card on heavy cream stock. "My secretary will contact you with my answer."

"Thank you," said Marie, very much aware of the contrast between his crisp efficiency and her own embarrassing display.

"Don't mention it," he said, smiling and turning to move along. "Have a nice day," he said, using an Americanism that seemed intentionally ironic. Marie stood, watching him step away, feeling her face turn red all over again.

Forward Operating Marine Base Riley, Near Baghdad, May 17

Ahmed Mosul snapped the grip and trigger housing back onto his M16; put away his cleaning rod, bore patches, and lubricant; and racked the gun beside him. Can't clean the rifle too much, the Americans told him. "Cleanliness is next to godliness, and it also just might save your life." The skinny Iraqi soldier sat back, wiping his brow. He was sitting on a bench in a patch of shade beneath the eaves of the barracks. These Americans, he thought, always busy, busy, always doing something. They just didn't understand a man's need for tea and a smoke, for pondering his fate in the world. He glanced at his new watch, a gift from his uncle after he was inducted into the police. Almost time for afternoon prayer, he noticed, his eyes wandering out over the perimeter fence.

"Ai!" cried Ahmed, standing quickly and grabbing his gun. He saw a man standing by the fence, struggling with something. Ahmed shouted again to the four Iraqi recruits near him and gestured to the periphery. The men argued for a few moments about what to do, but eventually headed out at a jog, Ahmed in the lead, running with his back straight, his chest out. As he approached, the man squirmed, hands up on the chicken-wire fence.

"His foot is caught in something!" one of the Iraqis yelled. "And watch out, he's got a knapsack!"

Ahmed got within twenty yards, raised his M16. "Drop the knapsack!" he shouted. The man didn't respond.

"Drop it or I'll shoot your knees!" shouted Ahmed. "You'll be one more filthy beggar crawling in the streets."

The man's face crumpled, and he slowly wriggled out of his knapsack, carefully dropped it to the ground, and Ahmed ran up and frisked him, then handcuffed him. Another man checked the bag. Inside was a metal pipe, a battery, some wires, and a clock. "Holy shit!" he shouted. "He's got a fucking bomb!"

Panic broke out. Ahmed tried to pull the young man away from the fence, but his foot was firmly wedged. A police officer put his hands around the man's leg and gave it a yank. The would-be bomber screamed with pain and Ahmed gave him a shot on the cheek with his rifle butt. They hustled him to the barracks.

Morgan Ensley first heard the shouts. He'd been given a desk with a telephone here until they found him a permanent office. Then there was the alarm, loud enough to rouse Nebuchadnezzar from his final rest.

Morgan stuck his head out of his borrowed office to see four Iraqi policemen wrestling a young man down the corridor, his white shirt pulled over his head and twisted around his arms.

The commanding officer, a Captain Hennig, also stepped out into the corridor. Ahmed pushed his prisoner forward.

"We found him at the fence," he said. "His foot was caught in a broken section. And we found a bomb in his knapsack, ready to go." Hennig looked at the man's ankles, both of which were bare. One had a nasty open gash.

After ordering a pair of marine bomb techs to disable the device, the officer gestured to the police to take the young man into the interrogation room. "Empty his pockets. Collect all ID, papers, business cards, notations. Everything."

Hennig turned toward Morgan. "Why don't you take charge of the interrogation? See if he's got any friends on their way behind him."

"Yes sir."

"You can use Comstock if you want," he said, gesturing to Morgan's colleague walking toward them down the hall.

Fucking Comstock, Morgan thought. His minder. A lame-assed muscle head, hanging around his neck like an old tire. Oh, he knew exactly why. The Bureau needed him because of what he knew, but they didn't trust him. So they stuck an enforcer on him.

Hennig gestured toward an interrogation room. Well, crap. How 'bout this now. Had to do an interrogation with Meathead by his side. Morgan stepped into the room, trying to focus on what he knew about Muslim psychology. He saw that the boy had a raised bruise on the side of his face that he hadn't seen at first glance. He looked young, maybe eighteen. His hands were cuffed behind his back. Comstock followed them in and stood by the door.

"All right, all right, stand back from him," Morgan told Ahmed. He asked everyone else, save Comstock and a senior Iraqi policeman, to step out of the room.

"Place the contents of his pockets on the table," Morgan said to the policeman, who set down one crushed cigarette, 10,000 dinars in bills, and 150 dinars in coins—about ten dollars—and a pack of matches.

Morgan walked around behind the young man and asked if everything he'd been carrying was on the table.

The boy nodded. Morgan lifted the tail of his white shirt enough to see his back pockets. There was something there. He pulled out a pair of spectacles. The boy tried to stop him with his manacled hands. Comstock stepped up and gave the kid a shot right to the chest. The kid gasped and crumpled to his knees.

Comstock pulled him back to his feet.

"What's in the other pocket?" Morgan asked the boy, who stood shakily and with some difficulty pulled out a white card. Morgan looked over a business card written in Arabic. He slipped it into his breast pocket, and Comstock sat the boy down in a chair.

"So, you thought you'd blow yourself up today," Morgan said. The policeman repeated his words in Arabic.

The boy sat steadily in his seat.

"But you screwed up. Got stuck." Morgan paused. "Anybody else coming behind you today?"

Though the boy wasn't answering, Morgan could see that he was afraid.

"You get paid to blow yourself up? Someone promise to take care of your mother if you blew yourself to hell?"

Still no answer.

"What's your name?"

Morgan was getting nowhere.

"Who paid you to blow yourself up?"

No response.

"What's your name?"

Shit, Morgan thought. Do I have to let the Iraqis take over? They were so much more resourceful. He'd done interrogations back home, but never a ticking-bomb case. And never interrogated a Muslim.

It hadn't started well.

"Ask him again if there are others," he said to the translator. Hell, I don't even know if this guy is translating what I'm saying, he thought. After a few more fruitless questions, he nodded to the policeman. "I'm going outside for a minute." He gestured to Comstock to follow him.

The boy started screaming almost immediately. Morgan felt sick. Telling himself he had no choice didn't help. He punched the wall in frustration. Damn! He paced his room for a couple minutes, then returned to the interrogation room.

"Stop," he said.

The policeman's face was darkened red with effort and excitement, his body emanating the animal heat of aggression. Morgan turned away. Not that the Americans didn't know how to punch someone's lights out, but they lacked the imagination of these guys.

"He say anything useful?" Morgan asked, struggling with his disgust.

The man stopped and turned. "He doesn't know about more suicide bombers. His orders were to detonate outside the mess hall at five p.m."

Morgan told him to return the prisoner to his cell. He walked into his office. Comstock followed him. Morgan put the evidence bag in a file cabinet and locked it.

"At least you found out nobody else is coming," said Comstock, accurately reading Morgan's frustration.

"I didn't find out anything. The policeman got the information with his big fat fist."

"The information you needed was gotten," elaborated Comstock. "I'm trying to support you here in case you hadn't noticed."

"Right," said Morgan. "Sure. All we know is that the guy *said* he didn't know about any others. We don't really know if there are more. Maybe he doesn't know. Maybe he does know and he's lying. How do you know if they're telling the truth? In any case, we need to keep the place on high alert. No vehicular approach, all that."

"Already done," said Comstock.

Morgan left his office and walked into what passed for a men's room: a hole in the floor and a sink. He had a cut on his knuckles from hitting the wall earlier. Shit. He washed his hands. He hadn't been prepared to interrogate the suspect. And he felt humiliated by the performance. He didn't know Arabic, so he couldn't communicate directly with the boy. With the translator between them, he couldn't control the interrogation. If they'd been in the U.S., he'd have known the suspect's rights and his own limits, but here he didn't know anything. What were the rules? If he didn't know them, he couldn't focus fully. Not to mention that it was the first time he'd looked in the eyes of a man determined to kill others by killing himself. Wild.

He was supposed to meet Marie Peterssen in two hours at the Al-Rashid for a drink. He hardly had time to get there, let alone finish his paperwork. He laughed at the absurdity of it. He finds a girl that he likes in this hole? And what was he going to do when he had to continue the interrogation tomorrow?

He went back to his office, took his revolver out of his desk and slipped it into his belt holster, strapped on his vest and helmet, and walked out.

Chapter Ten

Marie sat in the passenger seat of a white Chevy Suburban with her new driver, Massud Ratib, trying to get back into Baghdad before dusk. She'd toured a new industrial zone west of the city, an outing organized by a consortium of Iraqi manufacturers.

Massud had told her that *Ratib* meant "arranger" and that she should rely on him to smooth her path. His English was good, though accented, and he seemed alert and on the ball. He was relatively tall, with light-colored skin and curly hair. He showed up on time and seemed to know the streets well. But today there was traffic. The U.S. Army was still periodically closing the roads, which caused traffic jams. Marie glanced at her watch. She was supposed to meet that FBI guy tonight and hoped she wasn't going to be horribly late.

Even if she was, he'd find plenty of Americans at the bar of the Al-Rashid. Of course there'd be people to avoid, like the ever-irritating French journalists, the Saudi princes, the American contractors. She shook her head. Part of her wanted to protect him from standing there, waiting for her, wondering if she was going to show. But why? He was an

FBI agent. He could take care of himself. But she'd seen a look in his eyes—just a fleeting look—of delicacy or perhaps sadness. He seemed, for a second, vulnerable.

She looked out the window again. The stench of sewage rose to her nose. They'd been sitting in the same spot for five minutes. Dusk was approaching, though it was still so hot she felt faint. Tempers were wearing thin. People pounded their horns, men got out of their cars to peer around traffic. As instructed by Massud and everyone else, she was wearing a helmet and flak jacket. And she was sweating. There was dust everywhere, in her clothes, in her ears, up her nose. She pulled off her helmet to cool out her hair and noticed a U.S. military vehicle trying to edge around the traffic on the dirt shoulder. She looked up and saw a Marine Corps driver and beside him, in a flak jacket himself, Morgan Ensley.

Marie put her fingers between her teeth and let out a wolf whistle. Morgan looked her way and she flashed him a big smile. He gestured to the driver to stop.

"You whistlin' at me there, darlin'?" he yelled over.

She nodded. "Why don't you come on over?"

"Can't," he said. "Against regulations. Ditch your driver and come here with me." She thought for a minute, then said to Massud, "There's the guy I'm supposed to meet. I think I'll get into his car. Is that okay?"

"No, miss. Not okay. My job is to return you back to the office. That is how I must fill out forms and get paid." Marie looked back over at Morgan, then back at Massud. She was silent for a few seconds to think.

"Massud, I'm going over with him." She reached over and put her hand on his forearm in a gesture of friendliness. "Please follow us. I'll tell the driver to keep you close. I'll meet you at the hotel and make sure all the paperwork gets done." She slipped out before Massud could object. She ran a few strides over to the American military vehicle. Morgan was watching her closely. Marie knew that men often looked at her. She didn't really know why. But the combination of a dancer's grace and a fencer's easy power gave her an interesting way of moving that tended to catch men's eyes.

"Put your helmet back on," said Morgan, smiling appreciatively and scooting over to make room for her. He took the helmet from her and placed it on her head. He turned to his driver. "Take us on to the Al-Rashid."

The private gave him a rueful smile and accelerated over the shoulder of the road.

"Please let my driver keep up with you," added Marie. "He's a good guy and he wasn't happy about my leaving his car." The private nodded his acknowledgment.

"So how are you doing?" Morgan asked her.

"Good, good. Glad I met you here, because I was going to be late."

He looked at her, green eyes humorous. "So was I. We were goin' on late together. Sounds like a song."

Marie laughed. Morgan dropped his sunglasses on the floor of the vehicle, and while he was leaning over to pick them up, a white business card fell from a pocket.

"Here," she said, handing it back to him.

"Thanks. That's important. Too bad I can't read Arabic."

"Show it to my driver. He'll translate for you."

Morgan looked at her, didn't say anything.

"You can trust him," said Marie. "He's a Kurd, for one thing."

"Oh yeah?"

"Give it to me and I'll ask him what it says. I won't let him know it's yours."

"All right," Morgan said, handing the card to her. "I'll need that back, though."

"I understand," she said, putting it into her backpack. "Now where'd you say you got it?"

"I didn't."

"That's what I remembered."

The traffic was moving now, and Massud was sticking close as the marine private wove dangerously across lanes. They slowed again when approaching the hotel, as they now had to wind through a maze of concrete checkpoints. The most dangerous outer layer was patrolled by the Iraqis. These were the troops who were the daily targets of car bombs and other insurgent attacks. Vehicles were directed slowly through short lengths of roadway, turning left and right around the concrete blocks and to the second layer, controlled by the Americans. The final layer, the sterile zone, the hotel grounds, were patrolled exclusively by American troops. This arrangement was helping Americans to reduce their own casualties.

When they finally arrived at the hotel entrance, Massud was right behind them. Marie got out and walked back to Massud's car.

"See? I'm here in one piece," she said.

Massud smiled weakly. Morgan walked up beside Marie.

"This is my aide-de-camp, Massud. Massud, this is Morgan Ensley."

They greeted each other. Massud, Marie noticed, gave Morgan a fairly serious once-over.

"Massud, can you translate something for me please?" She handed him the business card that had fallen out of Morgan's pocket.

Massud said, "It's the name of a man and his business. A scrap-metal business, called Thaqib. The man's name is Qassim Rashid. The business is in Rutba, in western Iraq."

Marie pulled out her notebook and wrote it all down. "Great."

Massud nodded. "Lots of metal there," he said.

"Lot's of what?" asked Marie.

"Metal."

"Really?" asked Marie.

"Saddam used to have a lot of factories there. They built tanks and heavy armor. The Americans blew it up in the first Gulf War, so there are tons of scrap metal lying around. They haul it away and sell it."

"That's interesting," said Marie, signing the car-service papers Massud handed her. "Who wants scrap?"

"The Chinese economy is exploding and the Chinese are buying steel from anyone selling it," said Morgan. "Steel prices are up worldwide, and scrap is valuable."

"And they're finding it in Iraq," said Marie. "Wow. That's just the kind of story I'm supposed to be digging up. Emerging businesses in Iraq."

She tipped Massud in American dollars. Morgan and Marie moved quickly into the hotel; loitering outside was a bad idea anywhere in the city. Despite being one of the most heavily guarded buildings in Baghdad, the Al-Rashid was vulnerable to rocket fire.

Marie steered Morgan toward a bar on the ground floor, and found a table near the wall and away from the gathering crowd. They shook off their flak jackets and placed them on the backs of their chairs. Marie was wearing a peach-colored T-shirt and khaki slacks with desert-colored army boots. Her hair was pulled back in a ponytail down toward the nape of her neck. He watched her slide off the band that held it back and shake her hair loose. It was black and shiny and fell just over her shoulders in a little flip. She went up to the bar and returned with the beer. He averted his eyes. He didn't want to scare her off.

She set down the bottles with a half smile.

"So where in the States are you from?" she asked.

"North Carolina."

"Your family been there for a long time?"

"Well, yeah, that's right," he said. "My great-great-great-grandfather on my mother's side, John Roach, was a relatively famous shipbuilder in Chester, Pennsylvania, during the 1800s and he built the first steel ships for the navy. One of them, an ironclad vessel, the *Huron*, ran aground in a severe storm on Ensley Island, off North Carolina. The island had been named after ancestors on my father's side. Through a strange series of events, Roach wound up summering there, and his daughter met an Ensley boy and one thing led to another."

"So your life began as the result of a shipwreck?" Marie asked.

Morgan laughed. "I guess you could say that."

She raised her bottle and he tapped his against it. "To shipwrecks," she said.

"You ever hear the country song 'Let's fall to pieces together. Why should we both fall apart?' I think that's my family's theme song," Morgan said.

"That's funny," said Marie. "What are the next lines?"

" 'Let's fall to pieces together. Right here in each other's arms.' "

Marie caught his eye and quickly looked away. "Who sings that song?" she asked.

"That would be George Strait," he said.

"Cool," said Marie. "He sings a great song called 'The Chair.'"

"The very same," he said. As Morgan put his bottle on the table, Marie saw that his hand was cut and swollen.

"What happened there?" she asked him, one eyebrow up in an expression of friendly skepticism that he thought was quite fetching.

"Oh, nothing," he said.

"Yeah, I can see it was nothing," she said.

"Well, you know what Thomas Jefferson said: 'The price of freedom is eternal vigilance.'"

"Vigilance or vigilantism?" she asked, her eyebrow arching playfully again.

He laughed. "I have the full force of the United States law enforcement establishment behind me. Now whether that's worth a pile of sand fleas here anymore, I don't know."

"You drove over to meet me in a vehicle driven by a marine, right?" said Marie.

Morgan nodded.

"And we heard today that an attempted suicide bomber was caught outside the marine base. So it all leads me to wonder whether you might have, let's say, spoken with the lad."

"You're a smart lady," he said, stalling for time. "And well informed. I'm having trouble keeping ahead of you here." He looked at her appraisingly, meeting her eyes. "For some reason I trust you. I'm not sure why, but I do. And it's not just that I think you're pretty as all get-out."

"Don't say that or I'll have to put on my chador," she said. "Muslim women say that covering up serves their interests too. It protects them from predatory males." She swigged her beer and laughed at her own little joke. "That'd be good. A woman in a chador drinking beer in a Baghdad bar."

"I have an idea," said Morgan, smiling. "I got the feeling you were interested in driving out to that town with the scrap metal. And I'm also interested in going there for my own reasons. Maybe we could do that together."

"What about my reputation?" she said, laughing. "Who are you going to be? No one will talk to me if you tell them you're an FBI agent."

"Your assistant," he said.

"Magazine reporters don't have assistants," she said, smiling.

"Okay then, your photographer."

"That could work," she said. "I do have a camera."

"Consider me hired."

"Well then," she said, raising her bottle.

"Good deal," he said.

"I'd better call Massud to make a plan. What time should we leave?"

"I'd say early, so we can get a good part of the trip done before it gets too hot," Morgan answered.

"Five a.m.?"

He nodded.

Marie glanced at her wrist. She wore a Swiss Army watch. Practical chic, he thought approvingly, her style.

"He's not home yet," she said. "I'll call from my room later."

Just then, Marie saw Morgan's associate Danny Comstock appear beside them.

"Jesus, Comstock," said Morgan

"That would be Danny," he said. "But it's a common mistake."

Marie laughed. She remembered meeting him at the airport, the same day she met Morgan. The guy was total beefcake.

"I'm Marie."

"Yeah, I remember," he said, tipping his hat. "Pleased to see you again, ma'am."

"So what's up, Comstock? You got something for me?" asked Morgan.

"I do."

"What is it?"

"Now, you know I can't talk about secret stuff in front of the lady."

"You're telling me you want me to leave with you?" said Morgan, straightening up.

Comstock nodded. "My apologies to Marie."

Morgan turned to Marie. "Can you believe it? This clown is my special responsibility. And I gotta do what he asks."

"Go to it," said Marie, standing up. "You still up for what we talked about?"

"You bet."

"I'll call if there's a problem with Massud," said Marie.

"Ten-four."

They both picked up their things, and Morgan trailed her out of the bar, his arm protectively behind her, not quite touching her back but as though making sure nobody else did. He stopped at the elevators and put out his hand.

"See you tomorrow."

Somewhere West of the Canary Islands, May 17

It was too good to last, thought Captain Hamid. The seas were calm, the sky blue. He was on the bridge, staring at a weather map that had just reached him by fax. An early tropical depression was forming off West Africa and might churn its way across the Atlantic. Too early for a hurricane in May, he thought, though it wasn't impossible. Was this the effect of global warming? Seas already warm enough to sustain a tropical storm?

"Nothing I can do," he said out loud.

"What, sir?" said the helmsman, a dark-complected, pimply Lebanese.

"Nothing I can do about the fucking weather. There may be a hurricane out there before we're through."

"I've never been through one of those, sir."

"No? May God spare you. The wind is deafening. The waves look like apartment buildings. And they keep coming at you. You manage to steer up the face of one and the next one is not far behind. You pray a lot."

And the hostages, he reminded himself. They will be tossed about like pieces on a chessboard.

Hamid began to wish he hadn't signed on for this voyage.

Al-Rashid Hotel, Baghdad, May 18

Marie walked out the front door of the hotel. Her head was clogged with sleep and the effects of uneasy rest. She saw Morgan illuminated by the outdoor lights, standing away from the building, rucksack on, helmet hanging from it. He was playing a harmonica.

"Hi, Morgan," said Marie.

" 'Good mornin', little schoolgirl, can I come home with you?' " he sang softly, working the blues riffs between the verses. " 'Tell your mama and your father, I'm a little schoolboy too.' " He walked toward her.

"Junior Wells?" she asked, raising her right eyebrow.

"Originally, Sonny Boy Williamson," said Morgan with a huge grin. "But doggone it, you're my girl just for knowing the damn song." He pulled an origami flower from the pocket of his vest and handed it to her.

"Oh my," she said.

"As pretty as you," said Morgan.

Marie laughed. "You seen my driver, Massud?"

"Not yet," he said, looking around. "But I do see something else." Walking toward them was Danny Comstock. "What is *up* with this guy?"

"He certainly knows how to exercise, doesn't he?" said Marie.

"Yeah, he used to be a navy SEAL."

"Wow," said Marie, turning now toward Comstock. "Nobody tougher than a SEAL."

"I don't want to break up this little party," Danny said, acknowledging Marie and her comment with a quick smile. "But I need just one word with your regular dance partner, Mr. Ensley here."

"Aw, I'm disappointed," she said, her sleepiness and the impending trip making her more playful than she might ordinarily have been. "I thought you wanted *me*."

"I do, darling," said Comstock. "I *do*! But this is business."

Marie laughed. "Don't hold him up for long, because here comes my driver."

Massud eased his vehicle toward them through the maze of cement barricades. Comstock pulled Morgan aside.

Marie lifted a cardboard container of tea and handed it to Massud.

"Thank you, miss," he said, taking the cup.

"We have to wait a minute," she said, nodding at the men, who were speaking intently to each other. After a few minutes, Morgan returned and climbed into the front seat of the Suburban. He was quiet and seemed in a bad mood, so Marie left him alone. "You know where we're going?" she asked Massud as he pulled away from the hotel.

He nodded.

She unfolded a map and spread it out on her knees. "Well, we have the map just in case."

The sun was not yet up and the sky was black. No one was stirring in the shadows of the shops or in the rutted roads. As they made their way out of Baghdad, they saw people beginning to move about, to collect water and retrieve animals from fields and pens.

Massud and Marie sipped from their cups. Morgan looked out the window, letting the breeze, such as it was, blow over his face.

"So, we're headed out where Jesus lost his sandals?" asked Marie.

Massud laughed. Morgan didn't. Marie was quiet. She realized she couldn't ask Morgan about his conversation here in front of Massud.

"I have a question. How do we explain to Rashid why we're showing up on his doorstep? Are we going to hand him his calling card and say we found it on the street?"

"Fine question," said Morgan.

Marie was beginning to think that Morgan was pretty cagey. He hadn't given her a thing, not what had happened to his hand or how he'd got the card with the name on it. She remained quiet. Morgan volunteered nothing further.

"How are we going to say we got his name?"

"You can use me, miss," said Massud. "Everybody from the area knows this business. You could say you learned it from your driver."

"That'll work," said Morgan.

Outside, the landscape was flat and monotonous, dotted with small cement-block houses, each shaded by a tree or two. Everywhere, hot sand. It covered the asphalt road in places. The highway was wide and well traveled, filled with all manner of trucks and eighteen-wheelers, most headed in the other direction, toward Baghdad.

Massud stopped after three hours so they could all stretch their legs. He pulled up to a small café selling kebabs, roasted stuffed lamb, and minced meat mixed with nuts, raisins, and spices. They ordered three heaping plates of meat and vegetables and ate in the shade of a tree out front. They piled the food onto pieces of flat bread and washed it down with sweet tea.

Fortified, they piled back into the car to continue their trip. Marie silently thanked God for the air conditioner, which Massud was now running, giving them what seemed just enough air to breathe to remain alive. The sun was relentless, its light changing from hazy to metallic. Sheep, goats, and the occasional dromedary could be seen in pens fenced in with mattress springs, tires, odd sticks. Here and there the earth became greener, and they saw garden plots and cultivated fields. In all directions there were rusted, burned military vehicles, some decades old, melting into the sand and undergrowth. The feeling here was of turmoil, endless destruction, but also a strange subterranean energy.

Morgan swatted at a sand fly that had landed on his hand. "You got bit by any of these yet?" he asked Marie.

"Yes," she said, pointing to a spot on her arm. "They hurt."

"The soldiers are covered with them," said Morgan. "And then some of them get sores."

"Yeah, I heard about them. It's caused by a parasite causing an illness called leishmaniasis."

"Hey that's pretty good. How do you remember that?"

"Oh, that's just the pack-rat mind of a reporter," she said, smiling. "We store all kinds of crazy things away just in case we might need them one day. Like right now."

"The soldiers call them 'Baghdad boils,'" Morgan said.

"Poor guys," said Marie. "As if the fighting weren't bad enough. Flies, boils, it all sounds so biblical."

"Hey, this is Mesopotamia, right?" said Morgan. "That parasite has probably been around since the time of Abraham."

Marie laughed.

They came to a crossroads, and Rutba was plainly marked on a hand-painted post. Massud rolled to a stop before turning, and Marie would think later of that scene many times: the car pulling up to a sign of yellow hand-painted Arabic letters on a brown background, looming twenty feet into the sky, and two roads stretching as far as the eye could see, making a huge crisscross on the earth, leading off, it seemed, to the ends of the world. She had read that Rutba had been a way station for caravans for thousands of years, part of an ancient trade route between Saudi Arabia, Turkey, and Europe via Syria. How many bushels of gemstones, cinnamon and cardamom, frankincense and myrrh, had passed here through the centuries? How many thousands of peddlers and pilgrims had ridden and walked through this outpost on their way to Jordan or Egypt and back to Baghdad, carrying how many thousands of stories of intrigue and mystery? And today it continued, an asphalt highway that followed the same ancient camel paths.

It was four more miles to town. As they approached, they saw evidence of destruction from the American-led invasion that began on March 19, 2003: smashed trucks and bombed-out buildings, everything now picked clean as a carcass in the desert. But also new construction: houses, a health clinic, and a water-treatment plant.

Marie pulled from her bag a file of papers that she'd printed out from the Internet the night before. She paraphrased as she read aloud:

"The town of Rutba was bombed by the Brits at the start of the war because of the strategic importance of its three air bases. Code-named H1, H2, and H3, they were built by Saddam Hussein and named for the oil pipelines and pumping stations nearby. H1 originally ran to the port of Haifa via Jordan and the British Mandate of Palestine. This route was abandoned after Israel's independence in 1949. The H2 pipeline ran through the Syrian Golan Heights and on to the port of Beirut. It was closed down after the Israelis gained control of the Golan Heights during the Six-Day War. H3 is still operational, pumping oil through Syria to the Port of Latakia."

Marie looked up from her papers. "Listen to this," she said. "'The British captured H2 and H3 at the start of Operation Iraqi Freedom because satellite photos showed missile launchers being moved into the area, and military planners thought Saddam planned to fire Scuds at Israel again, as he had in the First Gulf War. Royal Marines landed here and helped demolish guard posts, communications equipment, and the missile launchers.'"

"Great," said Morgan. "These folks will be thrilled to see a couple of Americans drive up to their front door."

"Well, maybe it would be nice if we brought something. I have some cans of coffee and packages of cigarettes in my bag. Maybe if we arrive with a gift, it will smooth things over."

"Coffee for an Arab? Seems like you'd be better off bringing booze they can't buy for themselves."

"This is Iraq, not Saudi Arabia. They have booze. But that's not the point. This culture prizes gestures of generosity almost as much as it requires hospitality."

"Whatever you say dear," said Morgan, reaching down to an ankle holster and pulling out a Glock 17, a special, small 9 mm pistol. He checked the clip and tucked it back into his holster. "But I'm preparing my own hospitality basket."

"That's pretty funny," said Marie. "I've brought coffee, and you're packing gunpowder."

"It's always good to back up the sugar with a little spice."

"Please try to avoid shooting Massud and myself."

"Will do," said Morgan. "What are you, some kind of gun-control nut?"

"Absolutely. Anyway, my weapon of choice is a foil."

"Tinfoil?"

Marie gave him a look. "I'm a fencer."

"Well now, I didn't know what you meant. That's interesting. Did you compete?"

"Yes."

"Did you win?"

"Yes."

"What did you win?"

"I was NCAA Division I champion the year I graduated. And I was an alternate for the 2004 Olympics."

"I'm impressed," said Morgan.

"Thanks," said Marie, shrugging. "I'm in training again. Maybe I can redeem myself in 2008."

"Wow, almost an Olympic athlete," said Morgan. "You're all right."

"Almost," said Marie. "Almost. Story of my life."

"Aw, hell. How many people get as far as you did? I think that's amazing."

"Thanks," said Marie, giving him a smile. "What were you before you became an FBI agent?"

"Variously an architect, a driver for the Dixie Chicks, and a cave diver."

"Well, I'll be damned," said Marie.

"We're almost there," said Massud, driving down the main street of the city until he reached its outer limits. He then turned west and continued. As they crested a hill, they saw in front of them a compound of cinder-block houses.

"I'll bet that's your baby right there," said Morgan, pointing to a small house. Next to it was parked a huge shipping container.

Massud stopped the car and they all climbed out. Marie watched Morgan. He had a loping stride, very boyish, she thought, an ease of carriage. He saw her watching him, but didn't let on.

Marie picked up her backpack and hung a camera around Morgan's neck. Massud led the way. As they approached the house, a chicken waddled over and pecked Marie's leg. She shooed it away with her hands, then stepped back against a discarded tractor tire and lost her balance. Morgan pulled her up. She brushed the dust off her pants, laughing.

"That, what you just saw, is me. I do this. This is my everlasting weakness."

"What, hens?" he asked.

"No," she said, laughing again, "pratfalls." These events embarrassed her. She wondered sometimes if she was getting Tourette's or something. What the hell? She was a good athlete, and she knew it. In her mind, pratfalls were a tic. They always came on when she was approaching a new situation; she thought of them as a reminder to stay alert, not to take anything for granted.

Just then the screen door opened and a short man with a big belly, bald head, and plastic glasses stepped out. He held the screen open with his foot.

"Hello," said Marie.

The man continued to look at them and not say a word. Massud greeted him in Arabic. The man looked in Massud's direction, then turned back to Marie and Morgan with an unblinking and not very friendly stare.

"Massud, would you please tell this man that we are looking for Qassim Rashid?"

"Yes, miss," he said, then translated. The man replied and Massud said, "He would like to know the purpose of your visit."

"Please tell him that I'm an American journalist writing about Iraqi business, and I heard of the work Mr. Rashid is doing collecting scrap metal and thought it might be interesting for a story I am writing for *Fortune* magazine." She thought it was ridiculous to mention the name of the magazine, as if the guy had ever heard of it.

Massud turned back to the man and spoke.

The man's face broke into a big smile and, suddenly animated, he replied to Massud.

"Mr. Rashid said that he is delighted to make your acquaintance and that his nephew, who went to school in England, once had a subscription to *Fortune* magazine and brought back to Iraq every single issue he had gotten for his subscription. The issues are still in the house, and Mr. Rashid continues to find them very interesting, even though they are now eight years old."

"That's wonderful," said Marie. "I'd be happy to sign him up for another subscription. A new one."

Massud stopped translating, assuming that if he could read *Fortune*, he hardly needed a translator. Mr. Rashid invited them into his house for tea. Marie introduced Massud and her "photographer," Morgan.

"How is it that you speak English?" she asked.

"I worked in Saudi Arabia for an American company," said Rashid. "I learned English there."

"Very nice," said Marie, nodding.

The living room was sparsely furnished but neat. The walls were painted powder blue, and pillows lined the floor, Arabian divan-style, for sitting. The walls were hung with calligraphy and battle scenes. Marie saw a middle-aged woman in Western dress preparing tea. And she saw that Morgan was trying casually to case the joint. Casting glances out the windows and toward Rashid. Massud stood watchfully in a corner. Marie wondered how Morgan was going to sit on the pillows and keep his ankle holster concealed. Maybe that's why these he-man types always stood around, she thought, because they needed to keep their weapons concealed.

The woman came in with the teapot and glasses on a tray. Mr. Rashid served his guests in silence. She read somewhere that once an Arab offers you food, you are safe. The famed Arab hospitality means that once you have been fed or refreshed, you will not be attacked—at least not by your hosts. Mr. Rashid spent quite a bit of time insulting the Royal Air Force for bombing Rutba and seizing the nearby airfields. He carried on about the occupation of Muslim land by infidels. Marie decided just to nod and write down what he said, so he would know she considered his words important.

When they finished their tea, Rashid asked if she would like to walk outside and see the fruits of his work. Yes, of course. Marie got up, as did Morgan, who had seated himself atop two pillows so that his ankle holster remained concealed. Rashid led them out to his yard and to a large shipping container. They walked around it and peered in—it was half filled with scrap metal of all kinds. But when they walked around the outside again, Marie noticed some writing on the wall of the container. It was in English. She pointed this out to Morgan. "Eastern Marine Dry Shipping," it said. He clicked a few photos.

"Is this an American shipping container?"

"Oh, yes," said Rashid, smiling broadly.

"Where is the metal going?" she asked.

"Sometimes it goes to America."

"And how is it being shipped?"

"Private shipping lines. The steel goes all over the world."

"And what is the method of collection?" she asked.

"People find things and bring them over. I pay them by the pound. If the piece is too big, I arrange for a truck and a winch—sometimes the metal needs to be broken down, so I send metalworkers to dismantle the pieces. There are many Rashids throughout the western area of Iraq, each collecting metal to sell—sometimes to the Americans or Germans or Russians or Chinese. It is a good business." He smiled as he spoke. He almost always smiled. He seemed very satisfied with his current situation. "But I have to hurry because the government of Iraq wants to stop the exports."

"Why is that?" asked Marie.

"The legislature passed laws forbidding the export of certain products. They feel we shouldn't send all our valuables abroad. I'm not too concerned, though. The rules are not enforced. Things change very slowly."

Marie looked down to the main road. Three white pickup trucks were pulling off and making their way up the rutted track toward them. Rashid noticed too. He walked out of earshot to meet the first driver as he stepped out of his cab.

"Let me just get the details of this exchange and then we can go," she said to Morgan.

He nodded. Marie walked toward the trucks. However, when Rashid saw her, he turned away from the driver to put himself between her and the vehicles.

"I thought I might interview the man bringing in the scrap," she said.

Rashid shook his head. "This man picked up weapons instead of scrap, and they have to be taken care of in another way."

"Do you sell munitions as well?" Marie asked.

Rashid smiled and shrugged his shoulders again. "How is it that you say—'off the record'?"

Marie wanted to pursue this, but Morgan appeared at her side, standing a bit too close, as if to tell her to watch it. She looked back at Rashid, thinking she'd ask one more question, but she saw a pitiless look in his eye and a new set to his jaw. She remained quiet.

Morgan walked her back to the Suburban. The mood of the meeting had changed abruptly, and Marie reminded herself that she was in a country still mired in war and chaos. She continued into the house to retrieve her backpack. When she came out, she thanked Mr. Rashid for his time and told him she'd get his *Fortune* subscription activated right away. Morgan and Massud said their good-byes, and the three climbed into the car. Massud backed into a gravel turnabout and carefully drove away from the house.

The streets were quiet and the sun was still high overhead. It was insufferably hot in the vehicle and the three sweated in the front seat, the wind from the windows offering no relief.

"What do you think he's up to?" Marie asked Morgan, wiping the sweat off her face. They'd gone a safe distance down the road.

"I think he's a gunrunner," said Morgan. "And maybe more. The tarp covering the bed of one of those trucks flipped back and I saw a wooden box with Russian lettering on it."

"Did you see in the kitchen?" asked Marie.

Morgan shook his head.

"There were brand-new kitchen appliances. And the best Dell laptop money can buy. I snuck a look when I went back to get my bag."

"He also had a satellite dish on the roof. Probably for high-speed Internet access. Somebody's paying him pretty well."

Marie was too busy thinking to respond.

Massud picked up speed once they got back onto the highway, weaving between huge eighteen-wheel trucks headed from Jordan to Baghdad. Marie watched the trucks for a while, noting the shipments: food, water, heavy equipment. After they'd gone about ten miles, she noticed Massud looking into his rearview mirror. She looked herself. A Land Rover had pulled up close behind them. There were three men inside, heads wrapped in kaffiyehs, their faces covered, looking at them intently.

"Oh boy," said Marie.

Morgan looked in the mirror, then out the back window. One glance told him everything he needed to know. "Shit," he said, reaching for his pistol.

Massud sped up and the Land Rover momentarily fell behind. The heavy tractor-trailer traffic had lulled, and the road was relatively clear. No trucks to dodge behind. As Massud gunned the engine, he, Marie, and Morgan watched the rearview mirror intently. The Land Rover gained on them. The Suburban, heavy from its armored floorboards and doors, struggled to accelerate. Massud pulled to the right lane to allow the Land Rover to pass. The Land Rover didn't pass. It roared up on them again, approaching too close.

"Jesus," cried Marie, panic filling her voice. "Isn't that the man who drove up to Rashid's in one of the trucks? The guy in the middle?" The man's kaffiyeh had pulled away from his face.

"Just one more fucking mustache to me," said Morgan.

The Land Rover made another surge forward and struck them from behind.

Marie yelped.

"Got a weapon?" Morgan yelled at Massud.

"Yes."

The Land Rover roared up alongside on the left. A semiautomatic rifle barrel appeared at the right front passenger window. A shot shattered the left window on the driver's side. A shard sliced into Morgan just below his left eye. He cried out, his skin burning with pain.

Marie lunged toward him, to assuage him. He pushed her away.

"Massud!" he shouted. "Can you steer through a spin?"

"Yes."

"You know what I'm thinking?"

"Yes!" shouted Massud, and pulled the steering wheel sharply to the left. Marie was thrown hard to the right but dug her feet against the floorboards and reached for the dash. Morgan wrapped his arm around her head and hugged her to his chest.

Massud swerved left then right through the turn and tried to avoid the Land Rover skidding toward them. The tires were screeching, the Land Rover's horn was blaring, and they all ducked as it shot past them. Massud slammed his foot on the brakes and brought the car to a shuddering stop.

Both men then sprang from the car, weapons drawn. Marie watched the Land Rover stop about fifty yards away. Marie saw the two passengers pick up machine guns.

"Get the fuck down, Marie!" Morgan yelled. She slid below window level just in time. A burst of automatic-weapon fire broke more glass and thudded into the side of the Suburban's door. Marie felt in the middle of a maelstrom of terror, the memory of the black gun barrel thrust through the window, the shattering of the glass, combining in an assault on her nerves.

Nothing in her life had prepared her for this. Still, she saw a dagger in a scabbard attached beneath the dash. She grabbed it and held it by her leg. It was useful only at close quarters, but if it came to that, she would know what to do with it.

A car engine turned over. It sounded like the vehicle was coming back toward them. She looked to her left. Massud was still there, crouching behind the door. He raised his weapon, took aim, and squeezed the trigger as the Land Rover roared by. Morgan fired too, and Marie thought she heard a shriek of pain from the Land Rover's open window. The vehicle accelerated, back toward Rutba.

As the engine's rumble receded, quiet fell over the roadside. Marie let out the breath she realized she'd been holding. Her chest burned. Her rib cage ached.

Amman, Jordan, May 18

Julian paced the floor of the second-story apartment on Taha Hussein Street in Amman. It looked out over the city from a whitewashed building in a bland mixed-use area of town. The apartment had a small balcony in back, covered with an arbor of bougainvilleas. Light streamed in and the scent of flowers sweetened the air, but it did nothing to ease the tension in the room. Gil Kizner and Benjamin Harel each sat hunched before computer terminals. Beside Kizner was an ashtray filled with butts.

"The target isn't moving!" cried Kizner, who was tracking the car carrying Marie, Massud, and Morgan. Julian had inserted a GPS device in the leather handbag he gave Marie in London, and it was this signal they were receiving. Julian glanced at the screen. The amber dot that was Marie was blinking, stopped in space. Julian clenched his fists, then ran a hand over his mouth and chin. The route they were on was rife with bandits. It was a very unsafe place to drive.

Julian had disapproved of the trip to Rutba, but he could think of no way to stop it. He muttered a string of expletives. Then he took a breath. A deep breath. Gabi, his wife, always told him to breathe. She was a believer in yoga and had tried to convince him, if not to take yoga classes from time to time, at least to stretch and relax, or breathe deeply when he got stressed. He was sure she was right. Picking up a cigarette from Gil's pack on the table, he lit it with a Bic lighter and inhaled. He felt a huge rush from his chest down to his toes.

He stepped out onto the balcony, savoring the drag, and looked out over Amman. It was a sleepy government city, a city that had no reason for being except to house the capital's bureaucracy and thousands of intelligence operatives from around the world.

"I'm going to run out and get a coffee," he said as he walked down the steps. I'm not going to do this, he thought, turning the butt in his hand. He'd quit. For two years already, and he wasn't going to start smoking again. Tobacco wasn't going to take over this time. Julian shook himself and threw the butt into the street. He turned on Ramadi Street, picked up a newspaper on the corner, and walked to a coffee stall nearby, whose owner gave him a look of surprise and a bear hug.

"Yassim!" Julian said as they embraced each other, and they immediately launched into a discussion of politics as if they had been doing this every day for years: another group of terrorists tracked down in Amman, more explosions in Iraq. Yassim placed a cup of thick, sweet Turkish coffee on the counter. Julian took a sip, savoring the sweet bitterness. Yassim then reached into a shelf beneath the counter and pulled out a chessboard complete with pieces saved midgame. Julian saw that it was covered with dust, and he recognized the play. The pieces were in the same positions they had been the last time they'd seen each other, a year ago. Men who fought together knew the small gestures capable of eliciting the deepest gratitude in each other. Killers could be the most sentimental lot in the world.

"Your move, I believe," said Yassim.

Baquba, Iraq, May 18

The guest wore the traditional robes of a primary instructor, and he was known among the boys as the kind one, for he observed them in their classes quietly, only occasionally leaning forward and inspecting a lesson, offering a word of encouragement. This madrassa in Baquba, fifty miles northeast of Baghdad, was new; its teachers had moved here from Karachi, Pakistan, after the Pakistani president closed it in a crackdown on Islamic extremism. The new school quickly enrolled hundreds of new students from the poor Sunni families of the region.

"The kind one," Master Mansour, had put on weight since his arrival from London. He wore darkened contact lenses, which covered his blue eyes, making them appear dark brown, almost black, but completely natural. And more important, completely common. As he listened to the boys chanting their Koranic verses, each sitting on the floor before a low desk, he nodded contentedly. He smelled delicately of jasmine.

Downstairs, in another chamber, older boys studied different lessons. And farther below that was a full-fledged military training ground. The madrassa had taken over the former Olympic buildings of Saddam's son, Uday. Deep underground were training grounds, classrooms, and preparation rooms for suicide bombers. In those rooms, the martyrs received their final indoctrinations, made films for their families, washed and shaved until they were hairless—all in anticipation of their promised trip to heaven.

Obaidi had been in and out of Baquba for three weeks, visiting the school and catching up on business developments with his primary aide, Mustafa Hanavi, who ran Obaidi's day-to-day operations. Today he would sit in on the classes with the little boys to make sure their lessons were taught properly. He believed that Islam's final victory would not come in his own time, but perhaps in the next generation, and if not then, then the generation after. It was inevitable, but God alone knew when it would happen.

In preparation for that blessed day and with God's help to bring on the holy miracle, Obaidi wanted to make sure the children were properly trained in jihad. No science, as it offered an alternative model with which to explain the world. No philosophy, as it was too Western oriented, even the Greek-inspired medieval Islamic philosophers of the Mu'tazila school. Of course, only boys were taught here; mixing of the sexes, so common now in schools in Muslim countries, was to Obaidi an abomination. In this madrassa, strict attention was given to the fundamentals. The boys were taught proper speech—*fusha*—the dialect of Arabic that was its classical literary language, as opposed to the *mu'asira*, the contemporary tongue, which was almost devoid of historical Islamic references.

In Obaidi's view, the world was in a state of barbarity, or *jahiliyya*. Humans had turned away from a vision of the world legitimized by divine grace. Instead, they'd turned toward a system of values that placed man and his needs at its center. The future of this direction was hedonism, materialism, unbridled individualism, and moral and social depravity. The secular nationalists like Saddam Hussein and Hosni Mubarak were the enemy within; they cloaked themselves in the mantle of Arabism, but they were really fighting truth—Islam: the only true support and pillar of the Arab world.

Another man, a few years younger than Obaidi, strode into the room. Mustafa Hanavi wore a red-checked kaffiyeh and white flowing robes. He embraced Obaidi and they walked out of the room together quietly, almost floating, though the children were very much aware of them, for Hanavi was their master, and one couldn't afford not to be aware of his every move.

The men walked to an elevator with thick stainless-steel doors and took it down two floors to a tearoom fragranced with lilies and draped with fabrics. The walls were hung with calligraphy, the letters of prayers and exhortations. On the floor was a huge Persian rug of red, pink, and navy, with a central design of an amber lily surrounded by delicate tendrils, a glorious example of the Shah Abbasi design, developed about 1600 CE. Obaidi's eye slipped over the boundaries of the rug and then to the center. He was unconsciously searching for the imperfections that are always evident in Persian rugs, as described by the old proverb "A Persian rug is perfectly imperfect, and precisely imprecise." Weavers were required to introduce slight irregularities into the designs because Allah was the only perfect being, and anyone attempting perfection would be claiming the position due only to the Almighty. Obaidi smiled with satisfaction when he found the error, this one on the outside border, an old game he'd played since childhood.

He leaned back on an upholstered bench against gold-embroidered pillows. Hanavi sat beside him. Almost immediately, a man arrived with tea in glasses set into silver filigreed holders. He placed them on a tray. Mint leaves soaked in the glasses of hot tea.

"Mustafa," Obaidi said. "We have only a few moments before prayers, but tell me, how are the preparations?"

"Everything is proceeding very well," said the man in a mellifluous voice. "Fifteen new recruits arrived just this week. They are well trained and motivated; all have been properly educated and are the finest examples of Muslim youth. They join the eighty-five already here, handpicked by me from the various jihadists who entered the country both before and after the American invasion. Many have already been active in Falluja and elsewhere. We have seventeen commanders now, most from Kuwait and Saudi Arabia, but several Moroccans and Tunisians as well. Other madrassas make similar, though not as ambitious, preparations.

"We have set up a company here in Baquba to supply the Americans and other foreigners with drivers and translators. So far, our company has become the most successful, and we get more business every day. It is important that we are reliable, polite, and cooperative. We want to have the trust of the foreigners so when we decide to strike, we will have a strong hand that reaches far into the foreign community. Our drivers have legitimate access to the foreigners' inner compounds and protected areas, and they will use this access when we need it in the future."

Obaidi nodded, his eyes closed, as if savoring a fine cigar.

"In our separate activities," Hanavi continued, "we keep up daily assaults on Iraqi collaborators and Americans whenever the opportunity allows. We will ambush them, we will shoot at them and lure them into traps. Our kidnappings are also useful, as they demoralize and weaken the enemies among us. Everybody knows the Americans have no stomach for death, especially random death. Like the Zionists, Americans love life too much. This is one of our greatest advantages."

"Wonderful news," said Obaidi. He closed his eyes and clasped his hands on his chest. "And how about our other preparations?"

Hanavi turned to face Obaidi. "I think you will be pleased. The package proceeds without trouble toward its recipient."

"May Allah be praised." Obaidi nodded to his lieutenant as the muezzin began the call to prayers, and his thoughts roamed back to the day he first set eyes on the bombs. He remembered it now as if he had been standing in the Kaaba itself in Mecca. But rather, he had been inside the cement-and-barbed-wire fences of a munitions depot in Uzbekistan, a year after the collapse of the Soviet Union.

Acres and acres of desert were laid with poured concrete slabs, like basketball courts. On the slabs were stacks of bombs. Everything you could imagine. Even then, in 1993, grass was growing through cracks in the concrete, the fearsome guard towers were empty, and the supervisors were of a decidedly lower rank.

At this site were tactical warheads, designed to be dropped from fighter jets. Hundreds of them, piled on top of each other like toys. Some with intact nuclear warheads, some not. The Americans and Europeans were trying to get the Russians to take off the nuclear tips and store them in more secure locations. The Americans were even buying the warheads to get them off the market. But the Soviet generals, knowing that the money lay elsewhere, assured the Americans that all the nuclear matériel was being treated with the utmost caution. At the same time, they were selling control of the depots to the local mafia bosses. The bosses knew what they had. Those with nuclear tips were dear.

Obaidi had been able to purchase only three. But that should be enough. Of course, they had their detonators removed, but for him that was no problem. He could fashion new ones in a matter of days, or use something else as a detonator. He chuckled to himself. What glory he would bring to Allah. A lifetime of planning, and now the goal was near.

"Allahu Akhbar!" The call of the muezzin rang through loudspeakers in the madrassa and from minarets throughout the city, a sound at once strident and haunting, soaring and abrupt. "God is great!"

"Let us go then," said Obaidi, "and pray together."

Rutba, Iraq, May 18

Marie slid the knife back into its sheath under the dash and stepped out of the vehicle. Her heart was pumping so hard she could feel her ribs jumping in her chest. When she stood up, she realized her entire body was trembling. Her vision seemed to close into narrow tunnels of light. The periphery was black. Morgan came over and put his right hand over her shoulder; the other held her by the upper arm. She felt weak on her feet.

"Hold on there, girl. Don't feel bad if you need to hurl. It happens to everyone. Massud, you good?" Morgan shouted, looking over at him.

Massud nodded, uttering a string of what sounded like Arabic expletives.

"Who was shooting?" asked Marie, her voice coming out in a strangled whisper. She saw that Morgan had a cut below his eye that was still trickling blood. His shirt was spattered with it.

"I was," said Morgan. "I wanted them to get their hairy asses out of here. What the fuck. They shot a couple rounds back, then cut and ran."

"Your face all right there, Morg? You got a little wound."

Morgan waved her comment away. "Can you stand now?" he asked, looking her in the eye. She nodded, and he gestured for her to lean against the hood. He pulled a padded nylon case out of the back of the truck, unzipped it, grabbed the M16, and opened its collapsible stock. He collected three boxes of bullets from his rucksack. "Come on," he said. "We gotta get out of here. Who knows when they're coming back."

Marie stepped away from the cab. Her leg began to shake.

"Look at that!" she said, as if she were remarking on something entirely unrelated to herself.

"Were you leaning on that leg?" asked Morgan.

Marie nodded.

"It'll stop."

Marie looked up at Morgan. "Why aren't *you* trembling anywhere?"

"Listen, darlin', even if my leg was jumping out of its damn socket, I wouldn't admit it. Gunplay is something that blows people's minds, especially if they're not used to it. Next time, you'll see it won't be half as bad."

"Next time?" she said. "Excuse my French, but I'm not planning on any fucking next time. Find somebody else to go out and play gunfight with."

"Whoa there, girl, I think this visit was your idea."

"Yeah, I'm making a note to myself: Do not ever again go with an FBI agent to visit a person whose name he found on a suicide bomber."

Morgan paused. "You're quick, girl. Gotta hand it to you. You're also unnerved. It's natural. Move that leg a bit and take a few breaths. You'll feel better, I promise."

She walked a few feet away, trying to ease her leg and stop its trembling, and deal with the fear that had erupted as anger. "Do you think Rashid sent them out to scare us off?"

Morgan shook his head. "Don't know. He seemed to want to talk to you while we were there."

"Maybe we saw something he didn't want us to see," said Marie.

"Those trucks," said Morgan. "He might not have expected them to arrive when you were there. Massud? What do you think?"

"It could have been anything," said Massud, slipping his gun into his pants at the waist. "Maybe Rashid told them to scare us. Maybe the guy from the truck was mad at the price Rashid offered him for his stuff. Maybe they were a bunch of thugs who just wanted to kidnap someone. They were shopping around, saw us, and thought we'd be a good catch. The local gangs sell hostages to other groups. When we started shooting, maybe it messed up their plans."

"Where'd you learn to handle a gun, anyway?"

"Jordan," Massud said, lying.

"They send all the Kurds over there for training?"

"Some of us," said Massud, in a tone that did not encourage further questions. Morgan wondered whom Massud was working for. He had to assume it was for "their" side, whatever that meant at this moment.

"What about gas?" asked Morgan.

"I have gas in the back of the truck. Enough to get us back," said Massud. "Also enough, if someone hits the tank with a grenade, to blow us to pieces."

They drove almost two hundred miles without speaking a word. At first, they braced for a fight any time a car entered their vision. Morgan kept his M16 in his hands and his pistol in his lap. By the time they got to the outskirts of Baghdad, their anxiety was beginning to ease up. Not that they were safe from attack or roadside bombs, but at least they saw the occasional Coalition or American patrol.

"So tell me," Marie said to Morgan, clearing her throat, bone-dry after two hours of desert heat. She drank from the two-liter bottle of water they had brought. "What are you doing here in Iraq?"

"Looking for an oud," Morgan said.

"A what?"

"It's a stringed instrument. I collect exotic instruments, and the one I want is made in Jordan."

"So why are you in Iraq if you need to go to Jordan?" she asked.

"It's on the way," said Morgan, smiling.

"Right. Sure, Morg. Iraq isn't on the way from anywhere." She stopped then and looked at him. "Except Afghanistan. But it's usually the bad guys who make that trip. Or maybe you're one of those special-ops guys. Or maybe a spook. A desk man. She raised her eyebrow in the way he liked. "Should I be calling you 'M,'" she said, "as in James Bond's boss?"

"Call me whatever you'd like, sugar, but call early and call often."

Marie smiled and took a deep breath. Her ribs still hurt.

"But to answer your question, I'm just a regular hippie cowboy. Nothing like the hero SEAL Princeton-educated super-duper HQer Comstock."

Marie gave him a look. "Where do you live?" she asked.

"A little hill near Fort Worth, Texas, called Vulture Ridge. I live there in a custom stainless Airstream International twenty-eight-foot model called a CCD, which stands for Christopher C. Deam, a San Francisco designer who made a high-tech-type interior which does justice to the legendary Airstream exterior."

"You have a horse out there?"

"Four half-wolves."

"You're something, Morg. You want some Coke?" she asked him, holding up a warm can she'd fished out of her bag. He'd said more in the past two minutes than he'd ever said. To her, anyway. Maybe that's what gunfire did for some people, she thought, loosened them up.

"No thanks. But that reminds me. Time to take my special extra-strength greens energy drink." He pulled a Ziploc bag filled with green powder out of a pocket and poured it into his canvas-covered canteen. Then he poured in an MRE packet of Kool-Aid. He swished it all around and glugged it down.

"Nasty!" said Marie.

"Oh no, it's good," said Morgan, politely wiping his mouth with a bandanna. "It has wheatgrass, barley grass, alfalfa and oat grass powder, spirulina, chlorella, a little seaweed, ginseng, echinacea, rice protein, apple pectin, and a bunch of other good stuff to keep me healthy."

Marie made a face. "So, I'm sorry, you were telling me what you were doing here."

"Title 18, U.S. Code, Section 2331 authorizes FBI extraterritorial investigations," said Morgan. "I was originally sent here to investigate smuggling and shipping irregularities. Because I happened to be at the marine base yesterday when that guy was caught with a suicide belt in his rucksack, I was handed that investigation."

"And why did you want to go out to Rashid's today?"

"You already guessed it, girl."

"Because you found his card on the suicide bomber."

"Correct."

"So you thought that Rashid might be a lead in your investigation into the attempted suicide attack."

"Yes ma'am."

"Do you think he is?"

"Don't know yet."

Marie was quiet, watching the endless sand stretching in all directions. People had trod these lands for so many years. "I can't make heads nor tails out of anything in this godforsaken place," she said after a while.

"Godforsaken is the one thing it isn't," said Morgan. "People are calling on God and talking to God and throwing bombs on behalf of God at every opportunity."

Marie laughed.

"I tell you," Morgan said, "I think there's some major bad shit going on in Rutba. I need to make contact with the military—I don't know if it's the army or the marines or the air force or the British who are officially in control there. Maybe I can find someone from CIA and see what they know. They have better contact with the armed forces."

"What do you think is going on?" asked Marie.

"At the least, there's gunrunning. Rashid told you as much. But I agree with something you said earlier. Those trucks drove up with something Rashid didn't want us to see. Maybe that's why he sent those men after us."

"And the suicide bomber had Rashid's card in his pocket," said Marie.

"Right," said Morgan. "So, unless the suicider was supplementing his income with a little scrap collection, Rashid's hooked up with the insurgency somehow."

"If Rashid is part of the insurgency, why would suicide-boy carry his card around? Aren't they supposed to sterilize themselves before an operation?"

"He fucked up?" Morgan shrugged. "Maybe he was called in as a substitute at the last minute and he forgot to check his pockets? He wasn't shaved and perfumed like the guys are supposed to be before they ride their rockets to the virgins."

"Very funny," said Marie, pausing to think. "Also interesting. Do you think the Coalition Authority knows about the steel and the salvage operations?"

"I don't know. But the presence of American containers means the U.S. government might be purchasing some of the steel itself. Or someone is contracting through the DOD. Maybe shipping stuff right back to the military depots. And what a perfect cover that would be," said Morgan. "What a perfect cover."

Tel Aviv, May 18

Shimshon Ashkenazy typed intently on the keyboard in his cramped Shabaq office. Responding to new orders from Julian to penetrate a computer network in Rutba, Shimshon was obliged to pull up maps of western Iraq just to see where it was. Next, he made a quick search of Internet providers in the area, and he saw that there was one, Uruklink, which operated by satellite.

Shimshon's plan was to break into Uruklink via the Internet and capture all the e-mail going into and out of Rutba. The easiest way for him to do that was through a little trick he'd developed years ago to exploit a bug in the routers—the devices that connect networks to one another. After he got in, he had access to e-mails, Web links, instant messages, anything that passed through the Internet link. He could then do whatever he wanted with what he found—read it, capture it, or even divert it.

When he originally found the bug, he was sixteen—too young for the army, but already out of high school and enrolled in college. He told Mamram, the Israeli army computer department, about the flaw. This was not entirely selfless, since he repeatedly got in trouble at college for his activities inside computers where he didn't belong. Giving the information to Mamram gave him a layer of protection. When the college computer department people came knocking on his door to ask if he had broken into a computer at Carnegie Mellon University or Berkeley, he would sheepishly acknowledge the truth but, as usual, explain that he hadn't taken anything and was only learning how the systems worked. Sometimes a discreet call from Mamram got the harassed university computer people to lay off him.

When he turned seventeen and a half, Shimshon joined the army, where he was recruited to an elite computer division. Now that he was working for internal security, at Shabaq, everything was all right. He couldn't get prosecuted. He could hardly believe he actually got paid for indulging his obsession. And he was continually surprised by how few people really understood the networks that ran the Internet, how few people had been in and out of a Cisco router as he had. Networks had acquired a reality that he could sense and feel and almost "see," although in reality they were no more than wires, cables, circuit boards. For him, they were alive, like his own nervous system, full of axons, dendrites, and the most mysterious places of all, the synapses between, where messages were carried by neurotransmitters that appeared and disappeared according to their own mysterious but thoroughly logical imperatives.

Shimshon had chuckled to himself just the other day when the Cisco bug he'd found all those years ago finally showed up on an advisory put out by CERT: the Computer Emergency Response Team, a panel of world experts that pooled its resources to investigate computer security issues. Now CERT and Cisco were preparing a patch for the problem, but it would be a long time before the patch ever made its way to Rutba. Since 9/11, security information was held a bit more closely.

Scanning the network, Shimshon discovered Rashid's IP address. Then he found the uplink provider for Iraq. Most Arab countries used companies in Switzerland or the Netherlands. He chose another router in Switzerland to use as a substitute link. His goal was to reroute all IP traffic destined for Rashid's computer through the network he had just constructed. He typed furiously for a few moments, giving commands to the router to pass the network traffic through the new router in Switzerland. A few more steps and he saw the material start flowing: there was every message from the Uruklink network passing into his computer.

He installed a sniffer to continue to collect all e-mails to and from Rashid. He found they'd been encrypted, but he could handle that. It took about ten minutes because, along with all the other e-mails, he found one with the PGP key that told him the decoding combination. After that, he could make no sense of the messages, because they were written in Arabic. He printed them out and walked with them down the hall to the Arab department, where he looked for Sarah Berendt. Luckily she was there, just finishing up a sandwich.

Shimshon leaned against the wall of her cubicle. One thing he liked about her was that she was as shy and awkward as he was. She wore pants and a sweater because the air-conditioning always blew at meat-locker levels in there. When she saw him, she hurriedly placed her sandwich onto its foil wrapping on her desk and blushed.

"Hi," he said. "How are you?"

"Fine," she said, looking down and wiping her mouth.

He could tell she was nervous, but he didn't know what to say to make her feel more at ease.

"Cold in here, isn't it," he said.

She nodded. "As usual. All the fat generals need the A/C way up."

Shimshon laughed. "Are you real busy?"

"What do you need?"

"I have some documents that need to be translated."

"Do you have them with you?"

"Right here," he said, handing her the e-mails.

She looked them over and saw that each was relatively short. "I'll get them to you as soon as I can. It might be another day. Is that all right?"

He nodded to her and gave her a goofy smile. "That's great. You're the best. I mean, thanks a lot."

She smiled, and blushed, too.

Al-Rashid Hotel, Baghdad, May 18

Marie slipped her key card into the hotel door, heard the mechanism click, and opened it. Her room was close and stuffy, but she was so relieved to be back in relative safety that she flopped down on the bed, exhausted. She was thinking that she wanted to get up and open the window, but before she did, she fell into a hot, deep sleep.

She awoke three hours later from restless dreams. Someone was pounding on her door. At first she was disoriented and wasn't sure where she was. The windows and blackout curtains reminded her she was in her hotel room. She glanced at the clock. It was 7:00 p.m.

"Just a minute," she called out, throwing her feet over the side of the bed. She flicked on the light and opened the door. It was a hotel attendant, the man who worked nights behind the front desk. He handed her an envelope.

"Letter for you," he said. He seemed excited and held the envelope out to her as if it were a package from the Queen of England.

Marie walked to her desk for some change. She picked up a thousand dinars, worth about a dollar that week, and handed it to the clerk. She carried the envelope back to the bed and looked at it.

The package was lettered in beautiful calligraphy and bore no postage. It had been delivered by hand. The return address was Olive Tree Partners. It was Obaidi, she realized, and felt a jolt of electricity in her stomach.

She reached onto her desk for a letter opener and slit open the heavy envelope. She pulled out a letter on thick cream-colored paper. The folds were crisp and strong, and she saw that the letter, too, was handwritten in calligraphy.

She scanned it quickly, and after all the flourishes and rhetorical exaggerations, she saw that through his secretary in Bahrain, Mr. Mansour Obaidi had agreed to meet with her for an hour interview. She was to report to a certain address in Baghdad along the Tigris River, tomorrow morning at 10:30.

Marie stood up and looked for her telephone. She had to reach Massud. She felt bad about asking him to go out tomorrow morning, since they'd had such a rough day today. She could take a taxi, but she probably needed Massud to interpret for her. Anyway, Julian would kill her if she went without Massud. He had made it clear that she was not to ride around Baghdad without her driver.

She found her Thuraya satellite phone. Massud answered promptly. She explained about the letter and asked if he could drive her to the meeting the next morning. He hesitated, but when she asked him if there was a problem, he said no, he'd pick her up at 9:30 a.m.

Marie sat at her desk, thinking about the day. They had surely uncovered *something* in Rutba. But what? She needed to sort out all that had happened, let her thoughts settle into some semblance of order. She flipped through her e-mails instead, and felt a sting of disappointment that there was nothing from Julian. Although she had known him for barely three weeks, she realized with some surprise that she missed talking with him, missed the sound of his voice. She felt safe in his presence.

She shook away the mood that that thought was bound to usher in. This was the first bite from Obaidi, her first chance to learn about him. She pulled over a pad of paper and began to jot down some questions. She wondered what it would be like to sit face-to-face with such a man. How do you talk to a mass murderer? How would he speak to her? He seemed perfectly nice on first meeting. But how would she keep him from sensing her thoughts?

After jotting down ten questions, certainly enough to get a conversation going, she stood up; she needed to walk around. She gathered up her questions and the letter from Obaidi and slipped them into a manila folder. She took it with her as she walked out of the room. When the door slammed behind her, she jumped.

Al-Rashid Hotel Lobby, Baghdad, May 18

Marie sat in the lobby. It was quiet, just a couple of contractors and their heavily armed security teams. She flipped open her folder and lifted Obaidi's letter to read one more time. She was so caught up in her thoughts that she didn't notice Danny Comstock sit down beside her.

"You're looking very serious," he said, and Marie started.

"Danny, what's up?" asked Marie.

"Just soaking up the atmosphere of this fine hotel and its fascinating clientele," he said, thinking she looked tired and drawn. "Where's your sidekick?"

"You mean Morgan?" she asked. "I don't know, but he's probably sleeping it off."

"Sleeping what off?"

"Well we had a pretty eventful day. It was probably hard on his deli-cate system," she said, smiling. She told Danny about the attack on the way back from Rutba.

"You shouldn't have gone without an armed escort," he said. "It's just too lawless out there."

"I know," she said. "But we did."

Danny nodded. "And why aren't you sleeping it off as well?" he asked, gesturing to the papers on her lap, which he'd had the chance to look over thoroughly.

"I have an interview tomorrow," she said.

"You got security?" asked Comstock.

"Yes," she said, gathering her papers together. "But you know, either there's a bullet out there with my name on it, or not. Either way, there's not much I can do about it."

"Don't get complacent about security measures. Because if you do, then you hand your fate from God to the bad guys."

"That's an interesting idea," she said, standing up. Comstock rose as well.

"Handing off my fate. Now there's a concept I need to sleep on. Good night, Danny."

"Ma'am," he said as she passed on her way to the elevator.

Aboard the *LB Venture*, Atlantic Ocean, May 18

Boutros Hamid looked down from the bridge to the center of the ship. One of the engines had been acting up. Nothing his engineers couldn't repair, but it had cost them two days of sailing time. Never mind that, it was over, and they might be able to make up for some of the lost time. But the delays and quieted engines had made it clear that the hostages were becoming a liability. Noise from inside a container would spook the crew. They had to keep quiet. But they wouldn't.

Of course Gandoor had already thought of this problem. Three crew members worked for him, and for him alone. The captain knew who they were. Nobody else did.

Their job was to guard the container with the hostages, in shifts, twenty-four hours a day. If anyone else in the crew asked why a container needed a guard, he would be told: This is a special cargo, a gift from a Saudi prince to a female lover in America. A beautiful big car, a Bentley. The prince specifically asked for security, and he would get it. Didn't want anyone vandalizing the radio, the leather seats, the crystal bud vases. The customer is always right.

Except that there were human beings inside the container.

On every shift, one of Gandoor's guards brought in fresh food. But the guards hated the duty and tried to avoid it. They seldom stayed the night. And who was going to force them? Hamid? He didn't want any part of it. Just earlier today he'd gotten a report from one of Gandoor's guards. When he'd gone in, a woman had begun wailing and screaming. She wanted clothes and blankets. She swore at the guard, and loudly.

"Tell her to shut up," the guard said to a man who appeared to be her husband.

The man motioned for her to quiet down, but she persisted.

The guard shrugged, put a silencer on his pistol, held it up to her forehead, and fired. She fell back against the container's wall, blood dripping down her face.

"Be quiet," he said to the rest of the hostages. "Or you'll wind up just like her."

He dragged the slack body out with him and locked the container door. On deck, he made sure nobody was looking, then threw the woman's body into the churning sea.

Al-Rashid Hotel, Baghdad, May 19

Marie was up before the alarm rang, her stomach already tight with nerves. Why did she feel so anxious? And then she remembered. The guys in the vehicle bearing down on them yesterday, so eager for a confrontation, the car spinning around and the gunshots and crouching below the dash staring at Massud's knife. And today, this was it. She was going to meet Obaidi.

The day had broken hot and bright and the light was shining in around the edges of the curtains. She threw the drapes open wide for a breath of fresh air. It was beautiful out, the sun just over the palm trees and shining on the sparkling river. On the streets, people were stirring. A few cars were about, some pedestrians, hundreds of stray dogs. She had read that several American servicemen had adopted dogs and sent them back home. Apparently not many dogs were kept as pets in Iraq, and there were no animal-welfare charities. She wondered where all the strays had come from. The soldiers seemed to be the only people caring for them. It was such an American gesture that it made her smile.

She dressed and went down to the lobby. A buffet of fruit juices, fragrant black tea, and potent coffee was offered every morning. There was always a spread of breakfast breads and pastries, many filled with dates, apricot jam, and fresh candied orange. She saw some journalists milling around, arranging their schedules. All she could swallow was some coffee. Her stomach was all butterflies. She carried her vest, helmet, and bags to the front of the hotel.

Outside, the temperature was already about twenty degrees hotter than when she'd awakened. Massud was waiting for her. She stepped into the car and felt the air-conditioning. Bless Massud!

The former beauty of the city was hardly visible, but on Rashid Street in the Rusafa district, one of modern Baghdad's oldest neighborhoods, one could sense its shadows. Conceived by the Ottomans in 1916, she had read somewhere, and modeled on Haussmann's grand Parisian boulevards, it wasn't quite Paris, but she could see the ambition.

Individual houses had been built in a variety of styles, from opulent Islamic classicism to modern Bauhaus design, the clashing themes somehow working together, showing an uneasy conversation between Arab and European influences. The street had been built parallel to the Tigris River, a break from the traditional orientation of Baghdad thoroughfares running perpendicular to the river so as to allow the cooling breezes to blow straight into the neighborhoods.

On Haifa Street, a cluster of 1930s-era houses faced the old British embassy. A colonial feel was created by covered loggias and Doric columns, but wealthy Baghdadis made the houses their own by creating inside, at the end of a series of rooms, a *hosh*, the traditional inner courtyard that formed the center of family life. From the *hosh* a narrow set of stairs led the family to an underground room where they traditionally waited out the fierce midday heat. None of this could be seen from the street.

Massud approached the river, turned away again into a small park, then through an electronic gate and up to a house shaded by date palms and lemon trees. The grand front door was ornate but new Islamic style. Marie looked up at the dark windows framing the door and noticed a guard opening a curtain.

Out of consideration for Muslim sensibilities, again she wore a long skirt and a long-sleeved shirt with a high neckline. Her hair was lightly covered by a white scarf. Marie lugged her bag and her briefcase up the front steps, taking extra care not to trip. She knew she was prone to these mishaps on entering buildings, especially when she was nervous, so she picked up her feet. At the top of the stairs, she felt her heart beating faster, but she hugged her bag close to her body and tried to recall the confidence she felt with Julian. She took a deep breath and the door opened just as she reached for the buzzer.

A man in a white shirt and slacks ushered Marie and Massud down a few steps to a sunken living room carpeted in white plush rugs. The furniture was imitation Louis Seize, painted white, upholstered in gold brocade. She and Massud were directed to a sofa, in front of which was a low coffee table. She placed her bags down, and the man left. An elaborate crystal chandelier hung overhead and a circular stairway led upstairs.

The man returned with a carved wooden tray and set it down on the coffee table. He removed three glasses and a teapot redolent of mint. Another man entered from a hallway to the rear. It was Obaidi, as dapper as he had been in the hotel. For the first time, she noticed the gray at his temples. He looked to be in his late forties, maybe a bit older.

She began to rise, but he stopped her, gesturing toward the sofa. He greeted Massud and pointed to the seat beside him.

"You are a very persistent reporter," Obaidi said as he observed her with careful curiosity.

"An occupational hazard," she said.

"I notice persistence," Obaidi said. "I might go so far as to say I admire it, though it's not a virtue emphasized in the Koran, because it runs contrary to faith. Do you know it is not mentioned even once in the text?"

"No, I didn't," she said. Her eyes drifted out toward the river, which flowed gently past the living-room window. "It's quiet and peaceful here," she said. Then she repeated the phrase softly in French. "Tranquille et serein." She was moved by the view of the Tigris, thinking of the range and depth of history that had taken place on its shores, not very much of it quiet or peaceful. "When Baghdad settles down, it will one day be a very nice place to live, won't it?"

"It will once *again* become a very nice place to live," Obaidi said directly to Marie, in French.

"Of course," she said, startled. "You speak French?" she asked.

He nodded. "The French had a very strong presence in the Middle East, as you know, in Syria and Lebanon. Iraq was part of the British Mandate, as was Egypt, but my father was a businessman, and he knew French. And what about you? An American girl who speaks a foreign language? Unusual."

"My mother was French," said Marie. "She was a dancer, and we traveled a lot in Europe and the United States, but I spoke French at home."

"Very nice," he said. "Very nice. A wonderful profession. A dancer, was she?"

"Yes," said Marie. It appeared that Obaidi wanted to ask more questions along these lines, but he stopped.

"So, you are quite familiar with Baghdad?" she asked, trying to get the conversation back on track.

"I have been in and out of Iraq for many years," he said, nodding.

"Now is a fortuitous time for you then?"

"Every calamity offers opportunity. Wartime offers its own."

"What businesses do you think will offer the most opportunity here in the next few years?" she said.

"Perhaps you would be interested in learning about our date crops?" said Obaidi, leaning back in his chair and stroking his beard. "That is a local industry. You may not know that there are eighty varieties of native dates, and it was once a thriving export. In fact, there were date palms throughout Baghdad until Saddam Hussein cut them down, fearing snipers could conceal themselves in the palm fronds."

Marie scribbled notes in her pad, nodding to Obaidi, as he outlined his hopes for increasing the yields in Diyala Province, north and east of the capital.

"Is agriculture your main interest?" she asked him.

"No. Only one of many," he said. "Iraq must grow in every direction. We have oil refining and chemical production; we make electrical equipment, furniture, bricks, and cement. We also produce fine leather goods, textiles, jewelry, and carpets. Not to mention tobacco and processed food and beverages."

Obaidi stopped. She had expected him to keep on talking, and didn't have a ready question. She looked up at him and found herself in the awkward position of staring at him. He was handsome, though he had a harsh look around his mouth. He was light skinned, with an aquiline nose. His eyes, bright blue, were intelligent, eager. Is this what a mass murderer looks like? she wondered. Pictures of the Munich crash site flooded her mind's eye, but she had trouble connecting this man with that horror. She looked away from him, afraid he might be able to read something in her eyes.

"You were born in France, then?" he asked her. She was startled that he had asked her a personal question.

She nodded. "Did you ever live in France?" she asked.

"No, unfortunately, I have not had the opportunity, though I have visited many times," he said.

Marie, who was fiddling with her pen as she listened to Obaidi, accidentally dropped it. It rolled right off the back of her hand and made a slow swan dive to the floor. "Zut," she said under her breath as she leaned over to pick it up.

When Marie raised her eyes to his, she saw a peculiar expression on his face, but later had trouble remembering it exactly because a huge explosion shook the house, and then another almost immediately. Obaidi reached for her, pulling her to the floor, and, as he threw his body over hers, another huge explosion boomed. The chandelier crashed like an icicle not far from them. Obaidi was knocked away from her. Pieces of plaster fell from the ceiling, and she covered her head with her hands. The next thing she remembered was hearing a car horn outside that seemed never to end.

Chapter Eleven

Turaybil Crossing, Jordan-Iraq Border, May 19

Julian slowed the Mazda as he and Gil Kizner approached the border crossing between Jordan and Iraq. Julian had decided to go to Marie immediately after receiving the call from Massud. The report about the attack in Mansour made him frantic. He needed to be beside her, determine the extent of her injuries, rethink the operation. Within hours, he and Gil were on the road.

Three Iraqi soldiers stood with M16s held waist high. One approached the car and took the papers from Gil. He returned quickly. The guard waved them through, not saying a word about the Dutch passports the Israelis showed. They drove silently, Kizner in his seat, taking up little space. He was able to adapt physically to the emotional demands of a situation; it seemed he could expand or contract accordingly. Right now, he was hardly taking up any space at all. He knew that Julian had plunged into one of his moods of intense self-questioning, and at those times, he needed to be alone.

Some commanders agonized for days or weeks making their plans, and as soon as the orders were given to proceed, didn't question the operational plan. Julian was not like that. He kept reanalyzing the data, reconsidering each piece and its location in the pattern he had constructed. He knew better than anyone that the picture which emerged from fragments of intelligence had an 80 percent chance of being incorrect in a crucial way. He felt it was essential to loosen one's attachment to the theory, what the Americans called "thinking out of the box." Julian was doing that right now, if Gil's intuition was correct, rethinking every angle of the operation.

This was his strength. It often allowed him to catch the flaw before a mistake was made. But on the downside, it wasn't any good for his health. His face got red, his body tense like a python's ready to strike. Kizner glanced over at him.

"Take a breath," he said, which at least got a laugh out of his old friend.

Julian slapped down the sun visor on the windshield. "Goddamned sun," he said, then realized why he was feeling so lousy. The day in Madrid when he had driven through the city trying to find Ari had featured this same high, hot sun, dusty wind, no air to breathe.

"This girl moves too fast for me to keep track of," he said. "One day she's in Rutba meeting with an arms dealer and an American FBI agent, and the next day she's sitting down for tea with a terrorist in Baghdad in a house that just happens to get shelled. Does she like danger, or does it just find her?"

Gil looked over at his partner. "Are you getting too involved in this personally?" he asked gently.

"Why do you ask that?"

"Because she's doing exactly what you wanted her to do," said Gil, "leading you to Obaidi."

"No, I don't think I'm involved more than any commander should be when his charge is in contact with the enemy. Marie may be clever and levelheaded, but she has no operational training or experience."

They drove along for several miles without speaking. The Arabic music station they listened to was interrupted by a thirty-second newsbreak. Julian reached over to turn up the volume. More Iraqis killed from a roadside bomb. Iraqi oil revenues down again. Then the broadcast of a new audiotape from al Qaeda. Julian and Gil listened to the Arabic. It included exhortations for continued struggle and several verses from the Koran. Julian looked at Gil.

"Do you think they're signaling their men with the tape?"

"Sounds like it."

Silence again. Julian descended into his intense musing. After a while, he turned to Gil and said, "It was good of you to accompany me."

"Forget it," said Gil. Julian didn't have permission from Tel Aviv to go over the border into Iraq. As soon as his boss learned he was missing, there'd be hell to pay. But there was nothing to do about it now.

Julian was all alone. Flying solo. Either he'd succeed and find out what Obaidi was planning next and possibly save people's lives, or he'd fail and face possible disgrace back home. Ben-Ami had made it absolutely clear that he didn't want any of Julian's more flamboyant problem solving on this mission. And he had meant it. In Israel, you didn't play with the system; it was too strong. But Julian felt he had no choice about going over the border. His feeling of responsibility for Marie was driving him now. And though he justified it with his experience and his personal regrets, he didn't see that his tangled feelings about the past were coloring his plans.

Gil was at risk too. He faced a possible reduction in rank, loss of retirement benefits, and worst of all, being shunned by the military, his family for the past twenty-five years. Being cut off would be as bad as an amputation. Yet in a strange conflict of loyalty, inculcated by the very system that might soon punish him, Gil believed his rightful place was beside Julian, his longtime commander.

Two and a half hours past the border, Julian began to stir. Beside the road, familiar terrain came into focus as they passed the gigantic Iraqi airfield known as H3. Julian and Gil looked at one another. They were quite familiar with this air base, as well as H2 to the east, and H1 to the northeast. Years ago they had been here for clandestine operations and seen this place when it was a fearsome symbol and tool of Saddam's murderous intentions, holding aircraft, missile launchers, and sophisticated electronics equipment for directing biochemical weapons. Now it was abandoned.

"Do you see any American troops here?" asked Julian.

"Not a one," answered Gil, whistling through his teeth. "No Brits or Iraqis either."

"How can they leave this place unsecured?" Julian asked. "Just look at it!" He felt aghast, insulted even, that a target should be treated with such indifference, when it had been so strategically important that he and his men had risked their lives—more than once—to perform missions here.

"Remember the bunkers?" said Julian, glancing over at Gil. "Hundreds of them all around here. Each one packed with thousands of tons of munitions and explosives. What do you think happened to all of that?"

Gil was quiet for a few moments shaking his head. "Either the Americans and their allies carried it off, or someone else did. Or is doing it right now. Looks like the neighbors haven't missed a beat," he said, looking out at the scavengers everywhere, pulling apart broken planes, missile silos, tanks, armored personnel carriers, and other assorted junk. Trucks were parked up on berms that had once marked off quadrants for military supplies, and men swarmed everywhere, like ants on sugar.

"There's no security at all," mused Julian, shaking his head again in disbelief.

"So far, I've seen license plates on trucks from Jordan, Syria, and Lebanon," said Gil. "Not to mention sea containers everywhere."

Julian drove up on the shoulder of the road to get a closer look. "Many of them are marked 'Thaqib.' That's the name of the company Massud gave us, isn't it? The company of the scrap man from Rutba."

Gil nodded. "Remember what Thaqib means?" he asked.

"Star, or shooting star, or something like that, right?" said Julian.

"Yeah," said Gil. "Sounds more fitting for an aerospace company than a junk collector."

"And they're packing the scrap into sea containers to boot," said Julian, incredulous. Then his face blanched. He hit the steering wheel with the heel of his hand. "Shit!" he shouted. "Shit! Shit!"

"What's the matter?"

"The plane crashes were decoys, goddamn it!"

"What are you saying?" asked Gil.

"That fucking Obaidi was trying to set us all off in the wrong direction," said Julian, his face reddening. "He wanted the airplane crashes to distract us from the big show. And he did it. Hundreds of millions of dollars are being spent—again—on ratcheting up airline security, building stronger planes, more secure airports. But Obaidi has already moved on. Don't you see? It's the new vector. Shooting star. Of course, shooting star. Maybe billowing mushroom cloud. He's got big plans. And lots of juice. He may be crazy, but he's smart. Do you remember the intelligence report we received just before leaving?"

"About the increased chatter on terrorist sites?"

"No. But that's important too. It included information suggesting another large shipment of arms to the Palestinians was coming by sea, something like the *Karin-A.*" Julian referred to a Palestinian-owned freighter filled with explosives and munitions that had been intercepted by Israeli commandos in 2002 in the Red Sea.

"But it appeared the chatter was going wider than it should for such an operation," said Gil.

"Exactly," said Julian, turning red again. "I think I understand it now, and it's much bigger than the *Karin-A*. It's not going to be a shipment of mortars and Katyusha rockets to Gaza. The next international terror attack will come from the sea. And it will be launched from Iraq. But it won't be headed anywhere in the Middle East."

Tel Aviv, May 19

General David Ben-Ami stood at the door to Julian's office and snapped on the light. There was no sign of him. He turned and marched out to Nadav Rosenberg, who was working quietly at his desk.

"Where's Granot?" he bellowed.

Nadav shook his head. "No idea."

Ben-Ami turned to Shimshon Ashkenazy, who, as usual, was buried in his computer screen.

"Shimshon," said Ben Ami.

Shimshon leaped to his feet. "Yes sir."

"Where's your boss?"

"Don't know sir."

"Where has that man gone?" Ben-Ami muttered as he walked out.

He asked his secretary to get Julian's wife on the telephone. When the secretary returned five minutes later to Ben-Ami's office, she reported that Gabi hadn't seen Julian since he returned from Munich, four days earlier.

Ben-Ami paled. He couldn't believe Julian would dare do this again.

Gerhard Wegener from Germany's national military forensics lab was calling with a question about fuses. He wanted to speak to Julian. Ben-Ami's gut told him that Julian was already past the forensics. For Julian, forensics was not a religion. Forensics often didn't tell the whole story. Forensics was more like poems which enfolded the truth. The situation made Ben-Ami furious. He couldn't tell Wegener that Julian was out of the country on a mission. Truth was, he didn't even know where the hell he was. He'd have to dig up some old information himself to answer Wegener's questions, send whatever they had just to keep up appearances. If word got out that Julian was not home, it could set up an international incident. Goddamn him!

Baghdad, May 19

Eleven hours after leaving Amman, Julian pulled up to a small kebab shop in northwest Baghdad. It was late and the place was almost empty. Julian sat down, back to the wall, in a position that afforded a good view of the place. Gil ordered for them in Arabic. They spoke quietly together until Julian saw a young man with café au lait skin and a confident manner approach. He sat up to allow easy access to the Glock 9 mm pistol he kept in a light holster at his waist. He kept his eyes on the young man's face until he reassured himself that he was friendly.

Julian knew that Massud had received some instruction in Israel, although he was controlled by the Jordanians. He appeared confident and well trained, and Fahed apparently held him in high esteem. Julian rose and gave him the traditional Arab greeting of kisses, as if they were life-long friends.

Julian pushed glasses of juice and water over to Massud and let him settle down. After he'd finished his drink and they'd exchanged pleas-antries for a few moments, Massud leaned toward them and spoke qui-etly. "As you requested, I returned this afternoon to the house where Marie had her interview. It's empty. Cleared out. No one's there."

Julian nodded.

Massud pulled a folder from his bag and handed it to Julian. "I thought you'd want this," he said. "I've tried not to handle it because there may be fingerprints."

Julian took the folder and tipped it open. The letter Marie had re-ceived from Obaidi was inside. "Ah," he said, eyes growing wide. "This is wonderful. Thank you. She left it at the interview site?"

"In the car." Massud then handed Julian an object wrapped in a linen napkin. "I also took a cup that Obaidi held in his hands. Maybe there are prints there as well."

"Good man, Massud," said Julian, smiling. "What did those Jordani-ans do, send you to the FBI academy?"

Massud smiled. "I've picked up some tips over the last few days." They laughed.

"How is Marie?" asked Julian.

"She's all right. When I brought her into the hotel, the other journal-ists called the doctor who's been tending to them. He said she had a con-cussion."

"Tell me what happened," said Julian.

"We were all sitting in the living room together this morning—Obaidi, Marie, and I—when the shells hit. Obaidi was closer to Marie and, I'm ashamed to say, quicker. He pulled her away from the window after the first blasts and managed to get her away from the chandelier that fell right after. As soon as the shelling stopped, he called his men and they left the house. I picked up Marie, brought her to the car, and drove her back to the hotel."

"The cause of the blasts?"

"When I went back this afternoon" said Massud, "a group of men were standing around the rubble. They were talking about a local dispute. A local Shiite imam on one side, a Sunni tribal leader on the other. Someone got some shells and decided they'd teach the other guys a lesson."

Julian turned to Gil. "A random explosion?"

"You're surprised?" said Gil. "Good morning, Baghdad."

"You know Arabs," said Massud, not lifting his eyes to see who might be listening. "Addicted to hopeless heroic gestures."

"And Kurds aren't?" Julian responded. Kurds never liked Arabs. And vice versa. Sunnis and Shiites hated each other. And it went on and on. It was the Middle East. "When can we see her?" he asked, suddenly impatient. Impatient with the whole bloody situation here. Impatient with himself.

"I can bring you over now," said Massud. "You'll just have to avoid the hotel lobby. Marie's getting a lot of attention at the moment. News of your arrival and speculation about who you are will travel fast. Those journalists are quicker than Iraqi intelligence ever was."

They took a few bites of food and drained their glasses. Julian left a few thousand dinars on the table.

Julian and Gil followed Massud to the hotel. Gil waited in the car while Massud brought Julian in through a rear entrance, up the back stairs, and down the hall to her room. Julian knocked lightly. Marie opened the door, and when she saw Julian, her face broke into a surprised smile. She stepped back and ushered the men in. She looked from Massud to Julian, struggling to make the connection. She had scratches on her face and her arms, a bad bump on her forehead, and a black left eye. But she was clearly intact. Julian exhaled his relief, gave her a tender hug, then stepped back to look her over again, holding her hands in his.

"How are you feeling?" he asked, his face lined with concern.

"I'm fine," she said. She was happy once again to feel his bearlike embrace. She wanted to disappear in it, in its comfort and protection, but then she remembered what was tormenting her: the explosion, Obaidi. She felt confused and frightened. "I guess I have to thank Obaidi I'm not dead." She stepped back and took her hands from Julian's.

"Why do you have to thank Obaidi?" Julian asked, looking her straight in the eyes. He looked angry.

"He tried to protect me."

"How did he do that?" he asked derisively. "Did he take you to a doctor? Did he escort you home?"

"No," she answered, only vaguely hearing the sarcasm in his tone. Obaidi had thrown his body on hers. "I only remember waking up here later that day." Julian frowned.

Marie closed her eyes. Her head was starting to hurt again. Julian guided her toward the bed. Usually, he'd insist on getting as much information as possible from informants as soon as possible, no matter their physical state. He knew what Gil would say. He argued with himself. Then he decided he wasn't going to push her.

"You should rest, Marie. We'll talk later. You need to get yourself better."

"Yes," she said, lying down on top of the covers, only too happy to shut her eyes again. She was very sleepy. It was past midnight.

He patted her hand and her eyes fluttered open. She grasped his fingers and looked down at his hands. They were covered with red freckles, she noticed, like a little boy's. She smiled. She didn't want to think about what had happened. Julian held her hands for a few moments, then placed them back on the blanket. He turned down the light, walked out, and gently closed the door.

Tel Aviv, May 20

Sarah Berendt placed the sheet of e-mails from Shimshon Ashkenazy on her desk. She looked them over quickly and saw they were written in the flowery language of traditional religious Arabic prose. The first one read, "If the hypocrites and those in whose hearts is a disease and the agitators in the city do not desist, we shall most certainly set you over them; then they shall not be your neighbors in it but for a little while."

She carefully translated the lines and copied them into her computer. She picked up the second e-mail. It read, "Cursed: wherever they are found they shall be seized and murdered, a horrible murdering." She wrote this down, then looked over the third. "Men ask you about the hour; say: The knowledge of it is only with Allah, and what will make you comprehend that the hour may be nigh."

These were lines from the Koran. Sarah looked over all three e-mails again to make sure she hadn't missed any punctuation that might affect the meaning. Then she got up and printed out the original Arabic as well as her translations, and put them in a folder for her records. She took the originals to Shimshon. He wasn't at his desk, so she looked for him near Nadav Rosenberg's office.

Sarah knocked lightly on the door. With Nadav's words, "Come in," she entered the office, causing Shimshon to all but jump out of his chair to greet her. Nadav laughed. Sarah blushed and giggled. Shimshon ran his hand through his unruly curls. She handed him the papers, accidentally touching his hand in the process, causing them both to blush even deeper. She nodded to him as he thanked her.

As she left, Nadav asked, "Have you asked her out yet?"

Shimshon exhaled and blushed anew. "I'm working on it."

"Working on it? There's no work to be done. She's like a fruit ready to be picked. All you have to do is raise your hand and she'll fall into your palm." Nadav held out his hand as if he were already holding the fruit.

Shimshon smiled, shook his head. "Easy for you to say. Easy for you to do. Maybe if I'd grown up in an orchard, I'd understand it all. But I didn't. And I don't." Nadav laughed and waved him out of the office.

Baghdad, May 20

Julian pulled the car into a carport beside a house on the outskirts of Baghdad's Karbala neighborhood, an area of homes for wealthy Iraqis and up-and-coming businessmen and foreigners. It was a bright, clear morning. Massud had found this house for them, and it seemed a good fit for their cover story as wholesalers of water purifiers. Massud had also put them up last night at his place, figuring the neighbors here would have been unsettled had Gil and Julian arrived in the middle of the night. The property was fenced and had a high locked gate out front, an essential precaution. It had a garage and its own private generator, another Baghdad necessity.

Julian and Gil walked through the house. It was furnished with a few rudimentary items. In the kitchen, plates, flatware, a few pots for cooking, and a coffeepot. In two downstairs bedrooms, new mattresses still covered in plastic. Kizner dropped his bedroll on the floor; Julian placed his in the other room on one of the beds.

"Why not?" he said to Kizner's raised eyebrows. Julian was a sensualist; Gil, an ascetic.

Julian began to boil some Arabic coffee while Kizner washed the kitchen table and plastic chairs. Julian swept the floor with a broom left in a closet. The two were like old housemates, dividing chores and working together, almost without a word. Language was a luxury, like a sweet they saved for a reward at the end of the day. Julian was carefully performing these mundane housekeeping tasks but his mind was elsewhere; he was trying to assimilate and process his hunch about Obaidi's next moves. He was tense and fraught; his chest felt as if he'd swallowed burning gasoline.

Julian heaved open a window to let in some fresh air, hot though it was, and pulled up a chair. Kizner set down two cups and two saucers and Julian placed the coffee, now ready, on the table.

"So where are we?"

"Back in Baghdad," said Gil, smiling. "In better accommodations than we're used to."

Julian grunted. "Better accommodations, but more dangerous. Remember how peaceful it seemed in the desert? And sneaking around a football field full of Scuds offered its own kind of comfort, right?"

Gil laughed. "That's not exactly how I remember it."

Julian opened his computer bag and pulled out his laptop. "I didn't have a chance to read your report on Obaidi before we left. Do you mind if I look it over now?"

"Be my guest," said Gil.

Julian slipped on his reading glasses and pulled a file up on his laptop screen.

"Born 1954, Cairo, Egypt," he read aloud. "One of seven surviving children of Gahiji, a shopkeeper, and Aziza, a teacher. When he was twenty-two years old, he was jailed as a member of Jama'a Islamiyya. Tortured and imprisoned with some of his future confederates, including Ayman al-Zawahiri. He was released in 1977. He sought safe haven in Iraq, where he studied at the University of Baghdad. He joined the PLO, and after proving his talents as a bomb technician, was recruited by Arafat to Force 17." Julian looked up at Gil, silently acknowledging Gil's decision not to mention Madrid here. He then turned back to the text. "He was sent to Bulgaria to study explosives in 1978 and was active in Western Europe and elsewhere. In 1983, he split with Arafat and joined Abu Ibrahim back in Iraq. Ibrahim decided soon thereafter Obaidi should go to Afghanistan to help the mujahideen. He did so, joining forces briefly with bin Laden.

"Quite the fast crowd, eh?" said Julian, scanning the rest of the text and paraphrasing aloud. "After the Soviet departure in 1989, Obaidi moved back to Iraq to build up his business interests. The sanctions imposed on Iraq by the West after Saddam Hussein invaded Kuwait in 1990 provided almost endless opportunities. Anyone who could bring wheat, rice, and cooking oil into the country could make millions. Later, when the sanctions were modified by the oil-for-food program, business got even better. Sometimes he paid cash, sometimes he bartered. He had a wide circle of business partners, including mafia gangs in Eastern Europe. Eastern Europe," repeated Julian, looking up.

"Everyone wanted to join the party," said Gil.

"And I wonder what *they* had to barter," said Julian; then he continued to read. "He set up truck routes through Syria and Turkey that easily moved goods around the checkpoints. He made lots of money."

"Now, you're coming to the juicy part," said Gil. "When the Americans bombed Iraq in the First Gulf War, some of Obaidi's property was destroyed. He was furious about that, but could rationalize it away. But when the Americans and their allies marched into Iraq in 1991, everything changed."

Gil was referring to information known to intelligence officers at the time, that most Arabs believed the incident between Kuwait and Iraq was purely a local matter. They were deeply suspicious when the U.S. took an active role in repelling Hussein's army. Who in his right mind would take up arms to protect the rotten Kuwaitis? No one, unless he had deeper aims. As everyone knew, the Americans came to steal Arab oil. It was the only explanation that fit the facts. Bin Laden had offered his own soldiers to the Kuwaitis to drive the Iraqis out. But his offer had been politely refused, a grave insult.

It was then that the ideas nurtured by Obaidi and al-Zawahiri and others in Egyptian prisons, and later refined by warriors in Afghanistan and Chechnya and the Sudan, were crystallized: jihad.

The moment had come. The eternal enemy, the infidel West, had set down its filthy boots on holy Islamic soil. Everyone knew what had to be done. The beauty of the plan was sublime. Once the movement began, it would be unstoppable. Worldwide jihad depended on no single man. If a leader was martyred, another would take his place. Networks were in place. The horse was out of the barn, and the stakes were no less important than heaven itself.

"And here's Obaidi," said Julian, "lining up to be a minister in the new government of Iraq."

Julian's telephone rang. He listened, said "Okay," and hung up. "That was Massud. Marie is awake and ready to see us."

Al-Rashid Hotel, Baghdad, May 20

Marie was back at her desk, typing on her laptop. Hot, dry light streamed into the room. Julian felt something strange as soon as he walked in, something he'd sensed the night before but hadn't been able to describe to himself or Gil. Now he saw it in Marie's face when she turned toward them. She was distracted, hazy, unfocused, unlike her normal self: so sharp and present. Her movements this morning were a bit slower, her reactions delayed by a fraction of a beat. She looked up at them, rising from her chair with an expression—was it dreaminess? Or preoccupation? Maybe she was still suffering the effects of her injury.

Julian took her hands in his and looked into her face. She returned his gaze, then turned away. Julian held on to one hand and introduced her to Gil. Marie said hello, then gestured toward the two chairs in the room.

"Please sit down," she said, politely but distantly.

"You look rested now, Marie," said Julian. "How's your head?"

"It's fine," she said, running her hand absently over the bump. "It's not really anything." She looked back to Julian. "You came a long way. Why did you come here?" she asked.

"We heard about your accident, and I was concerned about you," he said. "I think the picture here in Baghdad is changing, and we might want to rethink our strategy."

Marie looked away. She had already guessed that Massud was telling Julian everything. But why? Was he on Julian's team too? Her head was too blurry to think about it.

"We found an interesting businessman in Rutba the other day," she said, changing the subject. "He's collecting scrap metal and sending it back to the U.S. on cargo ships."

"Tell us what you saw," Julian said quietly, settling back in his chair.

She liked the way he said that. It was inviting. It made her want to talk.

She told him about her trip to Rutba with Massud and Morgan Ensley. She told him about Rashid and his collection of eight-year-old *Fortune* magazines. She described sitting on pillows on his living-room floor while Rashid explained the business of collecting scrap metal and selling it all over the world. And she told him about the pickup trucks that drove up whose contents Rashid didn't want her to see. "Morgan thought he was buying or selling weapons of some kind," she said, "but you should ask him what he thought about that. I haven't had a chance to talk to him since we got back."

"Who's Morgan Ensley?" asked Julian. He knew of course, from Massud, but wanted to see how she answered the question.

"He's an American, an FBI agent. We met at the airport during a function my first week here. He's the one who came up with Rashid's name." Marie glanced at Julian to check his reaction.

"What kind of weapons do you think were being brought to Rashid in the trucks?" asked Julian. He seemed to be distracting himself from his emotions by focusing on the details, as she was.

"I don't know. He wouldn't let us get close. But Morgan said he saw a big metal crate with Russian labels."

Julian looked over at Gil. "Did he say anything else?" Julian asked.

"About the crates? No. But I should tell you what else we saw."

"What's that?" said Julian.

"American shipping containers all over the place. And Mr. Rashid is making some kind of money, because his house has new appliances and a satellite dish, and he has a new laptop computer."

"What else happened in Rutba?" Julian asked.

"A bunch of thugs chased after us when we left. We couldn't tell if it was Rashid's men, or freelancers wanting to kidnap us, or what."

"How many of them were there?"

"Three."

"The FBI man—Morgan, right?" asked Julian. "What was his interest in going there?"

Marie tried to read his expression. He seemed perfectly calm but clearly eager to hear her answer. "Morgan Ensley. He found a calling card in the pocket of a suicide bomber who failed to blow up a marine base. The card was Rashid's. When Massud told us that Rashid was a well-known scrap dealer in that area, I thought it might make a good story and I wanted to go out there. Morgan wanted to go for his own reasons, and he said he'd pretend to be my photographer."

"Did Rashid appear surprised to see you there?" asked Julian.

"Oh yes," said Marie. "Judging from his body language, he was not happy to see Americans drive up. Massud had to calm him down. Why do you ask?"

Julian didn't answer.

"There was a lot of activity in Rutba," said Marie, "and there was a menacing quality to some of the interactions we saw. The men who drove up weren't just carrying some old World War II rifles they'd found buried in the ground." She looked away and up the wall to the ceiling, where her eyes settled momentarily on a crack in the plaster.

"I met Obaidi, you know," she said, suddenly shifting the subject.

Julian was quiet. It seemed she had no memory of his visit the night before. Must be the effects of the concussion. He thought it was interesting that she made the mental connection between the activities in Rutba and Obaidi. He nodded and listened.

"He gave me a very funny look," she said. "I keep thinking about it."

Julian knew she had more to say.

"It was just before the shell exploded." Marie stopped.

"What happened?" asked Julian.

"I dropped my pencil. I said 'Zut' as I leaned over to get it, and after I picked it up and looked back at him, I saw the strangest look on his face."

"What do you mean?"

"It was as if he thought he knew me."

Julian watched her carefully.

"Right after that, there was a huge noise and the house shook and he pulled me away from the window. When I got up, I saw the glass chandelier had fallen down right where I would have been."

"That was thoughtful of him," said Julian drily.

"Well, by the way, he saved my life. And I need to see him again," said Marie.

"Why is that?" Julian asked, suppressing a growing feeling of impatience with the girl.

"Because we hardly said hello."

"That wouldn't be prudent," said Julian.

"Why not?" asked Marie.

"Too dangerous," said Kizner.

She had almost forgotten he was there. "What's too dangerous?" she asked, looking back to Julian.

"Obaidi is a killer," said Julian.

"He was a killer when you recruited me for this job," she said. "What's changed?"

"The situation's changed," said Julian. "For one thing, there's no one left in the house in which you met Obaidi."

"You mean it was simply a meeting place?" asked Marie.

"A dead drop."

"A dead drop for what?"

"Documents, for one thing. Instructions, orders," said Julian, "for a group of foreign terrorists. Something's up. A big operation is in the works. And when big operations are under way, people get more unpredictable. They get more dangerous."

"Listen," said Marie, standing and walking to the window. Julian noticed she had lost weight since her arrival, but she still moved quickly, purposefully, like the athlete she was. "Even if this guy is the worst terrorist since Genghis Khan, *I'm* going to be the one to write about him, okay? This is *my* story. I didn't come all the way out here to Iraq to turn and run when the walls started shaking. I've come this far, and I'm not turning back."

"Marie," said Julian, running a hand through his hair and standing himself with impatience. He put his hands on his hips at his belt and paused, searching for the right words. "Obaidi's most recent operations have killed seven hundred thirty-nine people, including one hundred sixty-nine children, almost a dozen of whom were younger than ten. He brought down four airliners. And from what I have gathered, this was just the overture. What he has planned next will make everyone forget these crashes ever happened."

Marie looked at him fiercely, her face reddening.

"Do you remember the mother and daughter you saw sitting in their seats in the field in Munich? Would they be impressed that the man who tossed them into the sky at thirty thousand feet pulled you away from a chandelier? You think it would soothe the skin burning off their bodies? Or make whole their bones, broken in a thousand pieces?

"Terrorists confuse, they sow doubt, they play on our expectations and then turn them upside down. Terrorism shakes up your life. It disrupts clear thinking. That's the whole idea of it."

Julian looked at Marie intently. He saw she was still resisting him.

Marie stood up and looked out the window. She crossed her arms delicately, like a ballet dancer, perhaps an unconscious echo of her mother. Just then, Julian caught himself admiring another woman, almost thirty years ago, looking out the window of *her* bedroom onto the Puerta del Sol in Madrid.

He thought of Jeanne Mercier's airy apartment, all windows facing the square. Yards of chiffon hung around her bed in a filmy canopy. She was a tiny thing, and her apartment was like a costume from a classical ballet, all bright and shiny, yet weightless, from her Limoges ceramics to the fabrics that hung from the walls.

She was a principal dancer for a French ballet corps, she told them, but had suffered an injury and taken a leave of absence to choreograph a ballet based on a painting in the Prado. Ari and Julian met her at a café one night. They saw her again a few days later at a dinner party, and they had both flirted with her, lackadaisically, because these entanglements, they both knew, were strictly prohibited.

Shaking himself from his memories, Julian had to pause. Marie did bear a haunting resemblance to her mother. Obaidi must have seen it as well. And Lord knows why, but Marie used that archaic expression *Zut*, just as her mother did. Marie said Obaidi had given her a strange look just after she'd uttered it.

Julian feared something had passed between Obaidi and Marie, something beneath the radar, some reverberation in the gut or the soul. Something Marie was withholding from him now. Maybe not even acknowledging herself. He could see Marie was struggling with it, and he knew there was nothing he could say to change it. This is what got men killed. And women.

Julian looked at Kizner, wanting to get them off the whole topic. "Maybe it's time for some tea, eh? I think we all need a little air, a stretch of the legs? Do you feel well enough to go downstairs, Marie?"

"Yeah, sure," she said. "I just need to remember where I left my shoes."

She rummaged about, pulling aside the bed skirt and looking under the bed, where she found a pair of green sneakers. She slipped them on.

Al-Rashid Restaurant, Baghdad, May 20

When Julian joined her, Marie had ordered an array of juice, coffee, and pastries for the table. A very late breakfast. She pushed a Turkish coffee over to Julian as he approached.

"Marie, it occurs to me that I am guilty of having displayed the worst manners," said Julian.

"How's that?" asked Marie.

"I've never asked you anything about your life. I don't know what you do in your spare time, whether you know how to cook, whether you like to ski. I don't know anything about your childhood, or even whether you have a boyfriend."

Marie laughed out loud, long and heartily, then swallowed her orange juice. She put down the glass, looked up at Julian, and said, her voice dripping with sarcasm, "My dear Julian, I thought you'd just never ask." She picked up a pastry and placed it on her plate. By now she knew that a man like Julian would never have sought her out without dredging up things about her she probably didn't know herself.

"But because we find ourselves in a situation of daily peril," she continued, "here in one of the world's most dangerous cities, I suppose it behooves us *all* to share—isn't that the word? You know: tell our deepest secrets; our worst fears. I mean, who knows how many more opportunities we'll get to spill our guts before some bloodthirsty lunatic does it for us? On video, of course."

"Oh, Marie, don't even joke that way," he said.

"Julian, haven't you already found out all you could about me?" Marie couldn't believe he was making this speech to her. She passed her hand over the bump on her forehead. It was starting to pound again. Her thoughts drifted off to the sound of her mother's high heels tapping along the hard floor of an airport. Click click click click, the lovely shoes, never worn down, always elegantly shaped, perfect. The ballerina always wore high heels. And there was Marie at age eight with her little round overnight case, her home in a bag, sitting beside her mother at the airport between cities, looking over her little treasures and pretending she had a sister and a brother, a dad, and a house with a backyard.

She thought of the last time she was in an airport with her mother. There they were, the two of them, as usual, preparing to board a plane. Except everything was different. Jeanne wasn't leading them, fashionable tote bag over her arm, her tiny, expressive feet flicking and turning. Marie was doing the leading, and her own footsteps were the only ones she heard.

Her mother wanted to be buried back in Bourgogne, in her family's ancestral village. And Marie escorted the body. Her mother was young, only fifty-five, when she died three years ago of lung cancer. Marie was twenty-five. The two of them had never spoken about anything as adult as mortality or wills or burial plans, so Marie learned of her mother's wishes from her longtime lawyer.

Marie looked straight at Julian. "You want to know if I might do something foolish, don't you? You're worried about the operation, and you're trying to figure out what I'm up to, if I might mess things up." She looked down, then back at him with disappointment on her face. "I haven't proved myself to your satisfaction?" She was determined to meet Obaidi again, and Julian probably knew it. He was trying to get a feel for how far she'd go.

Julian looked at her face. It was angry and closed.

She'd also learned, on the day of her mother's death, that her mother had left her the brownstone on West Eighty-third Street and Riverside Drive. The house had been given to Jeanne by the famous choreographer for whom she'd served as muse for much of his life. At one time, Marie had had great dreams about that house, hoping her mother and she would finally settle down, that she would go to the neighborhood school and have friends like all the other children.

The building was beautiful, playful, irreverent. It had an elaborate Victorian facade, and her bedroom on the top floor opened onto a terrace surrounded by a decorative lip of keyholes and turrets. The balcony was large enough for six small trees and beds of flowers. This was Marie's place, where she made up stories and ballets and staged them in the shadowed, breezy lair overlooking the Hudson River.

But as luck would have it, Jeanne stayed with the city ballet for only three years before returning to Europe to dance and, increasingly, to choreograph. So Marie and her mother passed their days in fancy hotels or the occasional villa lent to them by an admirer or patron of Jeanne's. Marie was taught by private tutors, some of whom she loved, others disdained. The brownstone became a guest house for ballet dancers. Out of deference to Jeanne, the dancers kept it up, oversaw repairs, and ensured that new tenants were as fastidious as the old ones.

"And why do you have this need to 'understand' me right now?" Marie asked Julian. Gil's expression was impassive.

"I need to know something about you because your job just became very dangerous in ways you can't understand." Julian paused, and stuttered, "Because there is information that you don't have."

"Like what?" she asked.

Julian took a long breath. He shook his head. "I am having the worst time figuring out how to say this," he said, looking off toward the wall.

She looked at Gil, and he batted her gaze back, neither a mirror nor a lamp.

"Marie, if I'd known what I know now, I would never have gotten you involved," began Julian, again, looking straight at her, calm, sure.

The worst words she could have heard.

"Did I make a mistake?" she asked, her face contorted with fear.

Julian exhaled and snapped his tongue against his teeth. "Not at all," he said. "Marie, it's nothing you did. Or didn't do. You have done an incredible job for us. Outstanding in every way."

Julian paused for a few seconds, trying to put his thoughts together. "When John Willoughby at the Port Authority Police first told me that you wanted to talk about airport security, I made a quick and possibly unwise decision to talk to you. I knew who you were from your aviation writing. I had read your stories over the years. But I also knew who you were before you became a writer. I've kept a distant watch over you since you were a baby."

Her open, curious expression made him stop.

"I don't understand. Why?" she asked, growing exasperated.

"Because I knew your mother. I knew her in Madrid when she was choreographing *La Danse d'Arachne* based on the Velázquez painting *The Thread Spinners*."

"You knew my mother in Madrid?" said Marie, her face reddening.

"No, no, not that way, Marie. I'm not . . ." An expression of pain swept over his face. He shook his head.

"My partner Ari Shiffrin and I were on a military operation in Madrid. We met your mother one night at a café. She was surrounded by a lively group of young people. One of them was a young man whom we knew then as Hassan. He was a low-level member of a terrorist cell from the Popular Front for the Liberation of Palestine—the PLFP. Or so we thought. We were trying to infiltrate the cell because we were interested in finding its leader, a dangerous bomb maker named Mansour Obaidi."

Marie sat up straight. "How can it be?"

Julian tipped his head and went on. "I've since learned that 'Hassan' was in fact Obaidi himself. I didn't learn this until after you began working for us, when I was shown a picture of the man known as al-Jizouri, the man who conducted the 'audit' on the repair shop in London."

Marie looked at Julian without saying a word.

"My partner Ari fell in love with your mother," Julian continued. "It was against all rules of conduct for him to be involved with a local woman while on a mission. We argued about it time and again. It seemed we had reached an impasse just at the time we were making inroads into the PFLP group. Then one day, without telling me, Ari went alone to a meeting with Hassan. And he was killed there."

With that, Marie, usually so stoic, lost her composure; her face seemed for a moment to lose its structure, the very supports that gave her cheeks their round, lively look. With this news, the brave front abandoned her. Her face crumpled.

Julian looked away. Was God playing tricks on him? Was this the divine comeuppance he had long awaited in a dark corner of his unconscious? Had God come to toy with him, dangle him in front of his conceits, reopen the pain of his past failures, and suggest the possibility of worse to come?

"My birthday is August 30, 1978," she said.

"Yes," said Julian softly. He saw the sad question in her face.

"I don't know," he said, demurring.

"Your partner could have been my father," she said, her voice becoming softer. Was this the point of it all? she wondered. Was this the reason I became a reporter? To find my father? Is this why I happened to call John Willoughby at JFK that day? Was it all pointed toward this?

"My mother became pregnant with me in Madrid," Marie said. "Not that she ever told me, but I figured it out."

Julian kept his eyes right on her, looking for Ari in her face.

"Who else could be my father if it wasn't your friend?"

This time, Julian was unable to maintain his signature expression of infinite patience.

Marie gasped. "Oh my God," she said, putting her hand on her mouth.

Julian looked away.

"Obaidi? Do you think that *he* and my mother . . . ?" She couldn't finish the sentence.

"I do not know that, either. Of course I wondered," said Julian.

Marie's head was swirling. For her entire twenty-eight years, she had never had a father. Not even the hint of one. And now, within a matter of a few minutes, she was presented with the possibility of two.

"Do I look like either one of them?" she asked.

"I don't know what Obaidi really looked like. He was a master of disguises. Even before the plastic surgery I know about. You resemble your mother."

Marie slumped back in her chair. She remembered sorting through her mother's things in the house after she died. There was the ethereal Lalique swallow given to her by the French ambassador after a performance of *Romeo and Juliet*; an English medal from Queen Elizabeth for something or other; a classical bust from her friend the antiquities dealer in Italy who entertained Marie and her mother one afternoon in his villa in the hills above Florence, offering them toast drizzled with olive oil pressed from his own olive trees. That was a lovely afternoon, the sun setting golden over the Florentine hills, a mild, sweet breeze scented with honeysuckle.

These were the artifacts she sifted through regularly, trying to make sense of her mother and their life together. Many of them she knew very well; where they came from, what they meant. But there were also a few things she was not the slightest bit familiar with. She found a medieval carving, which she later learned was a misericord, a carving from the underside of a seat in a medieval choir stall. She found a Venetian glass chandelier packed away in an old steamer trunk. And beneath a panel at the bottom of the same trunk, she found two items that caught her attention more than any other, not because of their value or beauty but precisely because they seemed to have been concealed.

"Julian, when I went through my mother's things after she died, I found a silver lapel pin with a fleur-de-lis on it, and a notebook hand-written in a language I couldn't read, an alphabet I didn't know. They were tied up in a velvet bag and hidden at the bottom of a steamer trunk. Now I wonder if the writing might have been Hebrew. I wonder if that notebook belonged to your partner."

Julian looked surprised. "Ari did keep a notebook or journal. But I never found it after he died. I questioned your mother about it, but she denied having it."

Julian pulled a pen from his pocket and reached for a napkin. He drew a raised sword flanked by wings that resembled a fleur-de-lis. He pushed the sketch toward Marie. "Is this what that pin looked like?" he asked her, sketching in a few more details.

"Yes," said Marie. "I think so."

"That is the insignia of the special reconnaissance unit Ari and I were in."

Marie took a breath and put her head down into her hands, in a gesture of surrender or defeat. She began to weep. Her shoulders shook, but she didn't make a sound. Julian walked over and gathered her into his arms.

"My whole life I wanted to find my father," she said, finally letting the tears flow.

Julian held her, rocked her like a child. She seemed small and light now, almost frail.

"I know. I know," he said.

"And now look what I found. One is a dead man and the other's a terrorist."

"I am sorry," said Julian. "I am so very sorry."

PART
THREE

Chapter Twelve

Morgan Ensley sat in a warren of temporary offices set up in one of Saddam's former palaces in the Green Zone. He and six other special agents from his unit now had a place to call their own, even if they had to share it with army intelligence. The building had the charm of a cheesy mausoleum. The massive marble walls were draped with plastic tarps, and the huge chambers were divided up by plywood cubicles, each equipped with international satellite phones and laptops. Highly sensitive information could be communicated through scrambled telephones, but one could get access to them only with a special request.

Three days ago, Ensley had helped interrogate a young man caught trying to blow himself up along with a unit of marines at chow time. Above all, that fact called for the completion of an FD 302 form, which he wrote and attached to an electronic communication, or EC. FBI agents did not communicate with each other via e-mail. In the mid-1990s, as the Internet transformed one sector of society after the other, the top brass approved a heroic last-ditch bid to keep the Bureau away

from the galloping communications revolution. Their stalwart vision re-
sulted in a homegrown internal network that had become—in less than
a decade—antiquated, cumbersome, and dangerously slow. "EC" referred
not only to the system, but also to the first page of any such communication, which included a synopsis, details, and administrative items.

Once the EC had been filled out in full, Ensley would forward it to
"in-the-know" parties who could then act on the sensitive information,
namely to the FBI legal attaché at the other end of the Green Zone.
This "forwarding" did not involve any of the FBI's proprietary technology.
But it did require Ensley to get up from his new desk and walk the floppy
disk over to the legal attaché, who would then send the documents—this
time by speed of light—to HQ for distribution to U.S. military and intelligence agencies. Was the suicide-bomb suspect already in the system? What did the Bureau know about him? In particular, was he
connected to any known terrorist group? If so, what was known about
the group's motivation, its past actions, its plans for the future?

These questions would, under normal circumstances, not be answered. Or they would be answered at some point mockingly close to
when they might have made a difference.

Which was not what Morgan wanted this time. So he picked up his
phone. He knew that in any normal place, he would make contact with
local law enforcement agencies—of course through the appropriate
FBI liaisons. But Baghdad was anything but normal. Whom was he supposed to request information from? The local Iraqi police? True, those
tenacious security forces had painstakingly, over the decades, assembled
extensive dossiers on all known or suspected political agitators. But, as
many of these same agitators either were dead or now held positions in
the American-sponsored Iraqi government, the files were of question-
able use. What about the new police force? Those people who had been
trained by the Americans and given smart new uniforms to boot. No
files. And no one was quite sure whom they worked for anyway.

Morgan put the phone back down and stood up. His eyes passed
over the few books he'd brought with him here: Two old Mickey Spillane
novels, *Day of the Guns* and *Death Dealers*, the books that had got him
fired up to be an FBI agent in the first place. Alexis de Tocqueville's

Democracy in America because it got everything right. For nostalgic reasons, he had brought a couple of how-to books on welding, boat building, and ecological house building. Then there was the stuff he needed for work: books on explosives and radiological weapons. He paced his cubicle, and finally determined to go to the one man out of all the Americans in Baghdad who was least likely to be of any help whatsoever: his boss, Gordon Hart, the supervisory special agent.

A minute later he stood at the door of Hart's office, hands on his hips, pushing back his jacket flaps. They were both wearing business attire as if at a hotel conference in Houston rather than in the middle of a bombed-out desert city. It was ridiculous. Morgan wore a navy blazer, khaki slacks, and loafers. All that betrayed his current address was the fact that his shoes were covered with dust night and day. It made sense to wear boots, as Jerry Bremer, Iraq's former American commissar, had famously done, but that was not regulation.

"What's up, Ensley?" said Hart, fifty-five, tall with a shock of white hair and wire-rimmed glasses, twirling toward him in his chair. Morgan looked around the office, noticing to his surprise that on the wall was a photograph of the big guy himself, J. Edgar Hoover, sitting rather coyly at the edge of a conference table. He knew that some of the old agents still admired Hoover for the institution he built and protected. But really, this was the twenty-first century. Morgan averted his eyes in embarrassment.

"I'm trying to feel my way around the case of the guy who tried to blow up the marine base," said Morgan. "I'm setting leads for indices searches on him in all our FBI databases."

"Have you filled out an FD 302?" asked Hart.

"Yes sir."

"And an EC?"

"Just finished it."

"And did you forward it to the legat?"

"On my way now, sir."

"Very good then," exclaimed Hart, turning to a stack of papers on his desk. "Good work, Ensley." He waved his hand to dismiss the young agent, but Morgan did not go.

"I thought it might be worth doing locally as well," he said. "I just wonder if this yahoo's got a record of any kind, or known associates. Who's our liaison with local law enforcement?"

"Ah, the local authorities," said Hart, tipping back in his chair. "It's like that line from *Casablanca,* when Captain Renault says, 'I'm shocked, shocked to find that gambling is going on in here.'"

Hart turned to Morgan with a smile of happy expectation. His face dropped when he saw Morgan's stony expression and realized that it was entirely possible that the young man had never seen the movie.

"I'll bet you never saw *Casablanca,* did you?"

"Oh yes I have, sir." Morgan was trying to hide the frustration he felt about Hart and the whole situation here. "Actually, I was thinking of another line," he piped up, trying to meet his boss halfway. "Also from Louis. How does it go? 'Realizing the importance of the case, my men are rounding up twice the usual number of suspects.'"

"Yes, yes," said Hart, smiling briefly, then finding something of overwhelming interest in the ornate designs on the walls. "Actually, it sounds like an excellent idea. Perhaps you should talk to our liaison about asking the local police to do just that."

"Rounding up twice the usual number of suspects, sir?"

"Yes, very good, Ensley. Thank you." Hart waved his hand again to dismiss Ensley, who by this point was bothering him to no small extent. He didn't get along with the young ones anymore. They were too ambitious and, frankly, hasty. Sometimes it was better to do nothing. Sit and wait. Hart took a deep breath and bowed his head. He placed his ten fingers together in a gesture of either prayer or surrender. Morgan wondered which.

"Sir," Ensley asked at last. "Have you got a name?"

Hart smiled, relieved at the opportunity to end the conversation quickly. "To answer your question," he said, "though local law enforcement here in Iraq is, shall we say, uneven, the federal level is better. I know someone over at the Iraqi Ministry of Defense who will run the name for you. And the Kurds up north keep their own law enforcement files, and the guys have a crack team. Called the Asayish. I know a guy there, too." Hart scribbled the names on a piece of paper and handed it to Morgan.

"Thank you, sir."

"Mr. Hoover would roll over in his grave if he saw us out trying to solve crimes in places like this, wouldn't he?" said Hart, tipping his head toward the photo of the man.

"It's not the cleanest work, is it, sir?"

"No, it's not. But not as dirty as what every other intelligence outfit in the world does. Including our friends across the Potomac."

"Yes sir."

"But the world is changing. And we have to change with it."

What is Hart trying to say? Morgan wondered.

He waited another few seconds for his boss to add something, but Hart did not.

Morgan returned to his desk and pulled the diskette from his computer. All he had to do now was walk it over to the legat's office. When he first came to the FBI and learned how primitive its communications were, he complained discreetly to a colleague, who told him the party line: it was aggravating, but safe. Safe as hell! They might be safe from computer hackers, since they weren't hooked up to anything, but the resulting limitations were terrifying. The bad guys sure as hell weren't putting their operations on hold while perfecting their own smoke signals.

In any case, Morgan's ECs would be forwarded to the National Joint Terrorism Task Force in D.C., Interpol, FBI field offices, the Terrorist Threat Integration Center, and the myriad databases set up to track terrorists. Morgan also requested that the information be sent to all friendly intelligence services in the area, which included those of Egypt, Jordan, Israel, Saudi Arabia, and Turkey; also to the Brits. Morgan marked it "Immediate," but he had no idea when anything would come back. It could be weeks.

Then he faxed the fingerprint card to the Criminal Justice Information Services Division in West Virginia, the location of the FBI's massive fingerprint repository. He knew that the fingerprint copy he sent would not be good, so even though it was marked "Urgent," it would take days for the CJIS to examine the fax and transpose its interpretation into numerical data which could be automatically searched.

The embassy was within walking distance, so Morgan headed out by foot across the Green Zone, an island of government offices and housing protected behind gigantic cement barriers and antimissile batteries. The

Americans and their allies had made a little home here, with swimming pools and air-conditioning. Hell, people even jogged here, women as well, in shorts and sports bras. Nowhere else in Baghdad would you see that. It didn't even smell like the same city. There was chlorine in the air from the swimming-pool complex, and the odor of ground beef sizzling in the new burger joint. Occasionally, you got a whiff of fresh-cut grass.

It was two in the afternoon and fairly quiet. Morgan held up his government tags, and a guard waved him into the embassy building from behind bulletproof glass. His destination: the office of the legal attaché, Richard Attanasio. Attanasio, an FBI veteran and a former supervisor, seemed remarkably youthful. He had red hair and a baby face. He seemed almost pleased to see Morgan.

"I need to send out some ECs," said Morgan. "I've got them all on a disk. Can I sit down at your desk?"

"Sure. I'm surprised to hear you've got everything ready to go. I usually have to write people's requests out for them."

Morgan shook his head, sat down, slid in the diskette, and sent off the forms. "I also have a request for information from friendly foreign intelligence," he said. "I've left the document up on the screen for you. I understand you need to send it off to your own counterparts."

"Well, it's not as though I don't have a lot of other stuff to do, but let me take a look." Attanasio set himself down at the computer and glanced over the summary. "Holy shit," he said softly. "You're right. We need an APB on this guy. I'll get right to it."

"Thanks," said Morgan. "Appreciate it."

"Okay. Be safe out there."

Morgan ducked out of the office. That was all he could do today. Now he was off to see Marie.

Al-Rashid Hotel, Baghdad, May 20

"It's pronounced 'AH-saad' not 'a-SAAAD,'" Julian said to Marie. They were in her room discussing the Syrian president. "The accent's on the first syllable."

"AH-saad," said Marie, jutting out her jaw like a Boston Brahmin. "AH-saad and AH-choo."

"It's not funny, Marie," said Julian. "If you can't pronounce the names of the people you are occupying, you'll never succeed at imperialism. Unlike the English, you Americans aren't cut out for it."

"That's the most reassuring thing you've said all day," said Marie.

"Oh, no, it's not reassuring at all," said Julian. "You like imperialism, but you don't do it well. You have no sense of history." Julian was still very anxious. The situation was not yet clear to him, and he was short tempered.

Marie looked blank.

He relaxed, and smiled. "Marie, Americans focus on the future. It's a strength, but also a weakness. It helps you develop wonderful technology. But it can backfire in world politics. You don't give a damn about the past, and so you have a hard time understanding people who do. Out here in the land of the Bible and the Bedouin, the past is all we have."

"There's always Faulkner," she said.

"William Faulkner?" asked Julian.

"Yes. The American novelist from Mississippi."

"I've heard of him."

"He said that for a southerner, the past is not only not dead, it's not even past."

Julian laughed. "William Faulkner could have been an honorary Arab, or even an honorary Jew."

"What about the Palestinians?" she asked.

"What about them?"

"Do they have a strong sense of their history?"

"It's about all they have, now that they've lost their land. Part of it is mythology, but we all mythologize ourselves. Probably even your Mr. Faulkner."

Marie smiled, then stared directly into Julian's eyes. "Do you feel sorry for them?" she asked.

"Sorry? No. They dug their own grave."

"So you like the status quo?"

"Marie," he said gently, "you haven't been out here long enough to understand. I don't feel sorry for the Palestinians, because they hate us. At the same time, I think they should have their own state."

"That surprises me," said Marie.

"Why? Come on. Suppressing them hurts us even more than it hurts them. It makes us into people we don't want to be."

"Wouldn't they attack you if they had complete control of their land, whatever that might be?"

"For a while, sure. But eventually they'd see that without Israel, their economy doesn't exist. Our mistake is that we haven't given them enough dignity to allow them to focus on economic reality. They make us crazy, so we make them crazy, so they make us crazy. It's a vicious cycle. And it's got to stop. The truth is we're bound to each other, whether we like it or not."

Marie was about to add something when there was a knock on the door. She opened it. It was Morgan.

"Well, hel-lo, soldier," she said with a grin.

In the background, Julian coughed politely.

"Am I . . . am I interrupting something?" Morgan asked.

"Not at all. We were just discussing American ignorance. Julian here has a dim view of our sense of other cultures."

Morgan looked confused.

"Oh, I'm sorry," Marie said. "You two haven't met." She gestured Morgan to come in and made the introductions, identifying Julian only as an Israeli airline security consultant. "Morgan works in law enforcement," she added, wanting to show the American that she could be discreet.

"What are you reading there?" Julian asked, gesturing to the book in Morgan's hand. Morgan turned up the cover and showed it was Bernard Lewis's *The Crisis of Islam*. He'd picked it up from a colleague headed back home.

"I'm impressed," said Julian.

"Impressed by what?" asked Morgan.

Julian glanced at Marie. "Impressed by people who read history. Though you know, of course, that the Muslims consider Lewis to be hopelessly biased."

"Doesn't matter. I'm willing to read anything that will help me figure out this place."

"It's an interesting world you've dropped into."

"You got that right," said Morgan, looking Julian up and down. The guy looks military, he thought. Strong. Extremely confident. "Airline security, huh?" he asked.

"Security. Also an interesting world. Especially these days."

"What aspect, if you don't mind my asking?"

"I don't mind at all," Julian said. "I look for holes in security systems. Vulnerabilities. Things that terrorists could exploit."

"Like how to plant explosives on airplanes?"

"Something like that," Julian agreed.

"Then why are you in Iraq? Shouldn't you be looking into those bombings?"

A tight smile crossed Julian's face. "Who says I'm not?"

Morgan realized he'd been too aggressive. "Sorry," he mumbled. "I was out of line there."

"No offense taken. But now I get to ask you: What is an American lawman doing in Iraq?"

"Pursuing some leads—about a terrorist, as it happens."

"Anyone I know?"

"I'm not authorized to discuss that with anyone outside my office."

Morgan realized that Julian was certainly intelligence. There were a few good people in the CIA, and Julian felt like one of them. Only more so. He exuded competence. For some reason, this annoyed Morgan.

Julian shrugged. "Suit yourself. But if you want to compare notes sometime, Marie can tell you where to find me."

That annoyed Morgan even more. Did this guy and Marie have something going on? Nah, the guy was too old. Old enough to be her father.

Marie sensed his thoughts. "Julian's a good friend," she said. "He's helped me on past stories. Maybe he can help you, too."

Julian nodded graciously. Morgan liked Marie, that was clear. That might be useful some day soon. In this business, you never knew.

Morgan was suddenly uncomfortable. "Look, Marie, I have to go," he said. "Why don't we catch up later? Maybe for breakfast tomorrow."

"I don't know," she said, laughing. "These morning meetings with you are getting a little too adventurous."

"I'll call you later and see what you're doing for dinner." Morgan smiled awkwardly and let himself out.

Marie turned to Julian. "So what do you think?"

"Are you asking if I approve of him as a suitor?"

She reddened. "No. I mean do you think he can be of value?"

"The thought had occurred to me."

"Are you going to open a file on him?" she asked.

"Who says we haven't already?"

Tel Aviv, May 20

Shimshon Ashkenazy read the e-mail again. He shook his head and printed it out. He read it again and walked back and forth across his small office. The note was from a member of Mamram, the IDF's computer branch, saying he'd picked up some information from a hacker chat room that might be of interest. Posted on a hacker bulletin board were messages offering money for help in getting into the Tunnel.

The Tunnel was a telephone switching station housed in a garrison of a building at 124 Eleventh Avenue in New York City, built in the 1960s to withstand any nuclear attack short of a direct hit. The Tunnel was a favorite target for hackers, a system so secure that getting into it instantly earned you your chops. Very few had ever done so, though Shimshon was one of them. Only the cognoscenti knew that. What a lamer this guy was, Shimshon thought, to ask for help and then offer money so crudely.

"Help me get into the Tunnel and you will be goodly rewarded," the message read. It had been posted three times over the past year, the last time about five months ago. The grammatical error did not escape Shimshon. But what was the significance of this posting? It could be just a lame-assed attempt to purchase some hacking tools, or it could be a serious probe into one of the most vulnerable points in the global telecommunications network.

It was a well-known vulnerability. The Tunnel was the last stop, the switching station, for all telephone, cable, and wireless communications to Europe via undersea cables. Sprint, Verizon, AT&T, MCI, Qwest, and Con Ed—whose fiber-optic cables carried a redundant data network for the New York Stock Exchange—all ran through the Tunnel. It was also a peering link, connecting calls from one cell phone provider to another. When the original networks were designed and built in the 1960s through the 1980s, security and fault tolerance were not issues at the forefront of the designers' minds.

But a better system had not yet been built. Every technology expert knew that the Tunnel was a gaping hole in national security.

Shimshon would have to do some digging to find out whether these messages needed attention. He wondered if he should alert his counterparts in the U.S. first. Pondering this, Shimshon headed out of his office to get a cup of coffee. As he walked down the hallway, he saw Sarah Berendt walking toward him. He froze. Okay, he said to himself, remember what Nadav said. "Ripe for the picking." That sounds disgusting, he thought. He tried to get a grip on his nerves, but when she passed him in the corridor, he just looked down and nodded as he rushed by.

He walked on a few paces and then stopped. "Sarah?" he called out. He walked back. "There's a great concert tonight at the Tel Aviv Jazz Festival," he said, one hand in his pocket, the other absently twirling one of his long curls. "Would you like to go?"

"Sure," she said, smiling.

"Really?" said Shimshon. "Did you just say yes?" he asked with a playfully wicked smile.

"Uh-huh." She nodded.

"Great!" he said, shocked for a few seconds into silence. "We can go over from here, I guess, direct from work."

"Okay," said Sarah, waving and walking on.

"Yeah," said Shimshon to himself. *"Oh, yeah."*

But first he had work to do.

Al-Rashid Restaurant, Baghdad, May 20

At dinner, Morgan pumped Marie for details about Julian. Was this guy really a consultant? Or was he some kind of intelligence agent, maybe Mossad or Shin Bet?

"I'm not too sure myself exactly what he does," Marie said. "I do know he knows what he's talking about. Maybe more than anyone I've ever met."

Something in her tone made Morgan look at her more closely. "Let me ask you something, Marie, and you can tell me to butt out if you don't feel like answering."

"Shoot."

"Do you have a thing for him?"

She colored slightly. She had always wished she didn't blush so easily. "For Julian? God, no. For one thing, he's married, with children."

"Hardly a deterrent in this day and age."

"For another, he's too old for me."

"Maybe."

"And third, I'm a journalist."

"So?"

"Whatever it is he does isn't compatible with what I do. If I learn secrets, I'm supposed to print them." She suppressed her guilty awareness of how close to the ethical line she had already gotten with Julian.

"Aha! So he is in some kind of secret service," Morgan said.

"I didn't say that. I suggested that what he does sometimes involves secrets he wouldn't want me to put in a newspaper."

He regarded her carefully. "So tell me this: why does he help you on your stories?"

Damn him! Marie thought. That was too close to the mark for comfort. Outwardly, she shrugged. "He likes me, maybe?"

"That's bullshit, Marie, and you know it. A man like Julian Granot doesn't do pro bono work. There has to be a payoff, either for him or for the people he works for."

"Okay, so maybe we swap information every now and then," Marie conceded. "Reporters do that all the time. It's called leveraging what you know." She paused. "The thing is, his information is always good—a lot better than mine, in fact. That's why I think you ought to get together with him. You might learn something you could never get out of the local cops. Or the Bureau's antiterrorism task force."

"Yeah, there's a lot of crap floating around Washington passing for intelligence."

"So you want me to set something up?"

Morgan thought for a moment. Fraternizing with foreign agents was not normally encouraged at J. Edgar's redoubt off Pennsylvania Avenue. But what the hell.

"Okay," he said. "Do it."

Al-Rashid Hotel, Baghdad, May 20

It was late that night when Morgan got back from his meeting with Julian. He found Marie in the bar. "What's that you're drinking," he asked, gesturing at the clear liquid in her glass. "Not water, I hope."

"Gin. Ice. Twist."

"Sounds good," he said, signaling the bartender and pointing to Marie's glass.

"So how'd it go?" she asked.

"Pretty intense. The guy knows a lot. But I got to be careful."

"Why?" asked Marie.

"Because Mossad is known for its cunning."

"How do you know he's Mossad?"

"Let's just say it's the safest assumption. The point is, we never know if their intelligence is straight or whether they're trying to manipulate us."

"Are you making much progress yourself?"

"No."

"Then you really shouldn't ask for help," she said, her voice dripping with sarcasm, "from one of our closest allies, one the president has praised for its record fighting terror over the past fifty years."

"Marie, working with Julian would be a direct violation of FBI rules and regulations. I said as much this morning."

"Yeah, I heard. But if you want to find out what's happening in Rutba, maybe you need to lift up the curtain and work together, think outside the box, break the rules. I have no doubt you'd learn plenty."

"Before or after I got fired?"

Marie shrugged. "Do whatever you want. I introduced you because I thought you might help each other. Your enemies here are the same." Marie took a swallow of her drink and looked Morgan in the eye. "So what are you going to do?"

"What do you think I'm going to do? I'm going to meet him again to-morrow," he said.

"Misgivings and all?"

"Misgivings and all. He said he'd help me question the suicide bomber."

"Great," she said, and gave him a quick hug before pulling away. "I'm tired, Morgan," she said. "I've got to go to bed."

Chapter Thirteen

Green Zone, Baghdad, May 21

Morgan stepped out of the trailer that was now his residence in the Green Zone. He'd gotten up early and worked out at the health club; he ran and lifted weights to help him be as sharp as possible. He got into his armored SUV and headed over to the Al-Rashid. He thought what a fine day it was. The temperature had yet to top one hundred degrees.

He arrived early and Julian was already waiting at the curb. He was taking everything in, as usual, in his calm way. He got into Morgan's vehicle. They hardly spoke on the short ride to Sahir Prison, where the suicide bomber had been transferred. There wasn't much to talk about; the two had already decided how things would go: Julian would help him get information from the prisoner, and Morgan would decide from there if he wanted to cooperate further.

Morgan pulled into one of the parking spots reserved for Coalition forces. He automatically reached for his briefcase, and was reminded by its absence that he could no longer take papers outside the office. All working documents in Iraq were restricted and classified, and many people would pay a lot of money to get their hands on them.

Carrying briefcases was too great a security risk. If he was attacked by terrorists, or if he found himself in a position in which he was called upon to protect someone else under attack, he would have to draw his weapon and find cover. In either case, he would have to drop the brief-case. Then it was ripe for theft. So he came up with his own solution: a notebook small enough to fit in his pocket.

The prison was a forbidding cement structure built by the Mukhabarat, Saddam's internal security force. It rose straight out of the sand, elicit-ing a feeling of dread and helplessness even in people who approached it with guns in their belts.

"Charming place," said Morgan, taking an appraising view.

"The Bates Motel in Baghdad," said Julian, putting his hand on Mor-gan's shoulder and guiding him toward the front door. Morgan grunted an uneasy laugh.

"Let me tell you a bit about the layout," said Julian, stopping for a moment. "I haven't been at this particular facility, but they're all the same. It's composed of four sections surrounding an inner courtyard. The first section, where we're headed, holds the interrogators' offices, where information gotten from the prisoners is processed, new ques-tions are prepared for the next round of interrogations, and information is shared and cross-referenced with others. The second section holds administrative offices, a kitchen, a dining room, and restrooms for the guards. The third makes up the prisoners' cells and the dungeons. The fourth contains the interrogation rooms and torture facilities."

"They take this pretty seriously, don't they?" said Morgan.

"You bet they do. This is how these people stay alive. The members of the Mukhabarat consider themselves to be professionals, almost a professional class unto themselves. They serve whoever's in power. It's easy to forget that yesterday it was Saddam, because today it's the Amer-icans. They're an institution, and their mission is to stay in the game."

"How do they do it?"

"The Mukhabarat run a business. They produce a high-value, real-time commodity: HUMINT, or human intelligence. You Americans need it because you can't produce it on your own. Because so few of you understand Iraqi culture or know Arabic. Also, you're more squeamish than the Iraqis. The Mukhabarat are experts at what they do, and the Iraqi people fear them. With good reason."

Julian turned and gestured Morgan to step up to the entrance. Morgan flashed his FBI credentials and announced that Julian was his guest. No further explanation was needed, as the system had been put in place to allow high-ranking U.S. intelligence officers to visit the facility incognito. It ensured a level of deniability.

As soon as they walked in the front door, Julian become very alert and sensitive; he tried to absorb as much as he could of the atmosphere and to adjust himself quickly to the jail mentality. He knew he'd have only one shot. His first approach had to be correct. But to determine which approach would be best, he needed to know a few things. First, what had the Mukhabarat interrogators already achieved with the prisoner and how had they handled his torture so far? He also needed to know the prisoner's current mental and physical condition.

Perhaps most important, Julian needed to know if the prisoner had become a *shahid* while in jail. Julian was well aware that suicide bombers who failed to blow themselves up—either after having second thoughts or because they were caught before reaching their targets—frequently developed this attitude in prison. It was intended to show the community that they were still loyal to the cause and to signal that although they hadn't fulfilled their terror mission, they weren't going to give up any information under interrogation. Becoming a *shahid* gave them a second chance at martyrdom. And it made questioning them quite difficult. When a prisoner decided he was willing to suffer rather than provide information, torture served his desires more than his captors'.

Julian and Morgan were led to the outside of an interrogation room. Through a small window in the door they saw a wide chamber equipped with implements of torture such as electrodes for administering shock to sensitive body parts and thick rubber hoses for beating the soles of the prisoner's feet. A ceiling fan rotated slowly. Pointing to it, Morgan whispered, "That fan isn't there to make people more comfortable, is it?"

"Oh, no," said Julian. "Sometimes they take a prisoner, lash his hands to the fan blades, and beat him with clubs as the fan rotates him."

Morgan shifted his view and saw that a prisoner, his back to the door, was being questioned. It was the would-be bomber. The man looked small and shaky. Morgan's stomach churned. After all, it was he who had delivered him into the hands of these men. "Shit," he said under his breath.

"They're just talking to him now, but they'll be working on him soon enough," Julian said quietly, so the guards walking by couldn't hear him. "But I don't want you to look at what they're doing. I only want you to look at the room.

"Do you see the table in the corner?" Julian asked, trying to orient him, give him something to hook his mind on. He could see that Morgan was losing his concentration. "There are two chairs there for the Mukhabarat interrogators, or for the U.S. intelligence officer and his Mukhabarat translator. They sit with their backs to the wall. Across from them sits the prisoner, facing them and unable to see the rest of the room.

"Behind the prisoner, two Mukhabarat guards sit or stand. At any time, at a hidden signal by the interrogator, the guards can hit the prisoner. The prisoner is therefore under constant psychological pressure. He's unable to prepare himself for the beatings.

"You see that stone bench behind the prisoner's seat?" Julian went on, rubbing his hand over his chin. "That's where he'll be taken if he isn't satisfying the interrogator. The guards will drag him to the stone, and he'll be beaten by one, two, or three guards holding plastic pipes. The bench works like a chopping block to increase the effect of the blows.

"And if that doesn't work, he might be dragged over to the 'bath.' You can see it behind the bench. He'll get pushed into it and held under the water's surface until he's about to pass out."

Just then a guard came to the door on the other side and, without acknowledging their presence, drew a blind over the window. The questioning was about to get more aggressive. Morgan stepped back. "Jesus Christ," he said.

"Yeah, I'm sure they would have taken him on as well," said Julian.

He turned to Morgan. By the way, what's your prisoner's name?" he asked.

"Abdel Kandil."

"Did you remember the bag with the stuff you removed from his pockets?"

Morgan pulled a bag from his vest. Julian examined it and grunted with satisfaction when he saw the spectacles. He took them out and returned the bag to Morgan.

Julian knew that any information about the prisoner he got from the guards wouldn't be dependable. What he could be sure of was that by inflicting uncertainty, fear, hunger, and intense pain, they had done their job: created for the prisoner a new planet on which he now resided. He had by this time—four unrelenting days—become acquainted with its rules and learned the behaviors that limited pain.

"Good," said Julian to Morgan. "Now get some food. A plate of fruit if there is any. And a pack of cigarettes. Get it now, so when I'm ready, it'll be available. Also, get a translator so you'll understand what's going on."

Morgan nodded and spoke to a guard.

"When we get into the room, just trust me," Julian said to Morgan. "I'll be using psychological tactics that you won't be familiar with, but you'll understand them quickly. I intend to create, suddenly and immediately, a new environment. It will cause the prisoner to lose his footing. He's just spent four days mastering the hell they've created for him, and his capacities for adjustment are now limited. The only way he'll be able to deal with what I throw his way will be to lean on my shoulder. Once I achieve this, he'll do as I say."

"Roger," said Morgan, his stomach on the verge of revolt.

"When we first enter, I'll ask you to do something for me. I want you to argue with me at the beginning, but then I want you to give up. By doing this, you'll help empower me in the prisoner's eyes."

A guard appeared with the plate of food. Julian instructed him to remain outside the door until called. Julian nodded to Morgan to follow him into the interrogation room as he opened the door and strode in, shouting, in a determined, deep voice, *"Stop!"* in Arabic.

The guards froze. Abdel Kandil, drenched and lying on the bench, was too caught up in his own misery to hear, and he continued to scream. Julian shouted again, *"Stop crying!"* in a voice so loud Morgan thought it would shake the windows. The guards looked up uncomprehending from their dirty work. Julian stepped into the middle of the room, fully establishing his dominance. The immediate effect was shocking to them all.

Before they had a chance to react, Julian delivered another order: "Seat the prisoner at the table. Guards out of the room." To one of them, he gave a discreet signal to remain behind the wet and shivering captive. After a few seconds, during which Julian assured himself that the prisoner had registered the guard behind him, he gestured to the interrogator to retreat to the bench and remain there, unseen. Julian and Morgan took their seats at the table. The Mukhabarat translator summoned Morgan to his place beside Julian.

"Unlock his handcuffs," said Julian to Morgan in English.

"That's not procedure," Morgan said, playing his role. "The protocols say that prisoners are always cuffed while outside their cells."

"Fuck procedure," said Julian. "I'll take the responsibility."

Morgan started to protest, but Julian silenced him. "Look, pal, right here and now in this room I'm the ranking officer and I say cuffs off."

Morgan shrugged, then snapped his fingers at a guard for the keys. When he reached down for Kandil's hands, the man flinched, expecting to be hit again. His hands were limp and cold to Morgan's touch as he removed the handcuffs. His face was ashen, his frame bony, as though he'd stopped eating well long before his arrest. He made a pathetic contrast with the beefy Americans Morgan had seen earlier in the day working out at the gym.

In Arabic, Julian ordered the translator to go out of the room and bring in the food. The man didn't want to respond to this command, as translators weren't servants. But he knew an iron will when he saw one. He went to get the food. Julian's authority was established. Kandil was almost ready.

The plate the translator brought back held an apple, a banana, and a glass of water. Julian took the plate and set it down just out of Kandil's reach. If anyone was going to be generous, it would be Julian.

For a few long moments he sat in silence. One of the Iraqi interrogation tactics was to deprive the prisoners of food and water. They were given enough food to keep them alive, but in a state of constant want. They were given nothing palatable to drink, but were allowed to lick from the toilets.

When Kandil flinched at Morgan's approach, Julian learned something: the man was not a *shahid.* He still feared pain. And maybe he recognized Julian's Arabic accent as that of an Israeli Jew. He would have heard the stories about the Israelis, how if you fell into their hands you should pray that Allah made your death quick.

It wasn't true, but the Israelis encouraged the idea. It played into their hands. They knew physical torture had limited effectiveness. Much more useful was the *fear* of torture.

He began to speak to Abdel Kandil in a calm, low voice.

"I'm not part of this prison," he said. "I'm not an American. I know they've hurt you and I want you to trust me. I'm the only one who can help you get out." The young man looked at him suspiciously.

Julian handed the boy his spectacles. His face, frozen, impassive, twitched. He hesitated.

"You may pick them up," said Julian, and the boy grabbed them hungrily. Julian imagined he hadn't been able to see a thing for days. He blinked a few times and seemed to take a few steps toward earth.

"Would you like something to eat?" Julian asked. "Yes?" He pushed the plate within Kandil's reach.

The young man hesitated, still suspicious. But Julian continued to speak to him in a soft, almost musical voice until the man gestured toward the apple. Julian pulled a knife out of his pocket and slowly cut the fruit into six pieces and gave the smallest one to the prisoner. Then he pushed the plate away. As the man chewed, Julian saw pain and hunger consume his face. Julian knew that the initial response to sweet food after long deprivation was an outpouring of saliva from the submandibular gland. This could be searingly painful.

"Tell me, my son," he said—*ya ibny* in Arabic—"what is your name? What can I call you?"

At that, the prisoner looked at him with surprise. Julian knew that the unexpectedly intimate words had sliced at his heart. Since the moment he entered the jail, he had been constantly terrorized by the guards; spent hours in interrogation rooms; been denied food and treated like a dog; was probably called a dog. In fact, he smelled like an animal, feces in his trousers and blood and sweat soaking through his clothes. Suddenly, from Julian's voice, he was hearing kind words. This man was not screaming or hitting him. Julian knew that the memory of comfort, of protection, of warmth, was bathing him where his nerves were frayed, the bruises most raw. Julian saw the young man's face go slack, and he suspected that something inside him was about to give way. The young man tried to hold on to it, but it was already gone. Kandil sobbed uncontrollably.

Julian sat quietly until Kandil calmed down.

Julian moved closer to him. "Listen to me. I can get you out of here. I just need you to tell me one thing. If you hold it in, they'll kill you. Or they'll get it out of you and then they'll kill you and throw your body into a field to rot. I've seen them do it a hundred times. I want you to tell me the location of your madrassa."

This proposition brought out of the young man an uncomprehending stare. He hadn't expected such a question. All the time he had been asked about his group, about the explosive and where he got it. What was the trick here? He had no time to think. The few breaks from torture he'd gotten had hardly offered enough time for him to calm himself, let alone renew his strength.

"Baquba," he whispered, and Julian gave him another piece of apple. When he finished chewing, Julian gave him the glass of water and let him drink.

"Describe the madrassa."

Morgan watched with fascination as the prisoner began to talk. Julian pulled out a piece of paper, and Kandil drew on it a map and plans. Morgan observed as Julian cajoled, argued, humored, and charmed his quarry. The prisoner told him that the madrassa was outfitted with training fields, dormitories, and classrooms and could hold up to a thousand fighters.

He continued to talk. He told Julian he was a student at the madrassa but not in military training. They'd needed a martyr for an operation and he had volunteered when a friend dropped out. Julian knew that most suiciders were cheap labor. They occupied the lower ranks of the terror gangs. But in disciplined organizations, they were usually isolated from other operatives and didn't know many operational details—either of their own missions or others. So Julian didn't expect Kandil to know much. On the other hand, Julian knew that in Iraq, where so many operations were ordered every day, the standards had become lax. The suiciders were being trained in groups, with less discipline about isolation and sterilization. It was chaotic and more improvisational than in disciplined terror organizations.

"Who is Qassim Rashid?"

The boy looked at him blankly.

"The scrap collector," said Julian.

The boy looked at him, puzzled. "How did you know that name?" he asked.

"My friend here found his card in your pocket," said Julian, gesturing to Morgan. Morgan put the card on the table.

The boy blanched. With everything that had happened to him, he'd forgotten about the American taking the card. He remembered the other one hitting him, though. The filthy dog. "I was supposed to throw the card away after picking up the bomb." He began to weep silently, at his mistakes, his oversights. His failures.

"And what is Mr. Rashid doing with the sea containers?" Julian asked.

"Sending them to the devil," said Kandil, suddenly focused, his eyes shining and the tears still dripping from his face. "He'll never see them coming, and they'll stick in his hide like a burr on a donkey."

Then Julian pulled out of his pocket a photograph of Obaidi taken in Thailand at the go-go bar. Mossad had infiltrated Bangkok's hotels and pleasure palaces. Photographs of men in their moments of downtime proved useful on occasion, as now.

"Do you know this person?"

At the sight of the photo, the boy froze.

"Okay, not a problem. I just want to make sure nothing happens to you. You are just a student, a willing soldier for Allah and for jihad."

Kandil turned to Julian. His face was white.

"That's not him," the prisoner said in Arabic. "It cannot be. This photograph is a fake."

"Okay," said Julian, pulling the pack of cigarettes from his jacket and turning it over in his hands. He unwrapped the cellophane from the pack. "I know he's your commander and I know he's a very important person for you. But the photo is real. I have more, if you'd like to see them. But the others are of a more intimate nature. You might find them distasteful."

Julian looked at the prisoner now: his face had fallen into a grin, a hollow grimace, really, his mouth hanging open in an expression of self-mocking defeat. He had reached the end of his resistance.

When Julian lit a cigarette and passed it to Kandil, Morgan knew the destruction of the man's ego was complete. For devout Muslims, smoking is *haram*, forbidden, because it destroys health and consumes wealth. Kandil's acceptance of tobacco from a stranger was evidence of a broken man.

Just then the muezzin's call was heard from a nearby mosque. The young man looked at Julian with an abashed plea in his eyes.

"Would you like to pray?" Julian asked. Kandil nodded. Julian walked to the door and banged on it until a jailer came. Julian walked out of the cell.

"What the hell is he doing?" said Morgan to himself. Julian was out of the room for a few minutes, and when he returned he was carrying a prayer rug and a copy of the Koran. He handed them both to the prisoner and signaled to Morgan to leave with him.

"Let's go," said Julian, and he and Morgan headed for the prison exit. An Iraqi policeman asked them what to do with the suspect.

"After his prayers, put him back in his cell," said Julian. "And no more interrogation."

"You told him you'd set him free if he gave you the information," said Morgan.

"Ach," said Julian. "We might need him for something else. Give him a decent meal and a blanket. Tell him we need to do some more paperwork first." Morgan got the joke but stayed silent. Julian and Morgan walked outside into the now blazing heat. The light seared their eyes.

They got into their armored SUV, Morgan at the wheel. Julian grabbed the door handle for balance as Morgan careered down the road. "Hey, if you've decided that you're on a suicide mission of your own, I'd just as soon you dropped me off right here," said Julian. "I'll walk."

"Sorry," said Morgan, slowing down. "I can't believe we're using those bastards to torture prisoners." He shook his head. "I mean, isn't that why the Americans invaded? To get rid of Saddam and his henchmen? To stop the torture and the murders?"

Julian exhaled.

"I know you didn't torture the guy yourself," said Morgan. "But your approach wouldn't have been quite as successful if the guys in black hadn't worked him over first. How do you do it?"

Julian said, "Because I have to."

"How often have you done interrogations like that?"

"Like that? Not very often. I seldom question a prisoner held in the custody of another country. But let me answer you another way. Do you have any idea how many suicide-attack attempts are made in Israel every month?"

Morgan shook his head.

"From twelve to eighty, depending."

"And how many do you stop?" asked Morgan.

"At the beginning of the recent intifada, we were stopping only three out of ten attempts. Now it's nine out of ten. But it's very expensive in terms of manpower and soldiers' lives. Also, as soon as one tactic works, the terrorists find a way to work around it. But what we do is we get information. We have informants. It's not pretty. And we've developed techniques of getting information from people who don't want to talk. Quite often we are dealing with final-countdown situations. You don't have those in the U.S. Not yet."

"Thank God for small favors," said Morgan.

"But you will. And you will have to have a discussion—as a society—about what you're prepared to do to get information to save lives. It's not easy. Not easy at all."

"Why are you here, Julian? I still don't get it," said Morgan.

Julian took a deep breath. "Why am I here? Two weeks ago, I was on vacation with my family. Retired. Now I'm back at the same shit I thought I'd left. I was asked by the government of Israel to investigate the causes of the four airplane crashes. I believe we've discovered how the terrorists blew up the planes and identified the mastermind: a terrorist I've met up with before. His name is Mansour Obaidi, and I believe he's now running a terror ring in this country. What's more, I think he has plans even grander than exploding four fully loaded passenger planes."

"May I ask you your position?" asked Morgan.

Julian hesitated before answering. "I retired as a colonel in the Israel Defense Forces."

"What service?"

"I served in a special reconnaissance unit. We operated in Iraq and Beirut and all over the Middle East. After fifteen years, I took a job with a special security unit that was in charge of protecting El Al as well as Israeli installations abroad. I became an expert in aviation security."

"So you're an agent operating on foreign soil."

"I was an agent. I'm retired, remember?"

"Why are you meeting with me?"

"Because of the scrap collection in Rutba. My gut tells me Obaidi is using it as part of a bigger scheme. I think his plan is to use a shipment of steel to the United States as a cover for delivering explosives."

"What kind of explosives?"

Julian looked at him. "What do you think? You saw the Russian markings on the crates. My guess is some kind of dirty bomb. Easier to assemble than a real nuclear device. And cheaper."

"What's the target?"

Julian looked out his window at the featureless landscape passing before them. "Let's think like a terrorist. You want targets of high symbolic value. Like the World Trade Center and the Pentagon were."

"New York and Washington."

"Exactly. Those are the cities with the most inviting opportunities. In this case we can rule out Washington because you can't get a container ship up the Potomac. So it's got to be New York."

"Like the Statue of Liberty?"

"Symbolically good, but psychologically bad."

"Why?"

"Because you want terrified people running around in front of TV cameras and against a background of smoke. You want ill-informed reporters speculating about radiation poisoning. You want viewers everywhere to be scared shitless. You won't get that from an explosion on Liberty Island."

"Wall Street?"

"The New York Stock Exchange. A promising target. Or maybe that nice new sixty-story building on Chase Manhattan Plaza. To sow panic in a bank would be most satisfying. A container ship could go off route on its way to the New Jersey ports and get pretty close to Manhattan Island before it was stopped—if it ever was stopped—and set off its load."

"And the effect would be only panic?"

"Well, you're the bomb tech. What would be the effect of a dirty-bomb detonation at the shores of the city?"

"Nobody really knows," said Morgan, shaking his head. "It's never been done. When people talk about dirty bombs, they mean small devices in which the radiation is dispersed by a conventional explosive like TNT."

"So how much damage?"

"From the explosion itself? Maybe a few thousand deaths. Radioactive contamination? Worrisome, but probably within a ten- to thirty-block radius. Deaths from radiation poisoning? It would depend on weather conditions and the source of the radiation. Cesium is easy to obtain but it's not very powerful. Weapons-grade uranium is powerful but hard to obtain. Either way, though, as you know, the point is not to kill but to terrorize." Morgan thought for a moment. "But Julian, we're not talking about a bomb at the stock exchange."

"Come again?"

"We're not talking about a truck. We're talking about a ship. A great big fucking container ship. How about the effects of, oh, three or five or twenty dirty bombs detonated simultaneously in lower Manhattan."

For the first time, Julian seemed unsure of himself.

"Or," Morgan went on, "suppose that the containers have different destinations. They could be off-loaded onto trucks or trains and deto-nated in the hearts of all the major cities."

"That would take a logistical genius to bring off," said Julian.

"And this Obaidi? Is he a logistical genius?"

Julian scratched his head. "Yes. He is. Damn him."

Morgan persisted. "And what if he's got a real nuclear weapon?"

The SUV was entering the outskirts of Baghdad. "Now you're think-ing like an Israeli," said Julian.

Bronx Zoo, Bronx, New York, May 21

Red stepped off the number 2 train at the East Tremont Avenue/West Farms Square stop. She wore a knit cloche today pulled low over her face and black bell-bottom stretch pants with a black-and-green vest that reached to her knees. She wore black boots. Had anyone looked, they might have noticed that she had unusually large hands and feet for a woman of her stature, but no one was looking. She climbed what seemed like a thousand stairs to the street and took a deep breath of air. She looked around the large intersection. The buildings were not as tall here. And there were many more African people. She found a street sign that said "Boston Road." Following the instructions on the Web site, she walked two and a half blocks to the zoo's Asia Gate, then inside and up to a small ticket booth.

She paid her admission in cash and followed the map she was given to the Butterfly Zone. She stepped in and looked around. Western music played softly in the background. So Germanic. How did they listen to it? Must increase productivity, she thought. She saw an arbor of cedar trees and followed it into a greenhouse filled with butterflies and flowering plants. It is so beautiful, she thought. Butterflies hiding everywhere.

On a screen she saw a running video of a butterfly emerging from its chrysalis. She sat down on a chair and watched the video through four times. After that, she watched through a window as the zookeepers cared for butterflies in cages, helping some who were having difficulty extricating themselves from their cocoons. She tried to ignore the many children running and playing and crying. The place is lost on them, she thought. She walked back to the video and watched it once more before walking outside and lying down on the grass beneath a huge oak tree. Won't be too long now, she thought. Not long.

Chapter Fourteen

Julian and Morgan regrouped at twilight. They sat at an outdoor table at an almost empty café on the banks of the Tigris with their cups of sweet, mud-thick Arabic coffee. Julian, operating as always out of channels, had a deal in mind.

"I still have access to my old staff," he said quietly. "But as an Israeli, I'm limited in what I can do on the ground here. You're not. But you don't know the culture or the language, so you're hamstrung. Plus, if I may be so bold, the FBI doesn't usually involve itself in the kinds of activities that produce real intelligence. And I understand why not. It's nasty. You Americans have no stomach for it. But without it, you don't get what you really need."

"Go on," said Morgan.

"I think we might be able to work together to stop Obaidi from delivering a shipment to your country that would be a disaster for us all. There are things you can do that I can't. There are things I can do to help you that you don't know how to do. Together, we can stop this bastard."

Morgan looked at Julian in silence for a few seconds. "I'm feeling all tied up here," he said. "I tell you, you know, you seem like a stand-up guy. You sure know a lot. But the FBI is pretty clear about what we are and aren't allowed to do. Cooperating with a foreign intelligence officer, even an ally, is way off base unless we have direct authorization to do so."

"I understand," said Julian. "You have commanders. I have commanders. We know the rules. And what comes from breaking the rules? We both know that, too. So be it."

They sat in silence for a good ten minutes. Julian guessed the quiet would work in his favor.

Morgan broke it. "Fuck this filthy coffee," he said. "Why don't we have a beer?"

"Now you're talking," said Julian. They walked back to the Al-Rashid and took a table at the back of the bar. Morgan went for the drinks.

He placed two bottles of Heineken on the table and sat down.

"What do you do for fun?" asked Julian.

Morgan laughed. "I haven't thought about it for a while, but my hobby is diving. Caving, looking for shipwrecks, stuff like that."

"I knew a guy once," said Julian. "He was an expert diver, but he was in the navy SEALs. Dennis . . . what was his name? Dennis McMenemy. We had a joint mission some years ago."

Morgan's eyes grew wide. "McMenemy?" he said. "That guy was a legend. I met up with him once, but heard lots of stories about him. Everyone knew of McMenemy."

"He had a peculiar ability to stay submerged for extremely long periods of time with no oxygen," said Julian.

"No shit," said Morgan, his torso tensing as if in recollection. "He left a couple of dive buddies in the drink, or close to it."

"I was once underwater with him in Turkey, and, I have to say he nearly killed me. But we succeeded at our job and we both survived," said Julian.

"You worked with him underwater? That's great, man. Amazing." Morgan took a long, appraising look at Julian.

"How long have you been in the FBI?"

"Ten years."

Julian took another pull on his beer. Morgan looked right at him.

"My father taught me to take a good straight look in a man's eyes," said Morgan. "If your gut tells you he's a good man, you should trust it. My FBI experience has taught me the same. Trust my gut."

Julian let him talk. He gave Morgan that same look of calm patience that had brought Marie out. It made Morgan feel comfortable searching for the words to describe how he felt.

"You clearly have experience that I don't have," he said. "You have done things I haven't even thought of doing. You knew McMenemy, and that's something in itself. I'm not proceeding very fast with my work, and I do believe it would go faster if I worked with you."

"But . . . ?" Julian asked, his voice trailing off. "I hear a 'but' coming."

"But I could get fired if I do. And I keep thinking about that, and I feel I've been in too many shit sandwiches in my life to have to put up with some moron bureaucrat jerking off at his desk."

Julian smiled. Desk men were the same the world over.

"I came here to investigate charges of port smuggling and the forging of ISPS codes. Federal agents all over the world are looking at this now. But then I happened onto the case at the marine base and followed a lead from the failed suicide bomber that led me to Rutba with Marie. I was spooked by the sight of the shipping containers. I thought an attack against a U.S. port was an incredibly dangerous possibility."

"Exactly," said Julian. *"Exactly."*

Morgan was quiet. He felt he'd said his piece.

"What I have," said Julian, "is twenty-five years of experience trying to stay ahead of criminal minds. The criminal mind is now inside me. It's not inside you. On the other hand, you organize well. Your logistics are superb. The combination of the devious Israeli mind and the American ability to work a big operation is what we need. And remember, the bad guys will always be one step ahead of us."

"And who are the good guys?"

"We are," Julian said.

"So you say. You're an Israeli. What about the Arabs? They don't see us as the good guys."

"No, they don't. And it's easy to understand why. Things never work out for them."

"What do you mean?"

"Look around you. Look at Iraq. You Americans got rid of Saddam. The typical Iraqi feared him, maybe even hated him. They were glad to see him go. But you overstayed your welcome. They don't like you being here anymore."

"So their view is, 'Thank you very much, now please leave'?"

"You put it well. This is an Oriental culture. They're losing face every day you remain on their soil."

Morgan leaned forward in his chair. "Do you think we've fucked things up?" he asked.

"Not exactly," said Julian. "You've just failed to get the background."

"Tell me."

"Well, think of our prisoner Kandil back in Sahir Prison. He's not likely to be on any international terror lists. He's not important enough. He is in fact nothing. And he knows it. It hurts him."

"Well shit, Julian, wouldn't that describe about 99.99 percent of the world? They're not important enough?"

"You don't understand," said Julian. "You're an American. You see people as individuals. Arabs are tribesmen. They see people as members of clans. They think: If I'm not important, my clan isn't important."

Morgan thought for a moment. "Or the other way around," he said. "If I strike against the infidel, I bring honor to my clan."

"Exactly. But there's more. Our friend Kandil, just like Obaidi, is an Egyptian. Egypt is a mess. Guess the average wage of an Egyptian."

"I can't."

"Well, let's just say that one Egyptian in five lives on less than two dollars a day. Food? Not good enough. Sanitation? Negligible. Clean water? Once you get outside Cairo, forget about it. And the hell of it is, so many of them are illiterate, they have no idea that their government could do better if it weren't so corrupt."

"So why is a kid like Kandil willing to blow himself up?"

Julian shrugged. "It's the Middle East," he said. "But seriously, Kandil is a believer. So when he asks why he's in the pond of shit that is his life, the imams tell him it's because Israel and the West are stealing money out of his back pocket while he's lying facedown in the street. They're stealing his birthright as an Egyptian."

"As an Egyptian?"

"Yes. The Pyramids, the Sphinx, the temples—these were all here when your ancestors were painting their faces blue and living in caves. Kandil may be illiterate, but he knows about Egypt's glory days. And then he flips on the television and what does he see? White faces, clean white faces, living in huge houses and driving big cars. And he sees beautiful women with their bodies uncovered and that is against his religion so he feels bad when he sees it, but he is also excited by it. And the women are wearing diamonds and jewels and he sees that what the imams say is all true."

"And so he straps a bomb on his back and dreams that this way he'll save his people?" asked Morgan, shaking his head. "Too simplistic."

"It is simplistic. But good enough for now."

Julian looked at Morgan, who seemed tense and worried. "All we have to do now is stop the people who tell us that Allah wants our annihilation. And the clock is ticking."

Al-Rashid Hotel, Baghdad, May 21

Marie was back at her desk on the computer, putting the finishing touches on a letter to Mansour Obaidi. She knew she shouldn't be doing this. She knew she should distrust that feeling in her gut pushing her forward. But she couldn't. And she didn't want to. She needed to know more about Obaidi, needed to be back in his presence.

In the letter, she explained that she wanted to finish the interview they'd begun and that had been so abruptly terminated. She tried to be businesslike but also friendly in her choice of words. When she felt she'd got the balance right, she printed the letter out on a small machine she'd bought off a departing journalist.

One snag: the only address she had for him was in Bahrain. And of course the house in Karada that got shelled. She folded the letter and put it into an envelope, remembering the finely handwritten note that she'd received from Obaidi just three days earlier. As the light turned from the harsh blast of midday toward evening, her thoughts unaccountably drifted far off, to her childhood home and to her mother's funeral three years ago.

Marie thought about watching her mother's coffin as it was unloaded from the plane in Paris and placed in the waiting hearse that would carry it to the village in which Jeanne was born. Marie's aunt Violette, who lived in Sancerre with her three children, picked her up. They drove in a small Renault through Normandy, the children chatting in the lovely tones of their beautiful French. Marie remembered playing with them when they were all children, this time in Paris in the Bois de Boulogne on the merry-go-round, holding out their wooden sticks to spear the brass rings. The kids were blond, two girls and a boy, with skinny long legs and a natural grace. She wondered why her mother never tried to recruit them for the dance, as they looked to be of the requisite proportions. Marie was not. Her torso was too long and at five feet ten inches she was too tall. No matter: having seen the world of ballet from the inside, she wasn't the slightest bit interested.

Finally she, her aunt, and her cousins stopped in Pont l'Eveque, at a farmhouse of dark wood, built around a central courtyard of sand in which her relatives parked their cars. Around the house were huge bushes of climbing roses, alternating red and white. As Marie got close, she saw that many of them were infected with powdery mildew—she pointed this out to her aunt and said there was a spray that could kill it, but her aunt waved her hand in a gesture of impatience and said, "There is only so much one can do to stop nature from taking its course," and led Marie into the living room, which was dominated by a huge stone hearth, two bright fabric-covered sofas, and various dark side tables covered with white cotton lace.

They were greeted by Bertrand and Lilly, her mother's parents. Lilly embraced Marie and showed her to one of the couches, bringing over a tray of cakes and tea. Her grandparents had run this farm for fifty years and it produced a fine Pont l'Eveque cheese that they sold to many Paris restaurants. Their view of the Americans was dim; they were but a noisy imitation of the tasteless English. There was a reason de Gaulle used to refer to both countries together as "les Anglo-Saxons."

Marie, in her sweltering Baghdad hotel room, continued to be drawn to the memories of these events of three years ago. She saw Lilly and Bertrand bringing food and drinks to her and the family, at the same time keeping up a running conversation with their dairyman, and also fielding calls from the local priest and their neighbors regarding the details of the service later that day. There was a lull after lunch, and Marie's younger cousin Guy took her by the hand as the afternoon wore on and brought her out to the stables, where he showed her the horses, one of whom she remembered from her childhood, a huge bay cart horse with hooves almost ten inches in diameter. She held her hand to his muzzle. He wiggled his lip into her hand and Marie giggled out loud.

"Viens," said Guy. "Shall we go for a little ride, get away from the gloom?" She agreed, and he threw bridles on two riding horses. They pulled themselves up bareback and headed out past the barn, along a path well trod by cows and goats, through a break in a rambling field-stone wall, and off into old woodcutters' paths through the forest. The horses were fresh and a bit feisty and broke into a canter at various spots. Marie laughed and held on. But the woods grew thicker and they returned to a walk, stepping for a time alongside a running stream, then turning into a grove of fir and emerging into a cleared field bordered by poplars.

They hardly spoke as they rode. Marie enjoyed the delicate country-side and the fragrant air redolent of lavender and peat. As she moved up beside her cousin, she saw him cast her a shy but inquiring look. She imagined she must be something of a curiosity to them all. Her mother was an original, just given her dance stardom, but she had also done her best to flout most rules of decorum. And then Marie, her little daughter with a father no one knew anything about. It must have been scandalous in this little village of Catholic farmers to contemplate such a life as theirs.

Past the row of poplars, Guy led them back into the woods along another path, toward a small clearing in which stood a cemetery of ancient stones. They were overgrown, but many of the markers, as well as a couple of vaults, were clear in their decorations. It was a Jewish cemetery, Marie realized, after seeing several Stars of David. They pulled up their horses, and Marie tried to get a better look at the little sanctuary which the sun, breaking through the overcast skies, had unexpectedly illuminated. Some of the stones dated back to the eighteenth century.

"This is quite an ancient place!" she exclaimed as the horses pushed on past a cluster of farmhouses and back to the poplar-lined field. The horses walked faster as soon as they turned toward home. Guy looked at Marie, and she said, "Let's go!" and they let the horses gallop across the field, jumping over tufts of grass and the low stone walls until they stopped, horses snorting and stamping, the two laughing, back at the farm.

It was only later that day, when they were standing in the stone sanctuary of the village church, the coffin of Marie's mother before them, draped in lilacs and roses, surrounded by carved and painted baroque images of biblical figures on the walls, and a huge crucifix above, that Marie wondered why Guy had brought her past that place. Why would he bring her to an ancient Jewish cemetery? Her mother was an atheist, or so she said, though she had requested to be buried here with her Catholic forebears.

But now, Marie wondered, Does he know something? Had her mother made a comment those many years ago to her sister or her mother that led them to believe Marie's father was Jewish? Did they know something she did not? Or was he just showing her an intriguing landmark?

Pulling herself out of her reverie, Marie stood up, then looked down at the envelope addressed to Obaidi on her desk. He was the only person she knew who might have the answers. She picked up the letter and headed to the door of her hotel room. She was going to bring it to her fixer at the front desk. She was sure he'd know where to deliver it.

Karbala District, Baghdad, May 22

The next morning, Morgan and Julian sat at the kitchen table of the house Massud had rented for them in Karbala. Julian was slightly disheveled, his shirt outside his slacks. Morgan, in a sweat-stained button-down shirt, chugged a can of Coke. The generator was working, but the air conditioner was struggling just to bring the temperature down to ninety. Gil Kizner sat behind them, a laptop on his knees. The men were reviewing research material sent from Tel Aviv.

"'There are three hundred sixty-one seaports in the United States,'" said Julian, reading from one of the documents. "'Ninety percent of U.S. imports by weight enter the country via ships. In 2005, more than eleven million oceangoing containers were off-loaded in U.S. ports.'"

"'In 2003,'" Morgan broke in, reading from a newspaper clipping, "'a labor dispute shut down the Port of Los Angeles for ten days. The losses were a billion dollars a day and it took months to clear out all the cargo that was held up. Some of it was unsalvageable.'"

"Think of the consequences if the port was destroyed," said Julian. "And what if the explosion ignited the ship fuel stored at the port? Hundreds, probably thousands, would die. Commerce would be disrupted from end to end. The trucking industry would be shot to hell. The railroads would be fucked. And the stock markets? Forget about it."

Morgan noted the American slang, and was both impressed and amused. But he thought Julian was being alarmist. "Look," he said, "we have some protection. Twenty-four hours before a container is even loaded onto a freighter headed for the U.S., Customs and Border Protection is notified of its contents. If there's anything funny about the

ship or the shipper, red flags go up all over Washington. Homeland Security begins a risk analysis—and this is before the ship even leaves
port."

Julian looked at Gil. Both men rolled their eyes. There was nothing
in American procedures an enterprising terrorist couldn't work around.

If Morgan noticed, he didn't show it, and went on. "We've got inspectors at nineteen foreign seaports from Vancouver to Rotterdam to
Singapore. They can screen containers and monitor shippers and cargos.
The coast guard uses real-time information to track high-risk vessels,
and boards suspect ships.

"I heard of a case where the CBP guys seized a cache of weapons on
a ship sailing from China to El Salvador. The cargo was listed as frozen
rainbow trout, except the container wasn't refrigerated."

Morgan sensed that he'd lost his audience, so he stopped. Julian and
Gil looked at him, saying nothing.

"What?" said Morgan.

Silence.

"Did I say something wrong?" said Morgan.

"Morgan," Julian said as kindly as he could, "your people are working
hard and they can certainly find a few rifles headed for El Salvador. But
it's easy to get around your law-enforcement records about shippers. All
a terrorist has to do is use dummy corporations within dummy corporations, and men like Obaidi know how to do that.

"Second, it's not hard to foil detection devices. A terrorist could line
a container with lead, and the most sensitive device in the world couldn't
detect any radiation.

"Third, your system depends on good intelligence, and the U.S. does
not have good intelligence in most of the really dangerous places in the
world.

"Fourth, it's impossible to check every container. Your own system
concedes that. It looks only at suspect ships and suspect containers. If I
were a terrorist on this kind of mission, I'd use a shipper and ship so
clean they'd look like Boy Scouts. So basically, a shipment of bad stuff
has a pretty decent chance of never appearing on your radar screen."

"Obaidi's on our radar screen," Morgan pointed out.

"Yes, but no thanks to American intelligence. It was sheer luck, your going out to Rutba with Marie. And it was Marie who stumbled across the connection between Obaidi and the airplane bombings."

Morgan looked glum. "You got any rum to put in this Coke?"

Julian pressed on. "And all your fancy scanning equipment, your last line of defense. Where is that located, do you know?" he asked.

"In the ports."

"Exactly. So what if the leader of one of the rogue states your president talks about decides to send a small nuclear bomb to New York? And your Homeland Security dutifully brings the container into its hangar to X-ray. But the bomb's already where it needs to be. The attack is a raving success. All the bad guys need to do is pull the trigger, because the bomb is already in your lap! New York will be radioactive for ten thousand years."

"Fuck," said a shaken Morgan.

Gil spoke for the first time. "I think that Obaidi has a much simpler scheme," he said, walking across the room, his thin, lithe frame gliding like a cat's. "He's already set up with shippers and forwarders. He's a well-known entrepreneur. He'll ship it in broad daylight under the noses of the inspectors, because they won't suspect him. His crew will be fully licensed, the ship or ships will be following protocol. You won't have any idea what he's up to. He'll look one hundred percent legit. For all we know, he's selling the steel to the Defense Department directly. Even shipping it back in government containers!"

Morgan got unsteadily to his feet. All of a sudden, he realized he was out of his league. "Let me go," he said, picking up his helmet and vest and M16. "We need to stop these ships. We need to find out which port Obaidi is shipping out of. I'll contact the British about Basra and see if they have any container ships docking there. And I'll contact Customs and Border Protection and warn them about a shipment of metal that could be booby-trapped." He walked to the back door.

"You're going to drive by yourself?" asked Julian.

"It violates protocol, I know," said Morgan. "But I won't make it in time if I wait for an escort."

Julian looked at him. "Be careful," he said. Morgan nodded grimly. "You might also inquire about shipments from the Port of Aqaba."

"In Jordan?" asked Morgan. Julian nodded. "Right, right," said Morgan, thinking quickly. "That makes sense."

Julian and Gil watched from the house until Morgan got into the car and drove down the street. Julian returned to the table and jotted down some numbers on a piece of paper.

"Those containers are forty feet long," he said. "They are all eight feet wide, and the height is eight foot six or nine foot six." Let's say there are ten containers. Let's leave ten feet on each end, so the explosives will take up twenty feet by eight feet by about nine feet. Each one can hold fifteen tons of explosives. Multiply that by ten containers, let's say, and that's enough explosive to make a blast as big as Hiroshima."

"Holy shit," said Gil. "But where will Obaidi send such a ship?"

"I think New York."

"We may have corroboration of that." Gil handed Julian an e-mail from Shimshon Ashkenazy that he had just printed out. "Shimshon captured three e-mails sent from Rashid's house in Rutba. They're all verses from the Koran." Julian read the verses that Sarah Berendt had translated from the Arabic.

"It's a version of the al Qaeda message we heard on Al-Jazeera when we crossed the border," Gil said. "But this one is more specific."

"Has Shimshon got any report from the code-breaking department?" asked Julian.

"Not yet. But he tracked down the computer that the messages were sent to."

"And where is that?" asked Julian.

"A computer in an apartment in Paterson, New Jersey. Ten miles west of New York City."

Green Zone, Baghdad, May 22

Morgan stepped into his trailer. He hadn't much time, but he needed a shower desperately. God he smelled bad. This heat was unbearable. And he was supposed to go back and meet Julian. And Marie.

When he stepped out of the shower three minutes later—hot water here was strictly rationed—he saw Comstock sitting in his living room.

"Holy crap, what are you doing here?" asked Morgan, toweling himself off. This was not the man he wanted to see. He was already late and he had to head back to Julian's this evening, something he was not about to mention to his nosy colleague.

"Just coming in to check on how you're doing," said Comstock. "What's with the guitar?" he asked, pointing toward an oud propped on a chair.

"That's an oud, you ignoramus," said Morgan, walking into his bedroom to dress.

"What the hell you get an oud for?" asked Comstock.

"It's a present."

"Some Iraqi girl singing love songs to you?"

"Fuck you, dogbreath. Haven't you got anyone else to pester? What about your own work?"

"I actually got a break in my case. Found the wallet and gun of a contractor who disappeared a month ago in the house of the suspect's brother. So that's something."

"Sounds like you still have a lot of work. Why you crowding me?"

"We've been over that a thousand times. You think I like it? Give me a break."

"Give *me* a break!"

"Who's the guitar for?" asked Comstock.

"Okay, here's the thing. I'll give you something good if you get out of my face. Is that a deal?" Morgan didn't want to be late getting back to Julian's place. He just wanted to get rid of Comstock as fast as he could. Maybe the best way to get rid of him was to throw him a bone.

"I'm waiting."

"All right, try this one, Comstock. For the last decade, while you've had your head stuck underwater in hell knows whose swimming pool, I've been keeping watch over some old missiles smuggled out of the

Soviet Union. Hot ones. The guy who's watching them for the bad guys is also taking money from me. The oud is an extra gift. Let him know how much I care. Okay? Now scram."

"Nuclear interdiction? Nobody told me you were in that unit, too."

"Nobody told you a lot of things, Comstock. Now why don't you go and inderdict somebody else. I got work to do."

Karbala District, Baghdad, May 22

With kitchen tongs, Gil picked up chunks of lamb from a marinade of vinegar, garlic, and scallions and placed them on the sizzling grill. Julian pulled well-filled salad bowls from the refrigerator and placed them on the table before Morgan and Marie.

The smell of grilling meat filled the room with a sweet garlicky aroma. Marie closed her eyes. "That smells so good, I think I may faint."

"If this is the catering service your officers get," said Morgan, stepping up beside her, "sign me up."

"Oh, come on," said Julian, giving them a quick glance. "This is nothing. You have to eat, no? And of course," Julian added playfully, "you have to drink." With that, he pulled several beers from the refrigerator and put them on the table. From a cabinet, he pulled a bottle of Jack Daniel's and four glasses.

"It's time for us to loosen up our thinking." He carried the glasses to the refrigerator and filled them with ice. He looked over at Morgan.

"Sure, hit me," Morgan said.

"And you, Marie? I remember once before you refused to drink bourbon with me," he said, smiling. But the look on her face surprised him. She appeared about to cry, but the expression passed across her features like a swift-moving cloud, and she quickly regained her composure.

"I would love to drink bourbon with you, Julian," she said, smiling wistfully.

He looked at Marie as he poured her a shot. Something about the mild intimacy of pouring her a drink made him realize how much he'd missed her and how agitated he'd been by her recent escapades. Maybe having Morgan around will calm her down, he thought. They seemed to like each other. But she was too good for him. I sound just like my father, Julian thought. Or worse, Grandpa. I really am getting old.

Julian placed on the table before Morgan and Marie the three e-mails of Koranic verses. "These verses were sent from Mr. Rashid in Rutba to a computer in Paterson, New Jersey," he said.

"They sound like a call to arms, don't they?" said Marie.

"I can get Washington to tap the Paterson apartment," said Morgan.

Julian looked up at him, his eyes heavy with concern. "Do you have sufficient cause to get it?"

"I think I do. There's something called the Foreign Intelligence Surveillance Act. It doesn't have as many restrictions as domestic wiretap law."

Julian sat at the table, pulled over a pad of paper, and started drawing up a time line.

"All right," said Julian. "How long will it take to get the tap?"

Morgan didn't want to tell Julian that the court responsible for approving these warrants met once a week, and they might already have missed this week's meeting. He didn't want to say that Bureau lawyers hated to have their requests turned down, so they grilled agents over and over about their requests before approaching the judge. Putting a rush order on the request might speed things up by three days. Morgan decided not to say any of that.

"It should be operational in four days," he said. "That's a guesstimate."

Julian nodded and looked at Gil, who frowned. In Israel, the tap would have been started yesterday.

"What about getting someone to watch the house?" asked Julian. "Do you have any agents who look Middle Eastern and speak Arabic? Two white guys in suits sitting in a Dodge Stratus in an Arab neighborhood in New Jersey would not look good."

"They would never be that stupid, would they?" Marie asked.

"Let me tell you about a little screwup the CIA made in Yemen," said Julian, his eyebrows raised. "They were hot on the trail of Ayman al-Zawahiri, bin Laden's right-hand man. This was a month before September 11. The CIA got a tip that al-Zawahiri was being treated at a hospital in Sanaa. What happened? The hospital guards saw a couple of white guys in suits videotaping the hospital. Before they finished their movie, al-Zawahiri was out of his hospital bed and back home in Afghanistan."

Marie burst out laughing. "Americans try so hard," she said.

"Why are you laughing?" Julian said, his voice lowering with anger. "Americans are oblivious. Oblivious of foreigners. Oblivious of history. Oblivious of geopolitical context of any sort beyond their backyard of Cuba. You two really have no idea how serious the threat is," he said.

Marie and Morgan sat up, their feelings bruised.

"It takes fifteen days to sail from the Middle East to the U.S.," Julian went on. "Twenty-five if you don't go through the Suez Canal. I'm pretty sure Obaidi will avoid the canal because of inspections. But I do think the ships are already at sea. Where they are, I don't know. But if my hunch is right, we have only a few days to stop an explosion that could make September 11 look like a skirmish."

"There have to be at least a handful of Arabic-speaking FBI agents in the United States, right?" asked Marie.

"One team should be planted outside the Paterson address," said Julian, looking at Morgan. "And the agents should do everything possible to determine who's receiving these e-mails. Even in the best of circumstances, it's going to take days to cultivate sources to get close to the guy. You have to start now."

"Roger that," said Morgan. "I'll send a physical surveillance request as well."

"Is that any faster to get than the wiretaps?" asked Julian.

"Yes. With physical surveillance there's no privacy issue. The target is viewed from public areas."

"Good." Julian turned to his time line and gave the government one day to put the physical surveillance in place.

"Marie," he asked, turning toward her. "Are you familiar with a place in downtown Manhattan referred to as 'the Tunnel'?"

She shook her head.

"It's a fiber-optic thruway," said Julian. "It hosts cables connecting all data and voice networks in New York before they pass under the sea to Europe and beyond. Basically, it's the last switching station for all communication to points east. And it's vulnerable to hackers."

Morgan and Marie listened carefully.

"One of my men in Tel Aviv stumbled on a request posted on a BBS five months ago offering to pay money for information on hacking into the Tunnel."

"Yikes," said Marie.

"Yikes for sure," said Julian.

"Julian," said Marie, "you just told us that motivational messages— or instructions—are being sent from Rutba to Paterson, which is not far from Manhattan. And also you believe that a shipload of explosives is heading to the U.S. from Iraq. And you're suggesting at the same time that someone is trying to hack into the central communications node for the entire East Coast. That sounds like someone is preparing a catastrophic attack and then making sure that chaos will follow. No phones. No computers. No communications. And the location of the attack has to be a port on the eastern seaboard."

"Bingo. And which one would that be, do you think?" he asked. "New York would get the most attention, of course."

"That's what we thought too," said Morgan.

Marie noted the "we," and pressed on. "I don't think there's an active container port in Manhattan anymore. There's at least one in Brooklyn, though. There's Port Newark and Port Elizabeth in New Jersey. I don't know if this would matter at all to Obaidi, but Port Elizabeth was the first American port built exclusively for container ships. That was in 1962. It's a very busy place."

"Would steel be shipped to New Jersey?" asked Morgan.

"I can look that up," said Gil, typing on his laptop. "I'll look at a scrap-iron and steel exchange Web site and see if New York or New Jersey is buying scrap." Gil was quiet as he scrolled down. "Kuala Lumpur, Shanghai, Hong Kong, Haiphong, Texas, New York, all want steel." He glanced up at the top of the page. "There are two hundred ninety-six entries just today. Steel scrap is going everywhere. Steel is being bought in Galveston, Norfolk, Boston, Charleston, New Jersey. There you have it. New Jersey. The answer is yes."

Julian took a breath. "Okay, Morgan," he said. "Did you find out whether the port of Basra is open for business?"

"I have *some* of that information," said Morgan. "After I left here earlier today, I got hold of the head of the American company that's now running the port."

Julian was pleased enough for now. "Excellent."

Morgan pulled out a notebook and consulted his notes. "First, the primary movement of goods in and out of Iraq is via containers. They're shipped through either Jordan or Syria. There are two companies, the Iraq-Jordan Trucking Company and the Syria-Iraq Trucking Company. These are both government-backed joint ventures, though they try to act like they're private enterprise.

"As for Basra, there's not much cargo movement these days. To get there you have to sail up the Shatt al Arab, which is clogged with ships sunk during the Iran-Iraq War. Also, it's only fifteen feet deep. Blue-water ships need at least thirty-five feet of water.

"South of Basra is the port of Umm Qasr," he continued. "It has four container cranes, all of which work. But here's the deal: there are lots of goods coming into the country via containers, but not too many going out. Any container shipment of any real size would be noticed. As far as my contact knew, there were no containers of steel passing through either Basra or Umm Qasr in the last month."

Marie interrupted. "Excuse me, everyone. This is all very interesting, but we have exactly zero evidence that any container ship is headed to the U.S. with steel. And even if we did, we'd have exactly zero evidence that explosives have been hidden inside the containers. We know next to nothing about any destination. If I went to an editor with a story like this, he'd laugh me right out of his office. If he was in a good mood."

"She ought to work for your organization," Julian said to Morgan.

"They'd never give her a job."

Julian laughed. "Too wild," he said. "But I'd give her a job in a special unit. A unit of one."

"Hel-lo, I'm here, you know," said Marie. "I can hear you."

"Look, Marie," said Julian, "we're not talking about police work here. We're not trying to make a case that can get a judge to grant us a search warrant. We're not looking for a prosecutor to seek an indictment. We've got to try getting inside the terrorist's mind. We have to ask what we would do next if we were him."

"We have to think like a criminal, you mean," she said.

"Exactly. And that's hard. There's too much stuff we just don't know about his capabilities. But to make it worse, some of these guys are not rational. Some are genuine nutcases."

"And some of them aren't."

"Right, and sometimes it's hard to tell the difference. In September 1998, the Unites States intelligence community circulated a report that someone had walked into an American consulate in East Asia ranting about a plot to fly aircraft bearing explosives into an American city. It was considered seriously by some, but dropped by others. A fatal mistake.

"In the summer of 1997, a year before the bombings of the American embassies in Kenya and Tanzania, someone walked into the American embassy in Nairobi—it turned out he was from al Qaeda—and told the CIA of a plot to bomb the embassy. The Agency thought the guy was out of his mind and ignored him. When you're thinking about these cases, trying to anticipate something that has not yet happened, you must take on an entirely new perspective. The thinking is almost reversed from that of ordinary logic. You can't rule out anything that is operationally possible.

"There's something we have to do right away," Julian said, looking at Morgan. "And Morgan, you know what it is."

Morgan said, "We have to locate all the ships coming from the Middle East with steel. Once we know what ships the steel containers are on, that's half the battle. Then we have to decide what to do about it. I'll contact Customs and Border Protection."

Julian nodded. "Good. You've earned your dinner. We'll reconvene later."

Gil walked to the table with a platter of sizzling lamb kebab spiced with rosemary, the perfume sweetening the room. He returned with plates of fresh herbs, tomatoes, eggplant salad, hummus, and fresh pita bread.

"Let's eat," said Julian, smiling and handing plates around the table.

Chapter Fifteen

The note came as the first one had, by messenger. When Marie answered the knock on her door later that evening and saw a letter written on the same heavy card stock with beautiful calligraphy, she felt her pulse racing. Carefully, she sliced open the envelope and slipped out a single sheet of paper.

Mansour Obaidi acknowledged receiving her letter and invited her to meet with him the following day. A chill ran through her as she imagined seeing him again, those strange blue eyes and the face that seemed too angular, too smooth. She knew that her impulse to see Obaidi again was unwise and dangerous. But she couldn't resist. If he was her father, she had to know.

She looked at her watch. Almost midnight. She started walking around her room, putting things in her bag, the one Julian had sent to her in London. She put into it her tape recorder, her Thuraya phone, notebook, and pens. It was awfully late to call Massud, she thought. Maybe she'd just take a cab over in the morning. But Julian would be furious. And of course it was risky. She called Massud.

He answered on the second ring. Yes, he was still awake. Yes, he would meet her tomorrow. When she hung up, she wondered where he lived, whether with family or in a boardinghouse with other single men working for the driving company. She felt bad about not asking him about his family and his life. She made a mental note to ask him.

Northern Iraq, May 23

The caravan of SUVs drove up the dusty road to Ibrahim al-Aziz's camp the same way the Isuzu trucks had come eleven days earlier. To al-Aziz, watching from his *madfeh,* the five tan trucks, machine guns bristling from the windows, resembled a line of camel spiders scuttling across the desert. He took another sip of tea.

The trucks stopped a polite distance from the camp. One man stepped down and walked over, Australian outback hat on, an oud under his arm. Al-Aziz smiled to himself. He had leveraged his knowledge pretty well on this one, hadn't he? Wasn't that the term the young ones were using? He poured a glass of tea for his visitor.

Al-Aziz stood as Morgan approached and gave him a Bedouin's embrace. Morgan stepped back and smiled, then handed him the oud. Al-Aziz murmured in satisfaction as he turned the pear-shaped instrument over and inspected its fine carving and inlays. Smiling broadly, he gestured Morgan inside.

They sat back against pillows on the new Persian rug that adorned the floor and drank tea in silence. When he had drained his glass, al-Aziz told Morgan that the metal boxes had been picked up.

"When?" asked Morgan.

"May 12."

Morgan sat in silence for a minute. Today was the twenty-third. Fuck. But of course, al-Aziz was getting paid by both sides. And of course his loyalties were to the other one. Morgan wondered for a moment just how much more they'd paid. Well, they'd got a healthy head start for their money. But just finding the bombs had been torture. And tracking this guy down was as convoluted as the 1001 Nights. Abracadabra. What was it he had just learned? The word came from the ancient Aramaic, *avra kedabra*, which meant "I will create as I speak." Poof. These desert dwellers had to use their wits, didn't they? What the fuck. He stood and removed an envelope of cash from his pocket and handed it to al-Aziz.

They embraced. Morgan figured better give the guy the hug. Might help him avoid a dagger in the back. As Morgan headed back to his vehicle, al-Aziz picked up his new oud. As he plucked the strings, he began to recite the ancient poetry for which the Bedouin are justly renowned. He chose the following lines from al-Khalil bin Ahmed:

> *If you knew what I was saying, you would have forgiven me. . . .*
> *If you knew what you were saying I would have blamed you.*
>
> *But you know not what I was saying, so you blame me. . . .*
> *And I know that you are ignorant, so I forgive you.*

Al-Rashid Hotel, Baghdad, May 23

Massud must be the only punctual man in all of Iraq, Marie thought as he pulled up bright and early in his white SUV. They greeted each other, and she gave him a cardboard container of tea from the hotel café.

"I was wondering last night, Massud, where do you live?" Marie asked as the SUV nosed into the busy Baghdad traffic. "With your family?"

"Ah yes, miss. I live with relatives."

"Are you married?" she asked. She felt bad that she hadn't asked him about his life before now.

"No, miss. I am not married. I have not been so fortunate. Not yet at least. I hope soon to earn enough money for a wife."

"A man like you will have no trouble finding a suitable woman," said Marie. She passed him a piece of paper with the address written on it.

"Yes, this is what you told me last night. It is not too far."

Massud drove through the city like a herder through old goat paths. He knew all the back routes and shortcuts, seeming to know how to push the traffic out of his way even as he was part of it. It was occasionally hair-raising. At times they splashed through ponds of raw sewage. Sometimes they came across dozens of people milling about on the streets, looking at Massud and Marie as if they'd intruded into a private lawn party. They let the SUV pass only reluctantly. And then there were animals and carts, not to mention the concrete barriers that were the bane of all drivers in Baghdad. If there was a complete roadblock, it meant backing out, some streets being too narrow to allow for even a U-turn.

Marie had great confidence in Massud. He knew the city well. They passed a school yard and what appeared to be a hospital, then rounded the corner to approach a slightly larger, paved road. As Massud slowed to turn onto it, Marie heard a thunderous volley of gunfire from the left. The vehicle jumped as if hit by a train. The gunfire came from a vehicle that had come up beside them on Massud's side. She ducked and grabbed her door handle to open it, but she was thrown onto the floor by what felt like a collision.

The car was still for a moment and the door finally opened. She saw a man directly in front of her. He leaned into the car and grabbed her arm. She tried to pull away from him, kicking out with her legs. She looked back at Massud.

She screamed. Massud was covered with blood and slumped away from her toward his door. Two more men in ski masks dragged him from the car. Marie heard herself screaming at the top of her lungs. "What are you doing?" over and over, her body filled with rage, as she hit the arms and chest of the man trying to lead her away. Another man pinned her arms behind her, and they hustled her away from the car into the back seat of a black SUV. Their grip on her was too strong to break, even though she tried, twice, twisting and kicking, using her weight.

A man sat on either side of Marie and two in front. They tied her hands in front of her. Someone tossed a sack over her head before the truck took off, tires spinning on the hot pavement, shooting gravel. She wondered where they'd put Massud, and whether he was alive. Her heart was pounding so hard it hurt. She tried to breathe because she didn't want to hyperventilate. She tried to calm herself down so she could think. Hysteria would not serve her well.

The best she could do, she thought, was to record and remember everything. The men were quiet; they didn't hit her or taunt her. After a few minutes, the guard to her left replaced the cloth over her head with a white blindfold, a change she didn't mind, because the air under the bag was getting old and she was afraid she might faint from lack of oxygen. But as soon as the white blindfold was on, her mind went suddenly to the gruesome television images of hostage beheadings. They were blindfolded in white cloths, too.

The car screeched along at breakneck speed, and she kept going over in her mind the first moments of the attack. She'd heard a volley of gunfire, and the car bounced forward and to the right. She wondered how it was that she didn't get hit. Could all of those bullets have gone into poor Massud? She thought of his sweet smile and the shy nod he made before speaking. Tears welled up in her eyes and were immediately absorbed into her soft blindfold. Why aren't these guys talking? she asked herself. Are they that well organized? Maybe they're afraid I know Arabic. They seemed to be wearing some kind of stiff uniforms, from the way they felt when they carried her.

Then she thought of Obaidi. She imagined him shooting his fancy monogrammed cuffs and glancing impatiently at his watch. What would be going through his head? But what if he was the one who had engineered this? That didn't make sense. Why would he kidnap her as she was headed to meet him? She took a deep breath.

The drive was long. She sat alert, listening. The men rarely broke their silence. Occasionally, she heard them pass a water bottle around, and she took a swig. She sensed one or another doze off from time to time, and she casually wondered whether she should try to reach over, open the door, and throw herself out. She'd get pretty well scraped up, and they'd just jump out and drag her back to worse consequences. If she grabbed at her blindfold, would she be able to get it off? Probably. They weren't tormenting her or roughing her up. But where would she run? Into the arms of even worse assholes, no doubt.

After another forty-five minutes, the car slowed and then stopped. Marie heard the driver speak to someone on his side of the car. The other men stepped out and the one on her right tugged on her arm. She stepped to the ground and ducked so as not to strike her head on the door frame. She felt gravel underfoot. When she stood up she could feel that it was very hot. There was no breeze, so she figured they weren't close to a river. She heard quite a bit of talking now. The man leading her indicated with a pull on her elbow that she was to follow him. She resisted and stood still.

"Why are you holding me?" she asked.

She heard more talking. The man pulled her by the elbow again.

"You are a prisoner of Saddam's Revolutionary Guard," said a voice, speaking English fairly well.

"And why am I a prisoner?" she asked.

More murmuring. Then the same man's voice again. "We're not privileged to know this level of answer. Our orders were to get you and bring you here."

"Where's here?" asked Marie.

The men laughed. They seemed to be joking with each other.

Then the same voice: "Don't worry. This is nowhere."

Karada District, Baghdad, May 23

Mansour Obaidi glanced at his watch exactly as Marie had imagined he would. He couldn't think why the girl would be so late—almost an hour—unless there had been an accident of some kind. Obaidi summoned his assistant. When he entered the room, Obaidi told him to place a call to the Baquba Car Service Company. He remembered that Marie had contracted with this company—his company, actually—for her driver and translator, Massud. He asked his assistant to inquire whether Massud had gone out with Marie Peterssen that morning.

The news, when it came back ten minutes later, jolted him. His face grew red and he stood up, arms shaking. Baathists attacked the car? A car from his transportation company? Were they out of their minds? They knew they weren't supposed to touch his cars. What an outrage. And where was the girl? No one knew yet. A search was being conducted. Obaidi paced the length of the living room.

"Get me General Mustafa al-Rassim on the telephone," he barked to his assistant, who bowed and walked backward out of the room. A few seconds later, he returned with a portable phone.

Obaidi spoke into it, a long stream of flowery invective. He didn't ask a single question. He let al-Rassim know in no uncertain terms that the girl was to be brought unharmed to him in the shortest time possible. He would provide an address as soon as al-Rassim had the girl in his custody. Obaidi would wait by the telephone. And then he hung up without waiting for a reply. Nobody disobeyed Mansour Obaidi.

Karbala District, Baghdad, May 23

Julian stood in the living room of the rented house, staring at a fifteen-inch black-and-white television sitting atop a greenish coffee table. Al-Jazeera was on and broadcasting an announcement that the Iraqi government had named a new minister of trade to replace Rassan Bagdadi, who had been assassinated by a car bomb a month earlier.

The new minister was Mansour Obaidi. He was described as a wealthy businessman with interests in Europe and Iraq, spanning the industries of electronics, agriculture, and energy. The appointee had previously been involved in the marketing of oil under the UN-administered oil-for-food program. Al-Jazeera reported that the appointment was approved by the Americans, as Obaidi had proved to be a reliable and able facilitator.

"Will you look at that," Julian said, hands on his hips. Gil appeared quietly at his side.

"Now he's untouchable," said Julian, shaking his head.

"What do you mean?" asked Gil.

"Now this mass murderer is a member of the international cast. And he just acquired free passage for his next attacks on the West. He basically just won a ticket to bypass the security systems. His containers will go unchecked through the ports."

Gil scratched his head. "If he's sending explosives to the U.S.," he said, "you can be sure he's carefully disguised the companies sending the steel. Look at him! He's moving up in the Iraqi government. He's got big plans for himself. And he won't jeopardize them by being careless now. There'll be so many layers of documents over that shipment that the cargo will never be traceable to him. Anyway, this confirms our suspicions that the ship or ships are already at sea. He wouldn't have accepted the job until the cargo had departed."

"Shit! Shit!" Julian hissed. Then he turned silent for several moments. "Yes," he finally said, "the ships have most certainly set sail. But how long ago?"

Julian stood up and paced the room. His thick, muscular body always seemed heavy from accumulated experience. Today, he moved like a man carrying a great burden.

"I think Mr. Obaidi needs a little kick," said Julian, stopping and turning toward Gil. "His joyride has gone on long enough. We have to knock him off balance. I think a telephone call to our old friend at CNN is in order."

Chapter Sixteen

Morgan walked out of his trailer to an army Humvee. He looked at the driver and grinned. "Black Jack, you son of a bitch, where've you been keeping yourself?"

"Hey," said Dennehy. "How you doin'? Eatin' well? Consortin' with the beautiful local ladies? Made your first million yet?"

Morgan laughed.

"Well, looks like you've taken some of my advice. That mustachio. Wooo! You could have been a double for one of Saddam's psycho sons. Too bad you missed out on the timing. Could have been the job opportunity of a lifetime."

Morgan tapped the dash. "Okay, my friend, let's go."

"Where you headed?" asked Dennehy. "Nobody tells me anything. You know, they're whispering to each other, 'Don't tell the dumb hillbilly nothing he don't know already.'"

Morgan laughed again. "It's hard to stay grim around you, I'll say that. I need to go to the British embassy."

"Righto then, we're off to London," said Dennehy. It was a short drive.

"Want me to wait?" he asked once they'd arrived.

"I'll just be a few minutes," said Morgan, stepping from the vehicle.

"I'll be right here," said Dennehy, pointing to a nearby parking lot.

"Roger that."

Morgan walked up the front steps and into the building. He announced he had an appointment with the MI6 station chief. He showed his ID and clearance, and after a whispered phone call he was escorted through the marble halls to a large reception area, where he saw the FBI legal attaché, Richard Attanasio, sitting in a chair. He put out his hand. Attanasio rose.

"Hey, thank you for coming over," Morgan said. "I really appreciate it."

"No problem."

"Is the station chief in?" asked Morgan.

Attanasio nodded and looked toward the receptionist. Morgan had told him he needed to see MI6.

"Mr. Armstrong will be right with you."

The two men stood, their impatience radiating tension that was out of proportion to their actual size, typical of Western men standing together, awaiting entrance.

Within a minute, Jack Armstrong, a man of medium build with a retiring demeanor but fiercely intelligent eyes, emerged from the office. "Ah, yes, Mr. Ensley and Mr. Attanasio," he said. "So glad you could drop by."

Armstrong gestured toward his office. The Americans preceded him inside. The office was furnished, astonishingly, in British colonial style: rattan and teak; linen curtains on the windows. The three men sat. A secretary set a tray holding glass tumblers and a pitcher of ice water on the table before them.

"I'm going to get right to the point," said Morgan. "We don't have much time."

"By all means," said Armstrong from the depths of his armchair. "What seems to be the trouble?"

"We've come to believe that certain terrorist elements are attempting to ship explosives out of Iraq in containers carrying scrap steel. We have actionable intelligence, though no shipping dates or specific information about which ports will be used. We need you to be on the lookout for the odd ship in the ports of Basra or Umm Qasr that may be on-loading material, particularly steel." The British controlled those two ports.

Armstrong walked to the window and looked out at a huge presidential palace, one of seventy or eighty such palaces scattered through Iraq. This one was now the center of the American presence in Baghdad. "Container traffic leaving Iraq? Shouldn't think there's much of that," he said. "Quite a bit coming in, though. All the same, I'll ask the harbormasters to keep an eye out. Never know what will turn up." Then he brightened. "Have you asked the Jordanians? If I were salvaging steel in western Iraq, Aqaba is the place I'd go. Speak with a Captain Abu Daloo there. Good man."

Morgan and Attanasio stood up. Morgan thanked him and handed him a card with a Thuraya satellite phone number scribbled on the back. "If you uncover anything that seems relevant, please call me."

Armstrong nodded and showed them to the door. "Good of you to involve us. Do everything we can, of course."

"That was interesting," said Morgan once they were outside Armstrong's office.

Attanasio nodded.

"Of course Aqaba would be the logical place to ship steel, especially if it was collected in western Iraq," said Morgan, remembering that Julian had already mentioned it.

"The British are good when it comes to former protectorates," said Attanasio. "You want me to send any ECs?"

"No," said Morgan. "Paperwork to follow. I've got some things to do first."

Tel Aviv, May 24

Shimshon Ashkenazy walked out of his cubicle. His curls hung down past his shoulders, and his long skinny frame, now unfolded, looked as if it needed to be pressed. He rubbed his eyes on entering the glare of the outer office, so accustomed was he to the dim light he preferred.

Nadav wasn't in his office but arrived soon, with a pizza box in his hand. Shimshon flashed him a sweet, mischievous smile. They could have been brothers with their Botticelli curls—Nadav's blond and Shimshon's dark brown—but Nadav was muscular and straight, and Shimshon skinny and stooped, his back rounded from days and nights peering into the computer throughout his formative years.

"Aw, Shimshon, I'm starving," said Nadav. Then with one rueful glance at his lunch, he slipped half the pie onto an extra plate and handed it to his younger colleague.

Shimshon devoured the food in a few hungry teenage bites. They shared a Coke, and Shimshon said, "I thought I'd come over and talk to you rather than send an e-mail," their normal form of back-and-forth. The twenty-first-century equivalent of shouting from room to room, the words tapped all but silently instead, the sounds all interior.

Nadav opened his eyes wide. "You, Shimshon, are actually seeking human contact?"

"It's a bit odd, I know," said Shimshon.

"What happened, they change your chip?" asked Nadav.

"Very funny. Maybe I just wanted to see if Sarah Berendt was around."

Nadav feigned astonishment. "I didn't know you had it in you," he said. "Well, good luck. She might appear, but generally she's as stuck to her chair as you are."

"There's always hope," said Shimshon.

"So what's up?" asked Nadav.

"Do you remember I told you I was alerted to a message left a few months ago on a hacker bulletin board asking for help getting into the major fiber-optic hub in New York?"

Nadav nodded.

"The person posting the note," Shimshon continued, "left an address from a Hotmail account. I traced the account and looked at the e-mails sent from it. In the early days, three months or so ago, he used an anonymizer."

"A what?" asked Nadav.

"Something to hide the identity of the computer sending his e-mails. Then he got lazy and stopped trying. Turns out he's accessing the Internet from a DSL provider in Paterson, New Jersey. That's how I found his address: 41 Remson Street.

"But then I did something else," Shimshon added with a smile. "I broke into the guy's computer and I read all his e-mails. I found out that someone had answered his post on the bulletin board and had helped him plant a Trojan horse in a computer of the Tunnel. The hacker was paid six thousand dollars. I've been keeping watch on the guy in Paterson, and this morning he tried to get in through his back door, but couldn't. Some security person at the Tunnel found and removed it. Now Paterson doesn't know how to get back in. The first hacker who helped him is no longer answering his e-mails. So I contacted Mr. Paterson myself, said I heard he needed some help. I anonymized the e-mail from a machine that I set up myself, so when he probed and pinged me, he would have no idea where I was. He did all that, as I expected. He's not very talented, but he does know a few things.

"So now I need direction. Shall I be his partner, so I can lead him wherever we want to lead him? Or should I withdraw and just watch him, set up a system to record all his keystrokes, so I know everything he's up to?"

Nadav nodded. "Good questions. I'll have to ask Julian. In the meantime, do both. Keep capturing the keystrokes, and let me know if anything interesting happens. Don't lose touch with Mr. Paterson. Lead him on for a day or so."

"Okay," said Shimshon, standing up. "I suppose this is none of my business, but shouldn't we inform the Americans?"

"In any sensible world, we should. But the FBI doesn't want to hear from us. They don't trust foreign intelligence gathering. If you want to get information to them, you have to go through informal channels. Julian's probably trying to do that."

Shimshon rose out of the chair, shaking his head. "Information is useful. More information is better. I don't get it." Nadav waved him away and he walked down the hall to his cubicle and the blinking computer screen through which he could—and did—travel anywhere on earth.

Green Zone, Baghdad, May 24

Morgan walked into his boss's office. Morgan hated to call anyone his "boss." Especially a potted plant like Gordon Hart. So he thought of Hart as his "supervisor." Even that seemed too good for him. Hart was reading reports at his desk, his face its customary florid pink, his blazer neatly folded on the back of a chair.

"Sir," said Morgan at the door.

Hart looked up. "Oh, Morgan. Come in, come in."

"We need to send an immediate NCIC alert. I believe a ship filled with explosives is headed for one of our ports on the eastern seaboard. Probably New York–New Jersey."

Hart sat back in his seat. "Well, where's your paperwork?" he said. "I haven't seen anything come over my desk about anything like this, no threat reports, nothing."

Morgan looked shocked. "I've sent you reports, sir, every step of the way. You know that sea containers full of scrap metal are being filled in Rutba. Some of them are American and most likely being put on return boats. I've uncovered evidence of weapons collection at the same site. And I included documentation from an interrogation at Sahir Prison that a leader of foreign fighters is financing a sea-bound terror operation."

"Morgan, to send out an alert through the National Crime Information Center, I need paper. The strength of the Bureau lies in its paper trail."

"Sir," said Morgan, exasperated. "I believe I've already made my case. An Israeli counterterror expert supports my conclusions and has added further information."

"Is this source documented?" asked Hart, sitting up and peering over his glasses. "Have you opened a file on him?"

Morgan was disgusted with himself for having brought it up. Of course Hart would jump on this technicality and fail to see the big picture. "With all due respect, sir, I've been in the field interrogating suspects and following up leads. We have a major situation here that requires action. I believe America is threatened with another catastrophic attack. Most likely to the country's third-largest port.

"I've sent a summary of my findings to Washington as part of a wiretap request. All that paper has gone across your desk. Included in it is information that someone in Paterson, New Jersey, is trying to break into a main telephone switching station in New York City. If that hub goes down, communications up and down the eastern seaboard could be disrupted or destroyed. If that communications blackout takes place at the same time as an attack on a port, I'm sure you'd have no trouble imagining the consequences. Sir."

"Morgan, I need the paperwork. You may have a great case, or you may be leading me down a rabbit hole. I'm happy to consider your request if you send me a lead on it. I need an EC."

Morgan stood up. "Again, sir, with all due respect," he said, his face reddening. "The clock is ticking. There's no time for typing."

Hart turned his back to Morgan and picked up a paper on his desk. Morgan was furious. He had to use all his self-control not to grab Hart's shirt and slam him into the wall. What an ass! He would rather piss in his pants than make a decision, a decision to do anything other than nothing.

"With all due respect, Morgan," said Hart, in a tone that made Morgan suddenly appreciate the concept of frontier justice. He forced his hands into fists by his sides. "In this company, if you want somebody in another office to help you, the standard operating procedure is to put a request in writing, so they can justify the time they'd spend on it."

"Mr. Hart," said Morgan, his jaw set, the muscles around his eyes tensed, "we are way beyond standard operating procedure. You know as well as I do that written requests can sit for days and not be answered. This boat or boats must be stopped before they get near American shores. Even if we're wrong, it's the right thing to do."

Hart looked back down at his desk and rustled some papers. He turned away from Morgan, who, incensed, walked out of the office. Morgan was doing everything he could not to shout. He stopped at his office to pick up his helmet and flak jacket. He'd go around his supervisor and get that NCIC alert sent out from the legat's office. That would alert the coast guard, customs, and the entire Homeland Security apparatus to the threat. Screw Hart! What was he waiting for, Osama bin Laden to show up with a container of popcorn and a schedule for Turner Classic TV?

Morgan opened the door of his SUV. He wasn't supposed to drive without an escort and a security detail, and he'd been reprimanded the day before when he was spotted driving solo. But screw that, too. He looked up as a small commuter plane took off from the airport. It ascended in a spooky spiral to gain altitude. None of the planes took off or landed with the usual long straight approaches. Too many missiles in the wrong hands. The planes remained within the airspace that could be protected from the ground, a relatively small area of the entire airport. Planes landing were quite the sight too, dropping out of the sky and corkscrewing down to the tarmac.

Morgan buckled on his jacket and his helmet and started up the SUV's engine. He wasn't going to wait for a convoy. He said three Hail Marys and put the car in gear. Hell, he hadn't said a Hail Mary since he was a kid leaving confession. He barreled off through the exit.

He knew that if he asked his colleagues what he should do, they'd all tell him it wasn't worth trying to be a hero, because he'd pay for it later, that he'd better not go outside the line of command, better wait and send the paper. But he couldn't do that. He had to do whatever it took, even if he'd pay for it. And what was a little bureaucratic hassle compared to the damage of doing nothing? What Julian had told him and Marie about preventing terrorist attacks seemed right. So maybe he'd fall on his sword. Fine. He'd get another job. At least he'd be able to sleep at night.

Paterson, New Jersey, May 24

The FBI men wore silky shirts and dress slacks with snakeskin belts. They sat in a white Nissan Maxima, talking. They both had black hair and olive skin. They ate sunflower seeds and drank Cokes while they kept their eyes trained on 41 Remson Street, a two-story clapboard house with a balcony and a pillared porch downstairs.

"There's Red again," said one, Joseph, nodding toward a man in his twenties with light skin and red hair emerging from the front door and walking down the street. "He's been in and out a couple times today."

"Looks Lebanese," said the other, Eddie. "What do you think, with that red hair?"

"Maybe."

"You taking pictures?"

"Yup."

"Got film in the camera?"

"Shut up."

"When are the guys coming to relieve us?"

"Soon. At eight a.m. Ten more minutes."

"Great."

"You write up the report last night of what we saw?"

"I'll do it today as soon as we get back."

"You better stay up on it. HQ is in on this case. Put a priority on it."

"I know, I know. I'll do it, don't worry."

"Don't piss them off on this. They'll have your head."

"Don't worry about it. It's as good as done. Okay, I see our replacements. They're coming up the north side of the street. They just slowed down now and they're parking. Let's head on back."

The agent in the driver's seat started up the engine and put the car in gear. "Get rid of these shells, will you?" He tried to pass his partner a handful of sunflower husks.

"Get rid of your own shells."

The driver opened his door and dropped the seeds beside the curb, slammed the door shut, and pulled the car out into the street.

Unknown Location near Baghdad, May 24

Marie sat on a broken, scratchy couch. It had been twenty-four hours since she was kidnapped. As far as she could tell, there was a man in the room with her. She could hear him shift in his seat, and she occasionally heard the sound of paper, as if he were turning the pages of a book. A literate kidnapper, she thought, how charming. She tried talking with him from time to time, but although he was quick to bring her anything she needed, such as food, water, or tissues, he would not engage her in any kind of conversation.

There was an air conditioner, hooked up to a noisy generator that seemed to be out back of the room. She thought there were two windows, each a regular sash that lifted up and down. She sensed that the adjoining room was a living room of some kind, with a kitchen beyond that. It seemed that her room stuck out into the yard and was attached to the house on only one wall.

She'd been brought here last night. Her kidnappers didn't harass her; in fact, they were disciplined and well behaved. They seemed to be waiting for orders about how to dispose of her. They cooked and ate a meal together, and brought her a plate of food. Her hands were kept tied, but loosened when they brought her something to eat or led her to the bathroom. She determined that there was a small window there, something she reminded herself to investigate further the next time it was possible.

She dozed off for a while on the couch, then awoke with a jolt, in her dreams seeing Massud getting shot again, blood everywhere, the loud pummeling of the bullets, the car screeching to a halt. She couldn't open her eyes because her blindfold was too tight, but she realized she was breathing hard and her heart was beating against her ribs. Sweat broke out on her forehead and under her arms. She put her head back against the cushions and breathed deeply. A wave of nausea hit her.

She remained awake. Every hour, the guard watching her was replaced with another. Nobody seemed to leave or enter the house. Occasionally, she heard the television droning in Arabic.

Green Zone, Baghdad, May 24

The soldiers at the checkpoint looked over Morgan's
tags and waved him in. He continued to the American embassy and
prayed to God—again—that the legat was free. He waited impatiently
to get through security and then ran up the stairs to the FBI office. He
looked expectantly at the secretary and she nodded. Attanasio was there.
The secretary buzzed the intercom and waved Morgan in.

Attanasio was standing in front of the television. He turned to Morgan and said, "Looks like your friend Obaidi here is moving on up the
ladder." Morgan turned toward the television, almost not comprehend-
ing, as he listened to a repetition of the news that Obaidi had been
named trade minister.

Morgan looked at Attanasio and back to the television. "I believe this
guy is a terrorist," he said. "I think he wants to blow up an American
port." Morgan paced the room, then turned to look at Attanasio again. "I
don't have that much experience as an investigator. I admit that. But I've
learned so much in the last few days that my head is spinning. And
my instincts tell me that something real bad is going down." Attanasio
started to say something, but Morgan stopped him with a raised finger.
"I came over here to send an immediate NCIC alert to customs, the
coast guard, the navy, and the FBI. I think a ship is on its way with containers full of explosives. I tried to get Hart's attention on the matter,
and he couldn't rouse himself from his paperwork. He told me to send
him paper. I could send him paper until the ships blew up at his door,
and he still wouldn't move his ass."

"You told him that?"

"Not exactly."

"I read your alerts about the Tunnel and the reports you wrote about
the scrap and weapons collection in Rutba," said Attanasio. "If you're

only halfway right, we're in deep shit. I'll send out the alerts you requested, and I'll place a call to a friend of mine at the coast guard in
New York. Any ships heading for New York ports have to get by him
first." Attanasio sat down at his computer.

"But let me advise you about something, Morgan. Cover your ass
and do the paperwork now. Just litter your boss with the paper he wants.
Otherwise, you're going to pay later for doing the right thing here. You
were right to come to me to get this out. Now go back and make sure the
paper trail is on your side."

Karbala District, Baghdad, May 24

"Use the girl," said Gil.

"What did you say?" Julian asked.

"Send her out to Obaidi. Let her lure him somewhere, and then we'll
blow the place up."

"What good would that do?"

"We'd be rid of the bastard."

"We'd also lose any chance to get information out of him."

"So we surround the place and grab him."

"I won't do that," said Julian.

"Why not?"

"Obaidi would take her hostage."

Gil looked at Julian in surprise. "What's going on with you? You're in
the middle of an operation. The target's in your sights."

"I know," said Julian. "But I can't do it that way. Not this time."

Gil looked at him for a long ten seconds. "Maybe your retirement
was the best thing. You've lost it."

"Who the hell are you to tell me how to run an operation?" said Julian, barely controlling his anger. "I taught you everything you know. But
I will not sacrifice the girl."

Gil stood his ground. "She's not one of us."

"She had no orders to come here and risk her life. She did it out of
free will."

"She did it out of ambition," said Gil.

"So what?" said Julian. "She was motivated by ambition and curiosity. Better reasons than we find in most people, no? She would never have been put in this situation if it hadn't been for me. She's a free woman, and she made a choice, and continues to make that choice every day she remains on the job, to risk her life for the operation. For what reward? A newspaper article? It's more than that." Agitated, Julian stood up and began to pace the room, running his hands in his hair.

"We'll lose him," said Gil. "And he'll continue his murderous rampage."

"If we can't find another way to get to Obaidi," Julian continued, "then I'll let him go. I'll let the Germans get him, or the Jordanians. They should have all they need to charge him with the aviation crashes now. Wegener did phone searches on the night before the first crash—the night of the so-called audit at Hajaera's—and found a web of calls between the Broadhurst shop and terror cells in London." He walked over to the kitchen cabinet and pulled out a bottle of Wild Turkey with two glasses.

"Help me figure out another way of flushing Obaidi out. If you're not interested, I'll do it myself."

"You're making a mistake, Julie," said Gil, taking a glass. "You're doing the same thing Ari did. You're letting your emotions get in the way."

"Well maybe Ari was right. Maybe finding the woman he loved was what he should have been doing when he was twenty-six years old, rather than hunting down terrorists and bomb makers. If he'd been able to live his life rather than rise to the constant demands of war and killing, then maybe he'd have something to show for it now."

"Ach, Julie," said Gil.

"Do you ever think about what you could have accomplished if you'd become a university professor or an archaeologist or a doctor instead of learning how to infiltrate and reconnoiter and kill?" Julian asked Gil.

"Remember what Bismarck said about settling the great questions of the day not with speeches and majority decisions, but with 'blood and iron.' Hasn't our own history borne him out?"

Julian swallowed a mouthful of whiskey. "I had a quick talk with my oldest son today on the telephone. He started this month training with the Navy SEALs, and he called to tell me that he passed his first dive. He was very excited, very happy. He's a great kid, a brave boy, and I'm sure if he's able to pass all the tests, he'll be a great Special Forces commando. But why?"

A long silence followed, broken finally by Gil. "Julian, tell me, are you in love with her?"

"In love with who?"

"Don't play games with me."

"How could I be? She is most likely Ari's daughter. That means she's almost my own daughter."

"You haven't answered my question," said Gil.

Julian was silent.

"Are you going to tell her that Ari was probably her father?"

"I don't have the heart."

"Better to know than to torture herself about whether it's the other one, no?"

"Well, it's served our purposes for her to wonder, hasn't it?" said Julian angrily, his face reddening, slamming his hand on the table and standing up. He walked across the room to the barred window. "And you criticize me for going soft."

After a quiet moment, Gil asked, "So why all this second-guessing?"

"I'm too old for this. I'm just thinking. Here I am playing with a brave, bright young woman who is prepared to put her life on the line for us because she had something to prove to herself. But since she's not an agent of ours, according to our protocol, she's expendable. More than that, she could be the daughter of one of our own comrades. Ari's daughter, of all people.

"And what if she weren't anybody's daughter, what if this bizarre collision of ghosts hadn't happened and she was just a bright, brave young woman who volunteered to help us out? Is it any less wrong to put her in harm's way?"

"Of course not," said Gil.

"Good," said Julian. "I knew you'd come around. I've been working up an operation."

Julian returned to the table and sat. Gil felt anticipation issuing from him like heat. Julian was a master plotter.

"I've already taken the first steps in putting it into action," Julian said. He reached for a piece of paper and sketched out three rectangles, three circles just below them, and a triangle in the middle. Gil refreshed the glasses. By the time the sun came up, the bottle was finished, and they'd completed their work.

Unknown Location near Baghdad, May 24

Marie's legs were cramping from hours of sitting on the couch, so she got up and began to stretch. Nobody knocked or asked her what she was up to, so she continued, then realized that the guard had left the room. She pulled off her blindfold. She looked around, squinting from the light. Two windows, the room jutting into the backyard, one door to the rest of the house. Her imagination had not been far off. She walked over to see if the windows opened. They did. No screens. She heard a noise outside and pulled her blindfold back on and slipped back to the couch. Not a minute later, the door opened and one of her captors returned with a plate of food.

He placed it into her hands on her lap and left. As soon as she heard him leave, she put the plate down on the coffee table and pulled off the blindfold again. Her guard had left the book he was reading on his chair. It was a copy of Hemingway's *Islands in the Stream.* How odd. She looked out the window, taking care not to be seen. She seemed to be in a semirural area. There were some goats and chicken outside. A road ran in front of the house, and she saw other houses nearby.

She heard footsteps again. She pulled on her blindfold, fixed her hair around it, and returned to her seat. Three men arrived.

"Don't like your food?" one asked.

"Not hungry," she said. Then two men took her by the elbows. They stood her up and walked with her out of the room.

"Where are we going?" she asked the man holding her left arm.

"There have been some developments," he said.

"Good ones or bad ones?" she asked.

"For who?"

"For me."

"You'll see," he said. "We're going back into the car. So please step up and lower your head." He placed his hand on her head to keep her from bumping it on the car door, just like cops do with criminals on TV, she thought to herself. It was reassuring in an odd, really messed-up way.

Tel Aviv, May 24

Shimshon Ashkenazy watched the keystrokes. He was following every letter that the young man in Paterson, New Jersey, typed into his computer, and he didn't like what he saw. He realized that the Paterson man, whose name was Ibrahim al-Amar, was typing "traceroute" and "show ip route" and "show config" commands to review the configuration of the routers in the Tunnel. Shimshon figured that al-Amar was trying to identify the physical location of a group of computers.

At first, Shimshon couldn't figure out what al-Amar was up to; then it dawned on him that he might be trying to develop a backup plan. In case he failed to get back into the system electronically, he was trying to locate the computers physically. What did he have in mind, Shimshon wondered, sabotage by fire or water? There were so many options. He had to keep close watch. What about a big truck full of explosives, like in Oklahoma City?

In a perfect world, Shimshon would be listening to al-Amar's telephone conversations. Was he calling a secretary or worker at the Tunnel and trying to social-engineer her? If so, what information did he want? He knew the FBI had a telephone tap on. He'd asked Julian if he could have access to the tapes. And Julian had told him no. No way. A million FBI reasons why not. No way would they share information. That was so stupid! How could they properly interpret the telephone intercepts if they couldn't see what the guy was doing on his computer?

Shimshon told Julian that if that's how the Americans were going to play, they had better batten down the hatches at the Tunnel because it looked like someone was planning to come at it with something more than great interest.

Baghdad, May 24

Mansour Obaidi sat at an ornate Louis Quinze–style desk in the library of the same house in which he had arranged to meet Marie the previous day, repeatedly tapping a letter opener on its marble top. He stared off into the middle distance, thinking. His attempts to locate her captors had proved fruitless; calls to local Sunni and al Qaeda commanders, also former Baathists and Revolutionary Guardsmen, brought nothing. No groups had claimed responsibility for the capture of an American journalist.

Obaidi wondered just how much the girl knew about him. It was too unlikely a coincidence that she would show up in Iraq looking for him just after writing a story about the electronics repair shop in London. Who was controlling her?

And what about that devilish distraction that had tormented him since he'd met with her? For some reason he couldn't quite put his finger on, she reminded him powerfully of the dancer he'd known in Madrid so many years ago. He thought about the moment he first saw Jeanne Mercier. He'd wandered into the theater one evening, bought a ticket, and sat down to a performance of a ballet called *La Bayadère*. Of course it was entirely blasphemous and based on a Hindu story. But he'd caught sight of that lovely creature, Jeanne Mercier, performing the role of the doomed temple dancer, Nikiya. He saw her at a café later and she drew him into her circle of friends.

He thought back to Nikiya's famous third act, the performance that made Mercier famous. It takes place in the Kingdom of the Shades when Nikiya dances in the dreams of the lover who betrayed her. Jeanne danced like a soul in heaven, effortlessly clear in her virtue and pureness of heart. She was light as air, delicate and supple. And he had fallen for her instantly, hopelessly, unfathomably. But things had gone wrong. Obaidi felt the anger rise in him.

And what had happened to the gang of them there? How many were now dancing or burning in the Kingdom of the Shades themselves? At least one other. The Jew in Madrid. And he, Obaidi, had sent him there.

It seemed so far away now, but it had been the start of everything. That killing had sent him off to Bulgaria, and it was there, in hiding, that he'd refined his ideas, built his plans. The Muslim movement needed a leader with independent financial means. Charity alone could not finance ambitious plans to restore Islam to its rightful place in history. Self-sufficiency was a value that he had absorbed in the airless, Soviet-strangled Bulgaria. The black marketeers ran their own microeconomy, had their own GNP, working entirely outside of the government.

He realized that this was a great lesson for the Islamists. They needed to set up a fifth column. He would have to finance his own revolution, and he would do so with his own skills and savvy. And he had done exactly that.

But where was Jeanne? And was this girl her daughter? If so, who was the girl's father? He hadn't even had time to discover her age. They'd only begun their conversation before they were interrupted by the mortar attack. That moronic firebrand cleric, firing off mortars in every direction. Idiocy clearly didn't respect religious boundaries.

Obaidi began to pace the room. His thoughts turned back to Madrid, to that evening when after many hours of food and talk, deep talk, he had walked Jeanne back to her apartment. He had anticipated that moment for months, and thought again and again about what he would do if he ever got the chance to be with her alone. She was so exquisite but at the same time warm and accessible. He wasn't uncomfortable around her as he was around other women. Being with her was like a dream or a dance, her dance, Nikiya among the shades. Up the stairs to her apartment, just inside the door, she teased him, kissed him, slipped her hands under his shirt and placed those exquisite fingers on his bare skin. On him.

Later, after she told him it was time to go, he walked slowly down the stone steps. But he was light-headed and not ready to leave that place. He pulled himself into the entryway of a building across the street to calm down. He sat and watched the light from her window and her shadow pass behind the curtain. He ran over and over in his mind what had taken place. He was filled with joy and gratitude and fell into an intense reverie, reviewing their entanglements while murmuring prayers to Allah. He prayed fervently for several minutes before he was distracted by the sound of footfalls. He looked up and he saw that man, the tall one with black hair, walking toward him. The Zionist.

At first, he couldn't believe it. Hassan, the only name by which Jeanne knew Obaidi, pulled himself back into the shadows and watched Ari Schiffrin turn into Jeanne's entryway and bound up the stairs, two at a time. He was going to her! And then the humiliation started, the humiliation that was like oxygen to the flames of his shame and degradation. The fury that had risen up years earlier in prison, that he'd batted down time after time out of a sense of self-preservation, now rose in full strength. It was then he became determined to kill the Jew. And he would do so where his whore would find the body. Then maybe she'd appreciate the depth of his passion.

U.S. Military Firing Range, Eastern Baghdad, May 24

"Ensley? He's out at the army firing range," said Hart when Comstock came looking for him. The range was just east of Baghdad, where the low-slung sand-colored houses and sheds gave way to the empty expanses of the Iraqi desert. Comstock caught a ride with a convoy of vehicles.

The vast, dusty field was fenced in by coils of concertina wire supported by wooden posts ten feet high. Just inside the gate was a small guardhouse. Beyond was a row of sandbags about a hundred yards from the entrance and after that, targets at varying distances.

He heard no gunfire and couldn't see Ensley. He walked into the hut and inquired. The guard pointed downfield to the east. "There's a guy way down there doing some damn thing."

Comstock squinted into the sun and dust and could barely make out a figure. He hiked down along the wire fence and after three hundred yards he saw Ensley looking through the scope of a .50-caliber sniper rifle, then typing away on a laptop. As Comstock approached, Morgan continued going back and forth, scope to laptop, not taking a shot.

"What the fuck're you doing, dude?"

Morgan didn't look up. "Checking the weather," he said, again scrutinizing the scope and going back to the laptop. Comstock watched this for another minute and pulled out some chaw. He stuck a wad in his cheek.

"Now there's a disgusting habit," said Morgan after Comstock spit a stream of brown juice into the dirt. "You HRT types just like the way it puffs out your lips, don't you?"

Comstock ignored the barb. "Checking the weather, you say? There is no weather in the desert. Look around you. It hasn't rained for weeks. There's no wind to speak of." The sun was blazing.

"I'm getting a feel for the weather patterns by looking through the scope at objects at various distances. I'm trying to measure stuff like changes in air density, all the stuff that affects the trajectory of a bullet over various distances. I do this most every day. Keeps me tuned in."

Comstock laughed. "You're full of shit," he said.

Morgan continued to look through the scope and at the laptop, scribbling down a few notes. "What about you?"

"You mean am I full of shit too?"

"No, I mean why are you out here? Aren't there any other hardworking agents you could be spying on?"

"I'm sure there are, but you're the one I'm interested in right now. I have a question for you. Why did I have to learn from Marie Peterssen, a newspaper reporter of all people, about an investigation into some containers of steel that are leaving Iraq for the U.S. of A.? And why did I have to learn—by reading over her shoulder—that she's also running after this lunatic named Mansour Obaidi?"

Morgan looked at Comstock. "Sorry, pal. I'm a little behind on my paperwork." He went back to his measuring.

"You're a complete case, Ensley, you know that? And you're driving me nuts." Comstock picked up a pair of binoculars and looked across the rock-strewn desert. He saw a target way downrange. He leaned over and rustled through Morgan's ammunition box and pulled out a bullet.

"May I?" he asked. He'd show Morgan a thing or two about shooting.

"Wrong weight for today's conditions," said Morgan. "There are a lot of subtle but erratic vertical wind shears today, so you'll need a heavier bullet to maintain its path. And you'll have to give it a little more arc to compensate for lower velocity." He stood up and got out of Comstock's way.

Comstock sneered, popped in his bullet, made some distance estimates, and performed a few adjustments on the scope. When he was ready, he squeezed off a shot.

He stood up and checked the target with the binoculars. The shot was just inside the bull's-eye. "Beat that, Enz. If you can," he said with satisfaction.

Ensley rooted through the ammo box, found a single archaic-looking .50-caliber round, and blew the dust off it. Then he polished the bullet with his bandanna and a little spit. He got into position on the ground, chambered the round, and made his own adjustments. He fired. Comstock looked with the binoculars and saw that Morgan's shot was out toward the edge of the target. He laughed.

"What's so funny?" asked Morgan.

"You suck, that's what's funny," said Comstock.

"Come on over and check through the scope again, squid." Morgan moved aside to make room. "See where it says 'Speer Firearms Products'?"

Comstock could barely see the logo of the manufacturer on the bottom edge of the target.

"If you look real close, you'll see a little bull's-eye next to the manufacturer's name," Morgan said.

"Bullshit."

Morgan dug through his things and pulled out a paper target. He put his finger on the Speer logo. Comstock looked back through the binocs and sure enough, there was the shot.

"Fuck you, Morgan."

"Fuck you, Comstock. Why don't you get off my back?"

"Do you think I like this? Do you think I left the SEALs to join the FBI because I wanted to babysit cowboys like you? Do you think I like following your ass around Baghdad? Fuck no. But the Bureau doesn't know what you're up to. And it's worried. So maybe we oughtta just cut to the chase. Why don't you tell me everything you know about this asshole Obaidi. And then you might explain who the foreign national is you've been visiting in Karbala?"

PART
FOUR

Chapter Seventeen

Mansour Obaidi relaxed in a window seat in the first-class cabin of Air France Flight 26, bound for Washington, D.C. He drank ginger ale and ate the Beluga caviar that the airline was still civilized enough to provide. He dabbed at his mouth with a napkin and adjusted his seat back. His body was taut with anticipation, but it was important for him at least to appear calm. All in all, it had been a satisfactory week. His ship had been at sea for twelve full days, and just about now would be making its northerly turn off the coast of Florida, ready to ride the friendly Gulf Stream waters. Happily, the expected hurricane had been downgraded to a tropical storm.

Four more days before New York would again feel the wrath of Allah. As soon as the *LB Venture* reached Ambrose Light and picked up the American pilot who would steer her to her berth, his throat would be cut. Then Captain Hamid would retake the controls. His orders were to sail the ship past the docks straight toward the petroleum tanks north of the port. He likely wouldn't make it all the way before being stopped by coast guard boats, but no matter. Obaidi would phone in the detonation codes, and with the help of the Almighty, all three triggers would work and the bombs would explode, obliterating the port and Newark airport. A radius of two miles would be leveled; tens of thousands of people would die immediately, some from the sheer force of the explosion, others burned and killed by the nuclear winds. Radioactive material would be spewed into the air and contaminate the ground and water for decades. Depending on the winds, millions in New York City would be in the fallout zone, suffering from radiation poisoning over the weeks and years to come, and leaving lower Manhattan a ghost town as far as Canal Street. Fires would rage and people would begin to die of radiation poisoning within weeks. Obaidi smiled to himself as he thought of the coup de grâce: a communications blackout. People would have helicopter images of the destruction, but no way of contacting loved ones. All emergency workers and first responders would be operating without a centralized command. Then, perhaps, America and her bull-riding president would rethink their determination to humiliate and subjugate Islam.

Obaidi put those thoughts aside for the moment. He was looking forward to his short stay in the American capital. With his new official status as the Iraqi trade minister, he had meetings lined up at the World Bank and the headquarters of the U.S. trade representative and, most important, with his old friend, Vice President Bill Cullum. And not just a meeting, but a meal at the vice-presidential residence, the former naval observatory on Massachusetts Avenue. These meetings would pay off later, when the Americans withdrew from Iraq. That wouldn't be long now. They'd turn to the businessmen they knew best to take over the important political and business roles in the newly independent republic. And Obaidi would be one of them.

He and the vice president knew each other from the United Nations' oil-for-food program, when Cullum was still a lawyer for a French company that brokered sales of Iraqi oil to, among others, two firms in the United States. Obaidi was well aware that a certain percentage of the profits found its way into Cullum's Cayman Islands bank account. But that was business. Who among his associates *didn't* have offshore accounts?

The week's only bad moment was that the Peterssen girl had failed to show up for their meeting in Baghdad. He didn't believe in accidents or coincidences. In his world, everything happened for a reason. In this case, he knew only that she'd been abducted at gunpoint and forced into a car. The vehicle had vanished.

Obaidi wondered what her abductors might know about him. Or might discover by applying a little pressure.

Unknown Location near Baghdad, May 24

Marie was feeling sick. For two hours, the vehicle had been rumbling over rutted roads with tight curves, and her empty stomach was sour. When her captors finally stopped the car, they met another group of men and fell into a heated discussion. Marie's fear was mounting by the minute. She'd been held for about thirty hours, she guessed. Deprived of her sense of sight and bundled from place to place, she was disoriented. How many times had she been forced into a car, pulled out, and then shoved back in? She was past the surprise and shock and now felt she was in the middle of what could be a long and grueling trial.

She thought of Julian, of his strong body and sympathetic face, the eyes that sometimes seemed as if they bore the sadness of the whole world. She wondered where he was, imagined him in his kitchen drinking coffee with Gil, and she started to cry, the tears wetting her cheeks but quickly absorbed by the blindfold, which suddenly afforded her something she was grateful for: privacy.

She thought how alone she was here in Iraq. Massud was probably dead. No one knew where she was or what had happened to her. She wondered how long it would be before Morgan or Julian realized she was gone.

The blindfold was wet and her nose was stuffed. She sniffed a few times, and her guard pulled her aside to stretch her legs, walking beside her along what seemed like a dirt path. Suddenly she stopped. Maybe he wasn't helping her stretch her legs. Maybe he was leading her to her execution. She pulled her arm away from him, and he asked her what was wrong.

"Where are you taking me?" she asked, her voice no longer completely in control.

"Don't worry. We're not going to hurt you." He spoke accented English. She was surprised and grateful for small favors. "I thought you might like to move around before we got back into the car. There are discussions under way about where you are to be taken."

"Who is discussing this?" she asked. "Who is holding me? Who are you?" She wondered if offering a little walkabout was what they did before putting the hostages on the floor in front of the video cameras, green flag with star and crescent on the wall behind them, just before the beheading. It had to be excruciating. And what if the knife wasn't sharp? That had to be one of the worst ways to die. On par with being eaten alive by a wild animal.

"I can't tell you," the guard said. "But don't be frightened. You won't be hurt."

These words did not reassure her. But his tone did, somewhat. So she tried to calm herself. What could she do? Make a break for it? She'd be caught in a second. She was surrounded by guards and she had no idea of the terrain. She'd just have to wait until she had a better chance.

Just then, her minder said it was time to get back into the car, and he handed her off to someone who led her back in. They drove for another two hours, when it occurred to her that they had reentered Baghdad. She recognized the smells and rhythms of the streets. Then she heard the sounds of jet airplanes and wondered if they were taking her to the airport. Her spirits began to lift. The sounds of the planes got louder and louder. The car stopped. The men on either side of her got out, and a moment later another man walked in. He took her arm and she felt a sharp prick.

"What are you doing?" she cried out, pushing him away, kicking him with her legs, and pulling off her blindfold. She saw a man beside her in a white coat with a hypodermic needle in his hands. She pushed him out of the way, jumped out of the car, and ran. Within a few steps, her head got cloudy. She saw she was near an American transport plane, and as the light began to fade, she thought she must be dying because she saw Massud loading her bags into the hold. And then, under its tail, she saw Julian, hands on his hips, his hair wild, his face a map of lines. She called out to him and he ran a few steps toward her before she fell to the tarmac.

Tel Aviv, May 25

Shimshon Ashkenazy played with Ibrahim al-Amar, "Mr. Paterson," like a cat with a mouse, first letting al-Amar think he had gotten into the Tunnel's network, then frustrating him by knocking him off. Shimshon had set up a fake network, a honeypot, into which he had lured al-Amar. Following Julian's instructions, Shimshon posed as a hacker named Kwiktiks who offered to show him a way into his destination. Instead, he took him on a tour of a computer network he had created himself, with familiar-looking, but utterly fake, signposts along the way, imitations of the telephone switches al-Amar so desperately wanted to enter.

So far it was working. As al-Amar found himself caught in a series of mazes, he sent off e-mails of increasing frequency asking Kwiktiks for help. Shimshon obliged, then frustrated him, took lunch breaks and naps and generally kept al-Amar on the hook.

Green Zone, Baghdad, May 25

"Convincing me that we have to stop that ship by any means possible is one thing," said Richard Attanasio as Morgan sprawled on the couch in his office, feet up on the coffee table. "Convincing Washington is something else entirely."

Morgan sat forward, looking at Attanasio intently.

"The first thing we have to do is supply them with a legal pretext, some reason for action that will allow the brass to cover their asses in case of a shit storm."

"Like what?"

"Well, I thought you should see a few documents I looked up."

Morgan took the papers.

"The first page is from U.S. Customs and Border Protection," Attanasio said, "regarding penalties for false identification of shipping containers. Why don't you read it aloud?"

Morgan began reading: "'Liability. Carriers can be held liable for penalties. Carriers should establish business relationships with shippers to ensure accurate information is provided.'"

Attanasio stopped him. "So, Morgan," he said, "how scared do you think your average international carrier would be by a penalty that 'can be' applied—and how biting is the suggestion that carriers protect themselves from falsified bills of lading by 'establishing business relationships with shippers to ensure accurate information is provided'?"

"Shiver me timbers," said Morgan.

"Exactly. And the next paper is testimony from a former naval officer who has been in the shipping business for twenty years. Can you please read me the underlined quotation?"

"'Everybody hides what they're shipping,'" read Morgan. "'Even legitimate shippers lie all the time about the bill of lading. It's a continuing problem.'" Morgan looked up. "Fuck! We can't be looking for just ships that say they're carrying steel!"

Attanasio nodded. "I have pages of additional documents supporting this. Now, do you think they're up to speed on this in D.C.?"

"I don't know," said Morgan. "But be my guest. *You* can make *that* phone call."

Port of Aqaba, Jordan, May 25

Colonel Fahed walked into an abandoned warehouse on the outskirts of the Aqaba port, escorted by three of his men from the King's Special Guard. The space was huge as an airplane hangar, dark and dusty and filled with cobwebs, rodent droppings, and roosting birds. He walked over to a handful of Internal Security officers who were standing around a tan-colored canvas tarp that seemed to be covering a human form.

"Dead bodies don't provide much useful information," he snapped to the senior officer, Major Qawar.

Qawar grimaced. "We had limited time, and we miscalculated his endurance," he said. "All three we picked up were jihadists, so they were going to die here or in prison." Fahed heard a commotion from the back of the warehouse, and when he looked up, he saw another prisoner being dragged in.

"We thought you might like to ask a few questions," said Qawar. "This one's talking."

Colonel Fahed looked away in disgust as the man got close. He was missing an eye, and the right side of his body seemed no longer in his control. He had burns on his hands, and it appeared he would soon join his compatriot in eternal rest.

Fahed looked at Qawar with distaste. "Who hired him?" asked the colonel, shifting his weight.

"Locals. We have their names and are tracking down their contacts."

"Name of the ship?" asked Fahed.

"*LB Venture,*" said Qawar.

"How many containers of explosives?"

"Five to ten."

"Of what kind?"

"Mixed up with scrap of all kinds, old mortars, missiles, grenades, rockets, ammunition."

"Where's the boat headed?"

"New York."

"Any unconventional weapons on that ship?"

"The prisoner seemed to have a lot to say on that matter earlier," said Qawar, who raised his voice and barked out a question to the prisoner. It wasn't clear if the man was resisting or didn't quite hear, but his guard wasted no time in finding out. He gave him a vicious kick in the kidneys. The man shouted "Allahu Akhbar!" and vomited over his torso and the legs that extended akimbo in front of him. Fahed jumped back in disgust. The man had vomited pure blood. There was no point in pursuing this line of questioning, because that cry to God would be the man's last.

Fahed turned to Qawar, his face red with anger. "This guard is no longer employed by you. Or me."

Fahed turned and walked quickly toward the door. Qawar ran after him. As soon as they exited the dark hangar into the sun, Fahed spoke, his mouth tensed in anger. "As for your future employment, we will discuss it in Amman. Tomorrow."

FBI Headquarters, Washington, D.C., May 25

Deep inside the forbidding, fortresslike J. Edgar Hoover Building on Pennsylvania Avenue, a task force convened to consider the alarming intelligence from Baghdad. Forty people in all, they met in the Strategic Information and Operations Center (SIOC) amphitheater. Reached through etched-glass doors, the chamber was formal, clean, practical. The front wall was dominated by a large video screen. To one side was a podium. Three rows of desktops formed a semicircle at the front, a phone at every other seat. Five tiers of theater seats rose behind them.

Morgan Ensley's urgent appeal had finally reached sympathetic ears in the form of one Dan Brown, deputy assistant director for counterterrorism. Like much business at the Bureau, this matter caught his attention by way of a phone call from a friend, a coast guard vice admiral who had been alerted to the matter by Baghdad legat Richard Attanasio. After speaking for several hours with Morgan on a secure telephone line, Brown decided to throw his own weight behind the case.

Still fit at forty-two, Brown had a commanding presence. As a former special agent and federal prosecutor, he enjoyed the respect of colleagues both above and below him. But even though he had carved out a flexible space for himself at the Bureau, he chafed at its hopeless parochialism.

It seemed as if half of official Washington had somebody in the room: the State Department, coast guard, Office of Naval Intelligence, CIA, and Counter-terrorism Center (CTC); the newly named Immigration and Customs Enforcement (ICE); and the Terrorist

Threat Integration Center (TTIC). Speaking for the FBI were several groups: the Hazardous Materials Response Unit (HMRU); members of the Joint Terrorism Task Force offices in New York and Washington; the Terrorist Financial Working Group, which tracked the monetary trail of outlawed organizations; and the Nuclear Inderdiction Unit.

Brown got straight to the point. "The reason I've called you here is that we've got a situation that, pardon my French, scares us shitless. This investigation is going to require many hands and quick but careful work."

He signaled to a technician, and a blown-up photo of a container ship appeared on the video screen.

"An FBI special agent on assignment in Iraq, Morgan Ensley, has uncovered evidence that a container ship laden with explosives from Iraq might be headed for the States, probably the eastern seaboard. There's a high probability that radioactive material is part of the shipment. In other words, a dirty bomb. Or worse. We've all known for years that seaborne freight is a huge hole in our security system. This is our nightmare coming true."

The coast guard man spoke up. "Do we know where this ship is going?"

"Our agent thinks New York or the Port of Elizabeth is the likely destination."

"And how close to the coast is the vessel?"

"Well, we believe it left Aqaba, in Jordan, around May 12. If it went around the Horn of Africa to avoid inspections in the Suez Canal, we can expect it in twenty-five days. That will give us twelve days to identify and stop it. However, if it passed through Suez, assuming sixteen days steaming time, maybe two and a half to three days away. That's an approximation. The boat could arrive in as soon as a day and a half."

It was the CIA's turn. "And I don't suppose your man has the name of this tub?"

"We're working on it. Do you have any idea how many container ships are in the Atlantic headed for the Americas at any given moment?" Brown answered his own question. "About a hundred."

There was a general shaking of heads.

"Of course, we're looking at all ships that made stops in the Middle East. And analyzing cargo manifests and shipper information. One other lead we have is a possible confederate in Paterson, New Jersey. For the last three days, he's been under physical surveillance by the FBI. Electronic surveillance has just been approved."

A photo of the man flashed on the screen at the front of the room. "His name is Ibrahim al-Amar," continued Brown. "Yemeni national. Preliminary travel records indicate he was in Afghanistan in 1999 and in Pakistan in 2003.

"Al-Amar had contact with a known computer hacker who was convicted of wire fraud and theft in Pennsylvania in 1999. The hacker is not known to have any prior terror ties. And he might be useful to our agents. His name is Paul Mundo." Another photo, a mug shot, flashed on the screen. The man was Caucasian, heavyset, with thick glasses.

"Al-Amar has also received visits from a red-haired Lebanese national named Farouk Abboud, who was identified by photographs taken during surveillance by the FBI. Abboud is on a watch list of foreign nationals who traveled to Afghanistan in the last four years. Our records indicate he studied construction of explosives." Several photos of Abboud, or "Red," went up, including those taken by agents outside the Paterson residence. In each, he wore men's clothing.

"Special Agent Ensley's asset, an Israeli computer expert, forwarded information that al-Amar is intensely interested in a building in lower Manhattan known as 'the Tunnel.' As some of you know, this is a hub of fiber-optic communications responsible for sending telephone and other electronic communications from the eastern seaboard to Europe and the rest of the world. The Tunnel also is responsible for peer linkage for the East Coast."

"Peer what?" asked the man from State.

Brown sighed inwardly. "Let's put it this way: if you're calling someone on a phone whose provider is different from your own, the call must go through this hub. The vulnerability of the Tunnel is well known to computer experts and law enforcement. There is no solution yet to the problem. The networks were built before our current security concerns."

Murmurs erupted throughout the hall.

"Yes, it's 9/11 meets the New York City blackout of 2003," said Brown. "The thinking is that the terrorists have some kind of explosion at a seaport in mind, with a simultaneous electronic attack on the Tunnel. If the Tunnel were tampered with or destroyed, the entire communications network of the eastern seaboard could be brought down. No one would be able to call family members, police would not be able to communicate with other agencies except through internal networks. Same with fire and hospitals and other emergency personnel. Communication between law enforcement and the government would be cut."

"Before we go any further, Dan," called out the CIA representative, a thin man in a gray suit with a clipboard in his hand. He stood up. "Do we have any solid evidence of this threat, or is it something cooked up by the Israelis to get us involved in a concern of theirs? I mean, I've looked over your man Ensley's ECs and I see Israeli prints all over it."

"Glad you brought that up, Bill," said Brown, who was not at all glad, though he was hardly surprised. "First, I'm not sure how protecting this country's seaports is of greater interest to the Israelis than to us—or, for that matter, any other country in the world. Global trade is a massive web that connects us all. Damage to the system would hurt every country from Cameroon to China. The estimated economic loss from a WMD attack on a seaport—any major seaport—is one hundred billion dollars."

"I just have to say," the CIA man interrupted, "I'm pretty damn tired of having our foreign policy read like a wish list for the Israelis."

And to think the CIA used to be on Israel's side, Brown thought. He took a deep breath to control his irritation. "I'm going to ask Joe Dolan from army procurement to address that, Bill. His answer might help you out here, though Lord knows it's not going to make any of the rest of us feel any better."

Brown looked across the room toward Dolan, a heavyset man of six feet with jet black hair and blue eyes. True black Irish. "Joe, you want to add your piece?"

Dolan nodded gravely. "As you all know," he said to the room, "millions of dollars of goods are being transported every day to Iraq from the United States. Our government pays for the transport, and since we don't buy much from Iraq, the ships are sailing back empty. However, some enterprising Iraqi businessmen have pursued the idea of sending shipments back to the States on these empty ships. It's cheap and there's space. Seems that the American hunger for scrap steel, and the military's need for it to build armor, has opened a nice opportunity for certain enterprising souls. When I was told of Special Agent Ensley's fear that explosives might be shipped back to the States on container ships, I looked into the possibility. And I found that the military has contracts with several different shippers to carry material from Iraq back to the States, some directly into our army depots. So this scenario is entirely possible. And I know personally that India, for example, has had trouble with explosions in its smelters from munitions mixed in with the scrap. If explosives can get mixed up in steel scrap by accident, it can happen on purpose."

The room was silent. The CIA man scribbled intently on his clipboard.

"All right then," continued Brown. "At this point, we don't know for sure where the suspected ship was loaded or if it will make intermediate stops. For that, we're depending on the coordination of shipping companies, our military liaisons, and friendly foreign intelligence.

"We may even be looking for more than one ship. This may require additional personnel and vehicles. Captain Whorley?" Brown said, raising his head to a grizzled seaman, a former captain in the merchant marine, brought in to advise them on commercial shipping. "Would you help coordinate searches and boarding of all high-interest vehicles with the coast guard?"

Captain Whorley looked up at Brown. "Aye sir."

"The Joint Terrorism Task Forces in New York and New Jersey," Brown continued, "might have information on ongoing criminal investigations at the seaports. Maybe they'll give us leads. You all know the drill. We have to look at everything, and I do mean everything, for any seemingly unrelated information that may now hold new significance.

"I want to emphasize that our mission here is prevention. We're trying to stop something and we don't have much time." He rapped his fingers on the podium. "Not much time," he repeated.

Brown took off his glasses and pinched the bridge of his nose. "A subgroup will be established right here in SIOC, 24-7," he said. "It will report to me. If you run into resistance in your investigations, come to me. If you have something to say, let me hear it. If you just want to do a brain dump, come see me. And another thing: there will be no interagency rivalries, no bullshit failure to talk to each other."

He stared at every single person in the room, one at a time. "Do I make myself clear?" he said.

Back in his office, Brown sat heavily into his chair and pulled up a map of Atlantic shipping lanes on his computer. His finger traced a route backward to Jordan, then north to Iraq. Iraq, he thought. It was time to bring Morgan Ensley home.

Chapter Eighteen

New York City, May 25

When Marie came to, it was to the throb of a vision-blurring headache. Her temples were pounding; her head felt as if it were swollen to double its size. She wondered if she'd been dropped in the desert to die of exposure. It was hot enough, she thought, moving her legs, but it certainly wasn't dry. She was sweating all over. She moved again and realized she was most certainly not lying in sand. She was in a bed. She lifted her head off the pillow, then sank back again with a groan.

A woman in a white coat appeared next to her and put her hand on Marie's forehead. "Easy there," she said. "Take your time waking up, and your head will hurt less."

"Who are you?" asked Marie.

"My name is Lucette."

"And what are you?"

"I'm your nurse," she said in a lilting Caribbean accent and with a reassuring smile. She looked up at the saline bag and checked the infusion machine that controlled the drip into her arm: 80 cc's per hour.

"Where am I?"

Lucette laughed. "Oh, you funny girl," she said, reaching for Marie's pulse and holding her wrist with a competent, warm grip. "You're in your apartment."

"Please," said Marie. "Don't tease me like this." She put her hands up to her eyes to feel for her blindfold. Her face felt soft and vulnerable, unaccustomed to exposure. But the blindfold wasn't there. She opened her eyes briefly, and could make out the outline of a glass door with flowering plants beyond. *Now* what were they doing to her? Making her nuts by placing her in a room that looked just like her bedroom, complete with the garden outside? Then she looked again, lifting her head to see. The headache slammed her once more, and she lowered her head right away.

Lucette put a digital thermometer into her ear canal, and got a reading in a single second. "Normal," she said. "And don't worry about the plants. I gave them a good watering this morning. You'll be able to go out tomorrow and tend to them yourself. But for now, try to rest a bit more. I'll wake you in a couple of hours and give you some broth. You'll feel better then."

Lucette checked the tiny needle taped into Marie's arm and pointed to a bag of fluid hanging from a pole. "Careful of the IV, now. You need it to keep you hydrated."

Marie's head whirled in confusion. The last place she could remember being was a broken-down farmhouse somewhere in Iraq. Then she had a dream in which Massud was still alive, and Julian waved at her while standing beside a U.S. military plane. Dreams as wish fulfillment indeed. She wondered how long she would stay dreaming. Compared with the pain of opening her eyes and looking out, it seemed the right thing to do, return to sleep.

Bensonhurst, New York, May 25

Four FBI agents arrived at a brick apartment building on Twenty-fourth Avenue in the Bensonhurst section of Brooklyn. On the second-floor landing, they drew their pistols and arranged themselves in a stack at the door. Special Agent Roberts gave a loud knock, then barked:

"FBI. Open the door." There was no sound from inside. The agents banged on the door again, and they heard bare feet shuffling toward them. The lock clicked open from the inside, and as soon as the door opened, the agents rushed in, Roberts first, and pinned a rumpled, black-haired white boy to the floor and handcuffed him.

"Are you Paul Mundo?" the lead agent asked, pulling him up off the floor.

"Yes," the boy answered, readjusting his glasses on his face. "Who are *you*?"

"Special Agent Anthony Roberts," he said, flashing a shield. "FBI." The other agents looked around the room, surveying the collection of computers, cables, servers, and routers.

Mundo was myopic, overweight, and wearing a rumpled T-shirt and sweatpants. It appeared he had been sleeping.

"I did my time," he said. "Why are you bothering me now?"

"You did time for computer theft," said Roberts. "You're in a lot more trouble now."

"What do you mean? I haven't done anything."

"Does the handle 'Terminal Man' mean anything to you?"

Mundo's face reddened. "Yeah, I knew him. Well I didn't really know him, but I communicated with him. He was an asshole."

"I can imagine he was. Did you help him break in anywhere?"

"No."

"Did he pay you six thousand dollars to break into the Tunnel?"

Mundo looked angrily into the eye of the agent. "I didn't help him break into the Tunnel. I sold him a simple Trojan horse. I needed the money to help out my mother and pay my rent, and the guy was such a lamer, I figured he'd never be able to do it."

"Good thinking, buddy boy. Turns out he did figure out how to use it. And now we're going to take all your computers and find out exactly what you told him and when."

"Hey, there's a lot of private stuff on there," Mundo began to whine.

The agents had gathered most of the equipment by now, and Roberts took Mundo by the arm. "Tough shit. You gonna slip on some shoes before we go?"

Mundo stuffed his feet into flip-flops. "Do I get a phone call?"

"Sure you do. You can make as many calls as you want. We'll dial the numbers. Let's go, pal."

Port of Hampton Roads, Virginia, May 26

Morgan Ensley walked toward the main container dock in Norfolk, Virginia, and looked out into the Elizabeth and James rivers. Before him was a gigantic container ship, as long as two football fields. Cranes whirred and clanked overhead, lifting containers from its deck to the railway cars or trucks that would carry them to their destinations.

It was like a bustling space city here, with most of the action taking place far above the ground. Yet the activity was most certainly down to earth: crude oil, salt, sulfur, earth and stone, machinery, wood, and fertilizer transported to and from all parts of the globe. Trains to dozens of cities several times a day, as well as accessible truck lines across the country, made Norfolk the most efficient port mover of goods in the country.

Morgan looked at the mountains of containers stacked on the ships in front of him and behind him in the holding areas away from the docks and shuddered. Stacked three and four high, stretching for hundreds of yards in every direction. Anything could be in those boxes and no one would know it. And right next door was the Norfolk Naval Station, the largest military base in the world.

"Morgan," said a low voice. Ensley turned and saw Danny Comstock approaching him on the shiny black tarmac. It was wet from an earlier rain.

"You just get in?" said Morgan, turning back to look at the port as Comstock stepped up beside him.

"Yeah," said Comstock. "Hitched a ride on a resupply plane. You?"

"Got into Langley this morning with a troop rotation."

They looked out into the harbor in silence. "You calculating the angle of takeoff for the submarine-launched missile we got to shoot at that container ship?" asked Comstock, thinking a joke might be in order.

"We gotta think of something pretty quick," said Morgan. "But it's not going to be a missile. There's something I need to tell you."

Comstock looked at him expectantly.

"We think there may be unconventional weapons on that ship."

"Biological or chemical?" asked Comstock.

"Nuclear."

"Fuck."

"Three crates of nuclear ordnance from the former Soviet Union that I've been tracking for the last dozen years were dug up recently from a Bedouin's camp in northern Iraq."

"Christ, Morgan. A dozen years. Why didn't we just grab the stuff?"

"It's been moving from one terrorist snake pit to another. Most of the time, we've been playing catch-up. And on the few occasions the bombs were within sight, we didn't have access. This last one was up in a Kurdish clan area. There's no way we could have launched a military operation there."

"Mother of God," said Comstock, digesting the information. "What was dug up?"

"Seventy-kiloton warheads. Three of them. Each packed in its own crate. And if my instincts are worth anything at all, they're closer to us than you think."

"Have they identified the ship yet?" asked Comstock.

"Narrowed it down. But I don't even know if the bombs are all together, or if they've been separated."

"Where does headquarters want us to hit it—or them?"

"Most of the boats crossing the Atlantic hitch a ride on the Guinea Current and then dip south to catch the Gulf Stream near the Florida coast. They ride the stream north. The special task force at HQ wants to try to stop the ship when it passes the shallow waters of the Diamond Shoals near Cape Hatteras, and scuttle it right there."

"That's where the Gulf Stream meets up with the Labrador Current, isn't that right?" asked Comstock. "Bad weather, very cold water, and a lot of historic wrecks in the sand."

"Roger that."

"It's shallow enough though, so we could sink her and salvage it later," said Comstock.

Morgan nodded and looked up to the cranes, the wharves. He shook his head. "They probably got enough octane on that ship to turn Mount Rushmore into garden pebbles," he said. "But all they need to cripple international trade is five sticks of dynamite in a container that kills four longshoremen."

"I know it," said Comstock.

"Shelves in Wal-Mart would be empty within a week," continued Morgan. "Show me the politician who would dare say, 'The ports are now safe.' Nobody could do it." He looked away from the docks. "But terrorists like big statements. Makes them feel important, I guess."

"Big time," said Comstock, setting his chin as he took one last appraising look at the huge ships. "Is this why HQ was suspicious of you? They didn't know you were working interdiction?"

"Of course they did."

"Nobody told me. Except you, when you were screaming at me over that oud or whatever it was."

"Yeah, I wanted you out of my place."

"Well why in hell didn't they tell me? It would have explained some of your weirder travels."

"Welcome to the world's premier information-gathering institution. But no lectures. They've made me operational commander."

"So I've been told," said Comstock. "Though you can't shoot worth shit," he said, deciding to show Morgan some respect by razzing him.

Morgan laughed. "Shooters aren't usually commanders. But because you were a SEAL, they're making you my number two. File your complaint later."

"First they set me on your tail, then they make you my commander," said Comstock. "Sounds almost religious. Forgive us our trespasses as we forgive those who trespass against us."

"Amen. We just need to find that ship and sink the sucker."

Hay-Adams Hotel, Washington, D.C., May 26

Obaidi walked through his suite at Washington's storied Hay-Adams Hotel. The view from his rooms looked across Lafayette Park to the White House. What a nice touch, he thought to himself. A view straight into the viper's den. And this after lunch today at the vice president's mansion, and afternoon visits with members of the United States Congress. Such magnificent, dark woodwork in those congressional office buildings, he thought. And the endless hallways. He smiled as he thought of the twists and turns of his own arduous route here.

He looked out the window again as he recalled his lunch. They'd reminisced about old times and talked about their hopes for the new Iraq. In many spheres, their interests overlapped quite nicely. In others, though Cullum hadn't a clue, they couldn't be further apart. But Obaidi had no hesitation working with the infidel. In fact, it gave him a mordant pleasure to think he was using the enemy's own tools to crush his very bones.

Obaidi glanced at the television where CNN was running silently. He started when he saw a picture of himself flash on the screen. He quickly turned up the volume. As he watched, he heard the newsman say that information leaked to CNN indicated that an Iraqi government official had been linked to the crash of the Royal Jordanian Airlines plane. Obaidi's face turned white as he watched. An electronics shop in London, the report said, was owned by a conglomerate whose major shareholder was Mansour Obaidi, the newly named Iraqi minister of trade. Obaidi stood motionless. He thought his heart had stopped.

"It's the girl," he said to himself. "It has to be. But who is behind her? Who is running her?"

Had he any idea that his old adversary Julian Granot was the one behind the girl—and the one who tipped off CNN—he'd likely have formulated a slightly different plan.

He called out to his aide, barely controlling his fury. "I will find her," he said to himself. "I must find out what she knows. There's still time to stop this." He suddenly felt faint and his eyes went black. He bent his head forward until the blood returned to his face. His hand went to the underside of his chin, to a tiny lump of skin, a bundle of scars from his first cosmetic surgery in Hungary. It was a habit he had, touching the scar, when he was unnerved. It reminded him of his reserves of strength. He stood up, emboldened, and shouted to his assistant working at the dining-room table. He walked toward the aide, who stood, cringing, and began to bark orders.

Town House Apartment, Norfolk, Virginia, May 27

"I got a report from HQ," said Morgan, checking his e-mail on a laptop. He and Comstock were sitting on their duffel bags in a two-bedroom apartment provided for them by SEAL team number 6 based nearby in Little Creek. Comstock knew some of the guys from 6, and they'd set him and Morgan up here so they didn't have to mess with the huge bureaucracy at Station Norfolk. They were preparing to train with the SEALs on a container ship at Port Norfolk that afternoon.

Comstock was throwing a toy ball into a miniature basketball net across the room.

"They just stopped two boats approaching New York," said Morgan. "Nothing on them."

"How many more are they after?" asked Comstock.

"Two other high-interest vessels are approaching the East Coast. Homeland Security is checking manifests and ship histories."

Comstock sat with his elbows on his knees. He flipped another ball into the basket. "Nice toy you got," he said. Morgan looked up at Comstock, who motioned with his head to the laptop.

"Couldn't work without it," said Morgan.

"Neither can the rest of us," said Comstock, laughing. The FBI still had no workable computer networks to connect agents with the Internet or the World Wide Web. Because Morgan was a bomb tech and needed real-time access to colleagues, he was a special case. He had a laptop, government e-mail, and Internet access.

"Hey here's a message," said Morgan, excited, sitting up. "They found three white trucks abandoned near the Port of Aqaba. They're testing them now for residues of explosives or radioactive material." He looked up at Comstock. "The bombs dug up in Iraq were driven away in three white pickups."

Morgan looked back down at his laptop. "Here's more. There's a container ship sailing up the Gulf Stream. Its port of embarkation was Aqaba, and the departure date is the one we're looking at, May 12. Name of the ship is the *LB Venture*. But what's this? Customs says they won't stop it because the manifest states it's filled with cotton shirts, and the shipper and forwarder are well known."

"That's just bullshit!" said Comstock, standing up quickly, his big body throwing off intense energy. "What else have they got?"

"One more ship, still halfway across the ocean, coming in from Syria," said Morgan. "From Latakia."

"But there are a thousand intelligence agents from a dozen different countries working the Port of Latakia," said Comstock. "No way would Obaidi send the ship from there. They're fooling themselves. Tell them about finding the trucks," said Comstock, pacing the floor.

"I did. They want the test results."

"Jesus! The fact that they're there is results enough, don't you think?"

Morgan nodded. "Probably."

"What's going on here?" said Comstock. "They're fucking with us. Something's not right."

"Or something's really right," said Morgan, shaking his head and looking up to Comstock. "Somebody's got things fixed really right."

Off Route 3, Rutherford, New Jersey, May 27

"The name of the ministorage is Store-Eze," said FBI Special Agent Joe Fortuna, sitting in the passenger seat of a GMC Jimmy. He was reading to his driver and partner, FBI Special Agent Eddie Martinez, from notes in his lap. "And it's right here off Route 3." He looked up. "Take a right on Wickett Avenue here. Tony said he'd meet us on the corner." Tony Delmonte was an explosives expert in the FBI's Newark office. "We'll go over to the storage place together."

"Got the warrant?" asked Martinez.

Fortuna rustled around among the papers on his lap. "Right here."

He held up a search warrant signed that morning for a storage unit rented by a red-haired Lebanese national named Farouk Abboud, observed entering and leaving an apartment located at 41 Remson Street and presumed to be an accomplice to a conspiracy to commit an act of terror against the United States.

"Okay, here we are at the corner. Where's Tony?"

"I don't know. What kind of car does he drive?"

"A Stratus, I think. Oh, now I see him coming down the hill." The Stratus pulled up beside the GMC truck. Delmonte rolled down his window.

"I'll follow you, okay?" Delmonte said. Fortuna pulled onto a highway access road and drove into a dilapidated ministorage center. They parked and got out of their cars and walked to the office. Fortuna went in with the warrant and came out with the manager, who was holding a large ring of keys.

"One forty-four is one of the large ones," the manager said. "It's way over this side in the old section."

The agents followed him. They drew their revolvers as the manager turned the key in the lock and opened the door. As the door swung open, Delmonte gasped.

Before them in the twenty-by-ten-foot room was a veritable chemistry lab. On a picnic table were beakers marked "nitric acid," "urea," and "sulfuric acid." On an open bookshelf behind, glassware was neatly stacked—beakers, pipettes, test tubes—along with test-tube racks. On the floor were wooden crates and plastic bags filled with bags of ammonium nitrate.

As their eyes adjusted to the dim light, they saw an additional worktable, this one with more chemicals and other paraphernalia: sodium cyanide; methenamine; wires; pumps; clumps of cotton wool; a bag of gunpowder and a propellant; sodium azide. The floor was marked with oddly shaped discolored rings.

They looked at each other and Delmonte spoke a single name: "Ramzi Yousef." The room looked just like the one that Yousef rented in 1993 to build the bomb that exploded in the World Trade Center. Even the same chemicals.

"Unbelievable," said Martinez. "These guys never give up."

"Let's start dusting for prints," said Fortuna.

"Get samples, too, and vendor info from the labels on all these bags and vats," said Delmonte. "Search the place for invoices. And look for anything like a notebook that might contain chemical formulas. We need to know how sophisticated this guy is. But do it carefully. We don't want him to suspect he's had any visitors. And for Christ's sake, put in a call to HQ to tighten up the surveillance."

SIOC Amphitheater, FBI Headquarters, Washington, D.C., May 27

Dan Brown was surprised that bedlam could appear so slow, so surreal, that its constituent parts could appear so without portent. It was almost amusing to watch people pouring coffee, tearing open envelopes of nondairy creamer, stirring their coffee in plastic foam cups. All while trying to thread a needle with rubber gloves in the pitch dark.

Through his reverie, he heard scraps of conversations. Coast guard captain: "A phone can be used as a trigger, but you need to hook it to a battery. . . . Satellite phones work all over the world, including on the open ocean, few points of no coverage. Use GPS as backup."

Someone new: "A GPS, for all its sophistication, is stupid. If there's a delay and the boat is directed to a new dock, the GPS won't lock on. Even if the ship is ten yards away from its target, it won't get the signal."

Another: "A human will control the explosion. You need visual identification of the ship."

One thing Brown was sure of: they didn't want that ship anywhere near the port terminals of New York. Between the waterways in the Kill Van Kull and Arthur Kill were huge storage tanks holding jet fuel for Newark, JFK, Logan, and La Guardia airports. Tanks holding hundreds of thousands of gallons of petroleum and chemical storage lined the shore. Ship and truck fuel as well. Inland was Newark Liberty Airport. And between them ran I-95, the most heavily traveled roadway in the

Northeast Corridor. An explosion there would kill thousands of people, create a tremendous fireball, and bring commerce in the eastern U.S. to a halt. World shipping would fall to its knees.

An FBI report identified the area as the ripest target for terrorism in the United States.

And the ship was heading straight for it.

Now it was up to customs to tell them where the boats were. Already three had arrived faster than expected, not honoring the ninety-six-hour notification of arrival. Nothing like testing the system in a crisis. And then there was the *LB Venture*, sailing up the coast, having gotten a green light from customs. Word had come down from the White House itself. Matter of respect, they said. "Important sensitive relations with the new government of Iraq. Hands off this one." Right from the vice president's office.

Great, thought Brown, just like the White House put the entire Saudi royal family on a 747 the day after 9/11. He thought that courtesy was wrongheaded then. And ten thousand times more wrongheaded now.

Chapter Nineteen

Marie Peterssen sat at her desk, surrounded by papers, reports, and her own notebooks. The first thing she did the day before yesterday when she awakened from her drug-induced slumber was to call Julian, but she couldn't reach him. Then she called Morgan, who didn't have too many answers for her about her kidnapping but let her know that her repatriation had been the result of a small miracle of diplomacy, although he wouldn't tell her a thing about it. He was thrilled that she had made it back home and he hoped to get back soon to see her.

Lucette the nurse, having determined that Marie was now fine, checked up on her only occasionally. Marie didn't even know what nursing agency she had come from or who had paid her. Although these questions nagged at her, she pushed her curiosity aside. She had time only to work on her story about Rutba and the steel.

The *Wall Street Journal* once again agreed to run her piece, and she wrote in a frenzy, yesterday stopping only for an occasional break to walk out to the roof and breathe some air. She suffered headaches from time to time, but when they descended, she put an ice pack on her head. She called Julian repeatedly. No answer.

Marie pulled out a folder of documents she'd printed out from the Internet the previous night. She'd found recently released reports about Iraq's oil-for-food program written by a private UN oversight agency. In them, she saw repeated mention of an Iraqi businessman with "ties in Western and Eastern Europe" who, in violation of sanctions, imported goods into Iraq. Elsewhere, three ships known to have been used to smuggle goods into Iraq were named. Some sections of the documents were blacked out, but it was stated that the boats were owned or operated by the businessman, who she had a hunch was one Mansour Obaidi. She picked up the phone and dialed Morgan. To her surprise, he picked up.

"Morgan," she said. "It's Marie."

"Hey, girl, how are you?"

"Good, good, thanks. Where are you?"

"Closer than you'd think."

"You in the States?"

"Something like that."

Marie was silent, her mind working. "Okay, first thing. Are you trying to stop the ship?"

"How would you come up with an idea like that?" Morgan asked.

"Oh, Morgan. Get over yourself. Get over your secret stuff. We don't have time for it."

"I can't talk to you on the cell. It's not secure."

"You near a land line?"

Morgan looked around the room. "There a phone in here?" he asked Comstock, who got up. Comstock found one in a bedroom, scribbled the number on a piece of paper, and handed it to Morgan.

"You home?" asked Morgan.

"Yup. You know the number?"

"I'll get it and call you right back."

"Don't blow me off, Morgan. I have some information that might help you. And if you're near a TV, turn on CNN, because there was a little piece implicating our friend Obaidi in the four plane crashes."

"Who got that story?" asked Morgan.

"I don't know, but I'm pissed. That's *my* story."

"I'll call you back." He hung up.

"Don't call her back," said Comstock. "She's not supposed to know any of this."

"Yeah, but she does."

"Not operationally sound. It'll just be trouble."

"Oh fuck off, Comstock. If it weren't for her, we wouldn't have got onto this thing in the first place."

Morgan got her number through the FBI database and called her back.

"Have you found the ship?" she asked.

"We're looking at all ships coming in from the Middle East, but we're not sure which one we're looking at."

"You want some names?"

"What do you mean?"

"I've got new UN files about the oil-for-food program. I believe Obaidi made a lot of money in that, and there's a man described in these papers that fits his description. Anyway, it mentions three of his ships. You want their names?"

"Shoot."

"Hold on a second here." She rustled through the papers. "They are the *Ohlalla J*, the *Oceanus Express*, and the *LB Venture*."

"*LB Venture?*"

"Yes."

"There's an *LB Venture* sailing in from Aqaba now. But we got an order to leave it alone. It's supposed to be carrying cotton shirts, and the shipper seems to know somebody important."

Marie couldn't say a word. She exhaled a long breath.

"We need help fast," said Morgan.

"Maybe I could publish something," she said, scrambling in her mind for an idea, pulling out the weapon that was closest at hand: the Web.

"We need help in a matter of hours, not days."

"Morgan, the world is a new place. News is a twenty-four-hour-a-day business. I can try to get a story posted on the *Journal's* online version."

"Like what?"

Marie stopped for a second as she gathered her thoughts. "Like an individual who made a fortune in kickbacks during Iraq's oil-for-food program has just been named minister of trade for the new Republic of Iraq. That the same man was just implicated by CNN as having ties to companies possibly involved in the recent airline crashes. That he is known to have operated three ships in his smuggling operations, the *Ohlalla J,* the *Oceanus Express,* and the *LB Venture.* And that one of the ships in question is headed for the States right now and considered suspicious by foreign intelligence agents."

"That might help break the logjam," said Morgan.

"Say a little prayer for me, Morg. With any luck, I'll be able to get something up within the hour."

Morgan hung up. "With a little prayer for us all, you mean," he said quietly, glancing at his watch.

International Airport, Larnaca, Cyprus, May 27

Colonel Gassan Fahed stepped off his private jet onto the tarmac of Larnaca International Airport. It was midnight but the tarmac was brilliantly illuminated by a full moon. Colonel Fahed didn't wear a uniform or travel with a security entourage, as he would have had he been traveling on official business. This trip was as unofficial as could be.

Fahed had flown in from Amman in response to an urgent request from his friend Julian Granot. He walked through the terminal and into a meeting room off the Cyprus Airways gates, where he found Julian sitting in a chair, nursing a drink, looking into space in his intense, pugilistic way, his unruly hair the only suggestion of inner turmoil. The two men embraced.

"Sorry to drag you away from home," said Julian. "But I thought you wouldn't mind flying over to Cyprus. Not a bad place to meet. Fresh air, nice landscape." He glanced out the window to the blinking lights on the tarmac.

"No time for bullshit, Julian," said Fahed, tired and agitated. "Sorry it took me so long, but the interrogations were difficult. My men eventually got the story."

Julian knew what that meant, but said nothing. It was better not to know for sure. "And they found?"

"Aqaba is busy these days because of all the extra shipping involving Iraq. We simply can't handle the traffic. The king has ordered an expansion, but it's not enough. As you can imagine, with so many ships passing through, there's a lot of room for smuggling and, let's say, side deals. And we can lose track of shipments for days at a time. The records are shit."

"But your men found something."

"Eventually. A ship set sail fifteen days ago. It was carrying ten containers of steel from Iraq. Headed for Newark." Fahed reached into a pocket and pulled out a piece of paper. "Here's the bill of lading," he said, handing it to Julian. "You'll notice it says the containers are packed with cotton shirts."

"Those ISPS codes are real enforcers, aren't they?"

Fahed shrugged. "It was piracy that brought the law of the sea into existence. In this case, I think the pirate is the Bahrain Sales Corporation. It was a major smuggler during the oil-for-food program. Your man Obaidi ran it. Shell companies. In layers. There was no paper trail back to him."

"So how do you finger Obaidi?"

"Do you forget how close Jordan and Iraq were at the beginning of the First Gulf War?"

"Of course not. But you had no choice, right?"

"Saddam had us by the balls. But backing Iraq had its benefits. One of them was that Obaidi left a few traces my dogs could scent."

Julian laughed. "Your dogs?"

"Yes, my dogs. They're very useful. In fact they interrogated the crew Obaidi brought to the docks to load the containers onto the ship. It was funny: the regular dockworkers weren't used. We only learned that after the harbormaster got a little persuasion. Anyway, the containers came in at night. As soon as they arrived, they went on board. Two of the men admitted they knew there were explosives in the containers."

Julian sat up straight. "How did they know?"

"Because of the special precautions."

"What special precautions?"

"Instructions not to drop anything. Hints of danger. No smoking. That sort of thing."

"Did the men say how many ships they loaded?"

"Sorry, I don't know. My men knew I wanted the information fast, so they used force. A little too much, I fear. The men didn't survive the interrogations. They died before I got everything I wanted."

"Shit!" said Julian. "Shit!"

"Blame it on Arab cynicism," said Fahed. "But hang on. The questioning points to one ship in particular."

"Oh?"

"Yes. A freighter named the *LB Venture*. As the Americans say, that's the good news."

"And the bad news?"

"There was one container loaded at the last minute filled with what appear to be—how shall I say?—unconventional weapons."

"What kind?"

"Small tactical weapons. In crates. We don't know how many might be inside each crate. The crates carried Russian markings."

"Battlefield nukes?" Julian was sick at the thought. Tactical nuclear weapons were a terrorist's dream. Nobody could steal an intercontinental ballistic missile. They were contained in their silos. They wouldn't work in any other setting.

Tactical weapons were another matter. They came in several shapes and sizes, some meant to be deployed in the close confines of a theater of combat. The West had dreamed them up as a deterrent to a Soviet invasion of Europe, back in the days of the cold war.

They were low-yield compared to the warheads used in intercontinental missiles, but they were enough to wipe out lower Manhattan. Worse, their safety mechanisms were easier to defeat. Their locks weren't as sophisticated.

NATO considered them "usable" because they couldn't flatten whole metropolitan regions. All they could do was kill tens of thousands of people and make a city uninhabitable for years.

Julian was not entirely surprised. He'd seen the arms depots in the former Soviet Union himself. "Battlefield nukes?" he said again.

Fahed nodded.

"And the Arab cynicism?" asked Julian.

"You couldn't find nuclear weapons in Iraq? In that case, we'll send them to you," said Fahed.

Julian gave Fahed a weak smile. "All in a day's work, eh?"

"Yes, and now that I've finished mine, I think I'll take a few breaths of that Mediterranean air before getting back on the plane."

"Ordinarily, I would love to join you," said Julian, placing his hand on Fahed's shoulder. He didn't finish his sentence. He pulled a floppy hat over his hair and walked from the terminal toward a small jet parked on the tarmac. Before he reached the plane, he pulled out his telephone and dialed a number.

He heard a noise at the end of the line.

"Morgan, it's Julian."

"What?" shouted Morgan. "Reception is terrible."

Julian raised his own voice. "Where are you?"

"Back in the States."

"I have information for you. You need to send this message up the line."

"Stop, Julian, this isn't a secure line, and you know it."

"We don't have time for secure lines. Given the sailing date from Aqaba, there may be as little as twelve hours before the ship gets to its destination. And there's lots of work to do, lots of tricky logistics."

"Okay."

"Now listen well. I want to get off this line as soon as I can."

"Roger that."

"First, the name of the ship is *LB Venture*."

Morgan was on full alert. "Got it."

"Wait," said Julian. "There's evidence that the shipment may include some nuclear matériel."

"What kind?" asked Morgan.

"Tactical weapons from the Soviet Union."

"Seventy-kiloton bombs?"

Julian paused. "How did you know that?"

"We picked up the movement of some nuclear material out of northern Iraq."

Julian was silent for a few seconds, wondering why Morgan hadn't told him this earlier. Well, at least they weren't headed to *his* hometown. Let the Americans play their games. "My source isn't clear if they're armed and able to detonate," continued Julian, "or if they're just meant to be part of dirty bombs. But if I were you, I'd plan for the former."

International Airport, Larnaca, Cyprus, May 27

Julian paused by the curtain to the cockpit of the Cessna Citation 10. His friend Uri was at the controls, working out flight plans. Julian stepped in and dropped into the copilot's seat, his knees wide, body slumped. "Can we fly directly to New York?" he asked.

Uri looked up at him, his lean, friendly face lined deeply by the sun. "You mean nonstop? No. You know that. This is the fastest plane in its class, the one with the longest range. But it can do only about thirty-six hundred miles without refueling. New York is close to fifty-five hundred miles from here."

"So what do we do?"

"We refuel at a private airfield outside Lisbon. It's all arranged. We land, gas up, take off. No police, no immigration control, no nothing. It'll add twenty minutes, a half hour to the flight, no more. And at six hundred miles an hour, we'll make it up."

"Even flying into the wind?"

"This baby can cruise at fifty thousand feet. Less resistance up there."

Julian was getting impatient. "Come on, Uri. How long to New York?"

Uri shrugged. "Ten hours, give or take a half hour."

Julian made a face. "We haven't got that kind of time."

"Hey, Julian. You want me to order up an F-18 for you? Or maybe you were thinking of *Air Force One.*"

Julian smiled. "I'd like that. Can you do it?"

"Oh, go fuck yourself, Granot."

"An anatomical improbability, but thanks for thinking of me. Look, I need some sleep. How long before we're in the air?"

Uri checked his watch. "Ten minutes, max. I've got to file our flight plan, which I'm doing . . . now." He clicked on a computer with a Wi-Fi connection to the tower. "And our copilot is crossing the tarmac. As soon as he's aboard, we're wheels up."

The Citation 10 was an opulent aircraft, with seats superior to first class on any commercial airline. There was enough legroom to allow a passenger to recline completely. With gratitude, Julian heaved himself into a seat in the forward cabin. He was hoping to hell Morgan had been able to mobilize his organization. He remembered all too clearly his own fruitless conversations with the Americans in July 2001, when he tried to warn them about a dangerous gentleman named Mohammed Atta.

Julian pulled out his cell phone and called his wife.

"Julie? How are you?" She knew never to ask him where he was, because he never answered.

"I'm okay," he said. "How are you and the boys?"

"Everybody's fine. Except I'm worried because Doron's going to a party tonight," she said about their younger son. "In a club in Tel Aviv."

"Don't worry about it. There'll be plenty of security. Also, it's hot weather. Harder to conceal a bomb under clothes when it's hot."

Gabi sighed. "I suppose you're right. But how's he going to get home? He agreed not to take a bus. I could always pick him up."

"At three in the morning?" said Julian. It wasn't that Gabi couldn't get up at that hour herself. She, like her husband, had been trained to be awake and alert whenever she had to. Rather, he was considering how his fifteen-year-old son would feel if his mother picked him up at that hour. Julian idly thought how odd that he was listening to domestic minutiae when the world was about to blow up. But again, that was life. The minutiae. In the face of everything else. Yet his personal minutiae regularly involved precautions against suicide bombers. Such a world.

"You might cramp his style," he said. "Otherwise, how are you?"

Gabi chatted a bit about departmental politics, and then her voice dropped. "I actually have some good news," she said.

"What's that?" he asked.

"My paper was accepted for publication by *Foreign Affairs* magazine." She'd been working on it for months. It analyzed Europe's newfound success in competing against U.S. hegemony in trade and finance and prognosticated about the future of European cultural and political influence in world affairs.

"That's great," said Julian. "Fantastic." He wondered how the Europeans would react to a port attack on America, seeing how vulnerable they were themselves. He shook the thought from his mind. "How about this? I'll cook you dinner as soon as I get back," he told her. "And we'll celebrate." Gabi chuckled happily.

Julian saw the copilot enter the cockpit. "Got to go," he said. "Give the boys a kiss for me, will you?" She murmured her assent. "And steal one for yourself."

Julian snapped closed the phone. She was a good girl, his Gabi. He pulled a vial of sleeping pills from his pocket and swallowed two of them. His claustrophobia made long flights painful, even in aircraft as comfortable as a Citation 10. Not to mention that he was headed to the same target as a few renegade nuclear devices.

In his forty-six years, he'd made it through too many close calls and impossible situations to count. But in most of them, he'd had some level of control, had access to resources and the best intelligence available. Now he was flying into vastly more unpredictable currents. The best thing he could do now was sleep. He stuffed two pillows under his head, adjusted himself, and waited for the pills to take hold. He didn't stir as the plane took off. He didn't even snore during the flight or awaken during the refueling stop. Not until the moment the plane touched down at MacArthur Airport on Long Island would he bolt wide awake.

·

Tel Aviv, May 27

Shimshon Ashkenazy stared at his computer screen, nibbling absently on the back of his wrist. It was a tic he had, a childhood habit he'd picked up when he read computer handbooks. His mother used to say that he needed nourishment, real nourishment, like literature. But Shimshon knew that the manuals were all the nourishment he needed. It was as if his mind were built to understand computers, as if it had been made in the image of the machines. Technology was indeed the continuation of evolution by other means.

Shimshon was racking his brain because what he looked at could not be broken down into logic gates and matrices or understood through graph theory. It was human, and that's what he had trouble with: humans when they weren't acting logically. Not the first time he'd grappled with the problem; nor the last, he knew. But he had a very particular problem right now.

He had found more e-mails, beyond those with the perorations from the Koran. The code-breaking department had done its work on the earlier ones, though the result was almost obvious—the call for an imminent attack, details of which offered clues to the location and timing. Code-breaking confirmed Julian's guess that the target was the port in New York and the event would take place in the next two days.

But what Shimshon was having trouble with were the lists and lists of phone numbers turning up in many of the e-mails. He would rather have shared the information with the FBI and asked the Bureau if it could find a pattern in the numbers. But Julian had warned him over and over that the FBI didn't play well with outsiders.

But these numbers. Shimshon felt the challenge eating at him. He had to figure out why there would be so many sat phone numbers being sent in e-mails to Paterson, New Jersey. Could all these numbers set off the explosion? Had they so many people sitting out there with their fingers on the bomb, so to speak? That made no sense from a tactical point of view. What was the relation among the numbers? And was there a relation between these numbers and the ship steaming toward Port Elizabeth?

Maybe it was a fail-safe mechanism.

Shimshon looked over the numbers again. Who was the provider for each of the phones? He looked up the phone numbers on a special reference directory. The first was Satcom. The second was the same. Also the third. Maybe he could hack into the company and disable the numbers.

Prevent the circuit from being closed. Prevent any explosions. Might be tricky.

Shimshon looked over the list again. Let's find these phones, he thought. They are in regular communication with the satellite, signals going in and coming back out, so they can be triangulated and located in space. This was a bit of an operation, but Shimshon wrote up a quick program to run the numbers. After an hour, he got the answer: the transmissions were coming from a vessel of some kind, off the coast of the United States, about one hundred miles from New York Harbor. It had to be the one they were looking for.

He waited a few minutes and took another reading. A third allowed him to plot a course.

He stood up and walked into Nadav's office.

"I think I've found the ship," he said.

That got Nadav's attention. "Where is it?"

"You're not going to like the answer."

"I haven't liked anything about this from the beginning. Go on."

"Looks like it's headed straight for New York."

Nadav stood up and walked to a map of the Atlantic he'd installed on a wall. "Where is it now?" he asked.

"A little more than seventy-four degrees west by thirty-nine degrees north. Or right about here," Shimshon said, with his finger on a point just off Cape May, New Jersey.

"Shit!" said Nadav. "That puts it—what? Six or seven hours away from the entrance to the harbor?"

"Something like that. Eight at the most."

Nadav stared hard at Shimshon. "Are you sure about this?"

"Of course not. You can never be sure without visual contact. But the signals from forty phones are coming from what looks like a boat at this location. And the phone numbers are included in e-mails from Iraq to a terrorist's apartment in New Jersey. So how many possible conclusions are there?"

"Right." Nadav called Julian's phone. It rang and rang. The answering service clicked on. Nadav left a message. He looked up to Shimshon. "This isn't good," he said.

"We need to tell the Americans."

"Yes we do. But I don't know how," said Nadav, exasperated.

"You can't exactly pick up the phone and ask the prime minister to ring up his friend the president of the United States, can you?" asked Shimshon.

"Ah, no. Julian's way outside channels on this one."

The two men looked at each other, the information weighing heavily in the air between them. Nadav again dialed Julian. No answer. Would New York blow up because they didn't know whom to call?

"Would you like me to send the information to the person who needs to know?" asked Shimshon quietly.

"Who would that be?" asked Nadav.

"Dan Brown, deputy assistant director for counterterrorism at the FBI."

"You could reach him?"

"I can make the phone that sits beside his right hand ring this minute," said Shimshon.

"How do you know that number?" asked Nadav.

Shimshon smiled. "It'd take a long time to explain."

Nadav shook his head, smiling in appreciation. He thought for a moment and said, "Why not? See if he'll listen to you."

SIOC Amphitheater, FBI Headquarters, Washington, D.C., May 27

The telephone beside Dan Brown rang. He picked it up. "Brown," he said. He listened in astonishment for a few seconds. "Where in hell did you get this number?" he barked.

"There's no time to get into that right now, sir. This is Shimshon in Tel Aviv. Remember me?"

Brown stopped dead. "The guy who told us about the house in Paterson." His tone became friendlier. "Have you got something more?"

Shimshon told him about the vessel, and gave its exact coordinates as of five minutes earlier. "You understand that I have no proof as such," he added. "Only a deduction. You're going to have to make a visual confirmation."

Brown glanced at the map in front of him, marked with the location of all known ships approaching U.S. ports. He saw the coordinates matched those of the *LB Venture*.

If Brown was irritated at the younger man's presumption, he didn't show it. "Nice work, son," he said, reestablishing his authority with a single word. "I'll put in a good word for you when all this is over."

The phone crackled. "Oh, please don't do that, sir," said Shimshon, sounding worried.

"Why not?"

"Let me say only that there has been some—what do you Americans call it?—*freelancing* over here."

Brown chuckled. "I have more subtlety than you give me credit for, young man. I won't burn you. But tell me: how did you get around our firewalls? This is a secure line."

"That was the whole point, sir," Shimshon said. "It's a secure line."

Shaking his head, Brown rang off. It's not good enough, he thought to himself. Those guys in the vice president's office don't want to hear it. And State has a bug up its ass about depending on the Israelis. He needed more proof. He had to think fast.

Now that he had the location of the ship, he could order a little surveillance of his own. He picked up the phone and dialed the manager of the small fleet of planes the FBI kept at Andrews Air Force Base. He ordered up a plane outfitted with a FLIR, an infrared, thermal-imaging camera, to fly over the ship, whose coordinates he gave. Results sent directly to him. Next, he called Ensley and ordered him and Comstock to get on a helicopter without delay and fly to Cape May. They'd missed their chance to stop that ship off Hatteras. Cape May was the last coast guard station from which to launch an operation before New York. They had lost ground. And time.

New York City, May 27

A young woman with a curly red wig, crushable hat, short skirt, and heavy-soled boots sat on a park bench across the street from the huge brick telephone building at 124 Eleventh Avenue, the building known to phreakers and hackers as "the Tunnel." She was petite and narrow, but she walked like a boy, her weight back at the hips, legs swinging forward from a more open, male pelvic joint. She opened up her knapsack and rustled through it, taking every chance she got to glance across the street. She observed a dozen police and SWAT team operators around the building. Employees were leaving for the evening now, but Red saw metal detectors had been set up at the doors. A hazardous-materials crew was posted with a bomb dog. All this security had appeared since yesterday, the last time she was here.

After a few minutes, she got up, slung her bag over her right shoulder, and walked away. She stepped into the subway and onto a car at the back of the downtown number 1 train. She slipped on some sweatpants, then pulled off the wig and the skirt and bundled them into her bag. Had the two Arab FBI agents been on the train, they would have recognized "Red," their name for the Lebanese man they photographed coming and going from 41 Remson Street in Paterson. At the next stop, he replaced his red wig with a blue wool cap and walked out of the car and into the midday light.

Special Agents Joe Fortuna, Eddie Martinez, and Tony Delmonte, having seen the chemistry laboratory he constructed under the name Farouk Abboud, would have been chagrined to see Red disappear into the crowd of young people at Astor Place.

SIOC Amphitheater, FBI Headquarters, Washington, D.C., May 27

Dan Brown was looking at the auditorium screen, studying a map of the continental shelf off the Atlantic Coast, when an aide stole in and whispered in his ear. "Bad news, sir."

"As opposed to the day's prevailing good news?"

The aide hesitated. "Sir?"

"Never mind. What have you got?"

"Yes sir. That surveillance mission you authorized?"

Brown nodded.

"Well, it picked up signs of life inside one of the containers."

"Meaning what?"

The aide took a breath. "We think there may be hostages on board."

Brown shot out of his seat, knocking over his water glass. "Hostages?" he roared in a voice loud enough to be heard in the hallway outside.

The auditorium fell silent. All eyes zoomed in on Brown. He calmed himself and walked to the podium. "Ladies and gentlemen," he said, "Special Agent Carter here has something to tell you that you're not going to like." He motioned Carter to come forward.

Carter coughed nervously. "At eighteen twenty hours," he began, "our surveillance overflight of the target vessel detected an anomaly."

Brown was impatient. "Cut to the chase, Carter," he snapped.

"Yes sir. Well, the infrared sensors found signs of life in places they shouldn't be."

"What do you mean?" called out Special Agent Leo Mazur of the Terrorist Financial Working Group. Brown waved him down.

"You expect to see life in the deckhouse, in the engine room, and maybe in the forecastle," said Carter. "But not amidships, where there are containers on deck."

"Maybe someone was having a smoke," said Duane Leroy of the Hazardous Materials Response Unit. "Or patrolling the cargo. Or maybe there was a little male extracurricular activity requiring privacy." The laugh he expected failed to materialize.

"No sir," said Carter. "The infrared suggested at least a dozen people, maybe more, huddled together inside one of the containers."

"How can you tell anything more than that there are signs of life in a container?" asked Mazur.

Brown broke in. "We can't for certain, of course. But ask yourself: how likely is it that a container ship whose manifest says nothing about animals is carrying goats or sheep? No, if there is life in that container, it's human. And if it's human, they're prisoners."

"So what?" said the HMRU's Leroy.

"Someone's considered the possibility that we would learn about the ship before it reached its destination," said Brown.

"And taken out an insurance policy."

"Exactly. He's counting on our thinking more than twice before we drop a bomb on that ship or torpedo it."

"Why should we?" asked Mazur.

"Why should we what?" asked Brown.

"Even think twice about sinking the fucker. Why don't we just do it? Now, before it's too late."

"You're prepared to sacrifice innocent lives?" asked Bob Malone, the State Department's representative.

"Why not? Better ten or twenty innocent lives now than thousands later."

It's not that easy," said Malone. "We don't yet know for sure there is a nuclear device on board. Shouldn't we wait?"

"Why take the chance?"

"Because we have to think about the Muslim world. How will it look if a ship leased and crewed by Muslims suddenly disappears practically in American territorial waters and, oh yes, killing a few innocent hostages in the bargain?"

"Oh, please," said Mazur. "As long as it happens out of sight of the media, who's going to know the cause? It just happened, that's all. Maybe it was bad weather. Come to think of it, didn't we just get briefed to the effect that there's going to be a nasty storm out there in a few hours?"

Malone shook his head. "You just don't get it," he said. "In an Internet world, you can't hide anything for long. Saying 'it just happened' won't cut it."

"Or," Brown interjected, "in an Internet world, we'll be blamed no matter what. You've got Al-Jazeera, you've got Arab blogs. The rumors about what the United States does are always worse than the reality."

Brown looked directly at Malone. "But Mr. Malone," he said. "There's a flaw in your argument about the Arab world. If the ship sinks and it becomes known that some of the dead were hostages, that is by itself evidence of criminal intent, don't you think? Criminal intent on the part of the shipper."

Malone answered quickly. "You need to spend some time in the Middle East."

The room was silent for a few seconds before Special Agent Carter cleared his throat, trying to get Dan Brown's attention again.

"Yes, Carter," snapped Brown, his mood decidedly darker.

"Interesting as it is, this talk may have just become academic," said Carter. "Here's a small item that just ran in the online version of the *Wall Street Journal*."

He handed a paper to Brown, who read Marie Peterssen's article aloud:

"'Iraqi businessman Mansour Obaidi finds himself embroiled in controversy just two weeks after his appointment as Iraq's new minister of trade. In an unconfirmed CNN report, Mr. Obaidi was identified as the owner, through an intricate web of overseas businesses, of an electronics repair shop that has been implicated in the downing of a Royal Jordanian passenger airliner. A former player in the UN's Iraqi oil-for-food program, Obaidi has negotiated lucrative contracts to deliver Iraqi goods to the U.S. via his own fleet of ships, one of which, the *LB Venture,* is currently under sail for the United States. Foreign intelligence sources confirm the boat is a "high-interest" vessel and is suspected of carrying contraband material. Nevertheless, Mr. Obaidi was a guest at the vice-presidential residence today, lunching with Mr. Cullum, who maintains he has "full confidence" in the new appointee.'"

Brown looked up. "I don't know who this Marie Peterssen is, but God bless her. This is our go-ahead. Mr. Malone, we're going to try to save your hostages."

Chapter Twenty

Morgan Ensley and Danny Comstock boarded the coast guard cutter *Mako* with four navy SEALs. The men, dressed in coast guard uniforms, strode up the gangway and joined four regular coast guard officers on deck. The day was overcast and cool.

"Dream come true," whispered Comstock to Morgan, leaning on the bow railing and grinning, looking out to sea. "Always wanted to be a coastie." Morgan rolled his eyes. Just minutes earlier, a VHF communication had been sent from the coast guard station at Cape May to the container ship *LB Venture* advising the captain that she would be boarded for a routine security and safety inspection. It would force the ship to stop, buying them a little time.

The radio crackled and the captain of the port announced that the *LB Venture* had agreed to be boarded. It was twenty miles off the coast. Within moments, the cutter's bridge rang down standby engines, tested its gear, eased out of its berth, and headed through the harbor out to sea. The sun was just going down, and the coastline was a rosy glow.

It took about forty minutes for the cutter to reach the container ship and prepare for boarding. The protocol was well worked out. Six men climbed aboard a Zodiac H-733, a rubber inflatable boat (RIB) designed for the military to inject commandos into situations at sea. It was a remarkably designed craft that could remain stable even as it was powering, or pacing, next to another boat. Once the men were seated, the boat davit was lowered over the side, dropping the craft into the water. As it hit and the davit was released, two 150-horsepower Evinrude outboard engines fired up and carried the men toward the ship.

Comstock stood behind Morgan in the stack as they approached the larger ship, and, adrenaline pumping, the men took turns grabbing the bottom of the Jacob's ladder and climbing up the thirty feet to the side port, a watertight door in the hull, through which they entered the ship. A second RIB carrying four more men from the cutter arrived. Morgan decided a slightly larger boarding party than the usual four to six men was warranted, since they didn't know if the crew would be hostile or not. After everyone was up the ladder, the two H-733s backed off and bobbed around in the lee of the ship awaiting orders.

The *LB Venture*'s master, Boutros Hamid, greeted them on deck. He shook hands with Mel Letourneau, a gruff, prematurely graying man with the rank of lieutenant commander, USCG. Hamid led Letourneau up the ladder of the house, a large whitewashed structure that resembled an apartment building at the aft of the ship. First they passed the rooms for the lower-level crew, then a floor that held the galley and mess hall. Above that were cabins for the junior officers and above that Hamid's quarters, a generous cabin that included a bedroom, bath, and large office. The office was decorated with scatter rugs and furniture that seemed to mark a seaman's travels across the continents: silk fabrics from Delhi, a rosewood sofa and tea cabinet from Bangkok, desk and chairs from Denmark. On the walls were framed photos of container ships and a calendar of naked Balinese women.

Hamid seemed uneasy. A cigarette hung from his lip.

"You know the drill," said Letourneau. "I need your crewmen's documents—passports, visas, everything. Do you have them all in one place?"

The captain shook his head.

"This may take a while, then. Have your security officer gather the documents together and bring them to me. Meantime, I'm going to read you the ISPS rules regarding the boarding of foreign ships. At the same time, my men will conduct an inspection. I'm also informing you that under the port boarding procedures, we will not be providing identification for our officers."

It was standard procedure. Hamid tried to seem bored as Letourneau read the rules. The coast guard officers spread out past him throughout the house and down to the deck, conducting the checks authorized under the new ISPS protocols. Morgan and Comstock made their way together up one deck to the wheelhouse atop the ship to find out who was in charge of the external communications systems. They saw a deckhand at the wheel and the main navigation controls, and a ship's mate at the controls of the INMARSAT, the International Maritime Satellite System, which runs the Global Maritime Distress and Safety System for communication with other ships and the shore. They observed that the ship was also outfitted with the required SAT-C system, a redundant communications apparatus.

They both memorized the mate's face to make sure they didn't kill him when they came back later that night. It was this man who likely was keeping in close communication with the commander of the operation, keeping him informed of their location and progress. It would probably be he, knowingly or not, who would signal when it was time to blow up the ship.

Morgan wondered how many of the crew even knew what cargo they were carrying. Maybe none of them. Maybe not even the skipper, though he seemed to be worried about something. But they had to know about the hostages. And if they did, they had to know someone was up to no good.

Morgan looked at Comstock and gestured him down the central staircase of the house, whose walls were gray metal, damp and dark. The junior officers enjoyed quite comfortable cabins with bedrooms and offices, like the skipper's, though smaller.

As they passed the mess and galley on the second deck, they noticed the evening meal had already been consumed, and the mess hands were finishing cleanup. On the main deck, where the crew bunked, most of the cabin doors were open partway and the men inside were talking or resting. Each crew member had his own bedroom, and almost every one had his own bathroom. Unions, thought Morgan. They've really done a good job for the merchant seamen. Morgan and Comstock counted the men as they went, checking them against the crew list provided by the ship before embarking. Then they continued down the ladders into the engine room. One man sat in the control room reading; another was making his rounds.

Back in Hamid's quarters, Letourneau droned on with his recitation of the ISPS code rules. Captain Hamid lit another cigarette.

"I'll read the questions I'm required to ask," said Commander Letourneau.

Hamid shrugged.

Letourneau was thinking there was enough laxity on board to kick in extraordinary measures right then and there and stop the ship. Hamid had been around long enough to know better how to keep up appearances. Maybe he'd fallen on hard times. In any case, Letourneau had been instructed from the top not to do anything but a routine board, and not—under any circumstances—to arouse suspicions that he was concerned about the ship's cargo. They didn't know if an individual on board was capable of setting off the explosions himself, or if there was some kind of self-destruct mechanism.

Morgan and Comstock left the house and walked onto the deck. They continued past the gangway along the port side of the main deck all the way to the forecastle at the bow, where they found the two huge anchor windlasses, over which the anchor chains were drawn. Morgan peered down over the side of the ship and saw that because the ship was heavily loaded, the hawse pipes, the holes through which the anchor chains ran from the windlass to the hull, were not too far from the water. It would be possible for the men to climb up the chains onto the boat through the hawse pipes if necessary.

They stepped through a watertight door in the forecastle bulkhead, a vertical wall at the bow of the ship just behind the anchor winches, and down a short flight of stairs into the bosun's locker. Morgan located the panel that controlled electrical power and hydraulic pressure to lower and lift the anchors. It was here in the bosun's locker where he'd hide when the others disembarked. Later, he'd guide them back onto the ship.

Morgan motioned to Comstock. He was ready. Comstock could go now. Comstock gave him a thumb's-up and headed back. To disguise Morgan's absence, he caught up with another group of officers making their rounds and accompanied them back to the house. When they arrived at the captain's quarters, they saw Letourneau holding two passports in the air.

"The U.S. visas of two of your crew members have expired," he said. "I'll have to find out from immigration and customs what they want to do about it. These crew members will not be allowed to disembark in port. I'll have to get back to you."

Hamid shook his head and shifted his weight. "Let me call my ship owners and the agent," he said. "I'll ask them what to do."

Captain Letourneau watched Hamid climb to the bridge. The Americans were spread out between the quarters and the deck, standing impatiently, legs out, arms folded. A few of the men gave each other looks, wondering if they should be expecting any monkey business. After five minutes, Hamid returned.

"I've been instructed to continue straight to New York, and we'll try to fix the visa problems before arriving there."

"As you wish," said Letourneau. "I have to remind you that a guard may be placed on the gangway if the visa problems aren't fixed, and some of your crew members may be kept from going ashore."

Hamid nodded and lit another cigarette. As the coast guard men began to descend the ladders to the main deck and the Jacob's ladder ashore, Letourneau reached for a sheaf of documents in his chest pocket.

"I'm so sorry," he said, pulling Hamid's attention back to the papers. "I forgot that I needed your signature on these also. And the signature of your security officer." Letourneau wanted to keep Hamid's eyes averted so he wouldn't notice that one coast guard man was missing. He kept Hamid busy signing papers until he heard the first RIB pull away from the ship. Then Letourneau gathered up the pages, shook Hamid's hand again, and descended to the remaining RIB, joining the rest.

Once the Zodiacs had all returned to the cutter and were safely stowed in their davits on board, the *Mako* set off a blast from her horn and headed back toward shore. It was 8:30 p.m. and dark.

"Most of those visas and passports were forged," said Letourneau. "I don't know how they made their way out of their last port and across the pond."

"I guess suicide missions don't attract the best sailors," said a SEAL dressed up as a petty officer.

"Are the visa irregularities enough to deny them access to the port?" asked Comstock.

"Unfortunately, no," said Letourneau. "Hamid is a clever old sea hand. The coast guard can't deny access to the port or stop him from continuing with only a crew visa problem."

"What do you need to stop him?" asked Comstock.

"A ship can be detained only with a mechanical problem on board. That would be damaged or deficient safety equipment, certificates out of date or improperly executed, steering gear not working properly, and so forth. We looked over the vessel. Her records and certificates were in order. The captain did his homework and crossed his t's and dotted his i's. Records of his last five port entries and his continuous synopsis record were reviewed. Everything was acceptable."

"What about the hostages? What about the weapons we believe are on board?"

"Truth is, we can detain any ship we want," said Letourneau. "But you don't want this ship stopped. You want it sunk. And that's why your man's on board."

Aboard the *LB Venture*, near Cape May, New Jersey, May 27

Crouching in the bosun's locker, Morgan Ensley heard the cutter's blast. He perked up his ears for sounds of running feet. This was the most dangerous moment of the operation. He was alone without backup and he didn't know if the crew had noticed a man was left on board. He knew it was more dangerous to move than stay put, but his skin was crawling. He knew that stowaways tended to head down to the bosun's locker and got caught when they ventured out for air. He understood why they moved. But he had to get out of there, if only for a few moments to get a feel for the situation on the ship.

He climbed the ladder to the forecastle, stepped onto the deck, and pressed himself against a stack of containers. He listened for the sound of a watchman making his rounds, but heard nothing. He couldn't see a thing. The containers were stacked four high all around him. Someone could be right around the corner of any of them. He slipped back down a ladder to the hold. There it was no better. Boxes were packed seven or eight high. He walked down a catwalk, along a canyon of containers. If there were explosives on this ship, they would be down here. The power of the blast would be maximized by the compression of the explosion created by the hull. He took out his PID, a handheld photoionization detector, which sensed the presence of volatile organic compounds, like explosives. It beeped. Positive. There were explosives on board the ship.

Morgan made his way back to the ladder, climbed up to the deck, and took out a small Geiger counter. The counter began to rattle. There was radioactive material on board. Morgan followed the counter to a container on deck, where the signal was strongest. He didn't see any guards, but as he passed a container standing by itself, he stumbled over a pile of rotten fruit peels. He continued. It was dark now and he had to be careful not to trip over the ropes lashing down the containers. There were no lights on deck. The ship was illuminated only by navigation lights: on the foremast, the stern aft mast, and one on each side of the bridge wings.

Morgan stopped beside a stack of containers piled six high. He proceeded slowly aft, stopping to listen between steps. Normally, a container ship would have two men on watch at night on the bridge. He stayed out of their line of sight.

Morgan took a breath and walked quickly to the stern. As he approached, he saw two men hanging from ropes along the transom. He ducked out of sight. When he came back for a quick peek, he saw what he hoped not to see: they were stringing nylon monofilament wire, common fishing line, across the transom, the SEALs' favored point of entry. No one, except the cognoscenti, suspected entry from the stern, since all eyes on a ship are forward. Sailors typically don't look aft.

The trip wires were strung into spring-loaded contacts, so anyone attempting to scale the stern would pull the nearly invisible wires from the initiating devices. The explosives were packed in oddly shaped boxes hung over the top rail of the stern. If Morgan was right, each side of the box was covered with steel shot, held in place by a thin layer of glue. If they were set off, they'd fire a wall of frag straight down. It would tear apart the men below.

Booby traps.

Morgan turned and walked quickly back along the deck rail to the bow. When he reached the forecassle deck, he stopped and caught his breath. The mission had just got a bit trickier. Entry would have to be at the bow.

Aboard the USGS *Mako,* near Cape May, May 27

Danny Comstock, eight SEAL commandos, and two drivers reboarded the H-733s and were lowered into the water off the *Mako.* They were heavily loaded down with gear: magnets for scaling the sides of the container ship, shaped charges for blowing holes in the sides, and rebreathers for working below the water line, as well as firearms, flares, and safety gear. The boats were riding deep in the water, but Comstock was confident they could handle the load.

The Zodiacs accelerated smoothly toward the *LB Venture.* Comstock sat beside the driver of the lead boat, GPS in hand, following the signal sent out by Morgan's beacon. Even if the ship went off course, they'd be able to follow it.

The sky was dark, the Gulf Stream water temperate, and the spray that kicked up from the boats did not chill their faces. Fifteen minutes out, the water began to change. Four-foot swells rolled past, and within minutes the ocean became choppy and rain began falling, first a few large drops, and then more, picking up so fast the sky was gray with water.

"I think we got ourselves a squall," shouted Comstock to the driver, Rick, who pulled his cap lower to keep the rain out of his eyes.

"Looks it," he said.

"This baby still cuts through a three-foot chop like a shark bearing down on its dinner," said Comstock.

Rick nodded. "Affirmative. We'll see what we get."

Aboard the *LB Venture,* Ten Miles North of Cape May, May 27

Morgan checked the forecastle one more time. He had to familiarize himself with the anchor mechanisms. Since the stern was booby-trapped, he'd signal the SEALs to enter the ship through the hawse pipes. He checked out the wildcat, on which the anchor chain hung like a sea serpent. Then he identified the dog clutch and the hatch to the chain locker, where the anchor chain self-furled. There was also the chain stopper, or "devil's claw," which he had to work properly to protect the men riding up the anchor. Each link of the anchor chain was almost twelve inches long. It could crush a hand in an instant if the chain was improperly secured.

Morgan slipped through the doors on the breakwater and back into the bosun's locker. He walked to the anchor controls. He flicked on a small flashlight, held his hand over it to constrict the beam, and searched the room. He located the motor controls and froze when he thought he heard footsteps outside. He turned off the light. He waited until he could make sense of the sounds and concluded that it was raining. He checked his watch: 9:00 p.m.

Morgan clicked his flashlight back on and looked for a place to conceal himself. He kneeled down to inspect a three-foot pile of mooring ropes. Maybe he could crawl around behind it. As he leaned forward to see over the top, he felt a sharp blow at the back of his head. The lights went out and he fell to the floor.

Atlantic Ocean, Eight Miles North of Cape May, May 27

Comstock held on for dear life to the Zodiac's center console rails. Twenty-knot winds were blowing the sea into a six-foot chop. Heavy rain fell and the wind whipped the waves into streaks of foam. The SEALs lashed down their gear. Comstock pulled out the handheld GPS from his belt to get a bead on the ship. The signal was gone. He shook it and looked again.

"Shit!" he said. "The GPS signal's out!"

The Zodiac helmsman, Rick, looked at him.

"I don't know how much more you want to put your men through," he shouted above the roar of the wind. "This shit's gonna be with us for another hour or so, and it'll get worse before it gets better. The tide and wind direction are against us."

"This operation will not be aborted over a fucking sun shower," said Comstock, who for this stage of the operation had replaced Morgan as commander.

"It's getting worse," yelled Rick, the rain lashing his face. "We may be putting the lives of these SEALs at risk if we continue to push."

"That's what they get paid for!" shouted Comstock. "There are many more lives on the line if we don't succeed."

"Well I get paid to get this boat and the fuckers in it back safely. So it's my duty to let you know we risk ripping the sides off one of these RIBs, or capsizing in this chop. *Sir.*"

The radio headset crackled to life and everyone in the boat lifted his head to stare at the console. It was the coast guard cutter *Mako*.

"Insertion team. Do you read?" asked Captain Letourneau.

"Taxi One, go," answered Rick.

"I have an order to abort the mission. The weather's too bad."

"Taxi One. Roger that we have an order to abort."

Comstock shook his head vigorously.

"Comstock requests your attention, sir," said Rick, keying his headset over to Comstock.

"This is Comstock. We have a man on the container ship. I can't abandon him. We're steady here. We can make it."

The reception crackled again. A huge wave crashed over the boat.

"Doppler radar readings look bad," said Letourneau. "A low-pressure system about a half mile wide is on top of you and moving very slowly."

"It's a rough ride, but we're making way. Give us twenty more minutes."

"Abort the mission and return to the cutter."

"Request permission to stay the course!" shouted Comstock. "We don't abandon our agents in a hostile field."

There was silence on the other end. The helmsman expertly worked the craft, steering over the peaks and troughs into the waves. The SEAL team leader in the back of the boat scrambled forward as the other men struggled to remain seated. Several had lashed themselves to the sides; others crouched as low as they could on the boat's floor. Comstock turned to the SEAL and looked into a set of intense eyes, a game face. He knew this face.

"Fuck 'em," the SEAL mouthed. "No turning back."

Comstock looked back to the horizon and searched for any sign of the ship's lights.

"We can regroup on the cutter and come back when the squall's over!" shouted Rick, again trying desperately to keep the boat heading straight into the waves.

"Goddamnit, helmsman, suck it up or we'll ask your husband to drive," growled the SEAL, who added a few more words into Rick's ear.

The radio crackled to life again. The SEAL team leader stood over Rick, his hand on the headset jack ready to jerk it out of the socket.

"Taxi One, do you read? Repeat, do you read?" Captain Letourneau again.

"Cutter *Mako*, this is Taxi One," said Rick, looking up at the huge SEAL beside him. "Cannot understand, repeat cannot understand." He cut the connection and put down the phone.

"Okay, Comstock," he said, turning angrily to the FBI man. "You have twenty more minutes. This is *your* ass now."

Comstock grinned. Rick turned back toward his console and radioed the helmsman of the other Zodiac.

"Taxi Two. Johnny, you there?"

"You bet your ass I'm here. Have you lost your mind? Captain's waiting for a response." He couldn't believe Rick had hung up on their commanding officer.

"Follow my lead and course, Johnny. I have an idea."

Aboard the *LB Venture*, Twenty Miles North of Cape May, May 27

When Morgan came to, he couldn't see for the light shining in his face. He reached instinctively to push it away, and realized his hands were tied. He shut his eyes and pulled his hands again, feeling they were bound to a pipe in front of him. The light moved away from his face, and Morgan saw that the person holding it was a midget.

No, it was a child! Dang! It was a kid with floppy black hair, couldn't have been more than nine or ten. Then Morgan saw that the kid had Morgan's own gun in his hand and was jacking around with his GPS beacon. And that's when he realized he was restrained with his own handcuffs.

"Dang there, boy!" said Morgan, and the boy looked at him with large scared eyes. "Give me that thing! You're likely to hurt yourself. Come on now."

The boy looked at him blankly.

"Oh boy. No English? No inglés?" Morgan laughed at himself. Why did Spanish come to mind?

"What are you, a stowaway?" Morgan's head was hurting at the back where the kid had whumped him. He sat quietly, knowing that every minute that beacon was out of service the mission was closer to being aborted, leaving him and the kid sitting on the biggest floating firecracker in history.

Morgan looked the boy right in the eye and tried to stand slowly.

"Come on there, buddy." Morgan kept talking, hoping to make some emotional contact with his voice, even though the boy didn't understand a word he was saying. He thought he might distract the boy with his hydraseal bag, a waterproof fanny pack that contained supplies and tools. "Open up this bag. I want to show you something. Lookie here. Undo this zipper."

The child tolerated the gibberish and opened the pack, then looked up at Morgan solemnly. He looked back down into the bag and searched it with his hands. He glanced back up at Morgan before grabbing a shiny-wrapped protein bar and hugging it to his chest.

"You're hungry, is that it?" asked Morgan. "It's yours." Morgan gestured with his chin to the boy, who opened the foil pack and gobbled down the bar.

"You just eat that down." Morgan let him finish before speaking again.

"Okay, buddy, please get the keys off my belt and undo my cuffs. Then we'll help each other off of this boat."

The boy looked at him with a puzzled expression.

"Maftach," said Morgan: Arabic for "key." He'd learned a bit of the language on a trip to Jordan for cave diving. A couple words floated back to him now. Morgan lifted up his cuffed hands to the boy and said it again, "Maftach."

The child took two steps away from Morgan, twirled, and sat down on his heels.

"You're gonna just sit there and watch me, huh? Watch me mess up this entire operation? Thing is, you don't know what the future holds for you, pal. Shark bait. If you knew that protein bar you just gobbled up was going to wind up in the stomach of a big fish down deep, along with you—you'd help me in a heartbeat."

Morgan took one last look at the kid and sighed. He thought for a minute of what implement he could use to free himself. He looked down at his shirt, saw the pen in his breast pocket, and smiled. He leaned over to grab it with his lips and teeth. He then dropped it carefully into his lap and grasped it with his hands. Three minutes later, having worked off the pocket clip, broken it, and sharpened it on the cement floor, he slipped the homemade shim between the ratchet and the shackle of one handcuff, sliding it open and releasing his hand. He did the same with the other and stood up. The child's eyes bugged out of his head. For a moment, Morgan pondered handcuffing the kid to the pipe, but then decided against it. Better to use the kid to navigate around the ship.

Morgan checked his watch. He'd lost twenty-five minutes. Shit! He picked up his gun and the GPS beacon from the floor and flipped the beacon switch back on. It started up again, but Morgan could see that the signal was weak. He had to get it above deck. Morgan rubbed the back of his head. Youch. There was an egg already.

Atlantic Ocean, Twenty Miles North of Cape May, May 28

"Twenty minutes," said Rick. "You got twenty minutes." His arms were so fatigued from holding the boat steady they were starting to shake. His eyes stung from the salt water. The rain continued to beat on them.

"Confirmed," said Comstock, picking up the GPS and giving it a shake. "The GPS is working again!" he yelled, turning back to the SEALs and holding it up. "It says we're a quarter mile from the ship."

The radio crackled again and Letourneau did not sound happy. "Taxi One, Taxi One, respond."

Comstock looked at Rick. Rick keyed over his headset to the FBI man.

"We have a visual, sir," Comstock lied. "Ship is within sight." Rick looked at Comstock, his face twisted in anger. There were no lights in sight. He was about to shout out something when Comstock put his hand on his pistol, removed it from his holster, and aimed it at the inflatable collar of the boat.

"We are proceeding, command," he said, and disconnected.

"I blow a hole in the collar and the boat'll sink like a stone," said Comstock, turning to the helmsman.

Rick, furious at this display, trimmed his engines and backed down on the throttles. Fucking cowboy Rambo jerkoff. Blew off a direct order, and now they were all in danger. This guy was playing with less than a full deck. "Listen, asshole, I killed my career just now when I didn't follow those orders from my commanding officer."

"I'm listening," Comstock replied, pistol still drawn.

"The only way I'm going to get you off my fucking boat and onto that ship is to place us just forward of the ship's bow wave and get a line onto the starboard anchor fluke. Once we're secured, the line will draw us alongside and up your guys go. I'll cut loose, and Johnny will follow my lead to get the other team on board."

"I take it you're with me then and I can put this thing away?" Comstock replied, waving his pistol.

"Don't flatter yourself, cowboy. I got on board when that SEAL leader told me he'd rip my head off and shit down my throat if I didn't get his men on that ship."

Aboard the *LB Venture*, Twenty-one Miles North of Cape May, May 28

Morgan followed the boy along the deck. Containers were stacked five and six high all around them, except for an area at the center of the ship, where two containers sat alone. The boy walked up to one and tapped softly on it. Morgan heard a voice reply inside, and the boy spoke for a good two minutes. It was the container Morgan thought might hold the hostages, because of the food scraps outside it on deck. Morgan wondered how many people were in that crate. They had been at sea for almost two weeks, and they must be miserable. He looked at the lock on the door and saw a wire leading to a plastic box. It looked like it was booby-trapped. He held up his PID. It registered positive. The booby trap was armed.

Just then, he heard a voice from inside say "Hello." It sounded firm but scared. You had to talk loud enough to be heard above the noise, yet nobody wanted the sound to carry to the bridge.

"Hello there," said Morgan.

"You are American?" asked the voice.

"Yes sir. I'm going to try to get you off this ship as soon as I can."

He heard a man's voice speaking inside, and then crying and wailing from many, then several voices trying to quiet the others.

"How many people are in there?" asked Morgan.

"Thirteen. The sanitary conditions are impossible. They take out buckets when they feel like it, but only every few days. People are sick."

"Now don't you worry. We want to get you out before the sun is up today. I have to ask you to please have hope. Now tell me, is this door booby-trapped?"

"Yes it is. There is a bomb attached right inside the door here. But it can be deactivated outside. There is a code for the battery switch." He explained that he'd heard the crewmen disarm it.

"Roger that. Thank you." Morgan opened up the plastic case outside the door and saw a small square pad with numbers on it, like a burglar alarm. "Uh-huh."

Morgan closed the box and returned to the door. "My name is Morgan. What's yours?"

"My name is Yassin al-Douri," said the man.

"Nice to meet you, Yassin. I have to make some preparations. I know it's terrible in there, but I'll have you out soon. Okay?"

"Yes sir."

"Yassin, how did you get into this box?"

"We were grabbed from a beach house in Aqaba. We are two families, Jordanians. We were on vacation. There's another group. Of ladies. Also grabbed from the same area of Aqaba." He cleared his throat. "We were forced into trucks and locked in here."

"I'm sorry to hear that. Please try to stay calm."

"Yes, we do it," said Yassin.

Morgan turned to leave, then thought better of it. He returned to the container. "Can you translate for me for a second with the boy?"

"Of course. His name is Hany."

"Good. Can you ask him how he got out of the box?"

Yassin said, "I can answer. One day, when they came to take out the waste, only one man came, and the ladies were screaming and pounding their feet and they made such noise about the conditions that the boy sneaked out and no one saw him."

"Ask him how he ate."

Yassin translated: "He says he stole food from the kitchen."

"So he's been all around the boat?"

Yassin asked the boy. "Yes, he says he has."

"Great. Buddy, come along with me," Morgan said, speaking to the boy. Morgan guided him along the deck to the other free-standing container. He saw that it too had an alarm pad on its door. Morgan held up a portable radiation detector he carried. The needle slammed itself into the end of the dial. Morgan let out a long, slow whistle.

I guess we know what we have in here, he thought. The Bedouin's bombs.

Morgan led the boy quickly away from the container forward to the bow. They were way off the rendezvous time. And there was some cloudy moonlight—a danger for them all. He'd better walk the anchor down now. He chose the lee side, less chance there of the anchors swinging and injuring his men.

Morgan and the boy walked aft to the bosun's locker; Morgan settled the boy in a corner with a piece of rope and a book of knots and hand directions to stay put. Morgan then started the windlass electrical power. Back up the ladder to the forecastle deck, where he released the devil's claw on the starboard side, pinning it away from the anchor chain. Before releasing the windlass brake, he activated the hydraulic motor to stop the anchor just as it reached the sea line. If it fell into the water, it would cause drag, which would be detected by the helmsman on the bridge. Worse yet, if he released the wildcat brake and let the anchor and chain run, it would wake up half of New York City. He slowly walked the chain down link by link to keep things quiet.

Once he spotted the SEAL team, he would let it down farther. They'd pull themselves up to the chain with grappling hooks, then scale the chain into the hawse pipe. Morgan walked over to the railing and looked at the water. The bow wave rolled out and slammed back with the movement of the ship. Not an easy trick. But they were SEALs. At least the storm had stopped, just as suddenly as it had started. He would wait here for the team, but there was one more thing he had to check first.

Atlantic Ocean, Twenty-five Miles North of Cape May, May 28

The Zodiac H-733 approached the ship from the darkness, and Comstock saw that the anchor on the starboard side had been lowered just above the bow wave. It was the sign telling him to go to Plan B, boarding through the hawse pipes. They approached the ship far to the starboard and in the hull's shadow, hoping to stay out of sight of anyone on the bridge. Comstock glanced over at Rick as the helmsman adjusted his course and speed, carefully studying the wake of the larger ship; it was time to make peace before the guns came out.

"Hey, Rick, you know I wasn't serious about shooting the boat, right?" he said.

"I have no idea what's brewing in that so-called brain of yours," Rick said, turning his head away from Comstock. "But you're crazy, I can tell you that. And if you hadn't been shooting the boat, you coulda' been aimin' a Taser at me and electrocuting us all. Who the fuck knows."

"Oh, stow it," said Comstock. "My partner back home has it worse. He has to deal with me all the time."

"Too bad for him," said Rick. "You're probably one of them sick motherfuckers eats bugs off the wall. You'd do just about anything to get what you need."

"You got that right," said Comstock, cheerful again, getting ready to settle into a story. "I do eat bugs. Once I walked into a 7-Eleven to get a cold Coke, and the cashier, a nice lady, was standing there behind the register saying she'd had a little unwelcome company that morning and she pointed up to this praying mantis perched on the wall. And I told her I'd take care of it and I picked it up and popped it in my mouth. I had an informant with me, a member of a Colombian drug cartel. The guy told me everything I needed to know after that. Sang like a fucking bird."

Rick shook his head. He was not amused. His arms had only just stopped shaking from the exertion of keeping the boat upright and on course.

"Aw, come on, cheer up," said Comstock. "We made it through the squall and it was all because of you and this awesome boat. You'll see. We'll wind up pals after this is all over."

"Pals like you and the praying mantis," said Rick. "No thanks."

The *LB Venture* loomed over them now, an intimidating metal wall. The approach was tricky because the ship was steaming ahead at seventeen knots and the tiny rubber craft had to maintain the same speed as soon as it jumped over the bow wave. The ship was heading north and the prevailing wind was blowing from the northwest, so the leeward side was starboard.

Comstock looked up toward the hawse pipes for a sign from Morgan. He reached into his bag and pulled out an infrared filter and looked again. Then he saw it. Morgan was signaling them from a special light that could be seen only through the filter. Two minutes later, Morgan flashed it again. Comstock responded with a similar light. Then Morgan sent a message tapped out in Morse code:

"Stern NFG." He sent the message twice until he got a reply indicating they'd received and understood. "Stern no fucking good."

Within a few minutes, the men saw the starboard anchor lower slowly to the water line. They jumped into action. Faces blackened, they adjusted their communications headsets, cinched their gear straps, and went to night scopes. They strapped on their packs and confirmed that their dry bags were sealed. Silencers were screwed onto their weapons.

Rick positioned the boat perfectly. One quick throttle boost and he was up over the bow wave. One of the SEALs tossed his grappling hook toward the anchor fluke. It caught. Rick then stalled the engine, and the Zodiac lurched like a slingshot and drew up tight against the ship's hull.

As each man stood to go, the SEAL leader slapped him on the shoulder. Each returned with a thumbs-up. Game time. Comstock led the way. It was good to be back in action, he thought. He felt fit and strong. Five years out and he felt as if no time had passed since his last mission. He reached up and stuck his climbing hook into the anchor chain. He pulled himself hand over hand to the hawse pipe, then squeezed himself through the space, some thirty-six inches in diameter.

"Comstock!" whispered Morgan on deck by the windlasses, reaching out a hand to the camouflaged, wet-suited man emerging from the hawse pipe.

"Hey, man," replied Comstock quickly, pulling himself onto his feet. "We thought we'd lost you back there when the GPS signal died. What the hell happened to you?"

"I was out ballroom dancing," said Morgan. "And I mean out. I'll introduce you to my partner later." Morgan reached down to help up the next SEAL, who was right behind. As soon as he was standing, Morgan felt a rush of adrenaline. Three men were now on board and a fourth was on his way. They had practiced an assault on a container ship similar to this in Norfolk. Each knew his job; the SEALs assumed a defensive stance around the deck, protecting the others as they boarded. Eight, nine, ten. When the last SEAL was up, Morgan directed them to gather in front of the breakwater, where they would be out of sight. The two Zodiacs drifted off into the darkness.

"There are two men on the bridge," Morgan said to the group tightly packed around him. "A watch and a lookout. The rest of the crew is in the house. Assume they're armed. In the center of the deck are two containers standing alone. One is carrying hostages. It's booby-trapped. The other one set off my Geiger counter like it was the end of days. Do not, I repeat, do not shoot firearms at either container. The hold is also full of explosives. We don't want to blow this firecracker up ourselves.

"We'll divide into two groups and storm the house from external ladders, one port, one starboard. There is also a central stairway, which we can use if necessary. Stay away from the stern transom. It's covered with booby traps. We'll clear rooms floor by floor. Bind and gag every individual subdued, so we can go quietly. After shots are fired, use your discretion. And shoot to kill."

At Morgan's signal, the men silently moved aft across the deck. It was midnight, and the black-clad forms snaked soundlessly over the deck and between the stacks of containers. At the bottom of the wheelhouse, the teams split in two. Morgan commanded the starboard group. The SEAL team leader took the port. Comstock grabbed the sniper rifle and split off to the base of the stack. He was going to climb up to the highest point of the ship aft to provide cover. The cover of an expert marksman.

Morgan and his team took off their night scopes and reached the first floor of the living quarters, which housed the low-level ratings. Each crew member had his own cabin, and as the SEALs burst in, weapons raised, the men were so surprised that they put up no fight. One was lying in his bed, reading. Another was folding his socks. The third and fourth were talking quietly together. Five more were asleep in their beds.

The crewmen were quickly gagged and handcuffed and the deck was secured. The commandos advanced up to the next level, which contained the galley and mess. Seven men were watching videos in the lounge. They were quickly overwhelmed.

Morgan's heart was beating hard now and the adrenaline was causing his vision to narrow. He was focused utterly on the goal, seeing only what mattered. With every step he took, he saw his physical surroundings— the gray-painted hallways, the equipment stowed on the walls, the fire doors leading back out to the outside ladders. He also saw them as the floor plan they had studied and practiced on, the two visions melding and separating, his plan and the reality working together.

He climbed up to the third level, the deck for the junior officers. As he prepared to open the fire door, Morgan signaled his men to stop. Then he pointed two fingers to his eyes. He tried to read the feeling in the air. It was ominously quiet. Morgan sensed there was organization. He pulled open the door. As soon as he stepped into the dark interior, he was smashed in the torso by what felt like a jeep. The SEAL behind him also went down. Morgan put his arms over his head and tried to keep breathing. A pummeling jet drove him back against the fire door. He and the SEAL were tangled together, water pounding them like wooden clubs.

The SEAL team on the port side burst through its door and advanced toward a crewman holding a fire hose with a suicide nozzle. The water shot out at a force of 120 pounds per square inch. One SEAL grabbed the crewman from the back, snapping his neck in one motion. The hose flew up in the air like an angry serpent before a second SEAL turned off the fire valve. Morgan was helped to his feet as the team regrouped and continued the deck search. They entered each of the three closed doors of the junior officers' cabins and captured the frightened men inside.

The SEALs were now swarming up the central staircase to the quarters of the senior officers. They formed two stacks along the stairs, and ran into the six cabins. They were empty. Morgan and the SEAL commander crouched in the staircase and took a minute to evaluate their position.

"They must be on the bridge," said Morgan. "Let's return to the outside ladders and approach again, from the outside." The two teams separated and Morgan gave the hand signal to continue up. They climbed the ladders to the bridge, stepped out on the top level, and stacked up at the two sides just aft of the bridge wings.

Through the windows, they could see two crew members manning the controls. Captain Hamid stood at the wing. As Morgan stepped forward, a bullet zinged past his head. He pulled back. Someone was above them, on the monkey island, with a rifle. The SEAL teams looked up but could see only satellites, radar antennae, and a binnacle. Navigation lights mounted on the after-mast put the flying bridge variously in bright lights or shadows. Morgan backed himself up against the house for cover, trying to catch sight of the gunman. He couldn't see a thing. Another crack rang out, and a SEAL on the port side groaned.

The headsets quietly responded. "Man down." There was silence again. One team member swiftly reacted and pulled his comrade safely into the shadows, placing one hand over his wound and one hand over his mouth.

Morgan heard three spits from the stack above him and saw a body fall. He knew the sound of a silenced rifle and looked up to see Comstock rise out of a firing stance on the stack. He'd got the sniper.

Morgan pointed to his eyes again and circled his hand above his head, motioning the SEALS to enter the bridge. They crashed and entered, guns raised. The crew stood in their places, motionless, facing them, including Captain Hamid, hands by his sides. Morgan shouted for them to put up their hands. Then, without warning, Captain Hamid removed a revolver from the small of his back and fired a shot into his temple. What looked like a cup of blood poured from the hole in his head as the ship's captain dropped to the carpet.

Morgan stepped back, shocked. Before he had a chance to react, one of the two crew members on the bridge beside the captain seized Hamid's gun from the floor and grabbed the man at the control panel. He held the gun to the crewman's head.

"Now what in hell?" Morgan said as the remaining SEALs raised their weapons and surrounded the perimeter of the bridge.

The man with the gun pushed his hostage over to the console.

"He's holding the comms guy!" said Morgan, suddenly realizing a potential hostage situation developing.

Just then a SEAL ran straight at the gunman, shouting at the top of his lungs, then threw himself on the floor and rolled across the width of the room. The crewman holding the hostage pushed his captive aside to free his arm holding the gun. A volley of spits emerged from the commandos, and both crewmen fell to the ground. The rest of the men in the room were grabbed by the SEALs.

"Shit!" shouted Morgan. "Shit, shit, shit!" he said, pacing back and forth. "Jesus fucking Christ, we shot the comms guy."

The SEALs stood around the bodies, shifting their weight on their feet, keeping eyes out for more assailants.

"Don't worry about it," said one. "One less asshole to worry about."

"One less asshole," said Morgan, "but this guy was probably ordered to stay in communication with the operational boss. If he stops communicating, the boat may have a self-detonate mechanism."

Morgan took a breath to ward off his anxiety. They were operating on the principle that a telephone call would set off the load. If the boat was underwater, the signal couldn't reach it. If there was a self-destruct mechanism, it could already be wired in the system. They certainly weren't going to look for it. The only thing to do was sink the ship. The water might interfere with any electrical circuit, and being underwater would muffle the force of the blast if it occurred.

"Okay, we're just gonna have to finish this deal real fast." Morgan looked up at the commandos ringing the room. They had boarded; they

had taken control. And now they needed praise. "Good job, men. I'll radio Cape May and get the choppers here. Let's get these hostages off
the ship and figure out how to sink this sucker.

"But first I need to scare up one little guy I left behind."

Atlantic Ocean, Thirty Miles from Ambrose Light, New York Harbor, May 28

The first chopper arrived within fifteen minutes of the
call. The coast guard was in charge, so Washington wasn't second-guessing
every move. Not yet.

After learning from the medic that he'd suffered only a flesh wound,
the injured SEAL didn't want to leave the mission. He'd be fine after a
little stitching up, he insisted. Morgan reminded him that the SEALs'
next job was underwater, and salt water on an open wound, even stitched
up, would be hell. Not to mention the infection he could expect later.
After more spirited protest, Morgan ordered the wounded man onto a
stretcher and lifted up to the bird.

The boy Hany was next to go. Morgan strapped a harness on himself,
then one over the boy, and hooked them together.

"Now, Hany," Morgan yelled to him over the roar of the rotors.
"They're gonna pull us right up into the helicopter." Hany, wrapped into
a too-large life preserver, didn't understand Morgan, but he knew one
thing: he was getting off that ship and would soon see his mother. He
looked around, his eyes filled with wonder. The chopper approached
and hovered overhead, sending down a rope for Morgan and the boy.

"Here we go, Hany-head-wacker!" said Morgan as they were lifted
into the sky. The boy looked alternately terrified and thrilled. They were
pulled into the open door of the UH-60 Black Hawk helicopter, where
they were grabbed by a coast guard rescue swimmer. He detached the
boy from Morgan's harness. Morgan gave Hany a pat on the head and
signaled the pilot to lower him back down on the winch. Hany grinned
and waved. Morgan dropped back to the ship, and as soon as he un-
strapped himself, the chopper flew away, harness trailing behind.

Under Comstock's direction, the commandos had spread themselves across the deck around the container of hostages, checking for pressure mines. If any had been set, simply lifting the box would set off an explosion. A magnet or a reed switch would do the trick, and both could be very small. Any device set up to disrupt the path—a transistor, a relay, or a collapsing circuit—could close the circuit and set off a bomb. The men shined their flashlights under the container, looking for anything unusual. It was difficult to see in the darkness. They worked in teams of two, then changed areas and checked again.

"I don't think they rigged this one," said Comstock to Morgan. "Did you see anything?"

"Nothing but a coupla dead rats and some lashing gear," he said, standing up. "But that reminds me, we gotta make sure these containers are tied down tight before we sink this sucker. We don't want them floating away."

"Good point. I'll issue the order," said Morgan. "But, Comstock, I need to thank you."

"What for?"

"Saving my ass. Taking out that sniper."

"Hell with it," Comstock said. "I'm sure you would have done the same for me."

"Yeah, 'cept you know, I'd need the fifty-caliber and my laptop to get a fix on the weather before I could squeeze off a shot," said Morgan, trying to keep a straight face.

"Speer Firearms Products!" shouted Comstock, raising his hands in the air, recalling the bull's-eye that Morgan had hit, way back in Baghdad on the firing range.

Morgan stood up and they shared a laugh. "Let's roll! There's lots to do and I don't want to stay out here any longer than I have to."

Morgan was scared as hell of what might set off the charges, since the communications protocol—whatever it might have been—with the operational commander, possibly Obaidi, had been disrupted. He dreaded a self-destruct mechanism. But on the other hand, he reasoned, Obaidi would certainly consider it a waste to blow up his load at sea.

Morgan picked up a sat phone that connected them with the coast guard and also Dan Brown's group in Washington. They were all in on the deal now. Morgan and Comstock couldn't make their own decisions anymore. Everything would be second-guessed in D.C.

"Request a chopper return to pick up the container of hostages," Morgan said into the phone. He knew Washington would have liked more time to hash out that decision. But they didn't have it. Getting the container of hostages off the *LB Venture* was the highest priority. The SEALs couldn't proceed with setting the charges on the hull until the hostages were off. And sinking the ship was everybody's concern. Comstock and Morgan walked swiftly back toward the wheel-house.

"This damn ship is still moving," said Morgan. "I ordered the engineer to stop it, but all he could do was slow it down."

"We need to find someone who can kill the engines," said Comstock as the two men surveyed the crew, sitting cross-legged beside the railing where their hands were cuffed. "Know any Arabic?" he asked.

"Some," said Morgan, assessing his available vocabulary. Then: "Aw, let's just try to do it ourselves. Let's go to the bridge."

"You know something about ships, don't you, Morg?" Comstock knew Morgan was configuring an old army boat for shipwreck salvage. He recalled a conversation they'd had waiting for orders in Norfolk. They walked together up the stairs to the bridge.

"It's an army combat support boat," said Morgan, "used for erecting bridges. That's why they call it an 'erection boat.'"

"Whoa there, pal," said Comstock. "I'll have you up on a sexual harassment charge faster'n you can ask 'How was it for you?'"

"It's a twenty-eight-foot aluminum beast," continued Morgan.

"Yeah, that's what all the girls say about you," said Comstock.

"Built in 1971 by Fairey Allday, a company in England that builds combat ships."

"A combat ship, of course. I would have expected no less," said Comstock, finally getting a smile out of Morgan. They walked up the many stairs to the bridge. Hamid's blood was still pooled on the rug. Morgan stepped carefully over the stain and they took their first careful look at the ship's control panels.

"Looks like the command post for a friggin' nuclear power plant," said Comstock, looking over the vast array of controls.

"These two are for the radar," said Morgan, walking past the two panels to the left. "We can ignore them. These are the ones we want"—he pointed to two on the right—"the automation panels." Then, walking over to the ship's steering stand: "Here's the autopilot." He pointed to a three-position switch labeled "Auto," "Hand," and "NFU."

"What's 'NFU'?" asked Comstock, joining him.

"Hell if I know. We should call Washington again," Morgan said, "see if they have an old sea captain who can help us control this ship. Get someone to walk us through it."

"What're you thinking?" asked Comstock.

"I'm thinking we need to sink this ship ASAP. As soon as it's underwater, no telephone signal can reach the triggers on the bombs. The guard or the army or the FBI can send bomb techs later to defuse the bombs when they're underwater. And if there's some other kind of trigger, the water will decrease the effect of the explosion."

Comstock nodded. "Let's divide up, then. You call D.C. and try to find someone to walk you through the ship controls. I'll get the men into the water to set the mines. We'll just work on a moving ship—harder, but not impossible."

"Ten-four," said Morgan. Just then, his phone rang. He answered, listened for a few seconds, then said, "Roger."

"The coast guard is sending a chopper for the hostages," he said to Comstock. The men heard the rotors of an approaching helicopter before they saw it in the light of the moon. Its nose dipped momentarily, as if not certain what was to come. Then it leveled off and hovered over the ship.

"Who's going to defuse the booby trap on the door?" asked Comstock.

"I guess some army sapper they're bringing in. They're taking the box to the old Brooklyn Navy Yard to work on it there in case things don't go well. They're putting it down in one of the old graving docks. Twenty feet of concrete around them. Built in the old days to withstand a nuclear explosion."

Comstock shook his head, trying not to think of the consequences if something went wrong. Poor Hany had been through enough without losing his mother too.

On deck, the SEALs were ready; they attached a container spreader and four lashing wires to hooks at the four corners of the container. The wires led to a large central ring. A SEAL clambered to the top of the container and held the ring as the Chinook lowered a large hook at the bottom of the cable it was dragging. The deck was fully illuminated by lights now, but the ship was still moving, making approach by helicopter difficult. The hook swung a few feet wide to port. The chopper turned and approached again. This time the pilot nailed it, and the SEAL scooped the hook right under the ring. The wire tightened, the SEAL lowered himself to the deck, and Morgan muttered a short prayer under his breath. The Chinook seemed to struggle for a few seconds, then lifted the box off the ship. Morgan and Comstock heard screams as well as cheers from inside the container as it sailed up into the sky.

Morgan smiled. "That's a good sight."

SIOC Amphitheater, Washington, D.C., May 28

"The *LB Venture* is thirty miles from Ambrose Light," said Captain Whorley, a whiskey-voiced man with a no-nonsense Bronx accent, referring to the buoy that marked the outer entrance to the ports of New York and New Jersey. "If it's not stopped, it'll get there in about two hours."

The number of people in Dan Brown's operations center had tripled in the last hour. Brown's tie was off, his shirt open. He sat in the front row.

"The hostages are off the boat," said Leo Mazur of the Terrorist Financial Working Group. "We should just torpedo it."

"Except we have two FBI agents and ten SEALs on board that ship," said Brown. "Not to mention the Indonesian crew, or what's left of it."

"Look," said Mazur, "At some point, if that boat isn't stopped, we'll need to take it out, no matter who's on it."

"How would you calculate that point?" asked Brown, his face reddening, his anger palpable. "We don't know the threat of the nuclear material on board. We can't even start to calculate nuclear clouds and potential deaths. We don't have any facts."

"None of it matters," said the HMRU's Leroy. "We know it's bad. We don't need to know how bad. We got the hostages off. One of our men was wounded in the attempt. We don't need to answer to anyone. For reasons beyond our control, the boat exploded. We torpedo or bomb the ship now and eliminate its chance of reaching New York."

"We have pilots at Otis Air Force Base readied to scramble at the president's order," said Major General Tom Beacham.

"From the reports I'm getting," said FBI director Tony Astante, stepping in, "the navy and FBI teams are working to sink that ship. They are proceeding according to plan. We believe that their operation is the most likely to achieve most of our goals in this matter. Saving the lives of those on board and sinking the ship to keep bomb detonators from receiving any telephone triggers. I think we're best served by giving them more time."

"How much more?" asked the man from State.

"That is a decision to be made by the president."

Atlantic Ocean, Twenty-five Miles from Ambrose Light, May 28

"Go to the autopilot switch on the wheel," said Captain Whorley on the telephone with Morgan. "Look where the rudder's positioned on the rudder-angle indicator."

"Hold on, sir," said Morgan. He was standing on the bridge of the *LB Venture*, scanning the automation panel in front of him. "Yes, it's at five degrees."

"Good," said Whorley. "Take the wheel in your hand and move it to five degrees. Then you'll match it to the autopilot."

Morgan looked at the wheel, turned it until the dial read five degrees. "Done, sir."

"Good man. Name's Bob."

"Okay, Bob," said Morgan.

"Now go to the autopilot switch on the steering wheel and turn it away from 'Auto' to 'Hand.'"

"Affirmative."

"Now you're steering the ship."

"Roger that."

"I'm told you want to stop the ship, correct?"

"Yes sir, Captain."

"I want you to go to the engine order telegraph. The switch next to it should say 'Bridge Control' or 'Engine Room Control.'"

"Got it," Morgan replied. "It's switched to 'Bridge Control.'"

"Good. That makes it easier. Now look for the lever that reads 'Full Ahead' or 'Half Ahead' or 'Dead Slow Ahead.'"

"I see it," said Morgan.

"Put it to 'Stop.' Pull the lever to 'Stop.'"

"Confirmed," said Morgan. He waited to hear the engines slow down. They did not.

"Engine did not stop," said Morgan.

"That's strange," said Bob. "We're going to need to take a step back and look at a few things."

Just then, Morgan heard an explosion somewhere below him and to starboard. His stomach dropped. Every nerve in his body steeled for a second explosion and then a chain reaction that would obliterate them all. He'd imagined it more times than he'd like to admit. Like white sulfur. But a million times hotter. A white hiss. Then nothing.

"What's up?" asked Bob.

"I heard an explosion downstairs, Skipper. I gotta get off the phone. Can you hold while I check?" Morgan was practically jumping out of his skin, desperate to get downstairs.

"You can't go anywhere, son. You're steering that ship."

"Jesus," said Morgan. He couldn't concentrate; he could hardly even hear the man because he was listening for it, his whole body anticipating another boom, a flash, then the big one. He felt the sweat rise on his chest and across his lower back.

"Listen to me," said the voice on the phone. "Walk over to the main panel and open the glass cover on the switch that says 'Emergency Stop Main Engine.'" Morgan pulled out the small hammer attached by a chain to the panel and lifted it in the air, preparing to smash it down on the plate glass. But then he saw just about the worst thing he'd ever seen. Small black wires running under the glass and around the edge of the emergency stop switch. When he leaned over and looked closely, he saw the charge, a small piece of gray Semtex, pushed up around the edge of the circular glass cover.

"Jesus fucking Christ," he said. "It's booby-trapped. The fuckers booby-trapped the emergency stop."

"Say again?" said Bob.

"The stop button is booby-trapped. I can even see the charge. But I can't cut the wires, because I've seen these kinds of deals—oftentimes they attach the wire to a relay." Morgan froze. He wasn't sure what to do now. He looked around, sure he smelled fire.

Comstock burst into the room. "One of the limpet mines went off prematurely, and a SEAL is hurt," he said, breathing hard from sprinting up the stairs. "And there's fire in the hold."

"We've got fire in one of the holds," said Morgan to the phone, his voice rising.

"Okay, son, listen to me. You need to stop the ship to control the fire. The moving ship is just fanning the flames. Depending on where the fire is, you might be able to put it out by flooding the space with CO_2. There are fixed CO_2 bottles in the engine room and elsewhere in the cargo spaces."

Morgan felt a glimmer of hope. "I have to find out where the fire is. Maybe the CO_2 will work. What can we do to stop the engine?" He was thinking out loud. "What if we try to disable the propeller?" he asked. "You know, like if you get fishing line wrapped around an outboard motor, you'll jam it. Could we drop one of the mooring wires of the stern back aft?"

"Possible but not practical. There should be an easier way."

"Let me put the ship back into autopilot and see if I can just slow it down."

"The engine order telegraph didn't work before," said Bob.

"It might be jury-rigged not to stop. Maybe it'll slow."

"Let's try it. Go to the telegraph and move it to 'Dead Slow.'"

Morgan moved the lever and heard the pitch of the engine slow. "Mother of God. The ship is slowing. I gotta go belowdecks and see what we got."

"Drop anchors when you get a chance," said Bob. "And go below and turn off the fuel pumps. That'll slow you down until the engine dies a natural death."

Lower East Side, New York, May 28

Red put his right foot into the tub in his bathroom at the Holiday Inn on Allen Street. He was small, his legs shapely, almost like a girl's, but covered with wiry black hair. He lowered his trim, taut body carefully into the steaming water. He loved hot baths. The one Western luxury he indulged in. Everything else was profanity and sin. You couldn't escape it. It was everywhere: on television, in the movies, in popular music on the radio. The Americans cheapened sexuality and worshipped senseless violence.

The young man pulled a bar of Ivory soap from its wrapper and lifted his lower leg out of the bath. He soaped it from ankle to knee and grabbed a Schick razor from the side of the tub. His first pass with the razor on his shin was tentative, and it hardly shaved any hair off. He soaped it some more, then scraped it a second time. The hair on his leg was coarse and thick, and it was harder to shave than he'd thought it would be. He'd worn thick black tights and long-sleeved shirts every day he dressed as a girl so as to avoid this chore, but now it was time to prepare for his passage to heaven. He had to be clean, hairless, and sweet-smelling when he took up his place beside the Prophet. And that was where the *shahids* sat, at the knee of Muhammad himself. Red thrilled with the thought. How many of them had thought and dreamed of this day? Many, but not all had made it. He grabbed a small scissors and tried snipping the hair first. He trimmed a small section, then tried to shave it. That was better. He ran his finger over his newly bare skin and his spine tingled. The skin felt different and new.

He recited prayers to himself, trying to cleanse himself of all but religious thoughts. "When He caused calm to fall on you as a security from Him and sent down upon you water from the cloud that He might thereby purify you, and take away from you the uncleanness of the Shaitan, and that He might fortify your hearts and steady your footsteps thereby." Red offered thanks to Allah that he had thought to buy more than one razor, because the first one became dull after he was only partly through with the first leg. He drank tea and continued with the other leg, then his forearms. He soaped his belly and carefully removed the hair there as well.

When he was finished, he let out the water from the tub, watching the hair wash down the drain as if it were washing away all the stains and dirt of the life he'd observed here. He then put on the shower and stood underneath it to rinse himself completely. After he had toweled himself off, he spoke several verses of the Koran into his cupped hands, and then rubbed his hands onto his body, so as to press the words into his very skin. Then he reached for the bottle of cologne he'd purchased the day before.

Red then pulled on his clothes: a snug-fitting top, tights, a tight-knit skirt, thick-soled boots. Again, the instructions stated that men should wear tight-fitting clothes, as that followed the ways of the Prophet Muhammad, who would tighten his clothes before battle. Red thought his disguise fit the bill quite cleverly.

Red looked over his will and last words, signed them, and placed them in the one bag he would leave behind. He checked his backpack, which held the bomb, and moved it away from the suddenly overheating radiator. He sat down on his bed and opened his copy of the Koran. Now was the time to continue his spiritual preparation, praying for God's mercy, strength in battle against the great Satan, and success over his enemies.

Atlantic Ocean, Twenty-three Miles from Ambrose Light, May 28

Morgan and Comstock ran down the stairs from the bridge two at a time to the main deck and looked around for the site of the explosion. The area around the *LB Venture* resembled a naval shipyard now, with helicopters overhead, divers in the water or clinging with magnets to the hull. The night was lit up with lights from the ship and beams from two coast guard cutters aiding the men setting the limpet mines. RIBs shuttled between the *LB Venture* and the cutters, removing the surviving crew members and the bagged bodies of the crew members killed during the assault, including Captain Hamid's.

"It's aft, on the starboard side," said Comstock as they made their way down the ladders toward the stern. He and Comstock stepped down to the dimly lit cargo surrounded by fifty-foot-tall walls of containers. It was like walking along Wall Street, the canyons of containers rising on both sides like skyscrapers. As they neared the ship's side shell, they saw flames flickering around a ragged hole above the waterline, lapping their way around the interior wall.

"Jesus. What else could go wrong?" asked Comstock.

"Let's just pray the explosives are in containers far away from here," said Morgan.

"I'm praying with all my might, Morg. I'm just forgetting the words."

A few more steps and the heat became unbearable. The men realized their approach was limited from this side and ran back up the ladders to the main deck. Once in the air, they ran to the ship's railing and looked over it toward the water. They saw a RIB bobbing beside the hull with several people aboard, including a diver who was prone and apparently hurt. Flames licked up the side of the ship, causing Comstock and Morgan to jump back from the rising heat. Morgan picked up his phone and called the coast guard.

"We've got a small fire in one of the cargo holds. We need a cutter with high-stream fire pumps and spray monitors. Highest priority."

Morgan hung up. "Dispatch says the cutter should be here. Its position is the same as ours. Can't see a damn thing of course, because of all the lights."

"We need to stop this goddamned ship and put out that fire! The CO_2 will snuff a fire in minutes in a closed space, but if that explosion punched a hole in the side shell, it won't do a damn thing!" shouted Morgan, who was feeling shaky. The operation seemed to be spinning out of control.

"Maybe if we can temporarily block the hole, a burst of CO_2 might be enough to put it out," said Comstock.

"How are you going to block the hole?"

"How about with a blast of water from a cutter?" asked Comstock. "It might be enough if the timing is right."

"Possible," said Morgan, who couldn't think of anything better. "I'll look for the CO_2 control room."

"Roger," said Comstock.

Morgan ran aft toward the accommodation forward bulkhead where Bob Whorley had told him the CO_2 was stored. As he jogged past the house, he saw a group of coast guard officers gathering evidence, placing materials in plastic bags. Good idea, Morgan thought as he kept moving. 'Cause pretty soon there'll be no more evidence. No more ship to investigate. Somebody was going to make a telephone call to a trigger and then there'd be no more nothing. He located the CO_2 room and kept the position in the back of his head.

Running forward on the main deck, he moved to the bosun's locker, his first point of refuge on the ship. He walked over to the panel that operated the anchors and hit the power switch. He heard the electric motors wind up and the air move through the pipes. He climbed back up to the forecastle deck where the two windlasses were located. He backed the chain for the starboard anchor up on the wildcat until it was slack. He shifted the dog clutch and turned the huge wheel to release the brake. The anchor chain flew out of the chain locker, rust and mud flying everywhere and the anchor disappearing into the sea. He repeated the action on the port windlass until both anchors were dragging deep in the ocean.

Morgan then ran back up to the bulkhead to the door marked "Fixed

CO_2." He pulled it open and found a large chamber filled with piping and about three hundred red-painted canisters of CO_2. On the wall he saw a schematic. "Jesus," he said. "Instructions in English." He could hardly believe his good fortune. He looked over the instructions, getting the idea pretty quickly. All he needed now was the confirmation from Comstock that the water was blasting at the hole.

Morgan stepped out of the room. He knew the SEALs were hanging off the sides of the ship, setting their mines below the waterline. The divers chose their spots from a map created for them before the assault by a structural engineer. They planned to set two mines each, a total of twelve. Even if one set failed, ten would be enough to sink the ship. The charges were shaped to cut round holes just below the waterline that would scuttle the ship quickly and evenly.

It was crucial to set all the charges at the same time. Then the ship would flood evenly, sinking straight down and not rolling over. The ends of the detonation cord at each mine were folded over out of the water and taped to make a cradle for the blasting caps. Each was double primed, meaning two caps were attached instead of one, wired in parallel, the second serving as a backup.

Morgan's phone rang. It was Comstock. "The cutter's here and spraying water at the fire."

"Ten-four," said Morgan. "I'll send the CO_2." He stepped back into the CO_2 closet, pulled the lever to the aft cargo hold, and slipped out the pin on the main valve. He twisted it to the open position, then pulled the release to send the CO_2 into the cargo hold. He heard a whooshing sound as the gas rushed through the tubes. He made sure all the available valves were open, then stepped back onto the deck, where the sharp breeze made him aware that his face and scalp were drenched with sweat. If the CO_2 didn't work, he had no other tricks up his sleeve. They'd have to abandon the ship. It'd blow, but with any luck most of them would be able to get off first.

His telephone rang again. "You did it, bud!" yelled Comstock. "The water held the opening closed long enough for it to work. The CO_2 put out the flames."

Morgan sagged for a moment against the ship's railing. His body was screaming with pain from the lashing he'd got from the fire hose during the assault. But he couldn't rest yet. There had been no communication from this ship for several hours. What had been the usual cycle? He had no idea. He put the phone back up to his head. "I want the ship evacuated now," said Morgan. "We'll set off the charges by radio control. I want everyone off."

"Ten-four, Morg," said Comstock, who was already running but not quite ready to follow Morgan's order. Comstock ran back to the bridge. How many times had he run the length of this deck today? This little sprint was almost a 440 itself. Thank God he'd been staying in shape, he thought, or he'd be dead meat by now. He climbed the stairs again, his legs heavy after the sprint, and up to the bridge. He was breathing so hard he had to stop for a moment and lean over. When he'd caught his breath, he walked over to the wheel and cranked it to twenty degrees, then ripped off a piece of cord from the back of the captain's chair and tied the wheel in place.

If this sucker wasn't going to stop, at least it was going to sail in a big circle. And that is exactly what it did.

New York City, May 28

Marie pushed away the covers and swung her feet to the floor. She'd fallen asleep, the first nondrugged sleep she'd had since returning home. She looked outside and saw with a start that it was morning. She stepped quickly to her desk and checked her e-mail and phone messages. Nothing. She'd sent in her story and there was nothing to do now but wait to hear from her editor. She walked into the bathroom and turned on the shower, stopping to look at herself in the mirror over the sink. She leaned in closer, then tipped her chin away from the mirror.

Whom did she look like? She looked at her face this way and that, then turned and walked into her bedroom. She opened the top drawer of her bureau. She lifted out a key ring and a card postmarked two days before. It was from Chelsea Mini Storage, informing her of a rodent problem and advising her to check her belongings for any signs of damage. She needed to go there anyway; she wanted to look for some old papers of her mother's.

Marie put the card from the storage place on the table in her entryway, propped against the telephone with her keys.

She turned on the shower and pulled off her clothes. How was it that a nice hot shower could make almost everything better, she thought, stepping in and letting the water run over the top of her head and down her body.

The bathroom door was half open, and she felt a brief draft, as if someone had opened a window or a door. She wondered if she had stupidly left the front door unlocked. She couldn't hear anything over the sound of the running water, so she turned it off and listened carefully for a few moments. She heard a scraping sound. It seemed to come from the hall outside. She felt the draft again, and, frightened, she stepped out of the shower, wrapped a towel around herself, and peeked out of the bathroom, down the hall to her front door. Nothing. She listened again, and heard the building's ancient elevator lumbering its way to the foyer.

She looked at the entryway table, and everything was exactly as she had left it. Being kidnapped could make a girl jumpy, she said to herself. Then she remembered an old saying she'd heard: "Even paranoiacs have enemies."

Marie got back in the shower and had a good scrub. Then she dressed quickly, slipped the key to her storage locker into her handbag, and went out the door. She took the stairs rather than waiting for the elevator, and hailed a cab.

"Chelsea Mini Storage please. Twenty-eighth Street and Twelfth Avenue."

She was still thinking about the *Journal* article, and in her concentration failed to notice a man watching impassively from across the street. He was elegantly dressed, his suit from a bespoke tailor on Savile Row. His dark hair was well trimmed, his skin a light olive. An observer might have described him as an Arab.

Lower East Side, New York, May 28

Red closed the door to her room at the Holiday Inn on the Lower East Side and walked down to the front desk. She pulled a backpack over her shoulder with a boyish tug and adjusted her skirt and tights beneath. She wore a wool hat with a small crocheted flower on it and heavy black patent leather boots. The desk clerk didn't say a word; cross-dressing was hardly unusual in this part of the city. Red walked to the F train stop at Second Avenue and entered with a Metrocard. She waited for three minutes for an uptown train and boarded, then slipped off at West Fourth and transferred to a downtown C train to Chambers Street. She walked the rest of the way to Eleventh Avenue, stopped at a small park two blocks from the target, and opened her backpack. She rustled around, setting the wires for the detonation, and when she was done, she pulled out a ChapStick and dabbed it on her lips. She hoisted the backpack over her shoulder again, tightened the lumbar strap, and continued down the street.

She had not received a call confirming that the *LB Venture* had arrived. But her orders were to proceed at the designated time nonetheless.

She approached the entrance of 124 Eleventh Avenue and noted the cement traffic blocks around the building and the SWAT team members with heavy guns posted at the perimeter of the building. Red walked up to the entrance as if she were an employee and pulled open the front doors. She walked toward the metal detectors and the guard dog, but then swerved out of line and headed into the lobby. A security guard called out to her to stop and show ID, but she kept walking, the rubber soles of her boots squeaking on the ground, her short skirt riding up the pink-and-black wool tights she wore beneath.

"Excuse me," the guard said again, this time with an expression of bewildered irritation as he walked after the red-haired young woman, holding on to his belt to keep his gun, flashlight, and handcuffs from banging against his leg. But by then she had made it halfway into the lobby, and before the dog could even bark she reached up to a pocket on her backpack and pulled a cord.

For several seconds, Red and a policeman and the security guard and the dog and two bystanders were up in the air together, gravity defied. Red was an expert, trained by Obaidi himself. The effect of the explosion was strictly mathematical and could be analyzed, before and after the fact, with simple three-dimensional vectors. Red had constructed the bomb to blow straight upward, because his aim was a computer on the second floor. It all went according to simple rules of physics. In fact, Red was able to visualize, just before pulling the cord, who would die, who would be wounded.

When they found his head later, the wig and hat blown off, he still had a smile on his face. One attendant at the morgue thought it was a smirk. The pathologist, a Pakistani Muslim, disagreed.

"It's joy," he said. "Paradise found."

Atlantic Ocean, Twenty-three Miles from Ambrose Light, May 28

Morgan Ensley and Danny Comstock stood next to each other on the deck of the Cutter *Resilient* one-half mile from the *LB Venture,* which was slowly circling in deep water. It had taken a small miracle of ship engineering and logistics, but everyone was now off the *LB Venture,* the mines all set.

They sat like city neighbors in lawn chairs, watching particularly interesting goings-on down the street.

"Forcing the ship to sail in circles. Un-fucking-believable." Morgan held up his hand and Comstock high-fived him.

They were waiting to get the order from the president to blow up the ship.

"This is pretty funny, if you think about it," said Morgan, sat phone in his lap.

"What's funny?" said Comstock.

"We're sitting here waiting for a phone call to tell us to set off some charges that'll sink that ship real slowlike," said Morgan. "And over there"—he pointed to the *LB Venture*—"is another phone, waiting to receive its own call that will blow it and everything in the ocean for a quarter mile to smithereens."

"And?" said Comstock.

"Well, I guess I feel seriously outgunned."

Comstock laughed. "Which one you think is going to come in first?"

The phone in Morgan's hand rang just then, causing them both to jump.

"Jesus," said Morgan. "Sweet holy Jesus."

"Answer it," said Comstock.

Morgan picked up the phone.

"Ensley," he said. Then, "Ten-four," and he hung up. He looked at Comstock. "We got the go-ahead."

They both looked down at the radio transmitter. Morgan put his hand in the air, hovering over the button. "You do it," he said, pulling away.

Comstock leaned over and pushed the button. They saw a line of spray around the hull and then bubbles as the det cord ignited; then they heard explosions underwater, heavily muffled.

"Thank the Lord," said Comstock. "We didn't set off the whole load."

They sat for a few minutes, watching.

"Is it sinking?" asked Morgan.

"Definitely," said Comstock.

They watched the ship turning, turning, taking on water. It seemed to begin to pitch slightly to starboard, the inside of the circle. "It's listing," said Morgan. "Not good."

"Yeah, but it's filling up fast," said Comstock. "And that *is* good." The two sat there, watching, almost hypnotized by the drowning ship. They heard some groaning steel, a few loud cracks. Everything was being recorded by satellite cameras on drones, they knew, and they'd see it all again later. But this was the best view anyone would ever get.

And then with a horrible sucking noise, in a final lurch, the *LB Venture* dipped beneath the surface, causing a boiling effect. Very quickly, there was nothing. Morgan had the distinct feeling his knees were about to give out.

"That'll show those religious freaks and their seventy-two virgins to mess with old Yin and Yank," Comstock said, raising his fist in the air.

"Oh yeah," said Morgan, sitting down hard.

"You ready for a beer?" asked Comstock.

"I'm ready for something just a little stiffer, thank you very much."

"Let's get *to* it," said Comstock. "Paperwork to follow, eh Morg?"

Chelsea Mini Storage, New York City, May 28

The mini storage company was in West Chelsea, an area now taken over by art galleries whose owners could no longer afford the high rents in SoHo. West Chelsea offered space in huge former maritime warehouses and in factories that once made products like paper bags and books. Of course, what some of the galleries gained in affordability, they lost in foot traffic from the sidewalks. They tended to be on upper floors, and unless you had a specific reason for going there, you were unlikely to find them. The buildings were that anonymous.

Chelsea Mini Storage was in one such building—but then, anonymity was a good thing in the personal-storage business. Who knew what might be in those lockers the size of a decent bedroom? The Drug Enforcement Administration was only one of the many interested government agencies.

Marie entered the office and approached an attendant behind a glass window. She told him the number of her storage locker and pushed her driver's license through a slot. He checked her on the computer, scribbled an identifying number on a name tag, and handed it back to her along with her license.

"Fourth floor," he reminded her. She thanked him, walked to a huge industrial elevator, and waited beside a couple of West African street vendors with a cart full of wood sculptures. The elevator operator entered and Marie watched as the doors closed from the top and the bottom, meeting at waist height. She remembered this from last time. Weird, but that was how all industrial elevators closed, she'd been told. She stepped out on the fourth floor. The hall was clean, the bricks painted a glossy battleship gray, with fairly new storage chambers on both sides. She checked the number on her key again, turned left, walked down a short hallway off the main passage to where she had rented a locker measuring sixteen feet by twenty feet.

It was more space than she really needed, but she kept a few bulky items there: the saddle of fine Spanish leather from the golden mornings she and her mother rode the bridle trails outside Cordoba; steamer trunks full of her mother's costumes; boxes of newspaper clippings, the ecstatic reviews that never failed to follow a performance by Jeanne Mercier. It was Marie who did the clipping.

In the locker she also kept some of her old fencing equipment.

This day, however, Marie had come for a box of old letters that dated from her mother's stay in Madrid. As a diva, Jeanne Mercier was deluged by fan mail and gifts. But she had not been a notably sentimental woman. Very little of the fan mail survived, and not many more of the personal letters. After her mother died, Marie read every one she could find. She remembered that there were a dozen from the same correspondent, written in a confident, all too obviously male hand. They alluded to luncheons in the countryside, postperformance suppers, and, it seemed to Marie, enough tender moments to amount to a love affair.

She opened her locker door and strode right to the box. She rummaged through it and found the packet of letters. Her mother had tied them together with purple velvet—a gesture quite unlike her, as Marie knew full well.

Seated spread-legged on the floor—a posture that always annoyed her mother, which was one good reason for doing it—Marie began reading. Surely somewhere among the letters was a clue to her father's identity.

She noticed the writer's veiled references to his necessary but unexplained departures. His English was good, but he made consistent grammatical errors, lumping future and conditional tenses together. But that was no help. Many foreigners did that when speaking English.

She got up and went back to the box. At the bottom, she found a green flannel bag closed with a silk cord. This is what she was looking for. After slipping her finger into the neck of the bag and easing open the cord, she tipped it open and out tumbled the silver pin she had described to Julian. Though she had remembered it as a fleur-de-lis, it was indeed just as Julian had described it: a dagger in the center surrounded by two wings. She looked it over again and slipped it into her pocket. Then Marie pulled out the brown paperbound book. She flipped open the pages and saw the writing, strange scratches of characters written from right to left. The book was only half filled, and either it was written in some kind of code, or it was poetry, for the lines were short and staggered in length. She looked at the last page of writing. The passage was a long one, as if a description or a story.

She closed her eyes and hugged the book to her chest. Here it was, before her, a book filled with words that might have been written by her own father! And she couldn't read them, even though right in her arms might be the answers to her long-unanswered questions. Her eyes filled with tears at the frustration of it. He was so close to her, but still completely out of reach. Was Ari anything like Julian? Julian told her his partner was handsome, very tall with brown eyes and dark curly hair. He was brave and stubborn. And also overly sensitive. He had played the flute. Tears dripped from her eyes now, and she doubled over the book. She wiped her eyes and took a deep breath when she realized that someone had walked down the hall and was now standing in front of the storage closet. She jumped up with a shout.

Three feet from her, dressed in business clothes, was Mansour Obaidi.

"I thought I might find you here," he said.

Marie fought to keep her breathing even, to slow her heart, which felt like it was beating its way out of her chest. Where was her composure? This was something she never imagined. Was he hunting her down? Did he know about her and Julian? Should she play dumb?

She chose bravado. "I expected to find you, too, though not here. In fact, I was on my way to meet you when my driver was shot. I was pulled out of the car and held captive for two days." She stopped and looked away for a moment. Then she looked back at Obaidi. "Actually, I thought it might have been you who kidnapped me."

"Me? Why would I do that? You were on your way to see me." His voice was low and clear, his accent baroque, ornamented. "When you didn't arrive, I called every former general and militia leader I knew in Iraq to find out what had happened, and no one knew."

"Well, I certainly didn't know. I was kept blindfolded, and then I was drugged and I woke up in my apartment back here."

"Improbable, I think."

"I'd have to agree with you about that," she said, allowing him a smile, "but it happens to be true."

What was even stranger was his coming to New York to look for her. She'd just escaped, if by no means of her own, a rather spectacular kidnapping in Baghdad. Was it her fate to be chased down, killed, and stuffed in her own storage locker beside the Hudson River?

She noticed that he was looking at her in an appraising way. It was not a friendly gaze. "You wanted to meet with me again," he said. "Why?"

Marie looked at him long and hard. She knew she was in grave danger and needed to play this right. She took a deep breath, and blurted it out: "I wanted to know if you were my father," she said. She wanted him to see her face softening. And she wanted to live.

What she saw on his face, for the first time, was an expression that was not artfully cultivated, controlled. He looked almost shocked, but she saw something else as well: pride.

"Why would you think that?" he asked.

"Because I think you might have known my mother. In Madrid a long time ago. Her name was Jeanne Mercier."

"She talked about me then, did she?"

There it was. He had figured it out. He had known she was connected to Mercier. Marie, lying, nodded. Her mother had never mentioned him.

"You used the past tense when speaking about your mother. Is she dead?"

"Yes. She died two years ago."

"I'm very sorry to hear that," said Obaidi. He ran a finger over his chin. His eyes wandered up the walls of the storage lockers. "Yes, I did know your mother."

To himself he said: I might even add that I was in love with her. Maybe. Maybe not. Perhaps I was confused at the time. He had been thrown off track by this talk. A shiver of emotion shook him, but he quickly righted himself.

Marie wanted to keep Obaidi's attention away from the book she held in her hands. That would be the end of everything. She also was avoiding the painfully obvious and frightening question of why he had followed her to the storage place and how he had gotten in. Had he pointed a gun at the guy downstairs? Did he have a gun now?

"Yes?" she said. "You said 'yes.'" Had he in fact said yes, or was she misremembering? "Is there any chance that you are my father?"

"That question is not a proper one for a woman to ask a man," Obaidi said.

"Did you come all the way to the United States to see me?" she asked quietly.

"I have governmental meetings here. I was named minister of trade for the Republic of Iraq shortly after our first conversation."

"Yes, I wanted to talk to you about that," Marie said.

"I am also here to clear my name of outrageous allegations made about me on American television."

Marie looked away, past Obaidi to the hallway. She thought she heard the elevator door open.

"I guess I didn't hear about them," she said. But he had caught the prevarication on her face.

He took a step toward her, and she took the opportunity to drop the notebook into the open box beside her, as if she were just going about her business. She was desperately hoping to go back about her business.

"You did some traveling when you were in Iraq," said Obaidi, standing a bit too close for comfort. "You were seen in Rutba and elsewhere in the company of an American."

Shit! thought Marie. What she said was, "Yes. I was continuing my story about successful Iraqi business ventures." She decided not to step back, not wanting to signal her fear.

"And what happened to that story?" he asked.

"I got kidnapped." She made a jagged smile. "Maybe now that we're here in the U.S., you and I will be able to finish an interview without any interruptions."

"I don't think so. That American you were with was an FBI agent. Who are you working for?"

"I work for an airline trade magazine. In Iraq, I was writing for other papers as well."

"Where did you get your information? How did you learn about the London repair shops? Why did you go there after the plane crashes?"

"Airlines are my beat. And I often write about crashes. It was a good subject to look into," she said.

"Somewhat too good," he said. "I think you need to come with me and we'll have a little talk somewhere more comfortable."

Obaidi reached for her wrist, but she turned quickly and he didn't get his hand on her arm.

"I'm quite fine here," she said, stepping sideways and knocking over the umbrella stand, where it looked surreal to begin with, holding her old foils, a few of which fell out onto the floor. Obaidi leaned over and grabbed one. But so did she. He tried to strike her with the sword, but she deflected his move easily.

Obaidi's eyebrows rose. "Ah, so you are trained in martial arts as well. Perhaps you are an *Israeli* agent."

Marie held her foil up, ready for him to move. "I'm an American," she said. "And a fencer. My choice. It's a sport. I don't know why you've picked up a foil, but I'll defend myself. And that won't be sport, I promise you." She was talking tough, but she was terrified because she had no idea what he had in mind. The foil was almost completely useless as a fighting tool. It didn't have a sharp blade, and the tip was blunt. Scoring in fencing came from hits marked by electronic sensors. Referring to these foils as weapons was outdated by a hundred years.

"A woman does not defeat a man. With a sword or anything else," said Obaidi with derision, stepping forward and swinging at her again. He was not skillful, but he was determined and angry. She deflected his hit and then went on the offensive. Her first strike was an open swipe that hit him on the arm. All she could do with the dull-edged foil was to make large slashing motions to bruise him, or cause a stinging burn. So that's what she did. He yelled and looked down at his foil, which he re-alized was not serving him well. With one quick movement, he put the tip to the ground and stomped the sword with his foot, breaking the steel shaft in half. Now he had a weapon with a jagged end.

With a sudden cold flash of understanding, Marie realized Obaidi was a dirty fighter, a street fighter, and this was probably how he'd fought when he killed her father.

"Now your skills will not be as handy as you thought," Obaidi said, charging her with the jagged sword. But the skill she had that he couldn't anticipate was footwork. She parried his attack and pulled back and away, causing him to lose his balance. She took advantage then and attacked, hitting his knuckles and his wrist with quick, repeated jabs until he shouted again and dropped the foil.

With a lunge, she attacked his head with big swings. He made a mis-take then, putting his hands up, and she continued to slash at them, making red welts. She pushed him back a few steps until she could reach down and grab the weapon he'd dropped. In reaction, he turned and reached under his jacket, and when he came back to face her, she saw with horror that he had a knife in his hand, a long one—it looked like it had a nine-inch blade. She wasn't sure how to defend herself against a dagger but decided she'd stick with her plan, an old Italian favorite: the coupe.

She placed her point down and then lifted it, making the usual moves to confuse: circulations, disengagements, beats. Then she raised her foil higher, making bell-shaped gestures over his head. He was watching the blade now. He was confused, almost hypnotized by it, not able to anticipate where it might land. That was good for her because the knife was harmlessly in his hand by his hip. What he didn't realize at that moment was that she was completely vulnerable. Her body was open, but all he could see was the blade whipping in and out over his head. Obaidi's instincts told him to wait until the blade stopped before reacting to it, but that was almost impossible to judge because the blade, her arm, and the point were going in opposite directions.

And that was the time for her to make her move. When the blade reached the top of the bell shape, she made a strong, firm counterwhip with her wrist that bent the blade 180 degrees, causing the tip to beat Obaidi on the back of his shoulder, a hard, stinging whack that, if she was lucky, would cause his whole arm to cramp. She liked this move because in addition to freezing his arm, it would destroy his confidence—he'd got hit from behind. After the blade smacked him, Obaidi shouted and reached for his elbow. She guessed she'd hit a nerve, a real one.

She then slipped her wrist and disarmed him, knocking his knife to the ground. In a real duel, this would have been the moment to throw a second hit at his chest and force him to kneel. But he would never kneel to her. He'd throw her more dirt, more street tricks, so she hit him on the head again, as hard as she could, jumping off the ground as she did so, one punishing blow, then another. Three blows and he fell to his knees. She took advantage of the moment and fled past him, sprinting down the short hall, a foil in each hand. Her heart was beating so fast that she couldn't hear a thing, but she had to get away. At the main corridor, she turned right toward the elevators.

And ran smack into Julian.

He grabbed her by the elbow and pulled her down a corridor, along another row of storage lockers and into a stairwell.

"You don't want him to see you with me," he said in a low voice. He was immensely strong. As he ran with his arm around her, practically carrying her off her feet, she felt his body strong as steel, yet nimble. At the next landing, he guided her out to another floor and toward another stairway. When they got to it, Julian found the door locked. He tried it again, then turned, puzzled. He had just checked this door and it had been open. What had happened? He knew that on this floor the only other stairwell was at the other end of the building, almost half a block away. He looked at the elevator and hesitated, then pushed the button.

The freight elevator arrived slowly, and when it reached them, it opened as usual horizontally from the middle—the top door pulling up, the bottom half pulling below the floor. They stepped in and the doors closed.

The elevator began moving, then ground to a stop.

"These aren't self-service elevators," said Marie quietly. "Where's the attendant?"

Julian pushed several buttons. The elevator didn't move. They waited quietly, thinking; Marie looked up at Julian and noticed that his face had turned ashen and he was sweating profusely.

"What's the matter?" she asked him, touching his arm. "Julian, are you all right?" His breathing seemed shallow and his hand was pressed against the wall behind him.

"I have trouble in enclosed spaces," he said, his words coming out slowly, his voice choked.

She looked at him, shocked by his instant transformation, lion into a tottering lamb. "Are you claustrophobic?"

He nodded, closing his eyes.

Realizing he was struggling, she became very calm and focused. "Is there anything that helps?" she asked in a quiet voice.

"Getting out."

She looked around the elevator. The ceiling was high. There might be a panel up there that could be pushed out. As she looked for something on the walls to catch hold of to climb up, the elevator suddenly began to move again.

Up.

On the next floor, the elevator stopped, and as the doors separated, the bottom one ahead of the top, she saw Obaidi's legs. This was her opening and her advantage. She bent her knees and lashed her foil as hard as she could across his groin. He screamed and she whipped him again. Because of the way the elevator doors opened, he couldn't yet reach her with fists or a firearm, if he had one. When the door opened far enough for her to see his chest and head, she saw that he did have a gun. But she'd knocked him off balance, and she didn't give him a second to react before she did what she had failed to do earlier. She aimed her foil, set her weight, and lunged. She drove the tip directly into his left eye. As she struck, she looked into his other eye, open wide, blue and affronted. He stood looking at her for a split second before going down, howling in agony, his face spurting blood.

Recovered now, Julian pulled Marie toward him and away from Obaidi, who lay unconscious on the floor. "Let's close up your storage locker and get out of here," he said in a low but urgent voice. As they rounded a corner, they saw the elevator attendant lying in a pool of blood. Marie screamed. Julian pulled her closer and continued to an open stairwell, down the steps, and back to the open door of her locker. He swung the door closed and snapped the padlock.

Marie's teeth started chattering violently. The adrenaline from the fight and her fear all imploded on her now. "How the hell did he get in here anyway?" she asked, feeling icy cold.

Julian placed his finger on her lips to keep her from talking. "I'm not supposed to be here. We've got to get out." He listened for running feet, in case Obaidi had come with a partner. If so, he hoped his own men in the building had found him.

"I need to call Morgan," said Julian, pulling out his phone. "He's got a direct line to the unified command. They've got to come and bring in Obaidi. I can't do it."

"What unified command?" asked Marie.

"There's a red alert at the ports."

"Oh God," she said, brushing her hair away from her face with the back of her hand. Oh good, she thought, suddenly realizing that maybe her Internet story had helped Morgan get things moving.

"The FBI would probably like that too," he said, pointing to the bloody foil she still held in her hand. She looked at it in disgust. She thought of the shocked angry blue eye staring at her. Her body was shaking now.

"Hey," he said to her, putting the phone down for a moment and searching her face.

She focused on him. Her eyes were large and questioning and wet with tears of anger and determination.

Julian opened his arms around Marie and gathered her into a hug. "You are my hero."

Department of Justice, Washington, D.C., May 28

The announcement given by Attorney General Bob Thompson was terse. He seemed nervous when he began to speak, but loosened up as his statement went along. He wanted to inform Americans that an explosion had taken place in lower Manhattan at a telephone switching station. Parts of the area were still closed and investigations were continuing, but it seemed to be an isolated incident, a possible terror attack that had been foiled by the authorities.

Though four people had lost their lives, including two law enforcement officers whose bravery and quick thinking had kept the damage to a minimum, the facility had suffered only minor damage. Limited phone and data lines were down for a few hours before they were rerouted to other computers. America had once again proven to herself and to the world not only that she would remain a symbol of freedom and liberty, a beacon to the rest of the world, but that her law enforcement and defense establishments were up to the challenge of the new world order.

He failed to mention that that information supplied to Red, the jihadist who bombed the building, by Mr. Paterson about the location of the target computer had been completely wrong. Stuck in Shimshon Ashkenazy's honeypot, Mr. Paterson never found any of the telephone switches. The only parts of the telephone infrastructure that had been damaged were cables running in the ceiling of the first floor, above the spot where the bomb had detonated.

The spokesman failed to mention these details because he didn't know them. Julian's team was accustomed to keeping its secrets. Even if Julian's superiors would have liked to score brownie points with the Americans by making them public, Julian wasn't cooperating.

As for the sinking of the container ship in the Atlantic, it was explained as an accidental explosion of flammable materials on board. The salvage operation, which began immediately, would be conducted under top-secret conditions, the findings, of course, classified.

New York City, May 28

"He'll be back, won't he?" Marie asked. She and Julian sat in her garden, their voices low, each in a wrought-iron chair, a round table between them. The moon was large and low in the sky.

"Once he gets his eye patched up and his face repaired? Yes, he will. I'm afraid you'll have to move."

"Move? Where?"

"Out of this beautiful apartment. Out of New York City. Somewhere you'll be safe."

"And where would that be? Israel?"

"We'll find someplace for you."

Marie felt shocked, momentarily disoriented. She struggled to pull herself back. "How is it possible that the FBI failed to find him? I mean, his eye was practically gouged out of his head. He had to go to a doctor."

"He probably had a medical contact set up before he arrived. One phone call and he got help. That's how it works with men like him. Then he snuck out of the country. There are many ways. Don't forget he has, or had at that point, diplomatic immunity."

"That's just unbelievable!" she said. "How can he just walk out of the country?"

"You've got very long, porous borders," said Julian. "And you're not used to defending them."

"What did Morgan say?"

"About Obaidi's slipping through the fingers of the FBI? Nothing. He said he was going on vacation."

"Vacation?" asked Marie.

"Diving or something like that."

"Oh, I'm sure he's diving. He's probably inside the *LB Venture* right now," Marie said. "That's his thing. He's a bomb tech and a cave diver. He helped investigate the bombing of the USS *Cole*."

Julian nodded.

"Anyway, there's no way he'd go on vacation without coming to see me first," she said.

"Oh, really?" said Julian. "Something going on I'm not aware of?"

"Considering your particular talents," said Marie, "unlikely. By the way, I'm still mad at you."

"For what?" he said, looking at her in alarm.

"Kidnapping me."

"Oh."

"That took a lot of chutzpih, don't you think?" said Marie, turning to look at him and frowning.

"What's that?" he asked, smiling in spite of himself.

"Chutzpih. Did I use that word right?"

" 'Chutzpah' I think is the word you were aiming for." Julian laughed out loud. "But that's okay. It's actually cute. I'll have to remember that."

"Sorry," said Marie, turning red.

"Never mind," said Julian. "But what made you think it was us?"

Marie took a long breath. "A few things didn't add up, but I'd have to say it was seeing one of my guards reading Hemingway. I mean, really. That had to be one of your guys."

"You were supposed to be blindfolded and bound."

"Well thanks a lot. With friends like you, who needs homicidal terrorist enemies? Anyway, they let my hands free. I pulled off my blindfold at one point and saw the book beside a chair where he'd been sitting."

"That is a fireable offense," said Julian. "I'll have to remember to let that man go. Make a note of that, will you? Now, how will I learn who was reading Hemingway in Baghdad?" Julian put his finger to his lip, considering.

Marie cleared her throat. "You're not off the hook with me yet, Julian. Why did you do it?"

"I had no choice."

"Not true."

"Obaidi proved I was right. He came after you. All the way here. What if he'd had a go at you in Baghdad? I wouldn't have been able to protect you."

"Protect me? How did you protect me here? I seem to remember being alone with him in my storage locker."

" 'Do I contradict myself? Yes I contradict myself.' Who said that?"

"Walt Whitman," said Marie.

"Exactly. You were alone with that man and that was regrettable," said Julian. "But you handled yourself excellently. As expected. I didn't anticipate the swordplay, but I had men all around Chelsea Mini Storage. And all around your apartment before, when Obaidi went there to find you."

Marie gave him a disbelieving look.

"That card you got in the mail from the storage facility about the rodents? Asking you to check your stuff? Who do you think sent that to you? Who do you think made sure Obaidi saw it? If you hadn't propped it on the table in your hallway, we would have made sure he'd noticed it elsewhere in your apartment. We had an extra one. And we were watching your every move."

"Why?"

"We wanted to get him out of there. We knew he'd find you one way or another, and we thought we could control the situation better at the storage facility."

Marie fell silent for a moment and stared at her flower beds, her climbing roses. Then she looked at Julian. "I'm sorry he got away. But still, we got lucky this time. The ship didn't explode. The Tunnel's still up."

"You were our luck, Marie." Julian looked straight at her. "Obaidi failed because of you. He never expected to cross paths with a young woman who, in a better world for him, might have been his daughter."

Marie looked at him quizzically.

"You were the only person on earth in a position to bring him down. Your biography has been your personal burden and, it seems now, your gift. You're the only person who could have drawn Obaidi out of his den. Because he is human. And he loved a woman once. And that woman was, of all people, your mother."

Julian was quiet. Marie looked at him, and she saw a smile playing around the corners of his mouth.

"Of course," he said, beginning a chuckle that turned into a belly laugh, "it didn't hurt that you're pretty handy with a sword."

Granot Family Farm, Outside Tel Aviv, June 8

The earth was soupy by the marigolds, where the loam was deep, the color of dirt the blackest. Julian, on his knees in the garden at his home, dug with his hands, ripping out weeds, resettling the earth around the flowers. Julian looked out at the overcast sky, thinking of his last memory of Obaidi. It seemed fitting that it was only a sound—a shout of aggrieved pain after being cut by Marie—as Obaidi was in so many ways a specter. He was gone again, as though vaporized out of the FBI dragnet in lower Manhattan. By now, Julian thought, he was no doubt in another disguise, in a new location, plotting another attack.

Julian's eyes turned closer to home, looking out at his boys, each working a different section of the two-acre garden. He warmed at the sight of them. The eldest, tall now and almost twenty, with dark wavy hair, crouched among the brushy tomatoes, staking and tying up the plants with a childish intensity. His little brother, just fifteen, with red hair and light complexion like his dad, checked out a section of the drip irrigation system that was leaking.

Julian grasped a clump of crabgrass and threw it to the edge of the garden. The boys, good sports and happy to be with their father, had gladly agreed this morning to help neaten things up. They weeded and hoed and repaired the tubes of an irrigation system Julian had dug when he himself was a teenager. Julian relished his time with them. He had been absent far too long during their childhoods.

Julian stood and rubbed the earth from his hands. He had begun his work this morning with gloves, but had dropped them somewhere. He heard a car coming along the drive and looked up.

Marie smiled at him out the car window and waved. Julian walked from the garden toward her. She parked and stepped out.

"It is so *beautiful* here," Marie said, giving him a long hug, then turning to look over the prolific garden, the houses nestled among cypress trees, a grove of fruit trees behind. "You live in paradise, Julian."

"Actually, I think the Garden of Eden was supposed to be somewhere else you've been recently—Iraq." Marie started laughing. Julian barked out a command in Hebrew and his two sons stood up. They shambled over with hoes and rakes and a burlap bag of weeds.

Julian introduced Marie to his sons and suggested that the boys go inside and shower. They had twenty guests coming for dinner in a couple hours and there was much to do yet. They ran off, chasing each other.

Julian looked at Marie.

"Would you like some tea? A soft drink?"

"Maybe later. I'm fine thanks." She looked at him, trying to be brave, but her lip was already trembling. "I just went to Ari's grave." She put her hands up to her eyes, suddenly weeping. "The graves," she said, tears rolling down her cheeks, "they look like little beds. And there are so many of them. Boys buried in tiny stone beds in beautiful gardens."

"Boy and girl soldiers killed," said Julian, "both."

When she stopped weeping, she said, "I put a pebble on his gravestone. Isn't that the custom?"

"Yes, it's a nice way to show you remember."

She opened her bag and pulled out a paperbound book.

"Uh-oh," said Julian, gesturing Marie to sit on a bench near the border of the garden. "Is this what I think it is?"

"You don't want to see it?" asked Marie.

"I'm not sure," said Julian. "I'm not sure I do."

"Well," said Marie, holding it in her lap, "you could just glance at it."

Julian had known this moment was coming. He dreaded looking into that black maw of the past. He was afraid of reading anything Ari might have written about his meeting with Obaidi. He was afraid of reading words of anger directed at him. He was afraid of reading Ari's pain. Above all else, he didn't want to learn that against all rules, Ari had kept a journal.

Marie looked into his eyes and saw the sadness. But he also seemed to be calculating something, and when he was done, his expression lightened.

"Okay," he said. "I'll look at it. I guess it's time."

She gently handed him the book. Julian flipped it over to read from the right. He turned the cover gingerly and glanced over the words. He began to smile as he read, turning the pages. He took a deep breath and turned to Marie.

"Your father left you a gift," he said. "There are no indiscretions here, no anger, no secrets. These are love poems to your mother."

"My dad was a poet?"

"Not a bad one either," said Julian. "I have a friend who's a translator. I'll ask him to write these out for you in English."

"My dad was a poet and I became a writer. How strange," said Marie. "Everything is so strange."

"And so right," said Julian. "When do you see your friend Popolovsky?"

"He's invited me to the Israel Philharmonic tomorrow night."

"What will they play?" asked Julian.

"Beethoven's Seventh Symphony in A Major," said Marie.

"That will be lovely," said Julian.

Just then a whistle was heard from the house. Julian looked up and saw Gabi gesturing to him with a big smile.

"That's my cue," said Julian. "Time to cook. Want to help?"

"Absolutely," said Marie, standing up.

Julian nudged a soccer ball out of the path.

They approached a farmhouse with trellises of roses clinging to its walls. The backyard was edged with a border of wildflowers.

"Everything will be okay," he said, putting his arm around her as they walked up to the house. "By the end of the day, everything will be okay. Now come in and meet everybody. As you can see, Gabi's eager to meet you. So are a couple of people who worked with you, Nadav Rosenberg and Shimshon Ashkenazy, the computer kid. He's with a new girlfriend, Sarah, so don't say boo in his direction or he might faint. Ari's sister is here and her children, your cousins. Ari's father, your grandfather, is here. Everyone's very excited. They've been waiting for a happy ending to this story for a long time."

Acknowledgments

In writing this story, I have been helped beyond measure by a source I first came to know as a journalist. For reasons that will surely be obvious, I cannot name him. But he is an important agent in the war against terrorism. Thanks to him, I learned more about the vulnerability of American ports of entry than I wanted to know. He opened doors to me that would otherwise have remained closed. I am deeply grateful to him for his help and his example. Of course, any misinterpretations or errors are mine alone.

Heartfelt thanks to Peter McGrath for his *Newsweek* assignments over the years, which have now led to three books. I also owe him thanks for his intrepid editing of this manuscript, informed by his many visits through the Middle East as *Newsweek*'s foreign editor.

Thanks to Ellen Kampinsky at *Glamour* magazine, whose assignments have offered me the opportunity to meet several exemplary individuals, including FBI Special Agent and SWAT Operator Jennifer Coffindaffer and U.S. Air Force Captain Chandra O'Brien, who flew her F-15C in Iraq and now trains on the Stealth bomber.

Robert Kunkel, with great good humor, helped me find my way around a container ship and manage a boarding party of SEALs. Peter

S. Shaerf was the maestro who put me in touch with Kunkel and several other men of the sea, including Jordan Truchan, a shipping expert, and John Gaughan, who offered hands-on knowledge of Iraqi ports. I owe debts of gratitude to several FBI agents, including the irrepressible and larger-than-life Special Agent Morgan Bodie, Supervisory Special Agent (Retired) Beverly Wright, and Special Agent Thomas O'Connor.

My literary agent and champion, Nick Ellison, fights like the pro boxer he once was. For that and his friendship I am the better. Many thanks also to his brainy group: Aby Koons, Sarah Dickman, and Arija Weddle. My thanks to Charles Spicer, Sally Richardson, George Witte, Matt Baldacci, Ronni Stolzenberg, and Yaniv Soha at St. Martin's Press for their enthusiasm, support, and good ideas. Heartfelt thanks to Joe Cleemann, young master of an old and indispensable art: line editing. Robin Lipshitz, M.D., offered important advice on physiology, and Vernie Simon lovingly held the chaos at bay. Marina Higgins helped provide a rooftop aerie, and Patrick J. Carroll kept the body tuned with his special SEAL workouts.

Paolo Rosselli, fencer and coach from the New York Athletic Club, and Peter Brand, fencing coach at Harvard University, provided fencing advice. My thanks to them for their artistry. Without Jeffry J. Andresen this book would never have been written. He also offered the key fencing move, holding, as he does so well, uncertainty at bay just long enough for clarity to shine through.